THE SCIENCE FICTION WEIGHT-LOSS BOOK

THE SCIENCE FICTION WEIGHT-LOSS BOOK

Edited by ISAAC ASIMOV,
George R. R. Martin,
and Martin H. Greenberg

Crown Publishers, Inc.　　New York

Published in the United States of America
Library of Congress Cataloging in Publication Data
The Science fiction weight-loss book.
1. Science fiction, American. 2. Obesity—Fiction.
I. Asimov, Isaac, 1920– . II. Martin, George R. R. III. Greenberg, Martin Harry.
PS648.S3S276   1983   813'.0876'08   83-19811
ISBN: 0-517-54978-6
Book design by Camilla Filancia
10   9   8   7   6   5   4   3   2   1
First Edition

ACKNOWLEDGMENTS

"Sylvester's Revenge" by Vance Aandahl copyright © 1975 by Mercury Press, Inc. Originally appeared in *The Magazine of Fantasy and Science Fiction.* Reprinted by permission of the author. ● "Fat Farm" by Orson Scott Card copyright © 1980 by Orson Scott Card. Originally appeared in *Omni Magazine.* Reprinted by permission of the Barbara Bova Agency. ● "The Stretch" by Sam Merwin, Jr. copyright © 1956 by Columbia Publications, Inc. Reprinted by permission of the Foley Agency. ● "Camels and Dromedaries, Clem" by R. A. Lafferty copyright © 1967 by Mercury Press, Inc. Originally appeared in *The Magazine of Fantasy and Science Fiction.* Reprinted by permission of the author and the author's agent, Virginia Kidd. ● "The Champ" by T. Coraghessan Boyle copyright © 1978 by T. Coraghessan Boyle. First appeared in *The Atlantic.* Reprinted by permission of Little, Brown and Company. ● "The Iron Chancellor" by Robert Silverberg copyright © 1958 by Galaxy Publishing Corporation. Reprinted by permission of the author and Agberg, Ltd. ● "The Man Who Ate the World" by Frederik Pohl copyright © 1956 by Galaxy Publishing Corporation. Reprinted by permission of the author. ● "Gladys's Gregory" by John Anthony West copyright © 1963 by Mercury Press, Inc. From *The Magazine of Fantasy and Science Fiction.* Reprinted by permission of the author and the author's agent, Robert P. Mills, Ltd. ● "Abercrombie Station" by Jack Vance copyright 1952 by Standard Publications, Inc. Reprinted by permission of Kirby McCauley, Ltd. ● "Shipping Clerk" by William Morrison copyright 1952 by Galaxy Publishing Corporation. Reprinted by permission of Mrs. Dorothy Samachson. ● "The Malted Milk Monster" by William Tenn appeared originally in *Galaxy of Science Fiction* magazine, copyright © 1959 by Galaxy Publishing Corporation. Reprinted by permission of the author. ● "The Food Farm" by Kit Reed copyright © 1967 by Kit Reed. Reprinted by permission of Brandt & Brandt Literary Agents, Inc. ● "The Artist of Hunger" by Scott Sanders copyright © 1982 by Davis Publications, Inc. Reprinted by permission of the author and the author's agent, Virginia Kidd. ● "Quitters, Inc." from *Night Shift* by Stephen King. Copyright © 1978 by Stephen King. Reprinted by permission of Doubleday & Company, Inc.

CONTENTS

FAT !

by Isaac Asimov

In general, there are three varieties of material objects that must be absorbed by the body if it is to maintain life: gaseous (air), liquid (water), and solid (food). Each presents a different problem and is handled in a different way.

Air is universally and continuously present on Earth's surface.

There are exceptional conditions, of course. Oxygen might be exhausted in a coal mine, in a locked vault, in the course of a fire. In the case of a fire, smoke, poisonous vapors, or heat might fatally contaminate the air supply. Such situations are, however, not a day-to-day matter and can be ignored. On the whole, we can assume that air is always present, so that human beings need simply breathe, steadily and automatically, all their life long. (This is also true of other land animals. The case of water animals and of plants is different in detail but not in essence.)

The result is that there is no real mechanism for storing air by land animals, notably the human being, because there is no need to develop such a mechanism. (Air-breathers that live in the sea—particularly the large whales—can remain submerged for extended periods by human standards, but even here the body-supply of air or, more specifically, oxygen, will last only a couple of hours at the most.)

For human beings, the body supply will last for, at most, five minutes. If breathing is prevented for that long, the human brain, oxygen-starved, will suffer irreversible damage and the human being will die.

Nor can a human being make himself less susceptible to suffocation by deliberate deep-breathing designed to permeate his body with oxygen. As I said, there is no reasonable mechanism for storage, and if you force your breathing, you will quickly grow dizzy and be compelled to stop.

Water is almost as common as air. To be sure, there are desiccated regions on Earth, where plants and animals must carefully conserve what water they do get, but human beings have evolved under water-

1

plentiful conditions and are not biologically adapted to desert life. The result is that their ability to conserve water is limited.

We must, therefore, drink water at frequent intervals to replace what is unavoidably lost through urination, defecation, perspiration, and expiration. Nor do we forget to do so, for the sensation of thirst is motivation enough, and it never fails to remind us.

Still, we can store water to a greater extent than we can store air. A good swig of water will satisfy our needs for several hours, usually; and, where necessity drives, a human being can go several days without water, although he will necessarily suffer agonies of thirst.

Nor can we protect ourselves against such an eventuality by drinking a great deal of water. We quickly sate ourselves so that further drinking becomes so unpleasant that even the fear of thirst cannot force us to continue; and much of the excess that we do ingest in this way is quickly lost through copious urination.

That leaves food. Food is less common than either air or water. Almost any animal is likely to face a situation where food becomes difficult to find over a period of time; either because there is a drought, or because it is winter, or simply because competition is temporarily too keen.

If a time should come, therefore, when a supply of food *is* encountered, it is important that as much should be eaten as possible, since one cannot tell when the next supply will be met up with. Animals that are easily sated and that satisfy themselves with their immediate needs only, as in the case of air and water, are quite likely to starve to death between widely spaced meals.

(Then, too, in the case of carnivores, a large kill cannot be allowed to remain largely uneaten, or it will decay and become inedible. The killers, therefore, eat all they can, while they can—and this goes for preindustrial humanity, too.)

Of course, huge meals will work only if the organism has an efficient way of storing food—and most organisms do. If food is ingested beyond immediate needs, it can be stored as starch (the usual case in plants) or, even more efficiently, as fat (the usual case in animals). What's more, the amount of food that can be so stored is surprisingly large. The result is that human beings can go without food, not for mere minutes (as in the case of air), or mere days (as in the case of water), but for weeks, and even months! (And they can be undernourished—if not zero-nourished—for years.)

An unusually large food-store eventually becomes difficult for an animal to carry about. An enormous fat supply will limit mobility, impair the functioning of organs, and, in particular, place an unacceptable burden on such particularly hardworking organs as the heart and kidneys.

Under ordinary circumstances, however, food storage is not likely to become a problem. An animal that becomes moderately fat under conditions of plentiful food is bound to encounter lean times soon enough and will then thin down.

Only the human being can so control the environment as to ensure a continuous plentiful food supply, and even then only for a relatively few. In most human societies, the bulk of the population has always had to scrabble for food, and to eat little more than is required to support life. Most people are therefore thin.

Once civilization was developed, however, there was usually a ruling caste—aristocrats, priests, successful merchants—whose food supply was reliable over an extended period of time and who could grow fat and *stay* fat. Since this was an unusual situation and since fatness bore visible evidence of high position and of success in life, it was viewed complacently.

A plump woman was clearly one who had been well cared for and whose family was therefore sure to be able to afford a good dowry, so that plumpness was a sign of beauty. It was very rarely, indeed, that any good could be seen in a starved and scrawny maiden. And a fat man was clearly a substantial provider whom any woman would be glad to marry.

After the Industrial Revolution, however, some societies prospered to such an extent that a large proportion of the population was in a position to store food and become sleek and paunchy. The most notable case is that of the United States of America in the twentieth century.

It is so easy for so many Americans to grow fat that there is no value to it. Fatness among Americans is too common to be much of a sign of success, so there is no economic motive for it to give rise to a feeling of aesthetic satisfaction, either.

In fact, since the ingrown instinct to eat everything in sight (in case of hard times ahead) is so strong, it is very difficult to maintain a slim outline in American society. If slimness *is* maintained, therefore, it is a sign of achievement, and if this is combined with signs of success *other* than fat—such as jewelry or a tanned and muscled body, bespeaking lots of leisure time—then slimness becomes the standard of beauty.

And that is the situation we have now in the United States of America. Surely there is no species of organism, other than the human being, that labors to deny itself available food in order to remain thin. Nor among human beings is there any society, other than the contemporary United States, in which this is done so extensively. In no other society is fatness so condemned, voluntary semistarvation so eagerly striven after, and pinched cheeks and gaunt limbs so idolized. And, to be sure, fatness *is* bad for health. A thin person is healthier, feels better, and lives longer than a fat person.

Now let's get personal. The three editors of this anthology—Isaac Asimov, Martin Harry Greenberg, and George R. R. Martin—are, all three, unusually handsome, remarkably intelligent, and enormously successful with the opposite sex—and have rather rounded silhouettes, too.

Mind you, we are not obese; we are not even really fat. We are merely plump, a little pudgy, perhaps. We do not suffer from under-nourishment, and we have healthy appetites. We are not among those whose plates are sent back to the kitchen only half emptied.

But we, too, wish to be slim now—if only to be in fashion. Being science fiction people, we wish to do it the science fiction way. That way is to put together a science fiction diet book.

What on Earth is a science fiction weight-loss book? Easy! It is a collection of science fiction stories that deal, one way and another, with the problem of overweight. It is that collection which you are now holding in your hand.

Are you overweight and do you wish to lose? Read this book. Are you *not* overweight and do you wish to feel good about it? Read this book.

But perhaps you had better not read this book too quickly. Not all at once. If you *do* read it all at once—you may never eat again.

And we wouldn't want you to underdo.

SYLVESTER'S REVENGE

by Vance Aandahl

The tale of revenge has a long and distinguished history in world literature. But rarely has revenge seemed as sweet as in this moving story.

Sylvester was dying. At 800 pounds he'd lost the ability to walk. He couldn't even sit up at 1,200. Now he weighed 2,000. An immense hunk of trapped and breathless blubber, naked except for an old blanket tossed across his sperm-whale hips, he lay flat on his back both day and night, his only movement an occasional roll to one side or the other. He hated himself, and now he wept as Dr. Fletcher held the mirror overhead and made him comb his hair.

He was resting in a deep eight-by-six-foot tile tub located in one corner of her basement laboratory. The tub was equipped with faucet and drain, and now, just as she did every morning after she'd make him comb his hair, Dr. Fletcher attached a shower hose to wash away his excrement.

"Stinko, stinko, honeybun!" she laughed. "Stinko, stinko, *stinko, stinko!*"

Then she squirted him with cold water till the tears poured from his eyes and he moaned desperately for her to stop. Abruptly she turned off the faucet and left him shivering and chattering, alone and naked and terrified.

And he was dying. He could feel his heart groaning under its burden. How much longer would the little pumper last? Another month? Or was it already just a matter of days?

If only Dr. Fletcher would abandon her experiment, it might not be too late for a starvation diet to save his life. He'd begged her and begged her, but she was completely crazy now, and he was helpless—absolutely helpless. He weighed a cool short ton, and it held him down like

5

a giant hand. He was pinned. Sylvester forced a tiny groan from his tortured, constricted lungs.

"What would you like for your eight o'clock feeding, honeybun?"

Just as her mind had dissolved completely in recent months, so too had her voice grown strange, half lilt and half whine; and though he couldn't see anything through his pig-squint eyes except the tops of three walls and nearly all of the dull olive ceiling, he knew by the sound's direction that she must be sitting down at her desk, probably to extract a few more milliliters of lowenicillin from the mourning cloak butterflies she'd collected last night. He waited until he heard the click of her instruments (he knew she was pinning the butterflies one by one to a board), then answered her, laboring for each word.

"Dr. Fletcher, please, I don't want to eat any more."

"Nonsense, punkins. Your next feeding's at eight."

"I know. But I'm too fat. It's killing me."

"Oh, poopsie, you know you need to eat. A body like yours requires fifteen thousand calories a day."

"But..."

Suddenly she appeared at the rim of the tub, leaned over, waggled her finger at him and clucked her tongue. "Poopsie—you know you're going to have your eight o'clock feeding whether you like it or not."

Sylvester hated that word *feeding.* Why couldn't she call it a meal? But there was no sense in arguing.

Eight months ago she'd seemed the soul of cool scientific reason. A noted biochemist at the University's Craigjacker Research Center, she'd hired him to serve as the first human subject in her obesity experiments. She'd explained that he would have to spend three months under constant observation at a secluded military laboratory, some thirty miles south of Elko, Nevada, that he would find the daily injections of lowenicillin somewhat painful, and that he might gain as much as 130 pounds during the course of the experiment. Maybe that's why she'd been having trouble finding a subject, and why she was now willing to pay Sylvester $8,500—more than enough to cover his expenses for the next two years while he finished his dissertation on the evolution of the Petrarchan sonnet. She'd also promised him all the Budweiser he could drink. So what the hell—Sylvester already weighed 260 pounds, and he'd figured that growing a little fatter at the wages Dr. Fletcher was offering sure beat teaching freshman comp for $800 a quarter.

In early June Sylvester had flown to Elko with Dr. Fletcher, then ridden with her in a rented Toyota to a World War II army base, which had seemed completely deserted except for an occasional jack rabbit and thousands—no, millions—of mourning cloaks perched on every branch and roof, dark-winged nymphs that had fluttered up like smoke wherever they'd walked. When Sylvester had seen that Dr. Feltcher's "military laboratory" was in fact a laundry room in the basement of a half-fallen barracks, when he'd seen the tub and the rig of lights and tubes and needles suspended over it, he'd known he'd made a big mistake. He'd told her to wait for a minute, that he'd left his glasses in the car. She'd shrugged and told him to hurry back; but when he turned to walk back to the Toyota to make his escape, something hard and black had dropped through his head, and when he'd awakened, he'd found himself chained to the bottom of the tub.

Now, eight months later in cold February, the chains were gone. His own weight held him prisoner.

He caught an acrid whiff of lowenicillin and blinked his eyes. Once again she was hovering overhead.

"Time for your medicine, dumpling! Try to be a big boy."

Sylvester gritted his teeth and closed his eyes. He knew what was. coming. A second later he felt the big needle plunge into his stomach— right through the diaphragm, like a rabies shot—and he screeched as the pain overwhelmed him. For a long instant of agony it seemed unendurable; then the lowenicillin reached his brain, and he fell spinning and nauseous through the dark chambers of his mind. He seemed to be floating in a black void, the vacuum of outer space. A huge slice of cherry cheesecake glided by like an asteroid. Suddenly he was surrounded by enormous portions of every imaginable delicacy—crackling rib-eye roasts, fluffy lemon meringue pies, peppery guacamole salads. Then he fell again, fell through the dark into a huge steaming vat of mashed bananas, calf brains, spaghetti drenched in melted lard, and tapioca pudding. Clinging to a boiled potato, he tried to keep from sinking, but the glop sucked him down like quicksand. He screamed and went under; he was suffocating in food, his nose filling with thick rancid gravy as he struggled not to breathe. He pushed away, swam deeper, deeper. He had to grope down, down to his childhood. There he stood alone, always alone, alone at the edge of play, a book of poems clutched in one hand, a chocolate bar in the other. His classmates ran. They skipped and jumped and bounded, they turned cartwheels, they even seemed to soar and glide like butterflies, their lean bodies whistling through the wind, their skinny arms and legs flapping up and down. They passed him in a breeze, then they were gone. He stood alone, choking in the unkicked cloud of playground gravel. He had to run, had to catch them. Putting his head down and clenching his fists, he lumbered into a slow waddle. Their voices came drifting back to taunt him:

"Fatty, fatty, two by four, couldn't get through the kitchen door! Fatty, fatty! Fatty, fatty!"

He tried to lift his feet higher, but the gravity of his bulk held him back like a giant hand. Then he couldn't run at all, couldn't walk, couldn't even move . . .

"It's almost time for your eight o'clock feeding, honeybun."

He lifted his head and slowly shook away the lowenicillin dream. The hallucinations that inevitably followed an injection of the obesity drug always overwhelmed him, but they rarely lasted more than a few minutes. As his eyes began to focus, he saw her overhead.

"Guess what's cooking! It's one of your favorites, sweetheart—tapioca pudding. Lots and lots, too!"

He waited till her footsteps disappeared into the barracks kitchen, then tried futilely to squeeze his sausage-fingers into fists. Tapioca was the worst. She wouldn't even let it cool before jamming the wide aluminum funnel into his mouth and pouring it down, cup after cup, quart after quart.

Once, about a month ago, Sylvester had tried a little rebellion: he'd locked his teeth, refusing to let her insert the funnel. Dr. Fletcher had frowned and tapped his incisors. Then she'd lifted the funnel and hacked down hard, gouging his gums. The pain had roared through his body, even through his rolling, nearly nerveless fat. He'd screamed. Then, whimpering, he'd opened wide. Mingling with the salt of his own blood, the first disgusting cupful of tapioca had slid down his throat like a gobbet of frog eggs.

"Chow time!"

He shuddered at the shrill of her voice.

"Ready or not, here it comes!"

He could hear the serving cart creaking closer under its heavy load, a two-gallon iron vat full to the brim.

"No, please, no . . ."

She leaned over him and scowled. As always, her skeletal face terrified him. The grayish yellow skin stretching from her pointed cheekbones to the jut of her jaw was scraped raw where her nails had been a-picking. She had no lips at all, only a thin fleshless slit. Her nose was a sharp hook, her eyes black holes. The tiny mourning cloak tattooed just above her left eyebrow seemed to glow like a preternatural death's-head, and her hair hung down in thin washed-out strands.

"Oh, poopsie, I was really hoping you wouldn't be a problem eater today! Why do you have to be such a big baby?"

As he raged against his bonds of lard, a searing fire suddenly exploded in his chest. Black waves rolled through his neck into his head, rolled up against the buzzing panic in his mind, pulling and pulling till only one thin beam of light still wavered in his brain and kept him from total darkness.

At last the pain eased and the black tide rolled back.

Did she know he was dying? He could feel the blood muscle flopping in his chest, slowing, fluttering like a powered wing, slowing again, beating its last feeble beats.

Moaning, he opened his mouth.

The cold aluminum touched his tongue, then probed deeper.

Bitterness flooded him. Why should he die like this? He wanted to do something forbidden, something wrong and perverse. He wanted to hurt her.

So when the first horrid glop of tapioca hit his throat, he blew it back.

It sprayed into her astonished face and stuck there, clinging to the drawn gray skin in steaming yellow beads. At the same instant he felt his heart rupture.

"YOU BAD BABY!" she howled, trying to rub the hot tapioca out of her eyes. Then her face seemed to blacken. Was it fury, he wondered, or just the fading of the light? Her screwed-up fists were pummeling his face—distant and trivial, like the summer rain on a patio roof—and even farther away, so faint he couldn't be sure, his stomach felt the bony sprawl of her elbows and knees. She'd jumped onto him.

It was then that inspiration came to Sylvester. He would begin his one movement—the long, certain roll.

Dr. Fletcher screeched and tried to clamber free, but too late: he'd already caught her between his belly and the side of the tub. He could feel his ton of blubber pressing her deeper and deeper, crushing her gaunt frame under great layers of suffocating fat. Then, a moment later, he was past caring, past enjoying the muffled shrieks beneath him.

And she was pinned. . . .

FAT FARM

by Orson Scott Card

What fat person hasn't dreamed of being able to walk into some miraculous little shop, and walking out a short time later without that extra baggage, made fashionably, painlessly, slim again? A whole new person, one might say. Well, it could be done . . . but there's a catch.

The receptionist was surprised that he was back so soon.

"Why, Mr. Barth, how glad I am to see you," she said.

"Surprised, you mean," Barth answered. His voice rumbled from the rolls of fat under his chin.

"Delighted."

"How long has it been?" Barth asked.

"Three years. How time flies."

The receptionist smiled, but Barth saw the awe and revulsion on her face as she glanced over his immense body. In her job she saw fat people every day. But Barth knew he was unusual. He was proud of being unusual.

"Back to the fat farm," he said, laughing.

The effort of laughing made him short of breath, and he gasped for air as she pushed a button and said, "Mr. Barth is back."

He did not bother to look for a chair. No chair could hold him. He did lean against a wall, however. Standing was a labor he preferred to avoid.

Yet it was not shortness of breath or exhaustion at the slightest effort that had brought him back to Anderson's Fitness Center. He had often been fat before, and he rather relished the sensation of bulk, the impression he made as crowds parted for him. He pitied those who could only be slightly fat—short people, who were not able to bear the weight. At well over two meters, Barth could get gloriously fat, stunningly fat. He owned thirty wardrobes and took delight in changing from

10

one to another as his belly and buttocks and thighs grew. At times he felt that if he grew large enough, he could take over the world, be the world. At the dinner table he was a conqueror to rival Genghis Khan.

It was not his fatness, then, that had brought him in. It was that at last the fat was interfering with his other pleasures. The girl he had been with the night before had tried and tried, but he was incapable—a sign that it was time to renew, refresh, reduce.

"I am a man of pleasure," he wheezed to the receptionist whose name he never bothered to learn. She smiled back.

"Mr. Anderson will be here in a moment."

"Isn't it ironic," he said, "that a man such as I, who is capable of fulfilling every one of his desires, is never satisfied!" He gasped with laughter again. "Why haven't we ever slept together?" he asked.

She looked at him, irritation crossing her face. "You always ask that, Mr. Barth, on your way in. But you never ask it on your way out."

True enough. When he was on his way out of the Anderson Fitness Center, she never seemed as attractive as she had on his way in.

Anderson came in, effusively handsome, gushingly warm, taking Barth's fleshy hand in his and pumping it with enthusiasm.

"One of my best customers," he said.

"The usual," Barth said.

"Of course," Anderson answered. "But the price *has* gone up."

"If you ever go out of business," Barth said, following Anderson into the inner rooms, "give me plenty of warning. I only let myself go this much because I know you're here."

"Oh," Anderson chuckled. "We'll never go out of business."

"I have no doubt you could support your whole organization on what you charge *me.*"

"You're paying for much more than the simple service we perform. You're also paying for privacy. Or, shall we say, lack of government intervention."

"How many of the bastards do you bribe?"

"Very few, very few. Partly because so many high officials also need our service."

"No doubt."

"It isn't just weight gains that bring people to us, you know. It's cancer and aging and accidental disfigurement. You'd be surprised to learn who has had our service."

Barth doubted that he would. The couch was ready for him, immense and soft and angled so that it would be easy for him to get up again.

"Damn near got married this time," Barth said, by way of conversation.

Anderson turned to him in surprise.

"But you didn't?"

"Of course not. Started getting fat, and she couldn't cope."

"Did you tell her?"

"That I was getting fat? It was obvious."

"About us, I mean."

"I'm not a fool."

Anderson looked relieved. "Can't have rumors getting around among the thin and young, you know."

"Still, I think I'll look her up again, afterward. She did things to me a woman should be able to do. And I thought I was jaded."

Anderson placed a tight-fitting cap over Barth's head.

"Think your key thought," Anderson reminded him.

Key thought. At first that had been such a comfort, to make sure that not one iota of his memory would be lost. Now it was boring, almost juvenile. Key thought. Do you have your own Captain Aardvark secret decoder ring? Be the first on your block. The only thing Barth had been the first on his block to do was reach puberty. He had also been the first on his block to reach one hundred fifty kilos.

How many times have I been here? he wondered as the tingling in his scalp began. *This is the eighth time. Eight times, and my fortune is larger than ever, the kind of wealth that takes on a life of its own. I can keep this up forever,* he thought, with relish. Forever at the supper table with neither worries nor restraints. "It's dangerous to gain so much weight," Lynette had said. "Heart attacks, you know." But the only things that Barth worried about were hemorrhoids and impotence. The former was a nuisance, but the latter made life unbearable and drove him back to Anderson.

Key thought. What else? Lynette, standing naked on the edge of the cliff with the wind blowing. She was courting death, and he admired her for it, almost hoped that she would find it. She despised safety precautions. Like clothing, they were restrictions to be cast aside. She had once talked him into playing tag with her on a construction site, racing along the girders in the darkness, until the police came and made them leave. That had been when Barth was still thin from his last time at Anderson's. But it was not Lynette on the girders that he held in his mind. It was Lynette, fragile and beautiful Lynette, daring the wind to snatch her from the cliff and break up her body on the rocks by the river.

Even that, Barth thought, *would be a kind of pleasure. A new kind of pleasure, to taste a grief so magnificently, so admirably earned.*

And then the tingling in his head stopped. Anderson came back in.

"Already?" Barth asked.

"We've streamlined the process." Anderson carefully peeled the cap from Barth's head, helped the immense man lift himself from the couch.

"I can't understand why it's illegal," Barth said. "Such a simple thing."

"Oh, there are reasons. Population control, that sort of thing. This is a kind of immortality, you know. But it's mostly the repugnance most people feel. They can't face the thought. You're a man of rare courage."

But it was not courage, Barth knew. It was pleasure. He eagerly anticipated seeing, and they did not make him wait.

"Mr. Barth, meet Mr. Barth."

It nearly broke his heart to see his own body, young and strong and beautiful again, as it never had been the first time through his life. It was unquestionably himself, however, that they led into the room. Except that the belly was firm, the thighs well muscled but slender enough that they did not meet, even at the crotch. They brought him in naked, of course. Barth insisted on it.

He tried to remember the last time. Then *he* had been the one coming from the learning room, emerging to see the immense fat man that all his memories told him was himself. Barth remembered that it had been a double pleasure, to see the mountain he had made of himself, yet to view it from inside this beautiful young body.

"Come here," Barth said, his own voice arousing echoes of the last time, when it had been the other Barth who had said it. And just as that other had done the last time, he touched the naked young Barth, stroked the smooth and lovely skin, and finally embraced him.

And the young Barth embraced him back, for that was the way of it. No one loved Barth as much as Barth did, thin or fat, young or old. Life was a celebration of Barth; the sight of himself was his strongest nostalgia.

"What did I think of?" Barth asked.

The young Barth smiled into his eyes. "Lynette," he said. "Naked on a cliff. The wind blowing. And the thought of her thrown to her death."

"Will you go back to her?" Barth asked his young self eagerly.

"Perhaps. Or to someone like her." And Barth saw with delight that the mere thought of it had aroused his young self more than a little.

"He'll do," Barth said, and Anderson handed him the simple papers to sign—papers that would never be seen in a court of law because they attested to Barth's own compliance in and initiation of an act that was second only to murder in the lawbooks of every state.

"That's it, then," Anderson said, turning from the fat Barth to the young, thin one. "You're Mr. Barth now, in control of his wealth and his life. Your clothing is in the next room."

"I know where it is," the young Barth said with a smile, and his footsteps were buoyant as he left the room. He would dress quickly and leave the Fitness Center briskly, hardly noticing the rather plain-looking receptionist, except to take note of her wistful look after him, a tall, slender, beautiful man who had, only moments before, been lying mindless in storage, waiting to be given a mind and a memory, waiting for a fat man to move out of the way so he could fill his space.

In the memory room Barth sat on the edge of the couch, looking at the door, and then realized, with surprise, that he had no idea what came next.

"My memories run out here," Barth said to Anderson. "The agreement was—what was the agreement?"

"The agreement was tender care of you until you passed away."

"Ah, yes."

"The agreement isn't worth a damn thing," Anderson said, smiling.

Barth looked at him with surprise. "What do you mean?"

"There are two options, Barth. A needle within the next fifteen minutes. Or employment."

"What are you talking about?"

"You didn't think we'd waste time and effort feeding you the ridiculous amounts of food you require, did you?"

Barth felt himself sink inside. This was not what he had expected, though he had not honestly expected anything. Barth was not the kind to anticipate trouble. Life had never given him much trouble.

"A needle?"

"Cyanide, if you insist, though we'd rather be able to vivisect you and get as many useful body parts as we can. Your body's still fairly young. We can get incredible amounts of money for your pelvis and your glands, but they have to be taken from you alive."

"What are you talking about? This isn't what we agreed."

"I agreed to nothing with *you,* my friend," Anderson said, smiling. "I agreed with Barth. And Barth just left the room."

"Call him back! I insist—"

"Barth doesn't give a damn what happens to you."

And he knew that it was true.

"You said something about employment."

"Indeed."

"What kind of employment?"

Anderson shook his head. "It all depends," he said.

"On what?"

"On what kind of work turns up. There are several assignments every year that must be performed by a living human being, for which no volunteer can be found. No person, not even a criminal, can be compelled to do them."

"And I?"

"Will do them. Or one of them, rather, since you rarely get a second job."

"How can you do this? I'm a human being!"

Anderson shook his head. "The law says that there is only one possible Barth in all the world. And you aren't it. You're just a number. And a letter. The letter *H.*"

"Why *H?*"

Because you're such a disgusting glutton, my friend. Even our first customers haven't got past *C* yet."

Anderson left then, and Barth was alone in the room. Why hadn't he anticipated this? *Of course, of course,* he shouted to himself now. Of course they wouldn't keep him pleasantly alive. He wanted to get up and try to run. But walking was difficult for him; running would be impossible. He sat there, his belly pressing heavily on his thighs, which were spread wide by the fat. He stood, with great effort, and could only waddle because his legs were so far apart, so constrained in their movement.

This has happened every time, Barth thought. *Every damn time I've walked out of this place young and thin, I've left behind someone like me, and they've had their way, haven't they?* His hands trembled badly.

He wondered what he had decided before and knew immediately

that there was no decision to make at all. Some fat people might hate themselves and choose death for the sake of having a thin version of themselves live on. But not Barth. Barth could never choose to cause himself any pain. And to obliterate even an illegal, clandestine version of himself—impossible. Whatever else he might be, he was still Barth. The man who walked out of the memory room a few minutes before had not taken over Barth's identity. He had only duplicated it. *They've stolen my soul with mirrors.* Barth told himself. *I have to get it back.*

"Anderson!" Barth shouted. "Anderson! I've made up my mind."

It was not Anderson who entered, of course. Barth would never see Anderson again, it would have been too tempting to try to kill him.

"Get to work, H!" the old man shouted from the other side of the field.

Barth leaned on his hoe a moment more, then got back to work, scraping weeds from between the potato plants. The calluses on his hands had long since shaped themselves to fit the wooden handle, and his muscles knew how to perform the work without Barth's having to think about it at all. Yet that made the labor no easier. When he first realized that they meant him to be a potato farmer, he had asked, "Is this my assignment? Is this *all?*" And they had laughed and told him no. "It's just preparation," they said, "to get you in shape." So for two years he had worked in the potato fields, and now he began to doubt that they would ever come back, that the potatoes would ever end.

The old man was watching, he knew. His gaze always burned worse than the sun. The old man was watching, and if Barth rested too long or too often the old man would come to him, whip in hand, to scar him deeply, to hurt him to the soul.

He dug into the ground, chopping at a stubborn plant whose root seemed to cling to the foundation of the world. "Come up, damn you," he muttered. He thought his arms were too weak to strike harder, but he struck harder anyway. The root split, and the impact shattered him to the bone.

He was naked and brown to the point of blackness from the sun. The flesh hung loosely on him in great folds, a memory of the mountain he had been. Under the loose skin, however, he was tight and hard. It might have given him pleasure, for every muscle had been earned by hard labor and the pain of the lash. But there was no pleasure in it. The price was too high.

I'll kill myself, he often thought and thought again now with his arms trembling with exhaustion. *I'll kill myself so they can't use my body and can't use my soul.*

But he would never kill himself. Even now, Barth was incapable of ending it.

The farm he worked on was unfenced, but the time he had gotten away he had walked and walked and walked for three days and had not once seen any sign of human habitation other than an occasional jeep track in the sagebrush-and-grass desert. Then they found him and brought him back, weary and despairing, and forced him to finish a day's work in the field before letting him rest. And even then the lash had bitten deep, the old man laying it on with a relish that spoke of sadism or a deep, personal hatred.

But why should the old man hate me? Barth wondered. *I don't know him.* He finally decided that it was because he had been so fat, so obviously soft, while the old man was wiry to the point of being gaunt, his face pinched by years of exposure to the sunlight. Yet the old man's hatred had not diminished as the months went by and the fat melted away in the sweat and sunlight of the potato field.

A sharp sting across his back, the sound of slapping leather on skin, and then an excruciating pain deep in his muscles. He had paused too long. The old man had come to him.

The old man said nothing. Just raised the lash again, ready to strike. Barth lifted the hoe out of the ground, to start work again. It occurred to him, as it had a hundred times before, that the hoe could reach as far as the whip, with as good effect. But, as a hundred times before, Barth looked into the old man's eyes, and what he saw there, while he did not understand it, was enough to stop him. He could not strike back. He could only endure.

The lash did not fall again. Instead he and the old man just looked at each other. The sun burned where blood was coming from his back. Flies buzzed near him. He did not bother to brush them away.

Finally the old man broke the silence.

"H," he said.

Barth did not answer. Just waited.

"They've come for you. First job," said the old man.

First job. It took Barth a moment to realize the implications. The end of the potato fields. The end of the sunlight. The end of the old man with the whip. The end of the loneliness or, at least, of the boredom.

"Thank God," Barth said. His throat was dry.

"Go wash," the old man said.

Barth carried the hoe back to the shed. He remembered how heavy the hoe had seemed when he first arrived. How ten minutes in the sunlight had made him faint. Yet they had revived him in the field, and the old man had said, "Carry it back." So he had carried back the heavy, heavy hoe, feeling for all the world like Christ bearing his cross. Soon enough the others had gone, and the old man and he had been alone together, but the ritual with the hoe never changed. They got to the shed, and the old man carefully took the hoe from him and locked it away, so that Barth couldn't get it in the night and kill him with it.

And then into the house, where Barth bathed painfully and the old man put an excruciating disinfectant on his back. Barth had long since given up on the idea of an anesthetic. It wasn't in the old man's nature to use an anesthetic.

Clean clothes. A few minutes' wait. And then the helicopter. A young, businesslike man emerged from it, looking unfamiliar in detail but very familiar in general. He was an echo of all the businesslike young men and women who had dealt with him before. The young man came to him, unsmilingly, and said, "H?"

Barth nodded. It was the only name they used for him.

"You have an assignment."

"What is it?" Barth asked.

The young man did not answer. The old man, behind him, whispered, "They'll tell you soon enough. And then you'll wish you were back here, H. They'll tell you, and you'll pray for the potato fields."

But Barth doubted it. In two years there had not been a moment's pleasure. The food was hideous, and there was never enough. There were no women, and he was usually too tired to amuse himself. Just pain and labor and loneliness, all excruciating. He would leave that now. Anything would be better, anything at all.

"Whatever they assign you, though," the old man said, "it can't be any worse than my assignment."

Barth would have asked him what his assignment had been, but there was nothing in the old man's voice that invited the question, and there was nothing in their relationship in the past that would allow the question to be asked. Instead, they stood in silence as the young man reached into the helicopter and helped a man get out. An immensely fat man, stark-naked and white as the flesh of a potato, looking petrified. The old man strode purposefully toward him.

"Hello, I," the old man said.

"My name's Barth," the fat man answered, petulantly. The old man struck him hard across the mouth, hard enough that the tender lip split and blood dripped from where his teeth had cut into the skin.

"I," said the old man. "Your name is I."

The fat man nodded pitiably, but Barth—H—felt no pity for him. Two years this time. Only two damnable years and he was already in this condition. Barth could vaguely remember being proud of the mountain he had made of himself. But now he felt only contempt. Only a desire to go to the fat man, to scream in his face, "Why did you do it! Why did you let it happen again!"

It would have meant nothing. To I, as to H, it was the first time, the first betrayal. There had been no others in his memory.

Barth watched as the old man put a hoe in the fat man's hands and drove him out into the field. Two more young men got out of the helicopter. Barth knew what they would do, could almost see them helping the old man for a few days, until I finally learned the hopelessness of resistance and delay.

But Barth did not get to watch the replay of his own torture of two years before. The young man who had first emerged from the copter now led him to it, put him in a seat by a window, and sat beside him. The pilot speeded up the engines, and the copter began to rise.

"The bastard," Barth said, looking out the window at the old man as he slapped I across the face brutally.

The young man chuckled. Then he told Barth his assignment.

Barth clung to the window, looking out, feeling his life slip away from him even as the ground receded slowly. "I can't do it."

"There are worse assignments," the young man said.

Barth did not believe it.

"If I live," he said, "if I live, I want to come back here."

"Love it that much?"

"To kill him."

The young man looked at him blankly.

"The old man," Barth explained, then realized that the young man was ultimately incapable of understanding anything. He looked back out the window. The old man looked very small next to the huge lump of white flesh beside him. Barth felt a terrible loathing for I. A terrible despair in knowing that nothing could possibly be learned, that again and again his selves would replay this hideous scenario.

Somewhere, the man who would be J was dancing, was playing polo, was seducing and perverting and being delighted by every woman and boy and, God knows, sheep that he could find; somewhere the man who would be J dined.

I bent immensely in the sunlight and tried, clumsily, to use the hoe. Then, losing his balance, he fell over into the dirt, writhing. The old man raised his whip.

The helicopter turned then, so that Barth could see nothing but sky from his window. He never saw the whip fall. But he imagined the whip falling. Imagined and relished it, longed to feel the heaviness of the blow flowing from his own arm. *Hit him again!* he cried out inside himself. *Hit him for me!* And inside himself he made the whip fall a dozen times more.

"What are you thinking?" the young man asked, smiling, as if he knew the punch line of a joke.

"I was thinking," Barth said, "that the old man can't possibly hate him as much as I do."

Apparently that was the punch line. The young man laughed uproariously. Barth did not understand the joke, but somehow he was certain that he was the butt of it. He wanted to strike out but dared not.

Perhaps the young man saw the tension in Barth's body, or perhaps he merely wanted to explain. He stopped laughing but could not repress his smile, which penetrated Barth far more deeply than the laugh.

"But don't you see?" the young man asked. "Don't you know who the old man is?"

Barth didn't know.

"What do you think we did with A?" And the young man laughed again.

There are *worse assignments than mine,* Barth realized. And the worst of all would be to spend day after day, month after month, supervising that contemptible animal that he could not deny was himself.

The scar on his back bled a little, and the blood stuck to the seat when it dried.

THE STRETCH

by Sam Merwin, Jr.

Then there are the people who really don't care that they are fat, they just don't want to look fat, the ones who are always buying loose clothing, always hunting for garments with flattering lines and stripes that run vertically, the ones who would dearly love to find something like . . . well . . . an interdimensional girdle.

Nita Barentz was lissome as a flame, and cold as dry ice. At the moment of barging into Paul Carden's office, she was angry as a quadruple scoop of hot lava. Flinging the nylon-and-Lastex girdle on his unoffending desk, she said, in her flat, husky Manhattan contralto, "What are you trying to do now, Cardy—strangle me?"

Since, at the moment, Carden was in the process of selling his next year's line of foundation garments to a pair of chain-store buyers from the Middle West, he considered her suggestion with something like pleasure. But since Nita Barentz was unquestionably the best girdle-display machine in the whole garment district, and was continually receiving enticing offers from his bitterest rivals in a cutthroat business, he sighed and picked up the offending girdle and asked her what was wrong with it.

"Wrong with it!" Nita's contralto rose a full notch. "Don't ask me—ask those Comanche-cut geniuses who design these instruments of torture. It pulls me this way"—with definitive hip-wriggle—"this way"—with another—"and *this* way at once. It makes me feel all torn up."

"That will be enough hula dancing during office hours," said Carden, removing his cigar. "Report to Miss Herrin and get something else to model."

He watched, not unappreciatively, the indignant flirt of nonexistent bustle with which Nita left the room. With an inward sigh, he saw that the two buyers were looking longingly after her. It was going to be quite a trick to get them back into the proper detachment of a buying mood. He got up, opened the cellarette against the far wall. He said, "Well, gentlemen, what'll it be?"

When they were gone, he tested the offending girdle, even held it against his own midsection in front of the mirror. It looked all right, it felt all right. It had both firmness and plenty of stretch. A little later, he summoned Miss Herrin and asked her if there had been any other complaints.

Bluebell Herrin, a large and very Junoesque ex-model who had graduated to higher estate as display manager for Cardenwear, shook her head and said, "I don't know what got into Nita, darling. You know how unpredictable she is."

"That's what I like about you, Bluebell," he said, slipping an arm about her willing waist. "You're always right on the beam."

Bluebell looked pleased. Then a hint of worry flickered across her smooth forehead. She said, with the trace of a pout, "I hoped you called me in to tell me you'd changed your mind about taking me to the Copa opening tomorrow night."

Carden sighed and said, "Honey, you know we can't risk being seen together in a place like that. Someone would be bound to tell Letitia, and then the fat would really be in the fire. We'll have to stick to your apartment. And that's not too bad, is it, honey?"

It was Bluebell's turn to sigh. She said, "Of course not, honey, but it's a hell of a way for a girl to waste the best years of her life."

"Don't worry, baby," said Carden, on familiar ground. "It won't last forever. Something's got to give soon."

"Meanwhile it seems to be me that does all the *giving*," said Bluebell, moving clear of his one-arm encirclement and sedately toward the door. Carden looked after her, frowning. All too evidently, this wasn't his day.

Because he was feeling mean, and because the girdle was still there on his desk at the end of the day, Carden had it wrapped up and took it home as a present to his wife. Letitia, plump and popeyed as usual, examined it with a distressed look and said, "It's very thoughtful of you, Paul, but I don't see how you expect me to get into it."

"Try," he said. "It's the latest thing." Like all successful makers of women's foundation garments, he possessed a sound streak of sadism. While he shaved, he listened with almost seraphic expression to the grunts and gasps of anguish that sounded sporadically from the bedroom at his back. He hurried through his shaving, anticipating a ringside view of the contest. Wife versus girdle—the battle of the century.

But when he finished mopping lotion dry and turned, he saw that, in some miraculous way, Letitia had won. She was actually wearing the girdle, standing before the pier glass and studying with disbelief the new trimness it gave her overfull hips, the phenomenal absence of compensating bulges.

"Darling!" she said, seeing his reflection. "I don't know how you've done it, but this is—is . . . *Unngh!*" She made a strange, spasmodic, writhing movement that Carden had never seen matched in burlesque hall or stag smoker.

"*O-o-oh!*" she gasped. "*Yipe!*" Undulating like a plump anaconda, she blinked furiously to keep sudden tears from spoiling her mascara.

"Hey!" Carden was alarmed. "Better take it off if it's not comfortable."

To which Letitia replied, somehow controlling another spasm, "Are you out of your mind?"

The following evening, when he took Letitia to the Copa, she had things under control. Happily she whispered while they were dancing, "I'm getting used to it. And did you see the way Mr. Markell looked at me just now?"

"That wolf!" said Carden self-righteously. Letitia giggled and wriggled happily in perfect mambo rhythm.

That night, after they got home, she disappeared. When Carden, wearing his pajamas and a case of heartburn, entered the bathroom to brush his teeth, his wife, clad only in the new girdle, was happily looking at herself in the pier glass. When he emerged, ready for bed, she had vanished.

Only the girdle remained, lying crumpled and clueless on the wall-to-wall carpeting.

The police talked of everything from another man to murder. The papers talked of Charley Ross and Judge Crater. Bluebell didn't talk about anything for a while. She merely looked at Paul Carden with an expression blended of worship and fear. Two weeks later, at the next Copa opening, she shared Carden's table.

Later, in the privacy of her apartment, she said, "Paul, we don't have to go on like this now, do we? I mean, it all seems so furtive and sordid.

I should think, with all the money Letitia left you, you could—well, we could afford something a little better."

"Did you see the size of that check I signed at the Copa?" he asked, aggrieved. "Get smart, baby. I've still got the cops on my tail. I don't know what happened to Letitia any more than they do—but they think I do. And if I give them any cause for suspicion . . ." He drew the edge of a hand significantly across his throat.

"Honey, you can tell me." She was close to him, almost overpowering him with the clouds of perfume that emanated from her lush ex-model's body. "What really *did* happen?"

He said, "If I knew, don't you think I'd tell you?"

And she said, "Oh honey, I don't know. That depends . . ."

He looked at her narrowly and said harshly, "Then you think like the cops do—that I murdered her."

She turned to jelly under his stern regard.

As time went on, Carden began to consider himself a lucky man. Thanks to the conditions of Letitia's disappearance, he would not be able to marry again for seven years—unless her body were found. Which, he thought, God forbid.

If he had to wait that long to inherit her fat estate, well, he still had the business and it was booming. Apparently, being suspected of having murdered his wife made him more interesting to deal with, rather than a pariah. He invented a whole new line of foundation garments, labeled them with somewhat sinister humor, *Invisible.* They sold like a flash fire.

If his domestic life was hardly ideal, it had not been perfection before. In fact, as time wore on and Bluebell's demands grew greater, he began to compare her unfavorably to Letitia. He even began to talk about it. "Look at you," he said one night when they were again in her apartment. "You're letting yourself go all to hell. You're getting rolls—and bulges. And you work for me, a girdle maker."

She began to cry and said, "It runs in my family; we all get fat after thirty. What can I do about it, Paul? What can I do?"

He looked at her with contempt. Then, as he turned away, he remembered the girdle that had done such wonders for Letitia, just before she disappeared. The next day, he had it dug out of the drawer in which it had been reposing, neatly folded, had it rewrapped and presented it to Bluebell.

"This may not be very comfortable at first," he told her, "but it will do wonders for you. You need a miracle. Here it is."

He wondered what it would do for her—certainly it had made the departed Letitia almost palatable. And, fugitively, he wondered if it would make Bluebell disappear, too.

The next day, when Bluebell came to work, she confessed to Carden that the girdle was killing her. "It makes me feel pulled all out of shape," she said, twisting a little.

"Throw it away then," he growled, eyeing her regained trimness of figure.

"Are you crazy?" she asked him, her blue eyes dancing. "Look what it does for me!"

Rolling the cigar in the corner of his mouth, he had to admit, grudgingly at first and then with rising interest, that it did make her look ten years younger of body—and Bluebell had always been young of face. He said, "Wait for me tonight, baby. I'll drop by about midnight."

She said, "Oh, Paul—*darling!*" She kissed him warmly and trailed out, humming a little happy tune to herself. At the doorway, she turned and said, "It's beginning to feel a lot better on me already. It's just a matter of getting used to it."

Scrubbing lipstick from his mouth with a handkerchief, Carden heard an inner alarm bell ring. The pattern was getting alarmingly close to that preceding Letitia's still unexplained disappearance. What if Bluebell . . . ?

When he reached her apartment, that midnight, he had decided to tell her to throw the damned thing away. But he was too late. Bluebell had vanished. Her blue-satin negligee and furred mules lay in a little heap in the center of her living-room floor. And, in the midst of the pathetic pile of clothing, was the girdle. Carden scooped it up and stuffed it into his overcoat pocket. Then he got out of there—fast . . .

He returned to the party he had unobtrusively left a few minutes earlier, thus establishing an ironclad alibi—since no one else had seen him enter or leave Bluebell's apartment, two short blocks away. It was a good thing he did so, for the cops, baffled by his connection with a second disappearance, were far more difficult to deal with. But, since they had no shred of evidence involving Carden, they were finally forced to give up.

Carden, frightened, behaved very well for a couple of months. Then, one afternoon, while discussing a display with Nita Barentz, who had fallen heir to Bluebell's job, he found himself asking her for a date that evening.

Nita regarded him critically over a cigarette. She said, "Six months ago, I'd have said yes and you know it. Now"—she blew a perfect smoke ring—"I don't see the point. I've got the job I want and you've gotten fat—too fat."

Carden blinked. His chair did embrace his hips more snugly than it had in the past. And the waistband of his well-cut trousers was cutting its daily red furrow in the flesh beneath. He said, knowing all at once that he wanted Nita as he had never wanted another woman in his life, "Honey, If I go on a diet and shed some lard, how about it?"

She blew another smoke ring, sat on the edge of his desk, revealing the impeccable slimness of her own hipline. She said, "I don't think you can make it, Cardy-boy. I've seen you stowing away the Chateaubriand with Bearnaise sauce. But if you do, I'll give it a spin. Let's face it— we're both heels and we might hit it off. Birds of a feather, and all that..."

Carden reached for his phone. "I'm joining an exercise club right now," he told her.

"You do that little thing," she said, with amusement in her light green eyes. Was there also a lurking affection? Carden tried desperately to sell himself on the idea. And, if he was nothing else, he was a very good salesman.

He exercised, he dieted, he starved—and, at the end of ten days, he was five ounces lighter. In his fury and frustration, he all but stamped on the bathroom scales. He was not, he told himself miserably, cut out for the life of a monk. He put his hands over the dome of his belly, seeking to squeeze it flat. He failed. He thought of Nita, so alluring, so casual, so hard to get—for him at any rate. He moaned.

Something was going to have to be done.

He pawed through his pajamas, pulled up the paper at the bottom of the drawer. There it was, a little creased and crumpled, a little the worse for wear—but not much—the girdle that had done so much for Letitia and Bluebell, just before they had disappeared.

He weighed it in his hand, marveling at its lightness. A damned fine piece of goods, even if he did say so himself. He didn't want to vanish like his wife and mistress. But if they had been just a little more careful, if their vanity hadn't caused them to wear it all the time . . .

So it was a woman's garment—did that mean *he* couldn't wear it? Carden, as the manufacturer, knew damned well that he could. Gripping his cigar tightly between his teeth, he held it low, stepped into it, pulled it up around his hips.

Save for its absurdity as a woman's garment on his male body, the girdle proved a magical cure for Carden's obesity. The convex curve of his stomach was miraculously flattened into a verisimilitude of its youthful contour. He eyed himself in the pier glass, thinking. *Look out, Nita, here we come. . . .*

"Yeeeow!" He almost shouted as anguish seized him. He felt as if his legs were being pulled from his body at impossible angles. He twisted and the pain was gone, stooped to pick up his bitten-through cigar from the carpet. And it hit him again, seeming to pull his insides outside. He gasped and grunted, feeling sweat burst out all over him. But even so, he caught a glimpse of himself in the mirror and was both flattered and pleased by what he saw.

He tore it off and, without again glancing at his reflection, flung himself on the bed. He was going to need his sleep. The morrow promised to be a difficult day.

He was gritting his teeth against sporadic discomfort when Nita entered his office. She said, "Cardy, what are you planning for the—" She stopped, her mouth half open, began to prowl around him like a big, sleek jungle cat around her prey. She said, "What happened to *you?* You look wonderful."

"I told you I'd do it," he said, somehow managing to make his voice sound normal. "For you, I think I'd do anything. I can tell you this—it ain't easy."

"Poor Paul," she said, patting his shoulder. Then she said, "Well, I'm off for the day."

"Where are you going?" he called after her.

She paused, spoke over shoulder. "If I'm having dinner with you tonight, Cardy, I'm going to give myself the works. See you at seven."

He opened his mouth to protest, then thought better of it. The girdle was still giving him fits. Fortunately, with Nita absent, there was a huge pile of orders and displays to occupy his attention. Not until six-thirty, that evening, did he draw a deep breath. And by then, to his mixed terror and delight, the girdle felt almost comfortable on him.

He looked at his watch and frowned. He could hardly afford to re-move it now, and show himself to Nita in all his avoirdupois; nor could he continue wearing it forever, lest he suffer the same fate as had befallen Letitia and Bluebell. He had, he decided, until midnight. Cin-derella in a glass girdle, he thought. When he asked the doorman down-stairs to summon him a pumpkin coach, the man looked at him as if he were out of his mind.

Nita looked enchanting as she opened the door for him. She said, "I thought it would be nice to have a drink here before we went out. Wait for me in the living room. I've got everything ready in the kitchenette."

He entered, owning the earth. Knowing Nita, he knew she wouldn't really care how plump he was in private—as long as he displayed a svelteness consistent with her own in public. He stood in front of a gilt-framed mirror and patted his vanished bulge complacently. The girdle was almost comfortable, almost—if he could just give it one little wrench, he felt certain he could forget he had it on.

He gave it a little wrench. . . .

He was standing in what looked like the inside of a kaleidoscope. Bizarre shapes and colors rose on all sides of him, opaque, transparent. They fused or belled out into a sort of gray nothingness above him in a manner utterly incomprehensible to him.

A figure that looked about as human as a sculptor's wire armature for a statue slid out of nowhere and a voice—or was it a voice?—sounded in his head. It said, "Oh, Lord! *Another* of them—and this one a man. How'd it happen, please?"

"Where am I?" said Carden, stupefied.

"You're in New York, of course," was the reply. "But you'd better put on some clothes before you're arrested."

Some strange-looking fabrics in even stranger designs and colors were handed him. As he looked down at his own limbs, he was almost paralyzed with terror. Nita had wanted him thin—but not this thin. He, too, looked like the mere twisted wire framework of a human being. He said, "Stop fooling, will you? What's going on around here?"

"That's what I'd like to know," was the reply and somehow Carden derived a distinct impression that this was a female of the species. "So will the authorities, I guess. Did you come through via that misplaced three-way-stretch girdle?"

"*Three*-way-stretch!" Carden gulped. "There's no such thing. It's impossible; in a three-dimensional world . . ." He stopped talking as the full implications sank home to him.

"Is this the fourth dimension?" he asked quaveringly.

"You might call it that," was the reply. "Come on, whatever your name is. I've got to get you downtown to the authorities. If my husband should find out that . . ." She left the rest of it hanging.

"You know," she added, helping him into the strange garments, "you're the third person who's come through in the past several lunars. It seems there was a mistake in the garment center and a girdle slipped through. Two women adjusted to it and made the jump. If you came the same way, what were you—a man—doing with it on?"

Letitia and Bluebell here ahead of him. The prospect was terrifying. He said, "My dear, do you have to turn me in? I mean—isn't there some other way of handling this? I promise you, if people wear girdles here, I can manufacture them. Why not help me get started." He squinted at her with what he hoped were his eyes, added, "I could do wonders for your figure—not that it needs much help, of course. But just a little added here, a little taken off there . . . it might prove profitable to us both."

The sound she made could only be laughter. She said, "How do you manage to keep so delightfully fat without a girdle? All the men I know are thin as rails. Why, without their girdles, they're nothing."

"It's a knack," he said modestly, trying to assimilate the eerie appearance of his hostess.

"It must be." She took two strange-looking cones from some sort of container, offered him one. Following her, he put the pointed end in his mouth, inhaled. It was some sort of fourth-dimensional cigarette—and it tasted a lot better than it looked.

He said, "Your husband . . . ?"

And she said, "Who? Oh, my husband. Don't worry about *him*. But I'll have to take you downtown, I'm afraid. Then, when you're all straightened out, perhaps we can make plans."

"Sure," he said. "Sure—I'm looking forward to it already." But he knew when he was licked. And besides, if Letitia and Bluebell looked like his hostess, it wasn't going to make very much difference. He wondered what was going to happen if Nita tried the girdle. It would be a donnybrook.

But Nita wasn't the sort of girl to need a girdle for a long time to come.

CAMELS AND
DROMEDARIES, CLEM

by R. A. Lafferty

Pregnant women have the most ephemeral sort of over-weight; they get to eat enough for two, grow larger and larger and larger, and then another person comes into the world and all that extra weight goes away. What if it worked that way for everybody? Or at least for Clem?

"Greeks and Armenians, Clem. Condors and buzzards."

"Samoyeds and Malemutes, Clem. Galena and molybdenite."

Oh here, here! What kind of talk is that?

That is definitive talk. That is fundamental talk. There is no other kind of talk that will bring us to the core of this thing.

Clem Clendenning was a traveling salesman, a good one. He had cleared $35,000 the previous year. He worked for a factory in a midwestern town. The plant produced a unique product, and Clem sold it over one-third of the nation.

Things were going well with him. Then a little thing happened, and it changed his life completely.

Salesmen have devices by which they check and double-check. One thing they do when stopping at hotels in distant towns; they make sure they're registered. This sounds silly, but it isn't. A salesman will get calls from his home office and it is important that the office be able to locate him. Whenever Clem registered at a hotel he would check back after several hours to be sure that they had him entered correctly. He would call in from somewhere, and he would ask for himself. And it sometimes did happen that he was told he was not registered. At this Clem would always raise a great noise to be sure that they had him straight thereafter.

Arriving in a town this critical day, Clem had found himself ravenously hungry and tired to his depths. Both states were unusual to him. He went to a grill and ate gluttonously for an hour, so much so that

30

people stared at him. He ate almost to the point of apoplexy. Then he taxied to the hotel, registered, and went up to his room at once. Later, not remembering whether he had even undressed or not (it was early afternoon), he threw himself onto the bed and slept, as it seemed, for hours.

But he noted that it was only a half hour later that he woke, feeling somehow deprived, as though having a great loss. He was floundering around altogether in a daze, and was once more possessed of an irrational hunger. He unpacked a little, put on a suit, and was surprised to find that it hung on him quite loosely.

He went out with the feeling that he had left something on the bed that was not quite right, and yet he had been afraid to look. He found a hearty place and had another great meal. And then (at a different place so that people would not be puzzled at him) he had still another one. He was feeling better now, but mighty queer, mighty queer.

Fearing that he might be taken seriously ill, he decided to check his bearings. He used his old trick. He found a phone and called his hotel and asked for himself.

"We will check," said the phone girl, and a little bit later she said, "just a minute, he will be on the line in a minute."

"Oh, great green goat," he growled, "I wonder how they have me mixed up this time."

And Clem was about to raise his voice unpleasantly to be sure that they got him straight, when a voice came onto the phone.

This is the critical point.

It was his own voice.

The calling Clendenning laughed first. And then he froze. It was no trick. It was no freak. There was no doubt that it was his own voice. Clem used the Dictaphone a lot and he knew the sound of his own voice.

And now he heard his own voice raised higher in all its unmistakable aspects, a great noise about open idiots who call on the phone and then stand silent without answering.

"It's me all right," Clem grumbled silently to himself. "I sure do talk rough when I'm irritated."

There was a law against harassment by telephone, the voice on the phone said. By God, the voice on the phone said, he just noticed that his room had been rifled. He was having the call monitored right now, the voice on the phone swore. Clem knew that this was a lie, but he also recognized it as his own particular style of lying. The voice got really woolly and profane.

Then there was a change in the tone.

"Who are you?" the voice asked hollowly. "I hear you breathing scared. I know your sound. Gaaah—it's me!" And the voice on the phone was also breathing scared.

"There has to be an answer," he told himself. "I'll just go to my room and take a hot bath and try to sleep it off."

Then he roared back: "Go to my room! Am I crazy? I have just called my room. I am already there. I would not go to my room for one million one hundred and five thousand dollars."

He was trembling as though his bones were too loose for his flesh. It was funny that he had never before noticed how bony he was. But he wasn't too scared to think straight on one subject, however crooked other things might be.

"No, I wouldn't go back to that room for any sum. But I *will* do something for another sum, and I'll do it damned quick."

He ran, and he hasn't stopped running yet. That he should have another self-made flesh terrified him. He ran, but he knew where he was running for the first stage of it. He took the night plane back to his hometown, leaving bag and baggage behind.

He was at the bank when it opened in the morning. He closed out all his accounts. He turned everything into cash. This took several hours. He walked out of there with $83,000. He didn't feel like a thief; it was his own; it couldn't have belonged to his other self, could it? If there were two of them, then let there be two sets of accounts.

Now to get going fast.

He continued to feel odd. He weighed himself. In spite of his great eating lately, he had lost a hundred pounds. That's enough to make anyone feel odd. He went to New York City to lose himself in the crowd and to think about the matter.

And what was the reaction at his firm and at his home when he turned up missing? That's the second point. He didn't turn up missing. As the months went by he followed the doings of his other self. He saw his pictures in the trade papers; he was still with the same firm; he was still top salesman. He always got the hometown paper, and he some-times found himself therein. He saw his own picture with his wife Ve-ronica. She looked wonderful and so, he had to admit, did he. They were still on the edge of the social stuff.

"If he's me, I wonder who I am?" Clem continued to ask himself. There didn't seem to be any answer to this. There wasn't any handle to take the thing by.

Clem went to an analyst and told his story. The analyst said that Clem had wanted to escape his job, or his wife Veronica, or both. Clem insisted that this was not so; he loved his job and his wife; he got deep and fulfilling satisfaction out of both.

"You don't know Veronica or you wouldn't suggest it," he told the analyst. "She is—ah—well, if you don't know her, then hell, you don't know anything."

The analyst told him that it had been his own id talking to him on the telephone.

"How is it that my id is doing a top selling job out of a town five hundred miles from here, and I am here?" Clem wanted to know. "Other men's ids aren't so talented."

The analyst said that Clem was suffering from a *tmema* or *diairetikos* of an oddly named part of his psychic apparatus.

"Oh hell, I'm an extrovert. Things like that don't happen to people like me," Clem said.

Thereafter Clem tried to make the best of his compromised life. He was quickly well and back to normal weight. But he never talked on the telephone again in his life. He'd have died most literally if he ever heard his own voice like that again. He had no phone in any room where he lived. He wore a hearing aid he did not need; he told people that he could not hear over the phone, and that any unlikely call that came for him would have to be taken down and relayed to him.

He had to keep an eye on his other self, so he did renew one old contact. With one firm in New York there was a man he had called on regularly; this man had a cheerful and open mind that would not be spooked by the unusual. Clem began to meet this man (Why should we lie about it? His name was Joe Zabotsky.) not at the firm, but at an after-hours place which he knew Joe frequented.

Joe heard Clem's story and believed it—after he had phoned (in Clem's presence) the other Clem, located him a thousand miles away, and ordered an additional month's supply of the unique product which they didn't really need, things being a little slow in all lines right then.

After that, Clem would get around to see Joe Zabotsky an average of once a month, about the time he figured the other Clem had just completed his monthly New York call.

"He's changing a little bit, and so are you," Joe told Clem one evening. "Yeah, it was with him just about like with you. He did lose a lot of weight a while back, what you call the critical day, and he gained it back pretty quick just like you did. It bugs me, Clem, which of you I used to know. There are some old things between us that he recalls and you don't; there are some that you recall and he doesn't; and dammit there are some you both recall, and they happened between myself and one man only, not between myself and two men.

"But these last few months your face seems to be getting a little fuller, and his a little thinner. You still look just-alike, but not quite as just-alike as you did at first."

"I know it," Clem said. "I study the analysts now since they don't do any good at studying me, and I've learned an old analyst's trick. I take an old face-on photo of myself, divide it down the center, and then complete each half with its mirror image. It gives two faces just a little bit different. Nobody has the two sides of his face quite alike. These two different faces are supposed to indicate two different aspects of the personality. I study myself, now, and I see that I am becoming more like one of the constructions; so he must be becoming more like the other construction. He mentions that there are disturbances between Veronica and himself, does he? And neither of them quite understands what is the matter? Neither do I."

Clem lived modestly, but he began to drink more than he had. He watched, through his intermediary Joe and by other means, the doings of his other self. And he waited. This was the most peculiar deal he had ever met, but he hadn't been foxed on very many deals.

"He's no smarter than I am," Clem insisted. "But, by cracky, if he's me, he's pretty smart at that. What would he do if he were in my place? And I guess, in a way, he is."

Following his avocation of drinking and brooding and waiting, Clem frequented various little places, and one day he was in the Two-Faced Bar and Grill. This was owned and operated by Two-Face Terrel, a double-dealer and gentleman, even something of a dandy. A man had just seated himself at a dim table with Clem, had been served by Two-Face, and now the man began to talk.

"Why did Matthew have two donkeys?" the man asked.

"Matthew who?" Clem asked. "I don't know what you're talking about."

"I'm talking about 21:1–9, of course," the man said. "The other Gospels have only one donkey. Did you ever think about that?"

"No, I'd never given it a thought," Clem said.

"Well, tell me then, why does Matthew have two demoniacs?"

"What?"

"8:28–34. The other evangelists have only one crazy man."

"Maybe there was only one loony at first, and he drove the guy drinking next to him crazy."

"That's possible. Oh, you're kidding. But why does Matthew have two blind men?"

"Number of a number, where does this happen?" Clem asked.

"9:27–31, and again 20:29–34. In each case the other gospelers have only one blind man. Why does Matthew double so many things? There are other instances of it."

"Maybe he needed glasses," Clem said.

"No," the man whispered, "I think he was one of us."

"What 'us' are you talking about?" Clem asked. But already he had begun to suspect that his case was not unique. Suppose that it happened one time out of a million? There would still be several hundred such sundered persons in the country, and they would tend to congregate—in such places as the Two-Faced Bar and Grill. And there *was* something deprived or riven about almost every person who came into the place.

"And remember," the man was continuing, "the name or cognomen of one of the other Apostles was 'The Twin.' But of whom was he twin? I think there was the beginning of a group of them there already."

"He wants to see you," Joe Zabotsky told Clem when they met several months later. "So does she."

"When did he begin to suspect that there was another one of me?"

"He knew something was wrong from the first. A man doesn't lose a hundred pounds in an instant without there being something wrong. And he knew something was very wrong when all his accounts were cleaned out. These were not forgeries, for they were hurried and all different and very nervous. But they were all genuine signatures, he admitted that. Damn, you are a curious fellow, Clem!"

"How much does Veronica know, and how? What does she want? What does he?"

"He says that she also began to guess from the first. 'You act like you're only half a man, Clem,' she would say to him, to you, that is. She wants to see more of her husband, she says, the other half. And he wants to trade places with you, at least from time to time on a trial basis."

"I won't do it! Let him stew in it!" Then Clem called Clem a name so vile that it will not be given here.

"Take is easy, Clem," Joe remonstrated. "It's yourself you are calling that."

There was a quizzical young-old man who came sometimes into the Two-Faced Bar and Grill. They caught each other's eye this day, and the young-old began to talk.

"Is not consciousness the thing that divides man from the animals?" he asked. "But consciousness is a double thing, a seeing one's self; not only a knowing, but a knowing that one knows. So the human person is of its essence double. How this is commonly worked out in practice, I don't understand. Our present states are surely not the common thing."

"My own consciousness isn't intensified since my person is doubled," Clem said. "It's all the other way. My consciousness is weakened. I've become a creature of my own unconscious. There's something about you that I don't like, man."

"The animal is simple and single," the young-old man said. "It lacks true reflexive consciousness. But man is dual (though I don't understand the full meaning of it here), and he has at least intimation of true consciousness. And what is the next step?"

"I fathom you now," Clem said. "My father would have called you a Judas Priest."

"I don't quite call myself that. But what follows the singularity of the animal and duality of man? You recall the startling line of Chesterton? —'we trinitarians have known it is not good for God to be alone.' But was His case the same as ours? Did He do a violent double take, or triple take, when He discovered one day that there were Three of Him? Has He ever adjusted to it? Is it possible that He can?"

"Aye, you're a Judas Priest. I hate the species."

"But I am not, Mr. Clendenning. I don't understand this sundering any more than you do. It happens only one time in a million, but it has happened to us. Perhaps it would happen to God but one time in a billion billion, but it has happened. The God who is may be much rarer than any you can imagine.

"Let me explain: my other person is a very good man, much better than when we were conjoined. He's a dean already, and he'll be a bishop within five years. Whatever of doubt and skepticism that was in me originally is still in the me here present, and it is somehow intensified. I do not want to be dour or doubting. I do not want to speak mockingly of the great things. But the bothering things are all in the me here. The other me is freed of them.

"Do you think that there might have been a sundered-off Napoleon who was a bumbler at strategy and who was a nervous little coward? Did there remain in backwoods Kentucky for many years a sundered-off Lincoln who gave full rein to his inborn delight in the dirty story, the dirty deal, the barefoot life, the loutishness ever growing? Was there a sundered-off Augustine who turned ever more Manichean, who refined more and more his arts of false logic and fornication, who howled against reason, who joined the cultishness of the crowd? Is there an anti-Christ—the man who fled naked from the garden at dusk leaving his garment behind? We know that both do not keep garment at the moment of sundering."

"Damned if I know, Judas Priest. Your own father-name abomination, was there another of him? Was he better or worse? I leave you."

"She is in town and is going to meet you tonight," Joe Zabotsky told Clem at their next monthly meeting. "We've got it all set up."

"No, no, not Veronica!" Clem was startled. "I'm not ready for it."

"She is. She's a strong-minded woman, and she knows what she wants."

"No, she doesn't, Joe. I'm afraid of it. I haven't touched a woman since Veronica."

"Damn it, Clem, this *is* Veronica that we're talking about. It isn't as though you weren't still married to her."

"I'm still afraid of it, Joe. I've become something unnatural now. Where am I supposed to meet her? Oh, oh, you son of a snake! I can feel her presence. She was already in the place when I came in. No, no, Veronica, I'm not the proper one. It's all a case of mistaken identity."

"It sure is, Clem Clam," said the strong-minded Veronica as she came to their table. "Come along now. You're going to have more explaining to do than any man I ever heard of."

"But I can't explain it, Veronica. I can't explain any of it."

"You will try real hard, Clem. We both will. Thank you, Mr. Zabotsky, for your discretion in an odd situation."

Well, it went pretty well, so well in fact there had to be a catch to it. Veronica was an unusual and desirable woman, and Clem had missed her. They did the town mildly. They used to do it once a year, but they had been apart in their present persons for several years. And yet Veronica would want to revisit "that little place we were last year, oh, but that wasn't you, was it, Clem?—that was Clem," and that kind of talk was confusing.

They dined grandly, and they talked intimately but nervously. There was real love between them, or among them, or around them somehow. They didn't understand how it had turned grotesque.

"He never quite forgave you for clearing out the accounts," Veronica said.

"But it was my money, Veronica," Clem insisted. "I earned it by the sweat of my tongue and my brain. He had nothing to do with it."

"But you're wrong, dear Clem. You worked equally for it when you were one. You should have taken only half of it."

They came back to Veronica's hotel, and one of the clerks looked at Clem suspiciously.

"Didn't you just go up, and then come down, and then go up again?" he asked.

"I have my ups and downs, but you may mean something else," Clem said.

"Now don't be nervous, dear," Veronica said. They were up in Veronica's room now, and Clem was looking around very nervously. He had jumped at a mirror, not being sure that it was.

"I am still your wife," Veronica said, "and nothing has changed, except everything. I don't know how, but I'm going to put things back together again. You have to have missed me! Give now!" And she swept him off his feet as though he were a child. Clem had always loved her for her sudden strength. If you haven't been up in Veronica's arms, then you haven't been anywhere.

"Get your pumpkin-picking hands off my wife, you filthy oaf!" a voice cracked out like a bullwhip, and Veronica dropped Clem thuddingly from the surprise of it.

"Oh, Clem!" she said with exasperation, "you shouldn't have come here when I was with Clem. Now you've spoiled everything. You *can't* be jealous of each other. You're the same man. Let's all pack up and go home and make the best of it. Let people talk if they want to."

"Well, I don't know what to do," Clem said. "This isn't the way. There isn't any way at all. Nothing can ever be right with us when we are three."

"There *is* a way," Veronica said with sudden steel in her voice. "You boys will just have to get together again. I am laying down the law now. For a starter each of you lose a hundred pounds. I give you a month for it. You're both on bread and water from now on. No, come to think of it, no bread! No water either; that may be fattening, too. You're both on nothing for a month."

"We won't do it," both Clems said. "It'd kill us."

"Let it kill you then," Veronica said. "You're no good to me the way you are. You'll lose the weight. I think that will be the trigger action. Then we will all go back to Rock Island or whatever town that was and get the same hotel room where one of you rose in a daze and left the other one unconscious on the bed. We will re-create those circumstances and see if you two can't get together again."

"Veronica," Clem said, "it is physically and biologically impossible."

"Also topologically absurd."

"You should have thought of that when you came apart. All you have to do now is get together again. Do it! I'm laying down an ultimatum. There's no other way. You two will just have to get together again."

"There *is* another way," Clem said in a voice so sharp that it scared both Veronica and Clem.

"What? What is it?" they asked him.

"Veronica, you've got to divide," Clem said. "You've got to come apart."

"Oh, no. No!"

"Now you put on a hundred pounds just as fast as you can, Veronica. Clem," Clem said, "go get a dozen steaks up here for her to start on. And about thirty pounds of bone meal, whatever that is. It sounds like it might help."

"I'll do it, I'll do it," Clem cried, "and a couple of gallons of blood-pudding. Hey, I wonder where I can get that much blood-pudding this time of night?"

"Boys, are you serious? Do you think it'll work?" Veronica gasped. "I'll try anything. How do I start?"

"Think divisive thoughts," Clem shouted as he started out for the steaks and bone meal and blood-pudding.

"I don't know any," Veronica said. "Oh, yes I do! I'll think them. We'll do everything! We'll make it work."

"You have a lot going for you, Veronica," Clem said. "You've always been a double-dealer. And your own mother always said that you were two-faced."

"Oh, I know it, I know it! We'll do everything. We'll make it work. We'll leave no stone unthrown."

"You've got to become a pair, Veronica," Clem said at one of their sessions. "Think of pairs."

"Crocodiles and alligators, Clem," she said, "frogs and toads. Eels and lampreys."

"Horses and asses, Veronica," Clem said, "elk and moose. Rabbits and hares."

"Mushrooms and toadstools, Veronica," Clem said. "Mosses and lichens. Butterflies and moths."

"Camels and dromedaries, Clem," Veronica said. "Salamanders and newts, dragonfly and damselfly."

Say, they thought about pairs by the long ton. They thought of every kind of sundering and divisive thought. They plumbed the depths of psychology and biology, and called in some of the most respected quacks of the city for advice.

No people ever tried anything harder. Veronica and Clem and Clem did everything they could think of. They gave it a month. "I'll do it or bust," Veronica said.

And they came close, so close that you could feel it. Veronica weighed up a hundred pounds well within the month, and then coasted in on double brandies. It was done all but the final thing.

Pay homage to her, people! She was a valiant woman!

They both said that about her after it was over with. They would admire her as long as they lived. She had given it everything.

"I'll do it or bust," she had said.

And after they had gathered her remains together and buried her, it left a gap in their lives, in Clem's more than in Clem's, since Clem had already been deprived of her for these last several years.

And a special honor they paid her.

They set *two* headstones on her grave. One of them said "Veronica." And the other one said "Veronica."

She'd have liked that.

THE CHAMP

by T. Coraghessan Boyle

The world is grossly unfair to the overweight. Not only are slim people considered more attractive, and not only do they live longer, but they also do better at nearly all sports, except sumo wrestling. Maybe what we need is a new professional sport for the large.

Angelo D. was training hard. This challenger, Kid Gullet, would be no pushover. In fact, the Kid hit him right where he lived: he was worried. He'd been champ for thirty-seven years and all that time his records had stood like Mount Rushmore—and now this Kid was eating them up. Fretful, he pushed his plate away.

"But, Angelo, you ain't done already?" His trainer, Spider Decoud, was all over him. "That's what—a piddling hundred and some odd flapjacks and seven quarts a milk?"

"He's on to me, Spider. He found out about the ulcer and now he's going to hit me with enchiladas and shrimp in cocktail sauce."

"Don't fret it, Killer. We'll get him with the starches and heavy syrups. He's just a kid, twenty-two. What does he know about eating? Look, get up and walk it off and we'll do a kidney and kipper course, okay? And then maybe four or five dozen poached eggs. C'mon, Champ, lift that fork. You want to hold onto the title or not?"

First it was pickled eggs. Eighty-three pickled eggs in an hour and a half. The record had stood since 1941. They said it was like DiMaggio's consecutive-game hitting streak: unapproachable. A world apart. But then, just three months ago, Angelo had picked up the morning paper and found himself unforked: a man who went by the name of Kid Gullet had put down 108 of them. In the following weeks Angelo had seen his records toppled like a string of dominoes: gherkins, pullets, persimmons, oysters, pretzels, peanuts, scalloped potatoes, feta cheese,

41

smelts, girl scout cookies. At the Rendezvous Room in Honolulu the Kid bolted 12,000 macadamia nuts and 67 bananas in less than an hour. During a Cubs-Phillies game at Wrigley Field he put away 43 hot dogs —with buns—and 112 Cokes. In Orkney it was legs of lamb; in Frankfurt, Emmentaler and schnitzel; in Kiev, pirogen. He was irrepressible. In Stelton, New Jersey, he finished off six gallons of borscht and 93 four-ounce jars of gefilte fish while sitting atop a flagpole. The press ate it up.

Toward the end of the New Jersey session a reporter from ABC Sports swung a boom mike up to where the Kid sat on his eminence, chewing the last of the gefilte fish. "What are your plans for the future, Kid?" shouted the newsman.

"I'm after the Big One," the Kid replied.

"Angelo D.?"

The camera zoomed in, the Kid grinned.

"Capocollo, chili and curry,
Big Man, you better start to worry."

Angelo was rattled. He gave up the morning paper and banned the use of the Kid's name around the Training Table. Kid Gullet: every time he heard those three syllables his stomach clenched. Now he lay on the bed, the powerful digestive machinery tearing away at breakfast, a bag of peanuts in his hand, his mind sifting through the tough bouts and spectacular triumphs of the past. There was Beau Riviere from Baton Rouge, who nearly choked him on deep-fried mud puppies, and Pinky Luzinski from Pittsburgh, who could gulp down 300 raw eggs and then crunch up the shells as if they were potato chips. Or the Japanese sumo wrestler who swallowed marbles by the fistful and throve on sashimi in a fiery mustard sauce. He'd beaten them all, because he had grit and determination and talent—and he would beat this kid too. Angelo sat up and roared: "I'm still the champ!"

The door cracked open. It was Decoud. "That's the spirit, Killer. Remember D. D. Peloris, Max Manger, Bozo Miller, Spoonbill Rizzo? Bums. All of them. You beat 'em, Champ."

"Yeah!" Angelo bellowed. "And I'm going to flatten this Gullet too."

"That's the ticket: leave him gasping for Bromo."

"They'll be pumping his stomach when I'm through with him."

Out in L.A. the Kid was taking on Turk Harris, number one contender for the heavyweight crown. The Kid's style was Tabasco and Worcester-

shire; Harris was a mashed-potato-and-creamed-corn man—a trench-
erman of the old school. Like Angelo D.

Harris opened with a one-two combination of rice and kidney beans;
the Kid countered with cocktail onions and capers. Then Harris hit him
with baklava—400 two-inch squares of it. The Kid gobbled them like
hors d'oeuvres, came back with chili rellenos and asparagus vinaigrette.
He KO'd Harris in the middle of the fourth round. After the bout he
stood in a circle of jabbing microphones, flashing lights. "I got one thing
to say," he shouted. "And if you're out there, Big Man, you better take
heed:

> I'm going to float like a parfait,
> Sting like a tamale.
> Big Man, you'll hit the floor,
> In four."

At the preliminary weigh-in for the title bout the Kid showed up on
roller skates in a silver lamé jumpsuit. He looked like something off the
launching pad at Cape Canaveral. Angelo, in his coal-bucket trousers
and suspenders, could have been mistaken for an aging barber or a
boccie player strayed in from the park.

The Kid had a gallon jar of hot cherry peppers under his arm. He
wheeled up to the Champ, bolted six or seven in quick succession, and
then held one out to him by the stem. "Care for an appetizer, Pops?"
Angelo declined, his face dour and white, the big fleshy nostrils heaving
like a stallion's. Then the photographers posed the two, belly to belly.
In the photograph, which appeared on the front page of the paper the
following morning, Angelo D. looked like an advertisement for heartburn.

There was an SRO crowd at the Garden for the title bout. Scalpers
were getting two hundred and up for tickets. ABC Sports was there,
Colonel Sanders was there, Arthur Treacher, Julia Child, James Beard,
Ronald McDonald, Mamma Leone. It was the Trenching Event of the
Century.

Spider Decoud and the Kid's manager had inspected the ring and
found the arrangements to their satisfaction—each man had a table,
stool, stack of plates and cutlery. Linen napkins, a pitcher of water. It
would be a fourteen-round affair, each round going ten minutes with a
sixty-second bell break. The contestants would name their dishes for
alternate rounds, the Kid, as challenger, leading off.

A hush fell over the crowd. And then the chant, rolling from back to front like breakers washing the beach: GULLET, GULLET, GULLET! There he was, the Kid, sweeping down the aisle like a born champion in his cinnamon red robe with the silver letters across the abdomen. He stepped into the ring, clasped his hands, and shook them over his head. The crowd roared like rock faces slipping deep beneath the earth. Then he did a couple of deep knee bends and sat down on his stool. At that moment Angelo shuffled out from the opposite end of the arena, stern, grim, raging, the tight curls at the back of his neck standing out like the tail feathers of an albatross, his barren dome ghostly under the klieg lights, the celebrated paunch swelling beneath his opalescent robe like a fat wad of butterball turkeys. The crowd went mad. They shrieked, hooted and whistled, women kissed the hem of his gown, men reached out to pat his bulge. ANGELO! He stepped into the ring and took his seat as the big black mike descended from the ceiling.

The announcer, in double lapels and bow tie, shouted over the roar, "Ladies and Gentlemen—," while Angelo glared at the Kid, blood in his eye. He was choked with a primordial competitive fury, mad as a kamikaze, deranged with hunger. Two days earlier Decoud had lured him into a deserted meat locker and bolted the door—and then for the entire forty-eight hours had projected pornographic food films on the wall. Fleshy wet lips closing on éclairs, zoom shots of masticating teeth, gulping throats, probing tongues, children innocently sucking at Tootsie Roll pops—it was obscene, titillating, maddening. And through it all a panting soundtrack composed of grunts and sighs and the smack of lips. Angelo D. climbed into the ring a desperate man. But even money nonetheless. The Kid gloated in his corner.

"At this table, in the crimson trunks," bellowed the announcer, "standing six foot two inches tall and weighing in at three hundred and seventy-seven pounds . . . is the challenger, Kid Gullet!" A cheer went up, deafening. The announcer pointed to Angelo. "And at this table, in the pearly trunks and standing five foot seven and a half inches tall and weighing in at three hundred and twenty-three pounds," he bawled, his voice rumbling like a cordon of cement trucks, "is the Heavyweight Champion of the World . . . Angelo D.!" Another cheer, perhaps even louder. Then the referee took over. He had the contestants step to the center of the ring, the exposed flesh of their chests and bellies like a pair of avalanches, while he asked if each was acquainted with the rules.

The Kid grinned like a shark. "All right then," the ref said, "touch midriffs and come out eating."

The bell rang for Round One. The Kid opened with Szechwan hot and sour soup, three gallons. He lifted the tureen to his lips and slapped it down empty. The Champ followed suit, his face aflame, sweat breaking out on his forehead. He paused three times, and when finally he set the tureen down he snatched up the water pitcher and drained it at a gulp while the crowd booed and Decoud yelled from the corner: "Lay off the water or you'll bloat up like a blowfish!"

Angelo retaliated with clams on the half shell in Round Two: 512 in ten minutes. But the Kid kept pace with him—and as if that weren't enough, he sprinkled his own portion with cayenne pepper and Tabasco. The crowd loved it. They gagged on their hot dogs, pelted the contestants with plastic cups and peanut shells, gnawed at the backs of their seats. Angelo looked up at the Kid's powerful jaws, the lips stained with Tabasco, and began to feel queasy.

The Kid staggered him with lamb curry in the next round. The crowd was on its feet, the Champ's face was green, the fork motionless in his hand, the ref counting down, Decoud twisting the towel in his fists—when suddenly the bell sounded and the Champ collapsed on the table. Decoud leaped into the ring, chafed Angelo's abdomen, sponged his face. "Hang in there, Champ," he said, "and come back hard with the carbohydrates."

Angelo struck back with potato gnocchi in Round Four; the Kid countered with Kentucky burgoo. They traded blows through the next several rounds, the Champ scoring with Nesselrode pie, fettucine Alfredo and poi, the Kid lashing back with jambalaya, shrimp creole and herring in horseradish sauce.

After the bell ending Round Eleven, the bout had to be held up momentarily because of a disturbance in the audience. Two men, thin as tapers and with beards like Spanish moss, had leaped into the ring waving posters that read REMEMBER BIAFRA. The Kid started up from his table and pinned one of them to the mat, while security guards nabbed the other. The Champ sat immobile on his stool, eyes tearing from the horseradish sauce, his fist clenched round the handle of the water pitcher. When the ring was cleared the bell rang for Round Twelve.

It was the Champ's round all the way: sweet potato pie with butterscotch syrup and pralines. For the first time the Kid let up—toward the end of the round he dropped his fork and took a mandatory eight count. But he came back strong in the thirteenth with a savage combination of Texas wieners and sauce diable. The Champ staggered, went down once, twice, flung himself at the water pitcher while the Kid gorged like a machine, wiener after wiener, blithely lapping the hot sauce from his fingers and knuckles with an epicurean relish. Then Angelo's head fell to the table, his huge whiskered jowl mired in a pool of béchamel and butter. The fans sprang to their feet, feinting left and right, snapping their jaws and yabbering for the kill. The Champ's eyes fluttered open, the ref counted over him.

It was then that it happened. His vision blurring, Angelo gazed out into the crowd and focused suddenly on the stooped and wizened figure of an old woman in a black bonnet. Decoud stood at her elbow. Angelo lifted his head. "Ma?" he said. "Eat, Angelo, eat!" she called, her voice a whisper in the apocalyptic thunder of the crowd. "Clean your plate!"

"Nine!" howled the referee, and suddenly the Champ came to life, lashing into the sauce diable like a crocodile. He bolted wieners, sucked at his fingers, licked the plate. Some say his hands moved so fast that they defied the eye, a mere blur, slapstick in double time. Then the bell rang for the final round and Angelo announced his dish: "Gruel!" he roared. The Kid protested. "What kind of dish is that?" he whined. "Gruel? Who ever heard of gruel in a championship bout?" But gruel it was. The Champ lifted the bowl to his lips, pasty ropes of congealed porridge trailing down his chest; the crowd cheered, the Kid toyed with his spoon—and then it was over.

The referee stepped in, helped Angelo from the stool and held his flaccid arm aloft. Angelo was plate-drunk, reeling. He looked out over the cheering mob, a welter of button heads like B and B mushrooms— or Swedish meatballs in a rich golden sauce. Then he gagged. "The winner," the ref was shouting, "and still champion, Angelo D.!"

THE TRUTH ABOUT PYECRAFT

by H. G. Wells

Every fat person wants to lose weight. "Gotta lose a little weight" could almost be considered a national slogan. But hold on a minute! Is weight really what needs to be lost?

He sits not a dozen yards away. If I glance over my shoulder I can see him. And if I catch his eye—and usually I catch his eye—it meets me with an expression....

It is mainly an imploring look—and yet with suspicion in it.

Confound his suspicion! If I wanted to tell on him I should have told long ago. I don't tell and I don't tell, and he ought to feel at his ease. As if anything so gross and fat as he could feel at ease! Who would believe me if I did tell?

Poor old Pyecraft! Great, uneasy jelly of substance! The fattest club-man in London.

He sits at one of the little club tables in the huge bay by the fire, stuffing. What is he stuffing? I glance judiciously, and catch him biting at a round of hot buttered teacake, with his eyes on me. Confound him! —with his eyes on me!

That settles it, Pyecraft! Since you *will* be abject, since you *will* behave as though I was not a man of honor, here, right under your embedded eyes, I write this thing down—the plain truth about Pyecraft. The man I helped, the man I shielded, and who has requited me by making my club unendurable, absolutely unendurable, with his liquid appeal, with the perpetual "don't tell" of his looks.

And, besides, why does he keep on eternally eating?

Well, here goes for the truth, the whole truth, and nothing but the truth!

Pyecraft ... I made the acquaintance of Pyecraft in this very smoking room. I was a young, nervous new member, and he saw it. I was sitting all alone, wishing I knew more of the members, and suddenly he came,

47

a great rolling front of chins and abdomina, toward me, and grunted and sat down in a chair close by me and wheezed for a space, and scraped for a space with a match and lit a cigar, and then addressed me. I forget what he said—something about the matches not lighting properly, and afterward as he talked he kept stopping the waiters one by one as they went by, and telling them about the matches in that thin, fluty voice he has. But, anyhow, it was in some such way we began our talking.

He talked about various things and came round to games. And thence to my figure and complexion. *"You* ought to be a good cricketer," he said. I suppose I am slender, slender to what some people would call lean, and I suppose I am rather dark, still—I am not ashamed of having a Hindu great-grandmother, but, for all that, I don't want casual strangers to see through me at a glance to *her.* So that I was set against Pyecraft from the beginning.

But he only talked about me in order to get to himself.

"I expect," he said, "you take no more exercise than I do, and probably you eat no less." (Like all excessively obese people he fancied he ate nothing.) "Yet"—and he smiled an oblique smile—"we differ."

And then he began to talk about his fatness and his fatness; all he did for his fatness and all he was going to do for his fatness: what people had advised him to do for his fatness and what he had heard of people doing for fatness similar to his. *"A priori,"* he said, "one would think a question of nutrition could be answered by dietary and a question of assimilation by drugs." It was stifling. It was dumpling talk. It made me feel swelled to hear him.

One stands that sort of thing once in a way at a club, but a time came when I fancied I was standing too much. He took to me altogether too conspicuously. I could never go into the smoking room but he would come wallowing toward me, and sometimes he came and gormandized round and about me while I had my lunch. He seemed at times almost to be clinging to me. He was a bore, but not so fearful a bore as to be limited to me; and from the first there was something in his manner—almost as though he knew, almost as though he penetrated to the fact that I *might*—that there was a remote, exceptional chance in me that no one else presented.

"I'd give anything to get it down," he would say—"anything," and peer at me over his vast cheeks and pant. Poor old Pyecraft! He has just gonged; no doubt to order another buttered teacake!

He came to the actual thing one day. "Our Pharmacopoeia," he said, "our Western Pharmacopoeia, is anything but the last word of medical science. In the East, I've been told—"

He stopped and stared at me. It was like being at an aquarium.

I was quite suddenly angry with him. "Look here," I said, "who told you about my great-grandmother's recipes?"

"Well," he fenced.

"Every time we've met for a week," I said—"and we've met pretty often—you've given me a broad hint or so about that little secret of mine."

"Well," he said, "now the cat's out of the bag, I'll admit, yes, it is so. I had it—"

"From Pattison?"

"Indirectly," he said, which I believe was lying, "yes."

"Pattison," I said, "took that stuff at his own risk."

He pursed his mouth and bowed.

"My great-grandmother's recipes," I said, "are queer things to handle. My father was near making me promise—"

"He didn't?"

"No. But he warned me. He himself used one—once."

"Ah! . . . But do you think—? Suppose—suppose there did happen to be one."

"The things are curious documents," I said. "Even the smell of 'em —No!"

But after going so far Pyecraft was resolved I should go farther. I was always a little afraid if I tried his patience too much he would fall on me suddenly and smother me. I own I was weak. But I was also annoyed with Pyecraft. I had got to that state of feeling for him that disposed me to say, "Well, *take* the risk!" The little affair of Pattison to which I have alluded was a different matter altogether. What it was doesn't concern us now, but I knew, anyhow, that the particular recipe I used then was safe. The rest I didn't know so much about, and, on the whole, I was inclined to doubt their safety pretty completely.

Yet even if Pyecraft got poisoned—

I must confess the poisoning of Pyecraft struck me as an immense undertaking.

That evening I took that queer, odd-scented sandalwood box out of my safe, and turned the rustling skins over. The gentleman who wrote the recipes for my great-grandmother evidently had a weakness for skins of a miscellaneous origin, and his handwriting was cramped to the last degree. Some of the things are quite unreadable to me—though my family, with its Indian Civil Service associations, has kept up a knowledge of Hindustani from generation to generation—and none are absolutely plain sailing. But I found the one that I knew was there soon enough, and sat on the floor by my safe for some time looking at it.

"Look here," said I to Pyecraft next day, and snatched the slip away from his eager grasp.

"So far as I can make it out, this is a recipe for Loss of Weight. ('Ah!' said Pyecraft.) I'm not absolutely sure, but I think it's that. And if you take my advice you'll leave it alone. Because, you know—I blacken my blood in your interest, Pyecraft—my ancestors on that side were, so far as I can gather, a jolly queer lot. See?"

"Let me try it," said Pyecraft.

I leaned back in my chair. My imagination made one mighty effort and fell flat within me. "What in Heaven's name, Pyecraft," I asked, "do you think you'll look like when you get thin?"

He was impervious to reason. I made him promise never to say a word to me about his disgusting fatness again whatever happened—never, and then I handed him that little piece of skin.

"It's nasty stuff," I said.

"No matter," he said, and took it.

He goggled at it. "But—but—" he said

He had just discovered that it wasn't English.

"To the best of my ability," I said, "I will do you a translation."

I did my best. After that we didn't speak for a fortnight. Whenever he approached me I frowned and motioned him away, and he respected our compact, but at the end of the fortnight he was as fat as ever. And then he got a word in.

"I must speak," he said. "It isn't fair. There's something wrong. It's done me no good. You're not doing your great-grandmother justice."

"Where's the recipe?"

He produced it gingerly from his pocketbook.

I ran my eye over the items. "Was the egg addled?" I asked.

"No. Ought it to have been?"

"That," I said, "goes without saying in all my poor dear great-grandmother's recipes. When condition or quality is not specified you must get the worst. She was drastic or nothing. . . . And there's one or two possible alternatives to some of these other things. You got *fresh* rattlesnake venom?"

"I got a rattlesnake from Jamrach's. It cost—it cost—"

"That's your affair anyhow. This last item—"

"I know a man who—"

"Yes. H'm. Well, I'll write the alternatives down. So far as I know the language, the spelling of this recipe is particularly atrocious. By the by, dog here probably means pariah dog."

For a month after that I saw Pyecraft constantly at the club and as fat and anxious as ever. He kept our treaty, but at times he broke the spirit of it by shaking his head despondently. Then one day in the cloakroom he said, "Your great-grandmother—"

"Not a word against her," I said; and he held his peace.

I could have fancied he had desisted, and I saw him one day talking to three new members about his fatness as though he was in search of other recipes. And then, quite unexpectedly, his telegram came.

"Mr. Formalyn!" bawled a page boy under my nose, and I took the telegram and opened it at once.

"For Heaven's sake come. —Pyecraft."

"H'm," said I, and to tell the truth I was so pleased at the rehabilitation of my great-grandmother's reputation this evidently promised that I made a most excellent lunch.

I got Pyecraft's address from the hall porter. Pyecraft inhabited the upper half of a house in Bloomsbury, and I went there as soon as I had done my coffee and Trappistine. I did not wait to finish my cigar.

"Mr. Pyecraft?" said I, at the front door.

They believed he was ill; he hadn't been out for two days.

"He expects me," said I, and they sent me up.

I rang the bell at the lattice door upon the landing.

"He shouldn't have tried it, anyhow," I said to myself. "A man who eats like a pig ought to look like a pig."

An obviously worthy woman, with an anxious face and a carelessly placed cap, came and surveyed me through the lattice.

I gave my name and she let me in in a dubious fashion.

"Well?" said I, as we stood together inside Pyecraft's piece of the landing.

" 'E said you was to come in if you came," she said, and regarded me, making no motion to show me anywhere. And then, confidentially, " 'E's locked in, sir."

"Locked in?"

"Locked 'imself in yesterday morning and 'asn't let anyone in since, sir. And ever and again *swearing.* Oh, my!"

I stared at the door she indicated by her glances. "In there?" I said.

"Yes, sir."

"What's up?"

She shook her head sadly. " 'E keeps on calling for vittles, sir. 'Eavy vittles 'e wants. I get 'im what I can. Pork 'e's had, sooit puddin', sossiges, noo bread. Everythink like that. Left outside, if you please, and me go away. 'E's eatin', sir, somethink *awful.*"

There came a piping bawl from inside the door: "That Formalyn?"

"That you, Pyecraft?" I shouted, and went and banged the door.

"Tell her to go away."

I did.

Then I could hear a curious pattering upon the floor, almost like someone feeling for the handle in the dark, and Pyecraft's familiar grunts.

"It's all right," I said, "she's gone."

But for a long time the door didn't open.

I heard the key turn. Then Pyecraft's voice said, "Come in."

I turned the handle and opened the door. Naturally I expected to see Pyecraft.

Well, you know, he wasn't there!

I never had such a shock in my life. There was his sitting room in a state of untidy disorder, plates and dishes among the books and writing things, and several chairs overturned, but Pyecraft. . . .

"It's all right, old man; shut the door," he said, and then I discovered him.

There he was, right up close to the cornice in the corner by the door, as though someone had glued him to the ceiling. His face was anxious and angry. He panted and gesticulated. "Shut the door," he said. "If that woman gets hold of it—"

I shut the door, and went and stood away from him and stared.

"If anything gives way and you tumble down," I said, "you'll break your neck, Pyecraft."

"I wish I could," he wheezed.

"A man of your age and weight getting up to kiddish gymnastics—"

"Don't," he said, and looked agonzied.

"I'll tell you," he said, and gesticulated.

"How the deuce," said I, "are you holding on up there?"

And then abruptly I realized that he was not holding on at all, that he was floating up there—just as a gas-filled bladder might have floated in the same position. He began a struggle to thrust himself away from the ceiling and to clamber down the wall to me. "It's that prescription," he panted, as he did so. "Your great-gran—"

He took hold of a framed engraving rather carelessly as he spoke and it gave way, and he flew back to the ceiling again, while the picture smashed on to the sofa. Bump he went against the ceiling, and I knew then why he was all over white on the more salient curves and angles of his person. He tried again more carefully, coming down by way of the mantel.

It was really a most extraordinary spectacle, that great, fat, apoplectic-looking man upside down and trying to get from the ceiling to the floor. "That prescription," he said. "Too successful."

"How?"

"Loss of weight—almost complete."

And then, of course, I understood.

"By Jove, Pyecraft," said I, "what you wanted was a cure for fatness! But you always called it weight. You would call it weight."

Somehow I was extremely delighted. I quite liked Pyecraft for the time. "Let me help you!" I said, and took his hand and pulled him down. He kicked about, trying to get foothold somewhere. It was very like holding a flag on a windy day.

"That table," he said, pointing, "is solid mahogany and very heavy. If you can put me under that—"

I did, and there he wallowed about like a captive balloon, while I stood on his hearthrug and talked to him.

I lit a cigar. "Tell me," I said, "what happened?"

"I took it," he said.

"How did it taste?"

"Oh, *beastly!*"

I should fancy they all did. Whether one regards the ingredients or the probable compound or the possible results, almost all my great-grandmother's remedies appear to me at least to be extraordinarily uninviting. For my own part—

"I took a little sip first."

"Yes?"

"And as I felt lighter and better after an hour, I decided to take the draught."

"My dear Pyecraft!"

"I held my nose," he explained. "And then I kept on getting lighter and lighter—and helpless, you know."

He gave way suddenly to a burst of passion. "What the goodness am I to *do?*" he said.

"There's one thing pretty evident," I said, "that you mustn't do. If you go out of doors you'll go up and up." I waved an arm upward. "They'd have to send Santos-Dumont after you to bring you down again."

"I suppose it will wear off?"

I shook my head. "I don't think you can count on that," I said.

And then there was another burst of passion, and he kicked out at adjacent chairs and banged the floor. He behaved just as I should have expected a great, fat, self-indulgent man to behave under trying circumstances—that is to say, very badly. He spoke of me and of my great-grandmother with an utter want of discretion.

"I never asked you to take the stuff," I said.

And generously disregarding the insults he was putting upon me, I sat down in his armchair and began to talk to him in a sober, friendly fashion.

I pointed out to him that this was a trouble he had brought upon himself, and that it had almost an air of poetical justice. He had eaten too much. This he disputed, and for a time we argued the point.

He became noisy and violent, so I desisted from this aspect of his lesson. "And then," said I, "you committed the sin of euphuism. You called it, not Fat, which is just and inglorious, but Weight. You—"

He interrupted to say that he recognized all that. What was he to *do?*

I suggested he should adapt himself to his new conditions. So we came to the really sensible part of the business. I suggested that it would not be difficult for him to learn to walk about on the ceiling with his hands—

"I can't sleep," he said.

But that was no great difficulty. It was quite possible, I pointed out, to make a shake-up under a wire mattress, fasten the underthings on with tapes, and have a blanket, sheet, and coverlet to button at the side. He would have to confide in his housekeeper, I said; after some squabbling he agreed to that. (Afterward it was quite delightful to see the beautifully matter-of-fact way with which the good lady took all these amazing inversions.) He could have a library ladder in his room, and all his meals could be laid on the top of his bookcase. We also hit on an ingenious device by which he could get to the floor whenever he wanted, which was simply to put the *British Encyclopaedia* (tenth edition) on the top of his open shelves. He just pulled out a couple of volumes and held on, and down he came. And we agreed there must be iron staples along the skirting, so that he could cling to those whenever he wanted to get about the room on the lower level.

As we got on with the thing I found myself almost keenly interested. It was I who called in the housekeeper and broke matters to her, and it was I chiefly who fixed up the inverted bed. In fact, I spent two whole days at his flat. I am a handy, interfering sort of man with a screwdriver, and I made all sorts of ingenious adaptations for him—ran a wire to bring his bells within reach, turned all his electric lights up instead of down, and so on. The whole affair was extremely curious and interesting to me, and it was delightful to think of Pyecraft, like some great, fat blow-fly, crawling about on his ceiling and clambering round the lintel of his doors from one room to another, and never, never, never coming to the club anymore. . . .

Then, you know, my fatal ingenuity got the better of me. I was sitting by his fire drinking his whiskey, and he was up in his favorite corner by the cornice, tacking a Turkey carpet to the ceiling, when the idea struck me. "By Jove, Pyecraft!" I said, "all this is totally unnecessary."

And before I could calculate the complete consequences of my notion I blurted it out. "Lead underclothing," said I, and the mischief was done.

Pyecraft received the thing almost in tears. "To be right way up again—" he said.

I gave him the whole secret before I saw where it would take me. "Buy sheet lead," I said, "stamp it into discs. Sew 'em all over your underclothes until you have enough. Have lead-soled boots, carry a bag of solid lead, and the thing is done! Instead of being a prisoner here you may go abroad again, Pyecraft; you may travel—"

A still happier idea came to me. "You need never fear a shipwreck. All you need do is just slip off some or all of your clothes, take the necessary amount of luggage in your hand, and float up in the air—"

In his emotion he dropped the tack-hammer within an ace of my head. "By Jove!" he said, "I shall be able to come back to the club again."

The thing pulled me up short. "By Jove!" I said, faintly. "Yes. Of course—you will."

He did. He does. There he sits behind me now, stuffing—as I live!—

a third go of buttered teacake. And no one in the whole world knows—except his housekeeper and me—that he weighs practically nothing; that he is a mere boring mass of assimilatory matter, mere clouds in clothing, *niente, nefas,* the most inconsiderable of men. There he sits watching until I have done this writing. Then, if he can, he will waylay me. He will come billowing up to me. . . .

He will tell me over again all about it, how it feels, how it doesn't feel, how he sometimes hopes it is passing off a little. And always somewhere in that fat, abundant discourse he will say, "The secret's keeping, eh? If anyone knew of it—I should be so ashamed. Makes a fellow look such a fool, you know. Crawling about on a ceiling and all that. . . ."

And now to elude Pyecraft, occupying, as he does, an admirable strategic position between me and the door.

THE IRON CHANCELLOR

by Robert Silverberg

Dieters are well aware of the temptations they face as they try to lose weight. Some people even place locks on kitchen cabinets. Another solution involves getting others to help the dieter fight the temptation—although, as Robert Silverberg shows us, there may be costs as well as benefits to this approach.

The Carmichaels were a pretty plump family, to begin with. Not one of them couldn't stand to shed quite a few pounds. And there happened to be a superspecial on roboservitors at one of the Miracle Mile robo-shops—40 percent off on the 2061 model, with adjustable caloric-intake monitors.

Sam Carmichael liked the idea of having his food prepared and served by a robot who would keep one beady solenoid eye on the collective family waistline. He squinted speculatively at the glossy display model, absentmindedly slipped his thumbs beneath his elastobelt to knead his paunch, and said, "How much?"

The salesman flashed a brilliant and probably synthetic grin. "Only 2995, sir. That includes free service contract for the first five years. Only two hundred credits down and up to forty months to pay."

Carmichael frowned, thinking of his bank balance. Then he thought of his wife's figure, and of his daughter's endless yammering about her need to diet. Besides, Jemima, their old robocook, was shabby and gear-stripped, and made a miserable showing when other company executives visited them for dinner.

"I'll take it," he said.

"Care to trade in your old robocook, sir? Liberal trade-in allow-ances—"

"I have a '43 Madison." Carmichael wondered if he should mention

57

its bad arm libration and serious fuel-feed overflow, but decided that would be carrying candidness too far.

"Well—ah—I guess we could allow you fifty credits on a '43, sir. Seventy-five, maybe, if the recipe bank is still in good condition."

"Excellent condition." That part was honest—the family had never let even one recipe wear out. "You could send a man down to look her over."

"Oh, no need to do that, sir. We'll take your word. Seventy-five, then? And delivery of the new model by this evening?"

"Done," Carmichael said. He was glad to get the pathetic old '43 out of the house at any cost.

He signed the purchase order cheerfully, pocketed the facism and handed over ten crisp twenty-credit vouchers. He could almost feel the roll of fat melting from him now, as he eyed the magnificent '61 robo-servitor that would shortly be his.

The time was only 1810 hours when he left the shop, got into his car and punched out the coordinates for home. The whole transaction had taken less than ten minutes. Carmichael, a second-level executive at Normandy Trust, prided himself both on his good business sense and his ability to come quickly to a firm decision.

Fifteen minutes later, his car deposited him at the front entrance of their totally detached self-powered suburban home in the fashionable Westley subdivision. The car obediently took itself around back to the garage, while Carmichael stood in the scanner field until the door opened. Clyde, the robutler, came scuttling hastily up, took his hat and cloak, and handed him a Martini.

Carmichael beamed appreciatively. "Well done, thou good and faithful servant!"

He took a healthy sip and headed toward the living room to greet his wife, son and daughter. Pleasant gin-induced warmth filtered through him. The robutler was ancient and due for replacement as soon as the budget could stand the charge, but Carmichael realized he would miss the clanking old heap.

"You're late, dear," Ethel Carmichael said as he appeared. "Dinner's been ready for ten minutes. Jemima's so annoyed her cathodes are clicking."

"Jemima's cathodes fail to interest me," Carmichael said evenly. "Good evening, dear. Myra. Joey. I'm late because I stopped off at Marhew's on my way home."

His son blinked. "The robot place, Dad?"

"Precisely. I bought a '61 roboservitor to replace old Jemima and her sputtering cathodes. The new model has," Carmichael added, eyeing his son's adolescent bulkiness and the rather-more-than-ample figures of his wife and daughter, "some very special attachments."

They dined well that night, on Jemima's favorite Tuesday dinner menu—shrimp cocktail, fumet of gumbo chervil, breast of chicken with creamed potatoes and asparagus, delicious plum tarts for dessert, and coffee. Carmichael felt pleasantly bloated when he had finished, and gestured to Clyde for a snifter of his favorite afterdinner digestive aid, VSOP Cognac. He leaned back, warm, replete, able easily to ignore the blustery November winds outside.

A pleasing electroluminescence suffused the dining room with pink —this year, the experts thought pink improved digestion—and the heating filaments embedded in the wall glowed cozily as they delivered the BTUs. This was the hour for relaxation in the Carmichael household.

"Dad," Joey began hesitantly, "about that canoe trip next week-end—"

Carmichael folded his hands across his stomach and nodded. "You can go, I suppose. Only be careful. If I find out you didn't use the equilibriator this time—"

The door chime sounded. Carmichael lifted an eyebrow and swiveled in his chair.

"Who is it, Clyde?"

"He gives his name as Robinson, sir. Of Robinson Robotics, he said. He has a bulky package to deliver."

"It must be that new robocook, Father!" Myra Carmichael exclaimed.

"I guess it is. Show him in, Clyde."

Robinson turned out to be a red-faced, efficient-looking little man in greasy green overalls and a plaid pullover-coat, who looked disapprovingly at the robutler and strode into the Carmichael living room.

He was followed by a lumbering object about seven feet high, mounted on a pair of rolltreads and swathed completely in quilted rags.

"Got him all wrapped up against the cold, Mr. Carmichael. Lot of delicate circuitry in that job. You ought to be proud of him."

"Clyde, help Mr. Robinson unpack the new robocook," Carmichael said.

"That's okay—I can manage it. And it's *not* a robocook, by the way. It's called a roboservitor now. Fancy price, fancy name."

Carmichael heard his wife mutter, "Sam, how much—"

He scowled at her. "Very reasonable, Ethel. Don't worry so much."

He stepped back to admire the roboservitor as it emerged from the quilted swaddling. It was big, all right, with a massive barrel of a chest —robotic controls are always housed in the chest, not in the relatively tiny head—and a gleaming mirror-keen finish that accented its sleekness and newness. Carmichael felt the satisfying glow of pride in ownership. Somehow it seemed to him that he had done something noble and lordly in buying this magnificent robot.

Robinson finished the unpacking job and, standing on tiptoes, opened the robot's chest panel. He unclipped a thick instruction manual and handed it to Carmichael, who stared at the tome uneasily.

"Don't fret about that, Mr. Carmichael. This robot's no trouble to handle. The book's just part of the trimming. Come here a minute."

Carmichael peered into the robot's innards. Pointing, Robinson said, "Here's the recipe bank—biggest, and best ever designed. Of course it's possible to tape in any of your favorite family recipes, if they're not already there. Just hook up your old robocook to the integrator circuit and feed 'em in. I'll take care of that before I leave."

"And what about the—ah—special features?"

"The reducing monitors, you mean? Right over here. See? You just tape in the names of the members of the family and their present and desired weights, and the roboservitor takes care of the rest. Computes caloric intake, adjusts menus, and everything else."

Carmichael grinned at his wife. "Told you I was going to do something about our weight, Ethel. No more dieting for you, Myra—the robot does all the work." Catching a sour look on his son's face, he added, "And you're not so lean yourself, Buster."

"I don't think there'll be any trouble," Robinson said buoyantly. "But if there is, just buzz for me. I handle service and delivery for Marhew Stores in this area."

"Right."

"Now if you'll get me your obsolete robocook, I'll transfer the family recipes before I cart it away on the trade-in deal."

There was a momentary tingle of nostalgia and regret when Robinson left, half an hour later, taking old Jemima with him. Carmichael had almost come to think of the battered '43 Madison as a member of the family. After all, he had bought her sixteen years before, only a couple of years after his marriage.

But she—*it*, he corrected in annoyance—was only a robot, and robots became obsolete. Besides, Jemima probably suffered all the aches and pains of a robot's old age and would be happier dismantled. Carmichael blotted Jemima from his mind.

The four of them spent most of the rest of that evening discovering things about their new roboservitor. Carmichael drew up a table of their weights (himself, 192; Ethel, 145; Myra, 139; Joey, 189) and the amount they proposed to weigh in three months' time (himself, 180; Ethel, 125; Myra, 120; Joey, 175). Carmichael then let his son, who prided himself on his kowledge of practical robotics, integrate the figures and feed them to the robot's programing bank.

"You wish this schedule to take effect immediately?" the roboservitor queried in a deep, mellow bass.

Startled, Carmichael said, "T-tomorrow morning, at breakfast. We might as well start right away."

"He speaks well, doesn't he?" Ethel asked.

"He sure does," Joey said. "Jemima always stammered and squeaked, and all she could say was, 'Dinner is served' and 'Be careful, sirr, the soup plate is verry warrm.' "

Carmichael smiled. He noticed his daughter admiring the robot's bulky frame and sleek bronze limbs, and thought resignedly that a seventeen-year-old girl could find the strangest sorts of love objects. But he was happy to see that they were all evidently pleased with the robot. Even with the discount and the trade-in, it *had* been a little on the costly side.

But it would be worth it.

Carmichael slept soundly and woke early, anticipating the first breakfast under the new regime. He still felt pleased with himself.

Dieting had always been such a nuisance, he thought—but, on the other hand, he had never enjoyed the sensation of an annoying roll of fat pushing outward against his elastobelt. He exercised sporadically, but it did little good, and he never had the initiative to keep a rigorous dieting campaign going for long. Now, though, with the mathematics of reducing done effortlessly for him, all the calculating and cooking being handled by the new robot—now, for the first time since he had been Joey's age, he could look forward to being slim and trim once again.

He dressed, showered and hastily depilated. It was 0730. Breakfast was ready.

Ethel and the children were already at the table when he arrived.

Ethel and Myra were munching toast; Joey was peering at a bowl of milkless dry cereal, next to which stood a full glass of milk. Carmichael sat down.

"Your toast, sir," the roboservitor murmured.

Carmichael stared at the single slice. It had already been buttered for him, and the butter had evidently been measured out with a micrometer. The robot proceeded to hand him a cup of black coffee.

He groped for the cream and sugar. They weren't anywhere on the table. The other members of his family were regarding him strangely, and they were curiously, suspiciously silent.

"I like cream and sugar in my coffee," he said to the hovering roboservitor. "Didn't you find that in Jemima's old recipe bank?"

"Of course, sir. But you must learn to drink your coffee without such things, if you wish to lose weight."

Carmichael chuckled. Somehow he had not expected the regimen to be quite like this—quite so, well, Spartan. "Oh, yes. Of course. Ah—are the eggs ready yet?" He considered a day incomplete unless he began it with soft-boiled eggs.

"Sorry, no, sir. On Mondays, Wednesdays, and Fridays, breakfast is to consist of toast and black coffee only, except for Master Joey, who gets cereal, fruit juice and milk."

"I—see."

Well, he had asked for it. He shrugged and took a bite of the toast. He sipped the coffee; it tasted like river mud, but he tried not to make a face.

Joey seemed to be going on about the business of eating his cereal rather oddly, Carmichael noticed next. "Why don't you pour that glass of milk *into* the cereal?" he asked. "Won't it taste better that way?"

"Sure it will. But Bismark says I won't get another glass if I do, so I'm eating it this way."

"Bismarck?"

Joey grinned. "It's the name of a famous nineteenth-century German dictator. They called him the Iron Chancellor." He jerked his head toward the kitchen, to which the roboservitor had silently retreated. "Pretty good name for him, eh?"

"No," said Carmichael. "It's silly."

"It has a certain ring of truth, though," Ethel remarked.

Carmichael did not reply. He finished his toast and coffee somewhat glumly and signaled Clyde to get the car out of the garage. He felt depressed—dieting didn't seem to be so effortless after all, even with the new robot.

As he walked toward the door, the robot glided around him and handed him a small printed slip of paper. Carmichael stared at it. It said:

FRUIT JUICE

LETTUCE & TOMATO SALAD

(ONE) HARD-BOILED EGG

BLACK COFFEE

"What's this thing?"

"You are the only member of this family group who will not be eating three meals a day under my personal supervision. This is your luncheon menu. Please adhere to it," the robot said smoothly.

Repressing a sputter, Carmichael said, "Yes—yes. Of course."

He pocketed the menu and made his way uncertainly to the waiting car.

He was faithful to the robot's orders at lunchtime that day; even though he was beginning to develop resistance to the idea that had seemed so appealing only the night before, he was willing, at least, to give it a try.

But something prompted him to stay away from the restaurant where Normandy Trust employees usually lunched, and where there were human waiters to smirk at him and fellow executives to ask prying questions.

He ate instead at a cheap robocafeteria two blocks to the north. He slipped in surreptitiously with his collar turned up, punched out his order (it cost him less than a credit altogether) and wolfed it down. He still felt hungry when he was finished, but he compelled himself to return loyally to the office.

He wondered how long he was going to be able to keep up this iron self-control. Not very long, he realized dolefully. And if anyone from the company caught him eating at a robocafeteria, he'd be a laughing stock. Someone of executive status just *didn't* eat lunch by himself in mechanized cafeterias.

By the time he had finished his day's work, his stomach felt knotted and pleated. His hand was shaky as he punched out his destination on the car's autopanel, and he was thankful that it took less than an hour to get home from the office. Soon, he thought, he'd be tasting food again.

Soon. Soon. He switched on the roof-mounted video, leaned back at the recliner and tried to relax as the car bore him homeward.

He was in for a surprise, though, when he stepped through the safety field into his home. Clyde was waiting as always, and, as always, took his hat and cloak. And, as always, Carmichael reached for the cocktail that Clyde prepared nightly to welcome him home.

There was no cocktail.

"Are we out of gin, Clyde?"

"No, sir."

"How come no drink, then?"

The robot's rubberized metallic features seemed to droop. "Because, sir, a Martini's caloric content is inordinately high. Gin is rated at a hundred calories per ounce and—"

"Oh, no. You too!"

"Pardon, sir. The new roboservitor has altered my responsive circuits to comply with the regulations now in force in this household."

Carmichael felt his fingers starting to tremble. "Clyde, you've been my butler for almost twenty years."

"Yes, sir."

"You always make my drinks for me. You mix the best Martinis in the Western Hemisphere."

"Thank you, sir."

"And you're going to mix one for me right now! That's a direct order!"

"Sir! I—" The robutler staggered wildly and nearly careened into Carmichael. It seemed to have lost all control over its gyro-balance; it clutched agonizedly at its chest panel and started to sag.

Hastily, Carmichael barked, "Order countermanded! Clyde, are you all right?"

Slowly, and with a creak, the robot straightened up. It looked dangerously close to an overload. "Your direct order set up a first-level conflict in me, sir," Clyde whispered faintly. "I—came close to burning out just then, sir. May—may I be excused?"

"Of course. Sorry, Clyde." Carmichael balled his fists. There was such a thing as going too far! The roboservitor—Bismarck—had obviously placed on Clyde a flat prohibition against serving liquor to him. Reducing or no reducing, there were *limits*.

Carmichael strode angrily toward the kitchen.

His wife met him halfway. "I didn't hear you come in, Sam. I want to talk to you about—"

"Later. Where's that robot?"

"In the kitchen, I imagine. It's almost dinnertime."

He brushed past her and swept on into the kitchen, where Bismarck was moving efficiently from electrostove to magnetic worktable. The robot swiveled as Carmichael entered.

"Did you have a good day, sir?"

"No! I'm hungry!"

"The first days of a diet are always the most difficult, Mr. Carmichael. But your body will adjust to the reduction in food intake before long."

"I'm sure of that. But what's this business of tinkering with Clyde?"

"The butler insisted on preparing an alcoholic drink for you. I was forced to adjust his programing. From now on, sir, you may indulge in cocktails on Tuesdays, Thursdays, and Saturdays. I beg to be excused from further discussion now, sir. The meal is almost ready."

Poor Clyde! Carmichael thought. *And poor me!* He gnashed his teeth impotently a few times, then gave up and turned away from the glistening, overbearing roboservitor. A light gleamed on the side of the robot's head, indicating that he had shut off his audio circuits and was totally engaged in his task.

Dinner consisted of steak and peas, followed by black coffee. The steak was rare; Carmichael preferred it well done. But Bismarck—the name was beginning to take hold—had had all the latest dietetic theories taped into him, and rare meat it was.

After the robot had cleared the table and tidied up the kitchen, it retired to its storage place in the basement, which gave the Carmichael family a chance to speak openly to each other for the first time that evening.

"Lord!" Ethel snorted. "Sam, I don't object to losing weight, but if we're going to be *tyrannized* in our own home—"

"Mom's right," Joey put in. "It doesn't seem fair for that thing to feed us whatever it pleases. And I didn't like the way it messed around with Clyde's circuits."

Carmichael spread his hands. "I'm not happy about it either. But we have to give it a try. We can always make readjustments in the programing if it turns out to be necessary."

"But how long are we going to keep this up?" Myra wanted to know. "I had three meals in this house today and I'm starved!"

"Me, too," Joey said. He elbowed himself from his chair and looked around. "Bismarck's downstairs. I'm going to get a slice of lemon pie while the coast is clear."

"No!" Carmichael thundered.

"No?"

"There's no sense in my spending three thousand credits on a dietary robot if you're going to cheat, Joey. I forbid you to have any pie."

"But, Dad, I'm hungry! I'm a growing boy! I'm—"

"You're sixteen years old, and if you grow much more, you won't fit inside this house," Carmichael snapped, looking up at his six-foot-one son.

"Sam, we can't starve the boy," Ethel protested. "If he wants pie, let him have some. You're carrying this reducing fetish too far."

Carmichael considered that. Perhaps, he thought, I *am* being a little oversevere. And the thought of lemon pie was a tempting one. He was pretty hungry himself.

"All right," he said with feigned reluctance. "I guess a bit of pie won't wreck the plan. In fact, I suppose I'll have some myself. Joey, why don't you—"

"Begging your pardon," a purring voice said behind him. Carmichael jumped half an inch. It was the robot, Bismarck. "It would be most unfortunate if you were to have pie now, Mr. Carmichael. My calculations are very precise."

Carmichael saw the angry gleam in his son's eye, but the robot seemed extraordinarily big at that moment, and it happened to stand between him and the kitchen.

He sighed weakly. "Let's forget the lemon pie, Joey."

After two full days of the Bismarckian diet, Carmichael discovered that his inner resources of willpower were beginning to crumble. On the third day he tossed away the printed lunchtime diet and went out irresponsibly with MacDougal and Hennessey for a six-course lunch, complete with cocktails. It seemed to him that he hadn't tasted real food since the robot arrived.

That night, he was able to tolerate the seven-hundred-calorie dinner without any inward grumblings, being still well lined with lunch. But Ethel and Myra and Joey were increasingly irritable. It seemed that the robot had usurped Ethel's job of handling the daily marketing and had stocked in nothing but a huge supply of healthy low-calorie foods. The larder now bulged with wheat germ, protein bread, irrigated salmon, and other hitherto unfamiliar items. Myra had taken up biting her nails;

Joey's mood was one of black sullen brooding, and Carmichael knew how that could lead to trouble quickly with a sixteen-year-old.

After the meager dinner, he ordered Bismarck to go to the basement and stay there until summoned.

The robot said, "I must advise you, sir, that I will detect indulgence in any forbidden foods in my absence and adjust for it in the next meals."

"You have my word," Carmichael said, thinking it was indeed queer to have to pledge on your honor to your own robot. He waited until the massive servitor had vanished below; then he turned to Joey and said, "Get the instruction manual, boy."

Joey grinned in understanding. Ethel said, "Sam, what are you going to do?"

Carmichael patted his shrunken waistline. "I'm going to take a can opener to that creature and adjust his programing. He's overdoing this diet business. Joey, have you found the instructions on how to reprogram the robot?"

"Page 167. I'll get the tool kit, Dad."

"Right." Carmichael turned to the robutler, who was standing by dumbly, in his usual forward-stooping posture of expectancy. "Clyde, go down below and tell Bismarck we want him right away."

Moments later, the two robots appeared. Carmichael said to the roboservitor, "I'm afraid its necessary for us to change your program. We've overestimated our capacity for losing weight."

"I beg you to reconsider, sir. Extra weight is harmful to every vital organ in the body. I plead with you to maintain my scheduling unaltered."

"I'd rather cut my own throat. Joey, inactivate him and do your stuff."

Grinning fiercely, the boy stepped forward and pressed the stud that opened the robot's ribcage. A frightening assortment of gears, cams and translucent cables became visible inside the robot. With a small wrench in one hand and the open instruction booklet in the other, Joey prepared to make the necessary changes, while Carmichael held his breath and a pall of silence descended on the living room. Even old Clyde leaned forward to have a better view.

Joey muttered, "Lever F2, with the yellow indicia, is to be advanced one notch . . . umm. Now twist Dial B9 to the left, thereby opening the taping compartment and—oops!"

Carmichael heard the clang of a wrench and saw the bright flare of sparks; Joey leaped back, cursing with surprisingly mature skill. Ethel and Myra gasped simultaneouly.

"What happened?" four voices—Clyde's coming in last—demanded.

"Dropped the damn wrench," Joey said. "I guess I shorted out something in there."

The robot's eyes were whirling satanically and its voice box was emitting an awesome twelve-cycle rumble. The great metal creature stood stiffly in the middle of the living room; with brusque gestures of its big hands, it slammed shut the open chest plates.

"We'd better call Mr. Robinson," Ethel said worriedly. "A short-circuited robot is likely to explode, or worse."

"We should have called Robinson in the first place," Carmichael murmured bitterly. "It's my fault for letting Joey tinker with an expensive and delicate mechanism like that. Myra, get me the card Mr. Robinson left."

"Gee, Dad, this is the first time I've ever had anything like that go wrong," Joey insisted. "I didn't know—"

"You're darned right you didn't know." Carmichael took the card from his daughter and started toward the phone. "I hope we can reach him at this hour. If we can't—"

Suddenly Carmichael felt cold fingers prying the card from his hand. He was so startled he relinquished it without a struggle. He watched as Bismarck efficiently ripped it into little fragments and shoved them into a wall disposal unit.

The robot said, "There will be no further meddling with my program tapes." Its voice was deep and strangely harsh.

"What—"

"Mr. Carmichael, today you violated the program I set down for you. My perceptors reveal that you consumed an amount far in excess of your daily lunchtime requirement."

"Sam, what—"

"Quiet, Ethel. Bismarck, I order you to shut yourself off at once."

"My apologies, sir. I cannot serve you if I am shut off."

"I don't *want* you to serve me. You're out of order. I want you to remain still until I can phone the repairman and get him to service you."

Then he remembered the card that had gone into the disposal unit. He felt a faint tremor of apprehension.

"You took Robinson's card and destroyed it."

"Further alteration of my circuits would be detrimental to the Carmichael family," said the robot. "I cannot permit you to summon the repairman."

"Don't get him angry, Dad," Joey warned. "I'll call the police. I'll be back in—"

"You will remain within this house," the robot said. Moving with impressive speed on its oiled treads, it crossed the room, blocking the door, and reached far above its head to activate the impassable privacy field that protected the house. Carmichael watched, aghast, as the inexorable robotic fingers twisted and manipulated the field controls.

"I have now reversed the polarity of the house privacy field," the robot announced. "Since you are obviously not to be trusted to keep to the diet I prescribe, I cannot allow you to leave the premises. You will remain within and continue to obey my beneficial advice."

Calmly, he uprooted the telephone. Next, the windows were opaqued and the stud broken off. Finally, the robot seized the instruction book from Joey's numbed hands and shoved it into the disposal unit.

"Breakfast will be served at the usual time," Bismarck said mildly. "For optimum purposes of health, you are all to be asleep by 2300 hours. I shall leave you now, until morning. Good night."

Carmichael did not sleep well that night, nor did he eat well the next day. He awoke late, for one thing—well past nine. He discovered that someone, obviously Bismarck, had neatly canceled out the impulses from the housebrain that woke him at seven each morning.

The breakfast menu was toast and black coffee. Carmichael ate disgruntedly, not speaking, indicating by brusque scowls that he did not want to be spoken to. After the miserable meal had been cleared away, he surreptitiously tiptoed to the front door in his dressing gown and darted a hand toward the handle.

The door refused to budge. He pushed until sweat dribbled down his face. He heard Ethel whisper warningly, *"Sam—"* and a moment later cool metallic fingers gently disengaged him from the door.

Bismarck said, "I beg your pardon, sir. The door will not open. I explained this last night."

Carmichael gazed sourly at the gimmicked control box of the privacy field. The robot had them utterly hemmed in. The reversed privacy field made it impossible for them to leave the house; it cast a sphere of force around the entire detached dwelling. In theory, the field could be penetrated from outside, but nobody was likely to come calling without an invitation. Not here in Westley. It wasn't one of those neighborly subdivisions where everybody knew everybody else. Carmichael had picked it for that reason.

"Damn you," he growled, "you can't hold us *prisoners* in here!"

"My intent is only to help you," said the robot, in a mechanical yet dedicated voice. "My function is to supervise your diet. Since you will not obey willingly, obedience must be enforced—for your own good."

Carmichael scowled and walked away. The worst part of it was that the roboservitor sounded so *sincere!*

Trapped. The phone connection was severed. The windows were darkened. Somehow, Joey's attempt at repairs had resulted in a short circuit of the robot's obedience filters, and had also exaggeratedly stimulated its sense of function. Now Bismarck was determined to make them lose weight if it had to kill them to do so.

And that seemed very likely.

Blockaded, the Carmichael family met in a huddled little group to whisper plans for a counterattack. Clyde stood watch, but the robutler seemed to be in a state of general shock since the demonstration of the servitor-robot's independent capacity for action, and Carmichael now regarded him as undependable.

"He's got the kitchen walled off with some kind of electronic-based force web," Joey said. "He must have built it during the night. I tried to sneak in and scrounge some food, and got nothing but a flat nose for trying."

"I know," Carmichael said sadly. "He built the same sort of doohickey around the bar. Three hundred credits of good booze in there and I can't even grab the handle!"

"This is no time to worry about drinking," Ethel said morosely. "We'll be skeletons any day."

"It isn't *that* bad, Mom!" Joey said.

"Yes, it is!" cried Myra. "I've lost five pounds in four days!"

"Is that so terrible?"

"I'm wasting away," she sobbed. "My figure—it's vanishing! And—"

"Quiet," Carmichael whispered. "Bismarck's coming!"

The robot emerged from the kitchen, passing through the force barrier as if it had been a cobweb. It seemed to have effect on humans only, Carmichael thought. "Lunch will be served in eight minutes," it said obsequiously, and returned to its lair.

Carmichael glanced at his watch. The time was 1230 hours. "Probably down at the office they're wondering where I am," he said. "I haven't missed a day's work in years."

"They won't care," Ethel said. "An executive isn't required to account for every day off he takes, you know."

"But they'll worry after three or four days, won't they?" Myra asked. "Maybe they'll try to phone—or even send a rescue mission!"

From the kitchen, Bismarck said coldly, "There will be no danger of that. While you slept this morning, I notified your place of employment that you were resigning."

Carmichael gasped. Then, recovering, he said: "You're lying! The phone's cut off—and you never would have risked leaving the house, even if we *were* asleep!"

"I communicated with them via a microwave generator I constructed with the aid of your son's reference books last night," Bismarck replied. "Clyde reluctantly supplied me with the number I also phoned your bank and instructed them to handle for you all such matters as tax payments, investment decisions, etc. To forestall difficulties, let me add that a force web will prevent access on your part to the electronic equipment in the basement. I will be able to conduct such communication with the outside world as will be necessary for your welfare, Mr. Carmichael. You need have no worries on that score."

"No," Carmichael echoed hollowly. "No worries."

He turned to Joey. "We've got to get out of here. Are you sure there's no way of disconnecting the privacy field?"

"He's got one of his force fields rigged around the control box. I can't even get near the thing."

"If only we had an iceman, or an oilman, the way the oldtime houses did," Ethel said bitterly. "He'd show up and come inside and probably he'd know how to shut the field off. But not *here*. Oh, no. We've got a shiny chrome-plated cryostat in the basement that dishes out lots of liquid helium to run the fancy cryotronic super-cooled power plant that gives us heat and light, and we have enough food in the freezer to last for at least a decade or two, and so we can live like this for years, a neat little self-contained island in the middle of civilization, with nobody bothering us, nobody wondering about us, and Sam Carmichael's pet robot to feed us whenever and as little as it pleases—"

There was a cutting edge to her voice that was dangerously close to hysteria.

"Ethel, please," said Carmichael.

"Please what? Please keep quiet? Please stay calm? Sam, we're *prisoners* in here!"

"I know. You don't have to raise your voice."

"Maybe if I do, someone will hear us and come get us out," she replied more coolly.

"It's four hundred feet to the next home, dear. And in the seven years we've lived here, we've had about two visits from our neighbors. We paid a stiff price for seclusion and now we're paying a stiffer one. But please keep under control, Ethel."

"Don't worry, Mom. I'll figure a way out of this," Joey said reassuringly.

In one corner of the living room, Myra was sobbing quietly to herself, blotching her makeup. Carmichael felt a faintly claustrophobic quiver. The house was big, three levels and twelve rooms, but even so he could get tired of it very quickly.

"Luncheon is served," the roboservitor announced in booming tones.

And tired of lettuce-and-tomato lunches, too, Carmichael added silently, as he shepherded his family toward the dining room for their meager midday meal.

"You have to do *something* about this, Sam," Ethel Carmichael said on the third day of their imprisonment.

He glared at her. "Have to, eh? And just what am I supposed to do?"

"Daddy, don't get excited," Myra said.

He whirled on her. "Don't tell me what I should or shouldn't do!"

"She can't help it, dear. We're all a little overwrought. After all, cooped up here—"

"I know. Like lambs in a pen," he finished acidly. "Except that we're not being fattened for slaughter. We're—we're bing *thinned,* and for our own alleged good!"

Carmichael subsided gloomily. Toast-and-black-coffee, lettuce-and-tomato, rare-steak-and-peas. Bismarck's channels seemed to have frozen permanently at that daily menu.

But what could he do?

Contact with the outside world was impossible. The robot had erected a bastion in the basement from which he conducted such little business with the world as the Carmichael family had. Generally, they were self-sufficient. And Bismarck's force fields ensured the impossibility of any attempts to disconnect the outer sheath, break into the basement, or even get at the food supply or the liquor. It was all very neat, and the four of them were fast approaching a state of starvation.

"Sam?"

He lifted his head wearily. "What is it, Ethel?"

"Myra had an idea before. Tell him, Myra."

"Oh, it would never work," Myra said demurely.

"Tell *him!*"

"Well—Dad, you *could* try to turn Bismarck off."

"Huh?" Carmichael grunted.

"I mean if you or Joey could distract him somehow, then Joey or you could open him up again and—"

"No," Carmichael snapped. "That thing's seven feet tall and weighs three hundred pounds. If you think *I'm* going to wrestle with it—"

"We could let Clyde try," Ethel suggested.

Carmichael shook his head vehemently. "The carnage would be frightful."

Joey said, "Dad, it may be our only hope."

"You too?" Carmichael asked.

He took a deep breath. He felt himself speared by two deadly feminine glances, and he knew there was no hope but to try it. Resignedly, he pushed himself to his feet and said, "Okay. Clyde, go call Bismarck. Joey, I'll try to hang onto his arms while you open up his chest. Yank anything you can."

"Be careful," Ethel warned. "If there's an explosion—"

"If there's an explosion, we're all free," Carmichael said testily. He turned to see the broad figure of the roboservitor standing at the entrance to the living room.

"May I be of service, sir?"

"You may," Carmichael said. "We're having a little debate here and we want your evidence. It's a matter of defannising the poozlestan and —*Joey, open him up!*"

Carmichael grabbed for the robot's arms, trying to hold them without getting hurled across the room, while his son clawed frantically at the stud that opened the robot's innards. Carmichael anticipated immediate destruction—but, to his surprise, he found himself slipping as he tried to grasp the thick arms.

"Dad, it's no use. I—he—"

Carmichael found himself abruptly four feet off the ground. He heard Ethel and Myra scream and Clyde's, "*Do* be careful, sir."

Bismarck was carrying them across the room, gently, cradling him in one giant arm and Joey in the other. It set them down on the couch and stood back.

"Such an attempt is highly dangerous," Bismarck said reprovingly. "It puts me in danger of harming you physically. Please avoid any such acts in the future."

Carmichael stared broodingly at his son. "Did you have the same trouble I did?"

Joey nodded. "I couldn't get within an inch of his skin. It stands to reason, though. He's built one of those damned force screens around *himself,* too!"

Carmichael groaned. He did not look at his wife and his children. Physical attack on Bismarck was now out of the question. He began to feel as if he had been condemned to life imprisonment—and that his stay in durance vile would not be extremely prolonged.

In the upstairs bathroom, six days after the beginning of the blockade, Sam Carmichael stared at his haggard fleshless face in the mirror before wearily climbing on the scale.

He weighed 180.

He had lost twelve pounds in less than two weeks. He was fast becoming a quivering wreck.

A thought occurred to him as he stared at the wavering needle on the scale, and sudden elation spread over him. He dashed downstairs. Ethel was doggedly crocheting in the living room; Joey and Myra were playing cards grimly, desperately now, after six solid days of gin rummy and honeymoon bridge.

"Where's that robot?" Carmichael roared. "Come out here!"

"In the kitchen," Ethel said tonelessly.

"Bismarck! Bismarck!" Carmichael roared. "Come out here!"

The robot appeared. "How may I serve you, sir?"

"Damn you, scan me with your superpower receptors and tell me how much I weigh!"

After a pause, the robot said gravely, "One hundred seventy-nine pounds eleven ounces, Mr. Carmichael."

"Yes! Yes! And the original program I had taped into you was supposed to reduce me from one hundred ninety-two to one hundred eighty," Carmichael crowed triumphantly. "So I'm finished with you, as long as I don't gain any more weight. And so are the rest of us, I'll bet. Ethel! Myra! Joey! Upstairs and weigh yourselves!"

But the robot regarded him with a doleful glare and said, "Sir, I find no record within me of any limitation on your reduction of weight."

"What?"

"I have checked my tapes fully. I have a record of an order causing weight reduction, but that tape does not appear to specify a *terminus ad quem.*"

Carmichael exhaled and took three staggering steps backward. His legs wobbled; he felt Joey supporting him. He mumbled, "But I thought —I'm sure we did—I *know* we instructed you—"

Hunger gnawed at his flesh. Joey said softly, "Dad, probably that part of his tape was erased when he short-circuited."

"Oh," Carmichael said numbly.

He tottered into the living room and collapsed heavily in what had once been his favorite armchair. It wasn't anymore. The entire house had become odious to him. He longed to see the sunlight again, to see trees and grass, even to see that excrescence of an ultramodern house that the left-hand neighbors had erected.

But now that would be impossible. He had hoped, for a few minutes at least, that the robot would release them from dietary bondage when the original goal was shown to be accomplished. Evidently that was to be denied him. He giggled, then began to laugh.

"What's so funny, dear?" Ethel asked. She had lost her earlier tendencies to hysteria, and after long days of complex crocheting now regarded the universe with quiet resignation.

"Funny? The fact that I weigh one hundred eighty now. I'm lean, trim, fit as a fiddle. Next month I'll weigh one hundred seventy. Then one hundred sixty. Then finally about eighty-eight pounds or so. We'll all shrivel up. Bismarck will starve us to death."

"Don't worry, Dad. We're going to get out of this."

Somehow Joey's brash boyish confidence sounded forced now. Carmichael shook his head. "We won't. We'll never get out. And Bismarck's going to reduce us *ad infinitum.* He's got no *terminus ad quem!*"

"What's he saying?" Myra asked.

"It's Latin," Joey explained. "But listen, Dad—I have an idea that I think will work." He lowered his voice. "I'm going to try to adjust Clyde, see? If I can get a sort of multiphase vibrating effect in his neural pathway, maybe I can slip him through the reversed privacy field. He can go get help, find someone who can shut the field off. There's an article on multiphase generators in last month's *Popular Electromagnetics* and it's in my room upstairs. I—"

His voice died away. Carmichael, who had been listening with the air of a condemned man hearing his reprieve, said impatiently, "Well? Go on. Tell me more."

"Didn't you hear that, Dad?"

"Hear what?"

"The front door. I thought I heard it open just now."

"We're all cracking up," Carmichael said dully. He cursed the salesman at Marhew, he cursed the inventor of cryotronic robots, he cursed the day he had first felt ashamed of good old Jemima and resolved to replace her with a new model.

"I hope I'm not intruding, Mr. Carmichael," a new voice said apologetically.

Carmichael blinked and looked up. A wiry, ruddy-cheeked figure in a heavy peajacket had materialized in the middle of the living room. He was clutching a green metal toolbox in one gloved hand. He was Robinson, the robot repairman.

Carmichael asked hoarsely, "How did *you* get in?"

"Through the front door. I could see a light on inside, but nobody answered the doorbell when I rang, so I stepped in. Your doorbell's out of order. I thought I'd tell you. I know it's rude—"

"Don't apologize," Carmichael muttered. "We're delighted to see you."

"I was in the neighborhood, you see, and I figured I'd drop in and see how things were working out with your new robot," Robinson said.

Carmichael told him crisply and precisely and quickly. "So we've been prisoners in here for six days," he finished. "And your robot is gradually starving us to death. We can't hold out much longer."

The smile abruptly left Robinson's cheery face. "I *thought* you all looked rather unhealthy. Oh, damn, now there'll be an investigation and all kinds of trouble. But at least I can end your imprisonment."

He opened his toolbox and selected a tubular instrument eight inches long, with a glass bulb at one end and a trigger attachment at the other. "Force-field damper," he explained. He pointed it at the control box of the privacy field and nodded in satisfaction. "There. Great little gadget. That neutralizes the effects of what the robot did and you're no longer blockaded. And now, if you'll produce the robot—"

Carmichael sent Clyde off to get Bismarck. The robutler returned a few moments later, followed by the looming roboservitor. Robinson grinned gaily, pointed the neutralizer at Bismarck and squeezed. The robot froze in midglide, emitting a brief squeak.

"There. That should immobilize him. Let's have a look in that chassis now."

The repairman quickly opened Bismarck's chest and, producing a pocket flash, peered around in the complex interior of the servo-mechanism, making occasional clucking inaudible comments.

Overwhelmed with relief, Carmichael shakily made his way to a seat. Free! Free at last! His mouth watered at the thought of the meals he was going to have in the next few days. Potatoes and Martinis and warm buttered rolls and all the other forbidden foods!

"Fascinating," Robinson said, half to himself. "The obedience filters are completely shorted out, and the purpose nodes were somehow soldered together by the momentary high-voltage arc. I've never seen anything quite like this, you know."

"Neither had we," Carmichael said hollowly.

"Really, though—this is an utterly new breakthrough in robotic science! If we can reproduce this effect, it means we can build self-willed robots—and think of what *that* means to science!"

"We know already," Ethel said.

"I'd love to watch what happens when the power source is operating," Robinson went on. "For instance, is that feedback loop really negative or—"

"No!" five voices shrieked at once—with Clyde, as usual, coming in last.

It was too late. The entire event had taken no more than a tenth of a second. Robinson had squeezed his neutralizer trigger again, activating Bismarck—and in one quick swoop the roboservitor seized the neutralizer and toolbox from the stunned repairman, activated the privacy field once again, and exultantly crushed the fragile neutralizer between two mighty fingers.

Robinson stammered, "But—but—"

"This attempt at interfering with the well-being of the Carmichael family was ill-advised," Bismarck said severely. He peered into the toolbox, found a second neutralizer and neatly reduced it to junk. He clanged shut his chest plates.

Robinson turned and streaked for the door, forgetting the reactivated privacy field. He bounced back hard, spinning wildly around. Carmichael rose from his seat just in time to catch him.

There was a panicky, trapped look on the repairman's face. Carmichael was no longer able to share the emotion; inwardly he was numb, totally resigned, not minded for further struggle.

"He—he moved so *fast!*" Robinson burst out.

"He did indeed," Carmichael said tranquilly. He patted his hollow stomach and sighed gently. "Luckily, we have an unoccupied guest bedroom for you, Mr. Robinson. Welcome to our happy little home. I hope you like toast and black coffee for breakfast."

THE MAN WHO ATE THE WORLD

by Frederik Pohl

Heavy consumption of goods and services is a problem of the rich, one that many of us wish we had. In the wonderfully titled story that follows, Frederik Pohl presents a stunning portrait of the ultimate in consumption and the costs involved.

I

He had a name, but at home he was called Sonny, and he was almost always at home. He hated it. Other boys his age went to school. Sonny would have done anything to go to school, but his family was, to put it mildly, not well off. It wasn't Sonny's fault that his father was spectacularly unsuccessful. But it meant—no school for Sonny, no boys of his own age for Sonny to play with. All childhoods are tragic (as all adults forget), but Sonny's was misery all the way through.

The worst time was at night, when the baby sister was asleep and the parents were grimly eating and reading and dancing and drinking, until they were ready to drop. And of all bad nights, the night before his twelfth birthday was perhaps Sonny's worst. He was old enough to know what a birthday party was like. It would be cake and candy, shows and games; it would be presents, presents, presents. It would be a terrible, endless day.

He switched off the color-D television and the recorded tapes of sea chanteys and, with an appearance of absentmindedness, walked toward the door of his playroom.

Davey Crockett got up from beside the model rocket field and said, "Hold on thar, Sonny. Mought take a stroll with you." Davey's face was serene, and strong as a Tennessee crag; it swung its long huntin' rifle under one arm and put its other arm around Sonny's shoulders. "Where you reckon we ought to head?"

79

Sonny shook Davey Crockett's arm off. "Get lost," he said, petulantly. "Who wants you around?"

Long John Silver came out of the closet, hobbling on its wooden leg, crouched over its knobby cane. "Ah, young master," it said reproachfully, "you shouldn't ought to talk to old Davey like that! He's a good friend to you, Davey is. Many's the weary day Davey and me has been a-keepin' of your company. I asks you this, young master: Is it fair and square that you should be a-tellin' him to get lost? Is it fair, young master? Is it square?"

Sonny looked at the floor stubbornly and didn't answer. My gosh, what was the use of answering dummies like them? He stood rebelliously silent and still until he just felt like saying something. And then he said: "You go in the closet, both of you. I don't want to play with you. I'm going to play with my trains."

Long John said unctuously, "Now there's a good idea, that is! You just be a-havin' of a good time with your trains, and old Davey and me'll—"

"Go ahead!" shouted Sonny. He stood stamping his foot until they were out of sight.

His fire truck was in the middle of the floor; he kicked at it, but it rolled quickly out of reach and slid into its little garage under the tanks of tropical fish. He scuffed over to the model railroad layout and glared at it. As he approached, the Twentieth Century Limited came roaring out of a tunnel, sparks flying from its stack. It crossed a bridge, whistled at a grade crossing, steamed into the Union Station. The roof of the station glowed and suddenly became transparent, and through it Sonny saw the bustling crowds of redcaps and travelers—

"I don't want that," he said. "Casey, crack up old Number Ninety-Nine again."

Obediently the layout quivered and revolved a half-turn. Old Casey Jones, one and an eighth inches tall, leaned out of the cab of the S.P. locomotive and waved good-bye to Sonny. The locomotive whistled shrilly twice and started to pick up speed—

It was a good crackup. Little old Casey's body, thrown completely free, developed real blisters from the steam and bled real blood. But Sonny turned his back on it. He had liked that crackup for a long time —longer than he liked almost any other toy he owned. But he was tired of it.

He looked around the room.

Tarzan of the Apes, leaning against a foot-thick tree trunk, one hand on a vine, lifted its head and looked at him. But Tarzan, Sonny calculated craftily, was clear across the room. The others were in the closet—

Sonny ran out and slammed the door. He saw Tarzan start to come after him, but even before Sonny was out of the room Tarzan slumped and stood stock-still.

It wasn't fair, Sonny thought angrily. It wasn't fair! They wouldn't even *chase* him, so that at least he could have some kind of chance to get away by himself. They'd just talk to each other on their little radios, and in a minute one of the tutors, or one of the maids, or whatever else happened to be handy, would vector in on him. And that would be that.

But for the moment he was free.

He slowed down and walked down the Great Hall toward his baby sister's room. The fountains began to splash as he entered the hall; the mosaics on the wall began to tinkle music and sparkle with moving colors.

"Now, chile, whut you up to!"

He turned around, but he knew it was Mammy coming toward him. It was slapping toward him on big, flat feet, its pink-palmed hands lifted to its shoulders. The face under the red bandanna was frowning, the gold tooth sparkling as it scolded: "Chile, you is got us'n's so worried we's fit to *die!* How you 'speck us to take good keer of you ef'n you run off lak that? Now you jes come on back to your nice room with Mammy an' we'll see if there ain't some real nice program on the TV."

Sonny stopped and waited for it, but he wouldn't give it the satisfaction of looking at it. Slap-slap the big feet waddled cumbersomely toward him; but he didn't have any illusions. Waddle, big feet, three hundred pounds and all, Mammy could catch him in twenty yards with a ten-yard start. Any of them could.

He said in his best icily indignant voice, "I was just going in to look at my baby sister."

Pause. "You was?" The plump black face looked suspicious.

"Yes, I was. Doris is my very own sister, and I love her very much."

Pause—long pause. "Dat's nice," said Mammy, but its voice was still doubtful. "I 'speck I better come 'long with you. You wouldn't want to wake your lil baby sister up. Ef I come I'll he'p you keep real quiet."

Sonny shook free of it—they were always putting their hands on you! "I don't *want* you to come with me, Mammy!"

"Aw now, honey! Mammy ain't gwine bother nothin', you knows that."

Sonny turned his back on it and marched grimly toward his sister's room. If only they would leave him *alone!* But they never did. It was always that way, always one darn old robot—yes, *robot,* he thought, savagely tasting the naughty word. Always one darn *robot* after another. Why couldn't Daddy be like other daddies, so they could live in a decent little house and get rid of these darn *robots*—so he could go to a real school and be in a class with other boys, instead of being taught at home by Miss Brooks and Mr. Chips and all those other *robots?*

They spoiled everything. And they would spoil what he wanted to do now. But he was going to do it all the same, because there was something in Doris's room that he wanted very much.

It was probably the only tangible thing he wanted in the world.

As they passed the imitation tumbled rocks of the Bear Cave, Mama Bear poked its head out and growled: "Hello, Sonny. Don't you think you ought to be in bed? It's nice and warm in our bear bed, Sonny."

He didn't even look at it. Time was when he liked that sort of thing, too, but he wasn't a four-year-old like Doris anymore. All the same, there was one thing a four-year-old had—

He stopped at the door of her room. "Doris?" he whispered.

Mammy scolded: "Now, chile, you know that lil baby is asleep! How come you tryin' to wake her up?"

"I won't wake her up." The farthest thing from Sonny's mind was to wake his sister up. He tiptoed into the room and stood beside the little girl's bed. Lucky kid! he thought enviously. Being four, she was allowed to have a tiny little room and a tiny bed—where Sonny had to wallow around in a forty-foot bedchamber and a bed eight feet long.

He looked down at his sister. Behind him Mammy clucked approvingly. "Dat's nice when chilluns loves each other lak you an' that lil baby," it whispered.

Doris was sound asleep, clutching her teddy bear. It wriggled slightly and opened an eye to look at Sonny, but it didn't say anything.

Sonny took a deep breath, leaned forward and gently slipped the teddy bear out of the bed.

It scrambled pathetically, trying to get free. Behind him Mammy whispered urgently: "Sonny! Now you let dat ole teddy bear alone, you heah me?"

Sonny whispered, "I'm not hurting anything. Leave me alone, will you?"

"Sonny!"

He clutched the little furry robot desperately around its middle. The stubby arms pawed at him, the furred feet scratched against his arms. It growled a tiny doll-bear growl, and whined, and suddenly his hands were wet with its real salt tears.

"Sonny! Come on now, honey, you knows that's Doris's teddy. Aw, chile!"

He said, "It's mine!" It wasn't his. He knew it wasn't his. His was long gone, taken away from him when he was six because it was *old,* and because he had been six and six-year-olds had to have bigger, more elaborate companion-robots. It wasn't even the same color as his—it was brown, where his had been black and white. But it was cuddly and gently warm; and he had heard it whispering little make-believe bedtime stories to Doris. And he wanted it, very much.

Footsteps in the hall outside. A low-pitched pleading voice from the door: "Sonny, you must not interfere with your sister's toys. One has obligations."

He stood forlornly, holding the teddy bear. "Go away, Mr. Chips!"

"Really, Sonny! This isn't proper behavior. Please return the toy."

He cried: "I won't!"

Mammy, dark face pleading in the shadowed room, leaned toward him and tried to take it away from him. "Aw, honey, now you know dat's not—"

"Leave me alone!" he shouted. There was a gasp and a little cry from the bed, and Doris sat up and began to weep.

Well, they had their way. The little girl's bedroom was suddenly filled with robots—and not only robots, for in a moment the butler robot appeared, its face stern and sorrowful, leading Sonny's actual flesh-and-blood mother and father. Sonny made a terrible scene. He cried, and he swore at them childishly for being the unsuccessful clods they were; and they nearly wept too, because they were aware that their lack of standing was bad for the children.

But he couldn't keep the teddy.

They got it away from him and marched him back to his room, where his father lectured him while his mother stayed behind to watch Mammy comfort the little girl. His father said: "Sonny, you're a big boy now. We aren't as well off as other people, but you have to help us.

Don't you know that, Sonny? We all have to do our part. Your mother and I'll be up till midnight now, consuming, because you've interrupted us with this scene. Can't you at least *try* to consume something bigger than a teddy bear? It's all right for Doris because she's so little, but a big boy like you—"

"I hate you!" cried Sonny, and he turned his face to the wall.

They punished him, naturally. The first punishment was that they gave him an extra birthday party the week following.

The second punishment was even worse.

II

Later—much, much later, nearly a score of years—a man named Roger Garrick in a place named Fisherman's Island walked into his hotel room.

The light didn't go on.

The bellhop apologized. "We're sorry, sir. We'll have it attended to, if possible."

"If possible?" Garrick's eyebrows went up. The bellhop made putting in a new light tube sound like a major industrial operation. "All right." He waved the bellhop out of the room. It bowed and closed the door.

Garrick looked around him, frowning. One light tube more or less didn't make an awful lot of difference; there was still the light from the sconces at the walls, from the reading lamps at the chairs and chaise longue and from the photomural on the long side of the room—to say nothing of the fact that it was broad, hot daylight outside and light poured through the windows. All the same, it was a new sensation to be in a room where the central lighting wasn't on. He didn't like it. It was —creepy.

A rap on the door. A girl was standing there, young, attractive, rather small. But a woman grown, it was apparent. "Mr. Garrick? Mr. Roosenburg is expecting you on the sun deck."

"All right." He rummaged around in the pile of luggage, looking for his briefcase. It wasn't even sorted out! The bellhop had merely dumped the lot and left.

The girl said, "Is that what you're looking for?" He looked where she was pointing; it was his briefcase, behind another bag. "You'll get used to that around here. Nothing in the right place, nothing working right. We've all got used to it."

We. He looked at her sharply, but she was no robot; there was life, not the glow of electronic tubes, in her eyes. "Pretty bad, is it?"

She shrugged. "Let's go see Mr. Roosenburg. I'm Kathryn Pender, by the way. I'm his statistician."

He followed her out into the hall. "Statistician?"

She turned and smiled—a tight, grim smile of annoyance. "That's right. Surprised?"

Garrick said slowly, "Well, it's more a robot job. Of course, I'm not familiar with the practice in this sector. . . ."

"You will be," she said shortly. "No, we aren't taking the elevator. Mr. Roosenburg's in a hurry to see you."

"But—"

She turned and glared at him. "Don't you understand? Day before yesterday I took the elevator, and I was hung up between floors for an hour and a half. Something was going on at North Guardian, and it took all the power in the lines. Would it happen again today? I don't know. But, believe me, an hour and a half is a long time to be hanging in an elevator." She turned and led him to the fire stairs. Over her shoulder she said: "Get it straight once and for all, Mr. Garrick. You're in a disaster area here. . . . Anyway, it's only ten more flights."

Ten flights.

Nobody climbed ten flights of stairs anymore! Garrick was huffing and puffing before they were halfway, but the girl kept on ahead, light as a gazelle. Her skirt cut midway beteen hip and knees, and Garrick had plenty of opportunity to observe that her legs were attractively tanned. Even so, he couldn't help looking around him. It was a robot's-eye view of the hotel that he was getting; this was the bare wire armature that held up the confectionery suits and halls where the humans went. Garrick knew, as everyone absentmindedly knew, that there were places like this behind the scenes everywhere. Belowstairs the robots worked; behind scenes, they moved about their errands and did their jobs. But nobody *went* there. It was funny about the backs of this girl's knees; they were paler than the rest of the leg—

Garrick wrenched his mind back to his surroundings. Take the guard rail along the steps, for instance. It was wire-thin, frail-looking. No doubt it could bear any weight it was required to, but why couldn't it look that way? The answer, obviously, was that robots did not have humanity's built-in concepts of how strong a rail should look before they could believe it really was strong. If a robot should be in any doubt—and how improbable, that a robot should be in doubt!—it would perhaps reach out a sculptured hand and test it. Once. And then it would remember, and never doubt again; and it wouldn't be continually edging toward the wall, away from the spider-strand between him and the vertical drop—

He conscientiously took the middle of the steps all the rest of the way up.

Of course that merely meant a different distraction, when he really wanted to do some thinking. But it was a pleasurable distraction. And by the time they reached the top he had solved the problem; the pale spots at the back of Miss Pender's knees meant she had got her suntan the hard way—walking in the sun, perhaps working in the sun, so that the bending knees kept the sun from the patches at the back; not as anyone else would acquire a tan, by lying beneath a normal, healthful sunlamp held by a robot masseur.

He wheezed: "You don't mean we're all the way up?"

"All the way up," she agreed, and looked at him closely. "Here, lean on me if you want to."

"No, thanks!" He staggered over to the door, which opened naturally enough as he approached it, and stepped out into the flood of sunlight on the roof, to meet Mr. Roosenburg.

Garrick wasn't a medical doctor, but he remembered enough of his basic prespecialization to know there was something in that fizzy golden drink. It tasted perfectly splendid—just cold enough, just fizzy enough, not quite too sweet. And after two sips of it he was buoyant with strength and well-being.

He put the glass down and said: "Thank you for whatever it was. Now let's talk."

"Gladly, gladly!" boomed Mr. Roosenburg. "Kathryn, the files!"

Garrick looked after her, shaking his head. Not only was she a statistician, which was robot work, she was also a file clerk—and that was barely even robot work, it was the kind of thing handled by a semisentient punchcard sorter in a decently run sector.

Roosenburg said sharply: "Shocks you, doesn't it? But that's why you're here." He was a slim, fair little man, and he wore a golden beard cropped square.

Garrick took another sip of the fizzy drink. It was good stuff; it didn't intoxicate, but it cheered. He said, "I'm glad to know why I'm here."

The golden beard quivered. "Area control sent you down and didn't tell you this was a disaster area?"

Garrick put down the glass. "I'm a psychist. Area Control said you needed a psychist. From what I've seen, it's a supply problem, but—"

"Here are the files," said Kathryn Pender, and stood watching him.

Roosenburg took the spools of tape from her and dropped them in his lap. He said tangentially, "How old are you, Roger?"

Garrick was annoyed. "I'm a qualified psychist! I happen to be assigned to Area Control and—"

"How old are you?"

Garrick scowled. "Twenty-four."

Roosenburg nodded. "Um. Rather young," he observed. "Maybe you don't remember how things used to be."

Garrick said dangerously, "All the information I need is on that tape. I don't need any lectures from you."

Roosenburg pursed his lips and got up. "Come here a minute, will you?"

He moved over to the rail of the sun deck and pointed. "See those things down there?"

Garrick looked. Twenty stories down the village straggled off toward the sea in a tangle of pastel oblongs and towers. Over the bay the hills of the mainland were faintly visible through the mist; and riding the bay, the flat white floats of the solar receptors.

"It's a power plant. That what you mean?"

Roosenburg boomed. "A power plant. All the power the world can ever use, out of this one and all the others, all over the world." He peered out at the bobbing floats, soaking up energy from the sun. "And people used to try to wreck them," he said.

Garrick said stiffly: "I may only be twenty-four years old, Mr. Roosenburg, but I have completed school."

"Oh, yes. Oh, of course you have, Roger. But maybe schooling isn't the same thing as living through a time like that. I grew up in the Era of Plenty, when the law was: *Consume.* My parents were poor, and I still remember the misery of my childhood. Eat and consume, wear and use, I never had a moment's peace, Roger! For the very poor it was a treadmill; we had to consume so much that we could never catch up, and the farther we fell behind, the more the Ration Board forced on us—"

Roger Garrick said: "That's ancient history, Mr. Roosenburg, Morey Fry liberated us from all that."

The girl said softly: "Not all of us."

The man with the golden beard nodded. "Not all of us. As you should know, Roger, being a psychist."

Garrick sat up straight, and Roosenburg went on: "Fry showed us that the robots could help at both ends—by making, by consuming. But it came a little late for some of us. The patterns of childhood—they linger on."

Kathryn Pender leaned toward Garrick. "What he's trying to say, Mr. Garrick—we've got a compulsive consumer on our hands."

III

North Guardian Island—nine miles away. It wasn't as much as a mile wide, and not much more than that in length. But it had its city and its bathing beaches, its parks and theaters. It was possibly the most densely populated island in the world . . . for the number of its inhabitants.

The President of the Council convened their afternoon meeting in a large and lavish room. There were nineteen councilmen around a lustrous mahogany table. Over the President's shoulder the others could see the situation map of North Guardian and the areas surrounding. North Guardian glowed blue, cool, impregnable. The sea was misty green; the mainland, Fisherman's Island, South Guardian and the rest of the little archipelago were a hot and hostile red.

Little flickering fingers of red attacked the blue. Flick, and a ruddy flame wiped out a corner of a beach; flick, and a red spark appeared in the middle of the city, to grow and blossom, and then to die. Each little red whip-flick was a point where, momentarily, the defenses of the island were down; but always and always, the cool blue brightened around the red, and drowned it.

The President was tall, stooped, old. It wore glasses, though robot eyes saw well enough without. It said, in a voice that throbbed with power and pride: "The first item of the order of business will be a report of the Defense Secretary."

The Defense Secretary rose to its feet, hooked a thumb in its vest and cleared its throat. "Mr. President—"

"Excuse me, sir." A whisper from the sweet-faced young blonde taking down the minutes of the meeting. "Mr. Trumie has just left Bowling Green, heading north."

The whole council turned to glance at the situation map, where Bowling Green had just flared red.

The President nodded stiffly, like the crown of an old redwood nodding. "You may proceed, Mr. Secretary," it said after a moment.

"Our invasion fleet," began the Secretary, in its high, clear voice, "is ready for sailing on the first suitable tide. Certain units have been, ah, inactivated, at the, ah, instigation of Mr. Trumie, but on the whole repairs have been completed and the units will be serviceable within the next few hours." Its lean, attractive face turned solemn. "I am afraid, however, that the Air Command has sustained certain, ah, increments of attrition—due, I should emphasize, to chances involved in certain calculated risks—"

"Question, question!" It was the Commissioner of Public Safety, small, dark, fire-eyed, angry.

"Mr. Commissioner?" the President began, but it was interrupted again by the soft whisper of the recording stenographer, listening intently to the earphones that brought news from outside.

"Mr. President," it whispered, "Mr. Trumie has passed the Navy Yard." The robots turned to look at the situation map. Bowling Green though it smoldered in spots, had mostly gone back to blue. But the jagged oblong of the Yard flared red and bright. There was a faint electronic hum in the air, almost a sigh.

The robots turned back to face each other. "Mr. President! I demand the Defense Secretary explain the loss of the *Graf Zeppelin* and the 456th Bomb Group!"

The Defense Secretary nodded to the Commissioner of Public Safety. "Mr. Trumie threw them away," it said sorrowfully.

Once again, that sighing electronic drone from the assembled robots.

The Council fussed and fiddled with its papers, while the situation map on the wall flared and dwindled, flared and dwindled. The Defense Secretary cleared its throat again. "Mr. President, there is no question that the, ah, absence of an effective air component will seriously hamper, not to say endanger, our prospects of a suitable landing. Nevertheless—and I say this, Mr. President, in full knowledge of the conclusions that may—indeed, should!—be drawn from such a statement—nevertheless, Mr. President, I say that our forward elements will successfully complete an assault landing—"

"Mr. President!" The breathless whisper of the blond stenographer again. "Mr. President, Mr. Trumie is in the building!"

On the situation map behind it, the Pentagon—the building they were in—flared scarlet.

The Attorney General, nearest the door, leaped to its feet. "Mr. President, I hear him!"

And they could all hear, now. Far off, down the long corridors, a crash. A faint explosion, and another crash; and a raging, querulous, high-pitched voice. A nearer crash, and a sustained, smashing, banging sound, coming toward them.

The oak-paneled doors flew open, splintering.

A tall, dark male figure in gray leather jacket, rocket-gun holsters swinging at its hips, stepped through the splintered doors and stood surveying the Council. Its hands hung just below the butts of the rocket guns.

It drawled: "Mistuh Anderson Trumie!"

It stepped aside. Another male figure—shorter, darker, hobbling with the aid of a stainless-steel cane that concealed a ray-pencil, wearing the same gray leather jacket and the same rocket-gun holsters—entered, stood for a moment, and took a position on the other side of the door.

Between them, Mr. Anderson Trumbie shambled ponderously into the Council Chamber to call on his Council.

Sonny Trumie, come of age.

He wasn't much more than five feet tall; but his weight was close to four hundred pounds. He stood there in the door, leaning against the splintered oak, quivering jowls obliterating his neck, his eyes nearly swallowed in the fat that swamped his skull, his thick legs trembling as they tried to support him.

"You're all under arrest!" he shrilled. "Traitors! Traitors!"

He panted ferociously, staring at them. They waited with bowed heads. Beyond the ring of councilmen, the situation map slowly blotted out the patches of red, as the repair-robots worked feverishly to fix what Sonny Trumie had destroyed.

"Mr. Crockett!" he cried shrilly. "Slay me these traitors!"

Wheep-wheep, and the guns whistled out of their holsters into the tall bodyguard's hands. *Rata-tat-tat,* and two by two, the nineteen councilmen leaped, clutched at air and fell, as the rocket pellets pierced them through.

"That one too!" cried Mr. Trumie, pointing at the sweet-faced blonde. *Bang.* The sweet young face convulsed and froze; it fell, slumping across its little table. On the wall the situation map flared red again, but only faintly—for what were twenty robots?

Sonny gestured curtly to his other bodyguard. It leaped forward, tucking the stainless-steel cane under one arm, putting the other around the larded shoulders of Sonny Trumie. "Ah, now, young master," it crooned. "You just get ahold o' Long John's arm now—"

"Get them fixed," Sonny ordered abruptly. He pushed the President of the Council out of its chair and, with the robot's help, sank into it himself. "Get them fixed *right,* you hear? I've had enough traitors. I want them to do what I tell them!"

"Sartin sure, young marster. Long John'll—"

"Do it *now!* And you, Davey! I want my lunch."

"Reckoned you would, Mistuh Trumie, It's right hyar." The Crockett-robot kicked the fallen councilmen out of the way as a procession of waiters filed in from the corridor.

He ate.

He ate until eating was pain, and then he sat there sobbing, his arms braced against the tabletop, until he could eat more. The Crockett-robot said worriedly: "Mistuh Trumie, moughtn't you hold back a little? Old Doc Aeschylus, he don't keer much to have you eatin' too much, you know."

"I hate Doc!" Trumie said bitterly. He pushed the plates off the table. They fell with a rattle and a clatter, and they went spinning away as he heaved himself up and lurched alone over to the window. "I hate Doc!" he brayed again, sobbing, staring through tears out the window at his kingdom with its hurrying throngs and marching troops and roaring waterfront. The tallow shoulders tried to shake with pain. He felt as though hot cinderblocks were being thrust up into his body cavities, the ragged edges cutting, the hot weight crushing. "Take me back," he sobbed to the robots. "Take me away from these traitors. Take me to my Private Place!"

IV

"So you see," said Roosenburg, "he's dangerous."

Garrick looked out over the water, toward North Guardian. "I'd better look at his tapes," he said. The girl swiftly picked up the reels and began to thread them into the projector. Dangerous. This Trumie was dangerous, all right, Garrick conceded. Dangerous to the balanced, stable world; for it only took one Trumie to topple its stability. It had taken thousands and thousands of years for society to learn its delicate tightrope walk. It was a matter for a psychist, all right. . . .

And Garrick was uncomfortably aware that he was only twenty-four. "Here you are," said the girl.

"Look them over," said Roosenburg. "Then, after you've studied the tapes on Trumie, we've got something else. One of his robots. But you'll need the tapes first."

"Let's go," said Garrick.

The girl flicked a switch, and the life of Anderson Trumie appeared before them, in color, in three dimensions—in miniature.

Robots have eyes; and where the robots go, the eyes of Robot Central go with them. And the robots go everywhere. From the stored files of Robot Central came the spool of tape that was the life story of Sonny Trumie.

The tapes played into the globe-shaped viewer, ten inches high, a crystal ball that looked back into the past. First, from the recording eyes of the robots in Sonny Trumie's nursery. The lonely little boy, twenty years before, lost in the enormous nursery.

"Disgusting!" breathed Kathryn Pender, wrinkling her nose. "How could people live like that?"

Garrick said, "Please, let me watch this. It's important." In the gleaming globe the little boy-figure kicked at his toys, threw himself across his huge bed, sobbed. Garrick squinted, frowned, reached out, tried to make contact. . . . It was hard. The tapes showed the objective facts, all right; but for a psychist it was the subjective reality behind the facts that mattered. Kicking at his toys. Yes, but why? Because he was tired of them—and why was he tired? Because he feared them? *Kicking at his toys.* Because—because they were the *wrong* toys? *Kicking—hate them! Don't want them! Want—*

A bluish flare in the viewing globe. Garrick blinked and jumped; and that was the end of that section.

The colors flowed, and suddenly jelled into bright life. Anderson Trumie, a young man. Garrick recognized the scene after a moment—it was right there on Fisherman's Island, some pleasure spot overlooking the water. A bar, and at the end of it was Anderson Trumie, pimply and twenty, staring somberly into an empty glass. The view was through the eyes of the robot bartender.

Anderson Trumie was weeping.

Once again, there was the objective fact—but the fact behind the fact, what was it? Trumie had been drinking, drinking. Why? *Drinking, drinking.* With a sudden sense of shock, Garrick saw what the drink was —the golden, fizzy liquor. Not intoxicating. Not habit-forming! Trumie had become no drunk, it was something else that kept him *drinking, must drink, must keep on drinking, or else*—

And again the bluish flare.

There was more; there was Trumie feverishly collecting objects of art, there was Trumie decorating a palace; there was Trumie on a world tour, and Trumie returned to Fisherman's Island.

And then there was no more.

"That," said Roosenburg, "is the file. Of course, if you want the raw, unedited tapes, we can try to get them from Robot Central, but—"

"No." The way things were, it was best to stay away from Robot Central; there might be more breakdowns, and there wasn't much time. Besides, something was beginning to suggest itself.

"Run the first one again," said Garrick. "I think maybe there's something there. . . ."

Garrick made out a quick requisition slip and handed it to Kathryn Pender, who looked at it, raised her eyebrows, shrugged and went off to have it filled.

By the time she came back, Roosenburg had escorted Garrick to the room where the captured Trumie robot lay enchained. "He's cut off from Robot Central," Roosenburg was saying. "I suppose you figured that out. Imagine! Not only has he built a whole city for himself—but even his own robot control!"

Garrick looked at the robot. It was a fisherman, or so Roosenburg had said. It was small, dark, black-haired, and possibly the hair would have been curly, if the sea water hadn't plastered the curls to the scalp. It was still damp from the tussle that had landed it in the water, and eventually in Roosenburg's hands.

Roosenburg was already at work. Garrick tried to think of it as a machine, but it wasn't easy. The thing looked very nearly human— except for the crystal and copper that showed where the back of its head had been removed.

"It's as bad as a brain operation," said Roosenburg, working rapidly without looking up. "I've got to short out the input leads without disturbing the electronic balance...."

Snip, Snip. A curl of copper fell free, to be grabbed by Roosenburg's tweezers. The fisherman's arms and legs kicked sharply like a galvanized frog's.

Kathryn Pender said: "They found him this morning, casting nets into the bay and singing '*O Sole Mio.*' He's from North Guardian, all right."

Abruptly the lights flickered and turned yellow, then slowly returned to normal brightness. Roger Garrick got up and walked over to the window. North Guardian was a haze of light in the sky, across the water.

Click, snap. The fisherman-robot began to sing:

> *Tutte le serre, dopo quel fanal,*
> *Dietro la caserma, ti staró ed—*

Click. Roosenburg muttered under his breath and probed further. Kathryn Pender joined Garrick at the window. "Now you see," she said.

Garrick shrugged. "You can't blame him."

"*I* blame him!" she said hotly. "I've lived here all my life. Fisherman's Island used to be a tourist spot—why, it was lovely here. And look at it now. The elevators don't work. The lights don't work. Practically all of our robots are gone. Spare parts, construction material, everything—it's all gone to North Guardian! There isn't a day that passes, Garrick, when half a dozen bargeloads of stuff don't go north, because *he* requisitioned them. Blame him? I'd like to kill him!"

Snap. Sputter*snap.* The fisherman lifted his head and caroled:

> *Forse dommani, piangerai,*
> *E dopo tu, sorriderai—*

Snap. Roosenburg's probe uncovered a flat black disc. "Kathryn, look this up, will you?" He read the serial number from the disc, and then put down the probe. He stood flexing his fingers, staring irritably at the motionless figure.

Garrick joined him. Roosenburg jerked his head at the fisherman. "That's robot work, trying to tinker with their insides. Trumie has his own control center, you see. What I have to do is recontrol this one from the substation on the mainland, but keep its receptor circuits open to North Guardian on the symbolic level. You understand what I'm talking about? It'll think from North Guardian, but act from the mainland."

"Sure," said Garrick, far from sure.

"And it's damned close work. There isn't much room inside one of those things. . . ." He stared at the figure and picked up the probe again.

Kathryn Pender came back with a punchcard in her hand. "It was one of ours, all right. Used to be a busboy in the cafeteria at the beach club." She scowled. "That Trumie!"

"You can't blame him," Garrick said reasonably. "He's only trying to be good."

She looked at him queerly. "He's only—" she began; but Roosenburg interrupted with an exultant cry.

"Got It! All right, you. Sit up and start telling us what Trumie's up to now!"

The fisherman figure said obligingly, "Sure, boss. Whatcha wanna know?"

What they wanted to know they asked; and what they asked it told them, volunteering nothing, concealing nothing.

There was Anderson Trumie, king of his island, the compulsive consumer.

It was like an echo of the bad old days of the Age of Plenty, when the world was smothering under the endless, pounding flow of goods from the robot factories and the desperate race between consumption and production strained the human fabric. But Trumie's orders came not from society, but from within. *Consume!* commanded something inside him, and *Use!* it cried, and *Devour!* it ordered. And Trumie obeyed, heroically.

They listened to what the fisherman-robot had to say, and the picture was dark. Armies had sprung up on North Guardian, navies floated in its waters. Anderson Trumie stalked among his creations like a blubbery god, wrecking and ruling. Garrick could see the pattern in what the fisherman had to say. In Trumie's mind, he was Hitler, Hoover and Genghis Khan; he was dictator, building a war machine; he was supreme engineer, constructing a mighty state. He was warrior.

"He was playing tin soldiers," said Roger Garrick, and Roosenburg and the girl nodded.

"The trouble is," boomed Roosenburg, "he has stopped playing. Invasion fleets, Garrick! He isn't content with North Guardian anymore, he wants the rest of the country too!"

"You can't blame him," said Roger Garrick for the third time, and stood up.

"The question is," he said, "what do we do about it?"

"That's what you're here for," Kathryn told him.

"All right. We can forget," said Roger Garrick, "about the soldiers— *qua* soldiers, that is. I promise you they won't hurt anyone. Robots can't."

"I understand that," Kathryn snapped.

"The problem is what to do about Trumie's drain on the world's resources." He pursed his lips. "According to my directive from Area Control, the first plan was to let him alone—after all, there is still plenty of everything for anyone. Why not let Trumie enjoy himself? But that didn't work out too well."

"You are so right," said Kathryn Pender.

"No, no—not on your local level," Garrick explained quickly. "After all—what are a few thousand robots, a few hundred million dollars' worth of equipment? We could resupply this area in a week."

"And in a week," boomed Roosenburg, "Trumie would have us cleaned out again!"

Garrick nodded. "That's the trouble," he admitted. "He doesn't seem to have a stopping point. Yet—we can't *refuse* his orders. Speaking as a psychist, that would set a very bad precedent. It would put ideas in the minds of a lot of persons—minds that, in some cases, might not be reliably stable in the absence of a stable, certain source of everything they need, on request. If we say 'no' to Trumie, we open the door on some mighty dark corners of the human mind. Covetousness. Greed. Pride of possession—"

"So what are you going to do?" cried Kathryn Pender.

Garrick said resentfully, "The only thing there is *to* do. I'm going to look over Trumie's folder again. And then I'm going to North Guardian Island."

V

Roger Garrick was all too aware of the fact that he was only twenty-four.

It didn't make a great deal of difference. The oldest and wisest psychist in Area Control's wide sphere might have been doubtful of success in as thorny a job as the one ahead.

They started out at daybreak. Vapor was rising from the sea about them, and the little battery motor of their launch whined softly beneath the keelson. Garrick sat patting the little box that contained their invasion equipment, while the girl steered. The workshops of Fisherman's Island had been all night making some of the things in that box—not because they were so difficult to make, but because it had been a bad night. Big things were going on at North Guardian; twice the power had been out entirely for nearly an hour, as the demand on the lines from North Guardian took all the power the system could deliver.

The sun was well up as they came within hailing distance of the Navy Yard.

Robots were hard at work; the Yard was bustling with activity. An overhead traveling crane, eight feet tall, laboriously lowered a prefabricated fighting top onto an eleven-foot aircraft carrier. A motor torpedo boat—full-sized, this one was, not to scale—rocked at anchor just before the bow of their launch. Kathryn steered around it, ignoring the hail from the robot-lieutenant-j.g. at its rail.

She glanced at Garrick over her shoulder, her face taut. "It's—it's all mixed up."

Garrick nodded. The battleships were model-sized, the small boats full scale. In the city beyond the Yard, the pinnacle of the Empire State Building barely cleared the Pentagon, next door. A soaring suspension bridge leaped out from the shore a quarter of a mile away, and stopped short a thousand yards out, over empty water.

It was easy enough to understand—even for a psychist just out of school, on his first real assignment. Trumie was trying to run a world single-handed, and where there were gaps in his conception of what his world should be, the results showed. "Get me battleships!" he ordered his robot supply clerks; and they found the only battleships there were in the world to copy, the child-sized, toy-scaled play battleships that still delighted kids. "Get me an Air Force!" And a thousand model bombers were hastily put together. "Build me a bridge!" But perhaps he had forgot to say where.

"Come on, Garrick!"

He shook his head and focused on the world around him. Kathryn Pender was standing on a gray steel stage, the mooring line from their launch secured to what looked like a coast-defense cannon—but only about four feet long. Garrick picked up his little box and leaped up to the stage beside her. She turned to look at the city. . . .

"Hold on a second." He was opening the box, taking out two little cardboard placards. He turned her by the shoulder and, with pins from the box, attached one of the cards to her back. "Now me," he said, turning his back to her.

She read the placard dubiously:

I

AM A

SPY!

"Garrick," she began, "you're sure you know what you're doing—"
"Put it on!" She shrugged and pinned it to the folds of his jacket. Side by side, they entered the citadel of the enemy.

According to the fisherman-robot, Trumie lived in a gingerbread castle south of the Pentagon. Most of the robots got no chance to enter it. The city outside the castle was Trumie's kingdom, and he roamed about it, overseeing, changing, destroying, rebuilding. But inside the castle was his Private Place; the only robots that had both an inside- and outside-the-castle existence were his two bodyguards.

"That," said Garrick, "must be the Private Place."

It was a gingerbread castle, all right. The "gingerbread" was stone-work, gargoyles and columns; there was a moat and a drawbridge, and there were robot guards with crooked little rifles, wearing scarlet tunics and fur shakos three feet tall. The drawbridge was up and the guards at stiff attention.

"Let's reconnoiter," said Garrick. He was unpleasantly conscious of the fact that every robot they passed—and they had passed thousands —had turned to look at the signs on their backs. Yet—it was right, wasn't it? There was no hope of avoiding observation in any event. The only hope was to fit somehow into the pattern—and spies would certainly be part of the pattern. Wouldn't they?

Garrick turned his back on doubts and led the way around the gingerbread palace.

The only entrance was the drawbridge.

They stopped out of sight of the ramrod-stiff guards. Garrick said: "We'll go in. As soon as we get inside, you put on your costume." He handed her the box. "You know what to do. All you have to do is keep him quiet for a while and let me talk to him."

The girl said doubtfully, "Garrick. Is this going to work?"

Garrick exploded: "How the devil do I know? I had Trumie's dossier to work with. I know everything that happened to him when he was a kid—when this trouble started. But to reach him, to talk to the boy inside the man—that takes a long time, Kathryn. And we don't have a long time. So . . ."

He took her elbow and marched her toward the guards. "So you know what to do," he said.

"I hope so," breathed Kathryn Pender, looking very small and very young.

They marched down the wide white pavement, past the motionless guards. . . .

Something was coming toward them. Kathryn held back. "Come on!" Garrick muttered.

"No, look!" she whispered. "Is that—is that Trumie?"

He looked.

It was Trumie, larger than life. It was Anderson Trumie, the entire human population of the most-congested-island-for-its-population in the world. On one side of him was a tall dark figure, on the other side a squat dark figure, helping him along. They looked at his face and it was horror, drowned in fat. The bloated cheeks shook damply, wet with tears. The eyes looked out with fright on the world he had made.

Trumie and his bodyguards rolled up to them and past. And then Anderson Trumie stopped.

He turned the blubbery head, and read the sign on the back of the girl. *I am a spy.* Panting heavily, clutching the shoulder of the Crockett-robot, he stared wildly at her.

Garrick cleared his throat. This far his plan had gone, and then there was a gap. There had to be a gap. Trumie's history, in the folder that Roosenburg had supplied, had told him what to do with Trumie; and Garrick's own ingenuity had told him how to reach the man. But a link was missing. Here was the subject, and here was the psychist who could cure him; and it was up to Garrick to start the cure.

Trumie cried, in a staccato bleat: "You! What are you? Where do you belong?"

He was talking to the girl. Beside him the Crockett-robot murmured, "Rackin she's a spy, Mistuh Trumie. See thet sign a-hangin' on her back?"

"Spy? Spy?" The quivering lips pouted. "Curse you, are you Mata Hari? What are you doing out here? It's changed its face," Trumie complained to the Crockett-robot. "It doesn't belong here. It's supposed to be in the harem. Go on, Crockett, get it back!"

"Wait!" cried Garrick, but the Crockett-robot was ahead of him. It took Kathryn Pender by the arm.

"Come along thar," it said soothingly, and urged her across the drawbridge. She glanced back at Garrick, and for a moment it looked as though she were going to speak. Then she shook her head, as though she were giving an order.

"Kathryn!" cried Garrick. "Trumie, wait a minute. That isn't Mata Hari!"

No one was listening. Kathryn Pender disappeared into the Private Place. Trumie, leaning heavily on the hobbling Silver-robot, followed.

Garrick, coming back to life, leaped after them. . . .

The scarlet-coated guards jumped before him, their shakos bobbing, their crooked little rifles crossed to bar his way.

He cried, "One side! Out of my way, you! I'm a human, don't you understand? You've got to let me pass!"

They didn't even look at him; trying to get by them was like trying to walk through a wall of moving, thrusting steel. He shoved, and they pushed him back; he tried to dodge, and they were before him. It was hopeless.

And then it was hopeless indeed, because behind them, he saw, the drawbridge had gone up.

VI

Sonny Trumie collapsed into a chair like a mound of blubber falling to the deck of a whaler.

Though he made no signal, the procession of serving robots started at once. In minced the maître d', bowing and waving its graceful hands; in marched the sommelier, clanking its necklace of keys, bearing its wines in their buckets of ice. In came the lovely waitress-robots and the sturdy steward-robots, with the platters and tureens, the plates and bowls and cups. They spread a meal—a dozen meals—before him, and he began to eat. He ate as a penned pig eats, gobbling until it chokes, forcing the food down because there is nothing to do *but* eat. He ate with a sighing accompaniment of moans and gasps, and some of the food was salted with the tears of pain he wept into it, and some of the wine was spilled by his shaking hand. But he ate. Not for the first time that day, and not for the tenth.

Sonny Trumie wept as he ate. He no longer even knew he was weeping. There was the gaping void inside him that he had to fill, had to fill; there was the gaping world about him that he had to people and build and furnish—and *use*. He moaned to himself. Four hundred pounds of meat and lard, and he had to lug it from end to end of his island, every hour of every day, never resting, never at peace! There should have been a place somewhere, there should have been a time, when he could rest. When he could sleep without dreaming, sleep without waking after a scant few hours with the goading drive to eat and to use, to use and to eat....And it was all so *wrong!* The robots didn't understand. They didn't try to understand, they didn't think for themselves. Let him take his eyes from any one of them for a single day, and everything went *wrong*. It was necessary to keep after them, from end to end of the island, checking and overseeing and ordering—yes, and destroying to rebuild, over and over!

He moaned again, and pushed the plate away.

He rested, with his tallow forehead flat against the table, waiting, while inside him the pain ripped and ripped, and finally became bearable again. And slowly he pushed himself up again, and rested for a moment, and pulled a fresh plate toward him, and began again to eat....

After a while he stopped. Not because he didn't want to go on, but because he couldn't.

He was bone-tired, but something was bothering him—one more detail to check, one more thing that was *wrong*. The houri at the drawbridge. It shouldn't have been out of the Private Place. It should have been in the harem, of course. Not that it mattered, except to Sonny Trumie's sense of what was right. Time was when the houris of the harem had their uses, but that time was long and long ago; now they were property, to be fussed over and made to be *right,* to be replaced if they were worn, destroyed if they were *wrong*. But only property, as all of North Guardian was property—as all of the world would be his property, if only he could manage it.

But property shouldn't be *wrong*.

He signaled to the Crockett-robot and, leaning on it, walked down the long terrazzo hall toward the harem. He tried to remember what the houri had looked like. It had worn a sheer red blouse and a brief red skirt, he was nearly sure, but the face....It had had a face, of course.

But Sonny had lost the habit of faces. This one had been somehow different, but he couldn't remember just why. Still—the blouse and skirt, they were red, he was nearly sure. And it had been carrying something in a box. And that was odd, too.

He waddled a little faster, for now he was sure it was *wrong.*

"That's the harem, Mistuh Trumie," said the robot at his side. It disengaged itself gently, leaped forward and held the door to the harem for him.

"Wait for me," Sonny commanded, and waddled forward into the harem halls. Once he had so arranged the harem that he needed no help inside it; the halls were railed, at a height where it was easy for a pudgy hand to grasp the rail; the distances were short, the rooms close together. He paused and called over his shoulder, "Stay where you can hear me." It had occurred to him that if the houri-robot was *wrong,* he would need Crockett's guns to make it right.

A chorus of female voices sprang into song as he entered the main patio. They were a bevy of beauties, clustered around a fountain, diaphanously dressed, languorously glancing at Sonny Trumie as he waddled inside. "Shut up!" he commanded. "Go back to your rooms." They bowed their heads and, one by one, slipped into the cubicles.

No sign of the red blouse and the red skirt. He began the rounds of the cubicles, panting, peering into them. "Hello, Sonny," whispered Theda Bara, lithe on a leopard rug, and he passed on. "I love you!" cried Nell Gwynn, and, "Come to me!" commanded Cleopatra, but he passed them by. He passed Dubarry and Marilyn Monroe, he passed Moll Flanders and he passed Troy's Helen. No sign of the houri in red. . . .

And then he saw signs. He didn't see the houri, but he saw the signs of the houri's presence; the red blouse and the red skirt, lying limp and empty on the floor.

Sonny gasped, "You! Where are you? Come out here where I can see you!"

Nobody answered Sonny. "Come out!" he bawled.

And then he stopped. A door opened and someone came out; not a houri, not female; a figure without sex but loaded with love, a teddy bear figure, as tall as pudgy Sonny Trumie himself, waddling as he waddled, its stubbed arms stretched out to him.

Sonny could hardly believe his eyes. Its color was a little darker than Teddy. It was a good deal taller than Teddy. But unquestionably, undoubtedly, in everything that mattered it was—"Teddy," whispered

Sonny Trumie, and let the furry arms go around his four hundred pounds.

Twenty years disappeared. "They wouldn't let me have you," Sonny told the teddy; and it said, in a voice musical and warm:

"It's all right, Sonny. You can have me now, Sonny. You can have everything, Sonny."

"They took you away," he whispered, remembering. They took the teddy bear away; he had never forgotten. They took it away, and they were wild. Mother was wild, and father was furious; they raged at the little boy and scolded him, and threatened him. Didn't he know they were *poor,* and did he want to ruin them all, and what was wrong with him anyway, that he wanted his little sister's silly stuffed robots when he was big enough to use nearly grown-up goods.

The night had been a terror, with the frowning, sad robots ringed around and the little girl crying; and what had made it terror was not the scolding—he'd had scoldings—but the *worry,* the fear and almost the panic in his parents' voices. For what he did, he came to understand, was no longer a childish sin; it was a *big* sin, a failure to consume his quota—

And it had to be punished. The first punishment was the extra birthday party; the second was—shame. Sonny Trumie, not quite twelve, was made to feel shame and humiliation. Shame is only a little thing, but it makes the one who owns it little too. Shame. The robots were reset to scorn him. He woke to mockery, and went to bed with contempt. Even his little sister lisped the catalogue of his failures. You aren't trying, Sonny, and You don't care, Sonny, and You're a terrible disappointment to us, Sonny. And finally all the things were true; because Sonny at twelve was what his elders made him.

And they made him . . . "neurotic" is the term; a pretty-sounding word that means ugly things like fear and worry and endless self-reproach. . . .

"Don't worry," whispered the teddy. "Don't worry, Sonny. You can have me. You can have what you want. You don't have to have anything else. . . ."

VII

Garrick raged through the halls of the Private Place like a tiger upon a kid. "Kathryn!" he cried. "Kathryn Pender!" Finally he had found a way in, unguarded, forgotten. But it had taken time. And he was worried. "Kathryn!" The robots peered out at him, worriedly, and sometimes they got in his way and he bowled them aside. They didn't fight back, naturally—what robot would hurt a human? But sometimes they spoke to him, pleading, for it was not according to the wishes of Mr. Trumie that anyone but him rage destroying through North Guardian Island. He passed them by. "Kathryn!" he called. "Kathryn!"

It wasn't that Trumie was dangerous.

He told himself fiercely: Trumie was *not* dangerous. Trumie was laid bare in his folder, the one that Roosenburg had supplied. He couldn't be blamed, and he meant no harm. He was once a bad little boy who was trying to be good by consuming, consuming; and he wore himself into neurosis doing it; and then they changed the rules on him. End of the ration; end of forced consumption, as the robots took over for mankind at the other end of the cornucopia. It wasn't necessary to struggle to consume, so the rules where changed....

And maybe Mr. Trumie knew that the rules had been changed; but Sonny didn't. It was Sonny, the bad little boy trying to be good, who had made North Guardian Island....

And it was Sonny who owned the Private Place, and all it held—including Kathryn Pender.

Garrick called hoarsely, "Kathryn! If you hear me, *answer me!*"

It had seemed so simple. The fulcrum on which the weight of Trumie's neurosis might move was a teddy bear; give him a teddy bear—or perhaps, a teddy bear suit, made by night in the factories of Fisherman's Island, with a girl named Kathryn Pender inside—and let him hear, from a source he could trust, the welcome news that it was no longer necessary to struggle, that compulsive consumption could have an end. Permissive analysis would clear it up; but only if Trumie would listen.

"Kathryn!" roared Roger Garrick, racing through a room of mirrors and carved statues. Because, just in case Trumie didn't listen, just in case the folder was wrong and the teddy wasn't the key—

Why, then, the teddy to Trumie was only a robot. And Trumie destroyed them by the score.

"Kathryn!" cried Roger Garrick, trotting through the silent palace; and at last he heard what might have been an answer. At least it was a voice—a girl's voice, at that. He was before a passage that led to a room with a fountain and silent female robots, standing and watching him. The voice came from a small room. He ran to the door.

It was the right door.

There was Trumie, four hundred pounds of lard, lying on a marble bench with a foam-rubber cushion, the jowled head in the small lap of—

Teddy. Or Kathryn Pender in the teddy bear suit, the stick-like legs pointed straight out, the stick-like arms clumsily patting him. She was talking to him, gently and reassuringly. She was telling him what he needed to know—that he had eaten *enough,* that he had used *enough,* that he had consumed enough to win the respect of all, and an end to consuming.

Garrick himself could not have done better.

It was a sight from Mother Goose, the child being soothed by his toy. But it was not a sight that fit in well with its surroundings, for the seraglio was upholstered in mauve and pink, and wicked paintings hung about.

Sonny Trumie rolled the pendulous head and looked squarely at Garrick. The worry was gone from the fearful little eyes.

Garrick stepped back.

No need for him just at this moment. Let Trumie relax for a while, as he had not been able to relax for a score of years. Then the psychist could pick up where the girl had been unable to proceed; but in the meantime, Trumie was finally at rest.

The teddy looked up at Garrick and in its bright blue eyes, the eyes that belonged to the girl named Kathryn, he saw a queer tincture of triumph and compassion.

Garrick nodded and left, and went out to the robots of North Guardian and started them clearing away.

Sonny Trumie nestled his swine's head in the lap of the teddy bear. It was talking to him so nicely, so nicely. It was droning away, "Don't worry, Sonny. Don't worry. Everything's all right. Everything's all right." Why, it was almost as though it were real.

It had been, he calculated with the part of his mind that was razor-sharp and never relaxed, it had been nearly two hours since he had eaten. Two hours! And he felt as though he could go another hour at least, maybe two. Maybe—maybe even not eat at all again that day. Maybe even learn to live on three meals. Perhaps two. Perhaps—

He wriggled—as well as four hundred greasy pounds can wriggle—and pressed against the soft warm fur of the teddy bear. It was so soothing! "You don't have to eat so much, Sonny. You don't have to drink so much. No one will mind. Your father won't mind, Sonny. Your mother won't mind. . . ."

It was very comfortable to hear the teddy bear telling him those things. It made him drowsy. So deliciously drowsy! It wasn't like going to sleep, as Sonny Trumie had known going to sleep for a dozen or more years, the bitterly fought surrender to the anesthetic weariness. It was just drowsy. . . .

And he did want to go to sleep.

And finally he slept. All of him slept. Not just the four hundred pounds of blubber and the little pig eyes, but even the razor-sharp mind-Trumie that lived in the sad, obedient hulk; it slept; and it had never slept before.

GLADYS'S GREGORY

by John Anthony West

The whole world is sports crazy and sports fans have become increasingly demanding and unforgiving of the players, officials, and their fellow fans. This may also apply to sports of the future, as John Anthony West shows us in the following story.

Ladies, members of the club, I am honored to be here today, to tell you about this year's contest in our community, and this year's contest winner, Gladys's Gregory. And I want to thank you all for your interest and for your kind attention.

I begin with statistics from the medical record. Gladys's Gregory upon his arrival at our community.

Height:	6′5½″
Weight:	242
Chest:	49″
Waist:	36″
Neck:	18½″

I anticipate your admiration, Ladies. Therefore, let me present the dark side of the coin immediately. Gregory, upon arriving, was twenty-eight years old, yet his weight had scarcely changed since his college days when he was an all-American football player. He had been married three *full* years. Club members! Please jump to no hasty conclusions. Hear me out before you heap blame on Gladys. Bear in mind that here, true, we have Gregory; 242 pounds of raw material. But his figure has not changed for *eight* years.

Unfortunately, I admit, the women of our community did not view the situation objectively either. "Gladys's fault," they shouted and indignation ran rampant.

We thought of Beth Shaefer who had brought her Milton from a gangling 164 to 313 pounds in less than three years; Sally O'Leary with three strikes against her at the onset, her Jamie an ex-jockey, fighting gamely nevertheless and bringing him out finally at 245; Joan Granz who nursed her Marvin to 437 and a second prize despite his dangerous cardiac condition. Certainly, all of you can appreciate our feelings.

Now, Gladys's Gregory was football coach and one day, driving past the stadium, the first clue to a nasty situation revealed itself. Gladys's Gregory was participating in the *actual* physical exercise.

I saw him hurl himself repeatedly at a stuffed dummy; saw him lead five minutes of strenuous calisthenics; then, undaunted, lead his team in a race around the track. The bitterest among Gladys's enemies would be forced to admit that perhaps it wasn't her fault entirely. To this day I see the flesh-building calories dripping from his pores in perspiration.

The next morning I paid a call on Gladys. She was a sweet young thing; far from the malicious vixen rumor had painted her. I recounted the stadium scene and poor Gladys knew it all too well. She had even stranger tales to tell. He mowed the lawn with a *hand* mower; played handball off-season; ran the two miles from the school to his home in a tracksuit. The girl was desolate.

We discussed his diet and I was shocked beyond words. Red meat! She fed him red meat; and fish, and eggs, and green vegetables....

"Eclairs!" I shouted at her. "Potatoes! Chocolate layer cake! Beer! Butter!"

But no. Gregory hated these things. Wouldn't touch them.

"He doesn't love you," I said.

"But he does," Gladys moaned, her voice cracking, "in his own way he does."

I suggested the strategy that was so often effective when contests had not yet gained their present popularity and opposition was stronger.

As we all know, we have more sexual stamina than our mates. A wife, subtly camouflaging her motives under the attractive cover of passion, can reduce a husband to a state of sexual fatigue in a matter of weeks. And a sexually sated husband is ripe for intelligent handling. Evening after evening he sits quietly. Eating. He marshals his energies for the night ahead and gradually he puts on weight. At a certain point his obesity interferes with his virility and at this point the intelligent wife begins to demand less. The husband, by this time swathed in comfortable flesh, is only too happy to be let alone. Now, the wife decreases her demands to nothing and the husband, carrying no burden of calorie-consuming anxiety, prepares for the contest.

With Gladys's Gregory, this method proved futile. After a month's trial Gladys was but a shadow of her former self while Gregory was seen everywhere, with his squad, mowing the lawn, his unsightly muscles bulging, a smug grin on his face.

At a special community meeting an ingenious plan was devised. We would make Gladys and Gregory the most socially prominent couple in the community. They soon found their social calendar booked solid; dinners, breakfasts, buffets, picnics . . . Gregory found himself seated down to tables groaning with carbohydrates. He was under constant surveillance. No sooner had he wiped the whipped cream from his lips before a plate mountain high in ice cream, bristling with macaroons, was thrust before him. His mug of beer never reached the halfway mark before some vigilant wife refilled it for him.

At this time, Ladies, I must point out that Gregory was in no way a conscious rebel; nor was he malicious or subversive. We must set aside his foolish notions of physical culture and regard him as he was; a charming man and an ideal husband; affable, reticent, and quite unintelligent. The militant fury of our community women soon gave way to a genuine solicitousness. And a beaming Gladys reported that he was wearing his belt out two notches.

A carefully coached Gladys waged psychological warfare. Magazines were left open about the house, all of them turned to calorie-rich advertisements. At parties she flirted openly with the heftiest husbands still allowed free.

By spring Gregory weighed an estimated 290. Bewildered, he still clung to his old notions. "Gotta get in shape for spring training," he would mumble, his mouth filled with chocolate *mousse.*

At 310 our cooperative spirit dwindled. The women, all at once, realized what they had wrought and were horrified by the prospect.

Meanwhile, Gladys, grown confident, moved swiftly and with brilliant technical strategy. She consulted a fortune teller who hinted to her that, given the chance, her Gregory would founder himself on Brazil nuts. She bought a trial pound and they were gone in five minutes.

Well, Ladies, Brazil nuts! It was the last straw. Calorie-filled Brazil nuts. Community spirit turned to a hostile chill and then to virulent envy. He couldn't stop eating Brazil nuts! Anxious eyes searched hopefully for the telltale signs of arrested development; the tight skin and fishy-eyed expression that signifies that a husband is nearing peak despite his apparent potential. We looked for hints of unsightly bloating. But at 325 Gregory was barely filling out. On his own he developed a taste for sweets.

The contest of that year was pure anticlimax. Jenny Schultz's Peter took a first at 423 but the prodigious Gregory was on the minds of all.

Shortly after, Gladys, contrary to expectation, put her Gregory into seclusion. It was the cause of hope. Certainly Gladys had overplayed her hand and had sacrificed strategy for youthful impetuosity. But her self-confidence incensed the ladies of our community.

For the first time in history our women banded together in an effort to counteract Gregory's impending victory. Surely the emotions that prompted this action were not entirely commendable but, Ladies, put yourself in our place. Would you be willing to undergo the heartache, the effort, even the expense of preparing a husband for a contest whose outcome was obvious in advance?

How long would it take her to prepare her Gregory? This was the burning question. The average husband takes three or four years, as we all know. Certainly Gregory was a special case. Four years for him would mean excess flab. Three years seemed most logical but with Gregory, two years did not seem impossible and Gladys had already displayed eagerness and impatience. It was the studied opinion of our community that Gladys would enter Gregory in two years. Therefore, it was but a simple matter for the rest to hold their husbands for a different year. Should Gregory be the only entry, his would be a hollow victory.

Our solution was bold but strong. The women made an agreement to enter their husbands the following year despite the fact that many would not have reached peak. It was felt that should a three-year plan misfire (as it might through a slip of the tongue, chicanery, a thousand reasons) four or five years of seclusion would be unbearable for all wives concerned and of course with husbands, decline is most rapid after peak has been attained. Women whose husbands had been in seclusion under a year were permitted to breach the contract.

A period of curious tension ensued. Gladys's arrogance was hidden beneath a cover of interest in community affairs while the other women masked their complicity and hatred under the guise of camaraderie in the face of healthy competition.

Gladys took to having provisions delivered; quarter kegs of beer, bushels of potatoes, sacks of flour. Oh yes! She would set a record in two years but it would be a wasted triumph.

And then she could outdo herself. We all remembered Elizabeth Bent's Darius who, several years earlier, having had almost the potential of a Gregory, and eager to set a record, had allowed himself to be pushed too hard. He died six weeks before the contest; a sensational but disqualified 621.

With the contest a month away Gregory was forgotten. True, this year's contest lacked the element of surprise. Everyone (but Gladys) knew which other husbands would be shown. The probable winner could be guessed with reasonable accuracy ... but still, a contest is a contest and the air was charged with the familiar bitter rivalry.

Contest day dawned hot and bright, and an excited crowd gathered at the stadium. This year, of course, there was little of that intense speculation: Who was entered by surprise; who was staying another year in seclusion?

But five minutes before the procession one question rippled through the audience. Has anyone seen Gladys? An expectant audience become a feverish one. Necks craned. Sharp eyes searched the crowd. She was not to be seen. A murmur of anger swept the stands. Could she have prepared her Gregory in a single year? No! No! It could not be done.

The band struck up and slowly the gaily painted, bunting-draped trucks passed before the stand. Twenty-six in all. How many women had entered the agreement to show their husbands. Twenty-five? Twenty-six? No one remembered.

The trucks circled the field. Attention was divided between the parade and the entrance to catch Gladys's expected tardy arrival among the spectators.

The fanfare rose brassy and shrill and the trucks halted. The wives debouched from the cabs and stood before their vehicles. We all know the tension of this moment; as the audience takes in the line of wives at a glance; sees two dozen or more women dressed in their best; tries, at the same time, to remember those who might have been there and are not. That tense moment when years of planning, hoping, working, scheming, unfold too quickly.... But in this split second all eyes focused on one person, and one person alone. Gladys.

She stood before her truck, stunning in white organdy, fresh as a daisy; showing nothing of what must have been a tense and lonely ordeal; not a single wrinkle was visible; not a strand of hair astray. I could feel hatred gathering in a storm.

The other wives in the contest glared helplessly at Gladys. The trumpet sounded and the wives released the covers of their trucks. It was the breathless instant when the husbands stood revealed. But this time, every eye focused on truck seventeen: Gladys's Gregory.

There was no applause; none of the usual wild cheering; nothing but an awed silence. In that single moment every wife present knew that her own small hopes were forever extinguished. Never, never in their maddest daydreams had they conceived of a Gregory.

He stood as though rooted to the back of the truck; monolithic. His face missed that bloated look usually found on the truly elephantine husbands; his brow was furrowed in thick folds of flesh; his cheeks, neither flabby nor swollen, hung in rich jowls like steaks. His neck was a squat cone leading unbroken into shoulders so gigantic that instead of easing into the inevitable paunch he seemed to drop sheer. He was perfect. A pillar; a block; a mountain; solid and immobile. He turned slowly, proudly. Front face, profile, rear view, front face. His weight was incalculable. He was bigger, heavier, more immense, more beautiful than anything we had ever witnessed. Hatred in the audience turned to despair. Our granddaughter might beg to hear about Gladys's Gregory, but _we_ had seen him. For us there would be no more contests. Not a woman among us thought of Gladys's original torments; her years of social ostracism. But how could they?

The weighing began and the audience cursed and fretted. Sixteen before Gregory. The winches lifted the husbands to the weighing platform and the results were announced: 345, 376, 268 (someone laughed), 417, 430 (someone clapped—a relative no doubt), 386, 344. Not a flurry of interest. The dismayed wives who had worked and schemed for years for this opportunity; who asked only for fair competition, wept openly. 403, 313. The wait seemed endless.

Gregory was next but Gladys had a surprise in store. As the men went to adjust the slings on Gregory, Gladys waved them off. She attached a strong pipe ladder to the truck and ponderously, but without hesitation, Gregory descended.

He was still able to walk!

Shoulders thrown back to balance his magnificent bulk, he swayed and lurched toward the stairs that led to the platform. He tested the frail banister and it sundered. Using a section of the rail as a cane he veered up the stairs while a breathless crowd waited for the sound of breaking planks. The stairs groaned but held and Gregory made his own way to the scale.

Well, Ladies, what difference does the actual figure make? It was all over. After seeing Gregory cold statistics were irrelevant. The figure, however, was 743 pounds.

Gregory turned slowly, proudly, on the scale and smiled. There was no applause but, first singly, then in groups, then en masse the audience stood. Even jealousy and hatred were powerless in the presence of the contestant who would stand as a monument to Gladys and our community, and as an inspiration to the world.

Now, Ladies, I wish, I only wish that I could finish this report on the note that such a performance deserves. Unfortunately one incident marred the perfection of Gladys's Gregory's victory.

Our club, like all others, has always adhered to the tacit but traditional practice: *The contest winner is permitted to choose the manner in which he would like to be served.*

Gladys's Gregory, however, out of sheer spite (the argument still rages on this point), or hearkening back to some primitive instinct, demanded to be served raw.

Having no precedent to act upon; and fearing to break so time-honored a custom we complied reluctantly with the request, creating acute physical discomfort for many and an acute physical revulsion in all. A motion is now under discussion in our community which will, in the future, relieve the contest winner of this responsibility. In view of our unfortunate experience, Ladies, it is part of my mission here today to urge you and your club, and all other clubs to pass a similar amendment at your earliest convenience.

I thank you for bearing with me, Ladies.

ABERCROMBIE STATION

by Jack Vance

Once upon a time, fat was a sign of prosperity and good health and was therefore considered a lot more attractive than it is today, now that we've enlightened ourselves about all the medical hazards of obesity. If there was a way to escape those hazards, however, might not the aesthetic reverse itself once again?

1

The doorkeeper was a big hard-looking man with an unwholesome horse-face, a skin like corroded zinc. Two girls spoke to him, asking arch questions.

Jean saw him grunt noncommittally. "Just stick around; I can't give out no dope."

He motioned to the girl sitting beside Jean, a blond girl, very smartly turned out. She rose to her feet; the doorkeeper slid back the door. The blond girl walked swiftly through into the inner room; the door closed behind her.

She moved tentatively forward, stopped short.

A man sat quietly on an old-fashioned leather couch, watching through half-closed eyes.

Nothing frightening here, was her initial impression. He was young—twenty-four or twenty-five. Mediocre, she thought, neither tall nor short, stocky nor lean. His hair was nondescript, his features without distinction, his clothes unobtrusive and neutral.

He shifted his position, opened his eyes a flicker. The blond girl felt a quick pang. Perhaps she had been mistaken.

"How old are you?"

"I'm—twenty."

"Take off your clothes."

She stared, hands tight and white knuckled on her purse. Intuition came suddenly; she drew a quick shallow breath. *Obey him once, give in once, he'll be your master as long as you live.*

"No . . . no, I won't."

She turned quickly, reached for the door-slide. He said unemotionally, "You're too old anyway."

The door jerked aside; she walked quickly through the outer room, looking neither right nor left.

A hand touched her arm. She stopped, looked down into a face that was jet, pale rose, ivory. A young face with an expression of vitality and intelligence: black eyes, short black hair, a beautiful clear skin, mouth without makeup.

Jean asked, "What goes on? What kind of job is it?"

The blond girl said in a tight voice, "I don't know. I didn't stay to find out. It's nothing nice." She turned, went through the outer door.

Jean sank back into the chair, pursed her lips speculatively. A minute passed. Another girl, nostrils flared wide, came from the inner room, crossed to the door, looking neither right nor left.

Jean smiled faintly. She had a wide mouth, expansive and flexible. Her teeth were small, white, very sharp.

The doorkeeper motioned to her. She jumped to her feet, entered the inner room.

The quiet man was smoking. A silvery plume rose past his face, melted into the air over his head. Jean thought, *There's something strange in his complete immobility. He's too tight, too compressed.*

She put her hands behind her back, and waited, watching carefully.

"How old are you?"

This was a question she usually found wise to evade. She tilted her head sidewise, smiling, a mannerism which gave her a wild and reckless look. "How old do you think I am?"

"Sixteen or seventeen."

"That's close enough."

He nodded. "Close enough. What's your name?"

"Jean Parlier."

"Whom do you live with?"

"No one. I live alone."

"Father? Mother?"

"Dead."

"Grandparents? Guardian?"

"I'm alone."

He nodded. "Any trouble with the law on that account?"

She considered him warily. "No."

He moved his head enough to send a kink running up the feather of smoke. "Take off your clothes."

"Why?"

"It's a quick way to check your qualifications."

"Well—yes. In a way I guess it is.... Physical or moral?"

He made no reply, sat looking at her impassively, the gray skein of smoke rising past his face.

She shrugged, put her hands to her sides, to her neck, to her waist, to her back, to her legs, and stood without clothes.

He put the cigarette to his mouth, puffed, sat up, stubbed it out, rose to his feet, walked slowly forward.

He's trying to scare me, she thought, and smiled quietly to herself. He could try.

He stopped two feet away, stood looking down into her eyes. "You really want a million dollars?"

"That's why I'm here."

"You took the advertisement in the literal sense of the words?"

"Is there any other way?"

"You might have construed the language as—metaphor, hyperbole."

She grinned, showing her sharp white teeth. "I don't know what those words mean. Anyway, I'm here. If the advertisement was only intended for you to look at me naked, I'll leave."

His expression did not change. Peculiar, thought Jean, how his body moved, his head turned, but his eyes always seemed fixed. He said as if he had not heard her, "Not too many girls have applied."

"That doesn't concern me. I want a million dollars. What is it? Blackmail? Impersonation?"

He passed over her question. "What would you do with a million if you had it?"

"I don't know.... I'll worry about that when I get it. Have you checked my qualifications? I'm cold."

He turned quickly, strode to the couch, seated himself. She slipped into her clothes, came over to the couch, took a tentative seat facing him.

He said dryly, "You fill the qualifications almost too well!"

"How so?"

"It's unimportant."

Jean tilted her head, laughed. She looked like a healthy, very pretty high-school girl who might be the better for more sunshine. "Tell me what I'm to do to earn a million dollars."

"You're to marry a wealthy young man, who suffers from—let us call it, an incurable disease. When he dies, his property will be yours. You will sell his property to me for a million dollars."

"Evidently he's worth more than a million dollars."

He was conscious of the questions she did not ask. "There's somewhere near a billion involved."

"What kind of disease does he have? I might catch it myself."

"I'll take care of the disease end. You won't catch it if you keep your nose clean."

"Oh—oh, I see—tell me more about him. Is he handsome? Big? Strong? I might feel sorry if he died."

"He's eighteen years old. His main interest is collecting." Sardonically: "He likes zoology too. He's an eminent zoologist. His name is Earl Abercrombie. He owns"—he gestured up—"Abercrombie Station."

Jean stared, then laughed feebly. "That's a hard way to make a million dollars . . . Earl Abercrombie. . . ."

"Squeamish?"

"Not when I'm awake. But I do have nightmares."

"Make up your mind."

She looked modestly to where she had folded her hands in her lap. "A million isn't a very large cut out of a billion."

He surveyed her with something like approval. "No, it isn't."

She rose to her feet, slim as a dancer. "All you do is sign a check. I have to marry him, get in bed with him."

"They don't use beds on Abercrombie Station."

"Since he lives on Abercrombie, he might not be interested in me."

"Earl is different," said the quiet man. "Earl likes gravity girls."

"You must realize that once he dies, you'd be forced to accept whatever I chose to give you. Or the property might be put in charge of a trustee."

"Not necessarily. The Abercrombie Civil Regulation allows property to be controlled by anyone sixteen or over. Earl is eighteen. He exercises complete control over the Station, subject to a few unimportant restrictions. I'll take care of that end." He went to the door, slid it open. "Hammond."

The man with the long face came wordlessly to the door.

"I've got her. Send the others home."

He closed the door, turned to Jean. "I want you to have dinner with me."

"I'm not dressed for dinner."

"I'll send up the couturier. Try to be ready in an hour."

He left the room. The door closed. Jean stretched, threw back her head, opened her mouth in a soundless exultant laugh. She raised her arms over her head, took a step forward, turned a supple cartwheel across the rug, bounced to her feet beside the window.

She knelt, rested her head on her hands, looked across Metropolis. Dusk had come. The great gray-golden sky filled three-quarters of her vision. A thousand feet below was the wan gray, lavender, and black crumble of surface buildings, the pallid roadways streaming with golden motes. To the right, aircraft slid silently along force-guides to the mountain suburbs—tired normal people bound to pleasant normal homes. What would they think if they knew that she, Jean Parlier, was watching? For instance, the man who drove that shiny Skyfarer with the pale green chevrets. . . . She built a picture of him: pudgy, forehead creased with lines of worry. He'd be hurrying home to his wife, who would listen tolerantly while he boasted or grumbled. Cattle-women, cow-women, thought Jean without rancor. What man could subdue her? Where was the man who was wild and hard and bright enough? . . . Remembering her new job, she grimaced. Mrs. Earl Abercrombie. She looked up into the sky. The stars were not yet out and the lights of Abercrombie Station could not be seen.

A million dollars, think of it! "What will you do with a million dollars?" her new employer had asked her, and now that she returned to it, the idea was uncomfortable, like a lump in her throat.

What would she feel? How would she . . . her mind moved away from the subject, recoiled with the faintest trace of anger, as if it were a subject not to be touched upon. "Rats," said Jean. "Time to worry about it after I get it. . . . A million dollars. Not too large a cut out of a billion, actually. Two million would be better." Her eyes followed a slim red airboat diving along a sharp curve into the parking area: a sparkling new Marshall Moon-Chaser. Now there was something she wanted. It would be one of her first purchases.

The door slid open. Hammond the doorkeeper looked in briefly. Then the couturier entered, pushing his wheeled kit before him, a slender little blond man with rich topaz eyes. The door closed.

Jean turned away from the window. The couturier—André was the name stenciled on the enamel of the box—spoke for more light, walked around her, darting glances up and down her body.

"Yes," he muttered, pressing his lips in and out. "Ah, yes.... Now what does the lady have in mind?"

"A dinner gown, I suppose."

He nodded. "Mr. Fotheringay mentioned formal evening wear."

So that was his name—Fotheringay.

André snapped up a screen. "Observe, if you will, a few of my effects; perhaps there is something to please you."

Models appeared on the screen, stepping forward, smiling, turning away.

Jean said. "Something like that."

André made a gesture of approval, snapped his fingers. "Mademoiselle has good taste. And now we shall see . . . if mademoiselle will let me help her...."

He deftly unzipped her garments, laid them on the couch.

"First—we refresh ourselves." He selected a tool from his kit, and, holding her wrist between delicate thumb and forefinger, sprayed her arms with cool mist, then warm, perfumed air. Her skin tingled, fresh, invigorated.

André tapped his chin. "Now, the foundation."

She stood, eyes half closed, while he bustled around her, striding off, making whispered comments, quick gestures with significance only to himself.

He sprayed her with gray-green web, touched and pulled as the strands set. He adjusted knurled knobs at the ends of a flexible tube, pressed it around her waist, swept it away and it trailed shining black-green silk. He artfully twisted and wound his tube. He put the frame back in the kit, pulled, twisted, pinched, while the silk set.

He sprayed her with wan white, quickly jumped forward, folded, shaped, pinched, pulled, bunched and the stuff fell in twisted bands from her shoulders and into a full rustling skirt.

"Now—gauntlets." He covered her arms and hands with warm black-green pulp which set into spangled velvet, adroitly cut with scissors to bare the back of her hand.

"Slippers." Black satin, webbed with emerald green phosphorescence.

"Now—the ornaments." He hung a red bauble from her right ear, slipped a cabochon ruby on her right hand.

"Scent—a trace. The Levailleur, indeed." He flicked her with an odor suggestive of a Central Asia flower patch. "And mademoiselle is dressed. And may I say"—he bowed with a flourish—"most exquisitely beautiful."

He manipulated his cart, one side fell away. A mirror uncoiled upward.

Jean inspected herself. Vivid naiad. When she acquired that million dollars—two million dollars would be better—she'd put André on her permanent payroll.

André was still muttering compliments. "—Elan supreme. She is magic. Most striking. Eyes will turn. . . ."

The door slid back. Fotheringay came into the room. André bowed low, clasped his hands.

Fotheringay glanced at her. "You're ready. Good. Come along."

Jean thought, *We might as well get this straight right now.* "Where?"

He frowned slightly, stood aside while André pushed his cart out.

Jean said, "I came here of my own free will. I walked into this room under my own power. Both times I knew where I was going. Now you say 'Come along.' First I want to know where. Then I'll decide whether or not I'll come."

"You don't want a million dollars very badly."

"Two million. I want it badly enough to waste an afternoon investigating. . . . But—if I don't get it today, I'll get it tomorrow. Or next week. Somehow I'll get it; a long time ago I made up my mind. So?" She performed an airy curtsy.

His pupils contracted. He said in an even voice, "Very well. Two million. I am now taking you to dinner on the roof, where I will give you your instructions."

2

They drifted under the dome, in a greenish plastic bubble. Below them spread the commercial fantasy of an outworld landscape: gray sward; gnarled red and green trees casting dramatic black shadows; a pond of fluorescent green liquid; panels of exotic blossoms; beds of fungus.

The bubble drifted easily, apparently at random, now high under the near-invisible dome, now low under the foliage. Successive courses appeared from the center of the table, along with chilled wine and frosted punch.

It was wonderful and lavish, thought Jean. But why should Fotheringay spend his money on her? Perhaps he entertained romantic notions. . . . She dallied with the idea, inspected him covertly. . . . The idea lacked conviction. He seemed to be engaging in none of the usual gambits. He neither tried to fascinate her with his charm, nor swamp her with synthetic masculinity. Much as it irritated Jean to admit it, he appeared—indifferent.

Jean compressed her lips. The idea was disconcerting. She essayed a slight smile, a side glance up under lowered lashes.

"Save it," said Fotheringay. "You'll need it all when you get up to Abercrombie."

Jean returned to her dinner. After a minute she said calmly, "I was —curious."

"Now you know."

Jean thought to tease him, draw him out. "Know what?"

"Whatever it was you were curious about."

"Pooh. Men are mostly alike. They all have the same button. Push it, they all jump in the same direction."

Fotheringay frowned, glanced at her under narrowed eyes. "Maybe you aren't so precocious after all."

Jean became tense. In a curious indefinable way, the subject was very important, as if survival were linked with confidence in her own sophistication and flexibility. "What do you mean?"

"You make the assumption most pretty girls make," he said with a trace of scorn. "I thought you were smarter than that."

Jean frowned. There had been little abstract thinking in her background. "Well, I've never had it work out differently. Although I'm willing to admit there are exceptions. . . . It's a kind of game. I've never lost. If I'm kidding myself, it hasn't made much difference so far."

Fotheringay relaxed. "You've been lucky."

Jean stretched out her arms, arched her body, smiled as if at a secret. "Call it luck."

"Luck won't work with Earl Abercrombie."

"You're the one who used the word luck. I think it's, well—ability."

"You'll have to use your brains, too." He hesitated, then said, "Actually, Earl likes—odd things."

Jean sat looking at him, frowning.

He said coolly, "You're making up your mind how best to ask the question, 'What's odd about me?'"

Jean snapped, "I don't need you to tell me what's odd about me. I know what it is myself."

Fotheringay made no comment.

"I'm completely on my own," said Jean. "There's not a soul in all the human universe that I care two pins for. I do just exactly as I please." She watched him carefully. He nodded indifferently. Jean quelled her exasperation, leaned back in her chair, studied him as if he were in a glass case....A strange young man. Did he ever smile? She thought of the Capellan Fibrates who by popular superstition were able to fix themselves along a man's spinal column and control his intelligence. Fotheringay displayed a coldness strange enough to suggest such a possession....A Capellan could manipulate but one hand at a time. Fotheringay held a knife in one hand, a fork in the other and moved both hands together. So much for that.

He said quietly, "I watched your hands too."

Jean threw back her head and laughed—a healthy adolescent laugh. Fotheringay watched her without discernible expression.

She said, "Actually, you'd like to know about me, but you're too stiff-necked to ask."

"You were born at Angel City on Codiron," said Fotheringay. "Your mother abandoned you in a tavern, a gambler named Joe Parlier took care of you until you were ten, when you killed him and three other men and stowed away on the Gray Line Packet *Bucyrus*. You were taken to the Waif's Home at Paie on Bella's Pride. You ran away and the superintendent was found dead....Shall I go on? There's five more years of it."

Jean sipped her wine, nowise abashed. "You've worked fast....But you've misrepresented. You said, 'There's five years more of it, shall I go on?' as if you were able to go on. You don't know anything about the next five years."

Fotheringay's face changed by not a flicker. He said as if she had not spoken, "Now listen carefully. This is what you'll have to look out for."

"Go ahead. I'm all ears." She leaned back in her chair. A clever technique, ignoring an unwelcome situation as if it never existed. Of course, to carry it off successfully, a certain temperament was required. A cold fish like Fotheringay managed very well.

"Tonight a man named Webbard meets us here. He is chief steward at Abercrombie Station. I happen to be able to influence certain of his actions. He will take you up with him to Abercrombie and install you as a servant in the Abercrombie private chambers."

Jean wrinkled her nose. "Servant? Why can't I go to Abercrombie as a paying guest?"

"It wouldn't be natural. A girl like you would go up to Capricorn or *Verge*. Earl Abercrombie is extremely suspicious. He'd be certain to fight shy of you. His mother, old Mrs. Clara, watches him pretty closely, and keeps drilling into his head the idea that all the Abercrombie girls are after his money. As a servant you will have opportunity to meet him in intimate circumstances. He rarely leaves his study; he's absorbed in his collecting."

"My word," murmured Jean. "What does he collect?"

"Everything you can think of," said Fotheringay, moving his lips upward in a quick grimace, almost a smile. "I understand from Webbard, however, that he is rather romantic, and has carried on a number of flirtations among the girls of the Station."

Jean screwed up her mouth in fastidious scorn. Fotheringay watched her impassively.

"When do I—commence?"

"Webbard goes up on the supply barge tomorrow. You'll go with him."

A whisper of sound from the buzzer. Fotheringay touched the button. "Yes?"

"Mr. Webbard for you, sir."

Fotheringay directed the bubble down to the landing stage.

Webbard was waiting, the fattest man Jean had ever seen.

The plaque on the door read, *Richard Mycroft, Attorney-at-Law.* Somewhere far back down the years, someone had said in Jean's hearing that Richard Mycroft was a good attorney.

The receptionist was a dark woman of about thirty-five, with a direct penetrating eye. "Do you have an appointment?"

"No," said Jean. "I'm in rather a hurry."

The receptionist hesitated a moment, then bent over the communicator. "A young lady—Miss Jean Parlier—to see you. New business."

"Very well."

The receptionist nodded to the door. "You can go in," she said shortly.

She doesn't like me, thought Jean. *Because I'm what she was and what she wants to be again.*

Mycroft was a square man with a pleasant face. Jean constructed a wary defense against him. If you liked someone and he knew it, he felt obligated to advise and interfere. She wanted no advice, no interference. She wanted two million dollars.

"Well, young lady," said Mycroft. "What can I do for you?"

He's treating me like a child, thought Jean. *Maybe I look like a child to him.* She said, "It's a matter of advice. I don't know much about fees. I can afford to pay you a hundred dollars. When you advise me a hundred dollars' worth, let me know and I'll go away."

"A hundred dollars buys a lot of advice," said Mycroft. "Advice is cheap."

"Not from a lawyer."

Mycroft became practical. "What are your troubles?"

"It's understood that this is all confidential?"

"Certainly." Mycroft's smile froze into a polite grimace.

"It's nothing illegal—so far as I'm concerned—but I don't want you passing out any quiet hints to—people that might be interested."

Mycroft straightened himself behind his desk. "A lawyer is expected to respect the confidence of his client."

"Okay. . . . Well, it's like this." She told him of Fotheringay, of Abercrombie Station and Earl Abercrombie. She said that Earl Abercrombie was sick with an incurable disease. She made no mention of Fotheringay's convictions on that subject. It was a matter she herself kept carefully brushing out of her mind. Fotheringay had hired her. He told her what to do, told her that Earl Abercrombie was sick. That was good enough for her. If she had asked too many questions, found that things were too nasty even for her stomach, Fotheringay would have found another girl less inquisitive. . . . She skirted the exact nature of Earl's disease. She didn't actually know herself. She didn't want to know.

Mycroft listened attentively, saying nothing.

"What I want to know is," said Jean, "is the wife sure to inherit on Abercrombie? I don't want to go to a lot of trouble for nothing. And after all Earl is under twenty-one; I thought that in the event of his death it was best to—well, make sure of everything first."

For a moment Mycroft made no move, but sat regarding her quietly. Then he tamped tobacco into a pipe.

"Jean," he said, "I'll give you some advice. It's free. No strings on it."

"Don't bother," said Jean. "I don't want the kind of advice that's free. I want the kind I have to pay for."

Mycroft grimaced. "You're a remarkably wise child."

"I've had to be. . . . Call me a child, if you wish."

"Just what will you do with a million dollars? Or two million, I understand it to be?"

Jean stared. Surely the answer was obvious . . . or was it? When she tried to find an answer, nothing surfaced.

"Well," she said vaguely, "I'd like an airboat, some nice clothes, and maybe . . ." In her mind's eye she suddenly saw herself surrounded by friends. Nice people, like Mr. Mycroft.

"If I were a psychologist and not a lawyer," said Mycroft, "I'd say you wanted your mother and father more than you wanted two million dollars."

Jean became very heated. "No, no! I don't want them at all. They're dead." As far as she was concerned they were dead. They had died for her when they left her on Joe Parlier's pool table in the old Aztec Tavern.

Jean said indignantly, "Mr. Mycroft, I know you mean well, but tell me what I want to know."

"I'll tell you," said Mycroft, "because if I didn't, someone else would. Abercrombie property, if I'm not mistaken, is regulated by its own civil code. . . . Let's see—" He twisted in his chair, pushed buttons on his desk.

On the screen appeared the index to the Central Law Library. Mycroft made further selections, narrowing down selectively. A few seconds later he had the information. "Property control begins at sixteen. Widow inherits at minimum fifty percent; the entire estate unless specifically stated otherwise in the will."

"Good," said Jean. She jumped to her feet. "That's what I wanted to make sure of."

Mycroft asked, "When do you leave?"

"This afternoon."

"I don't need to tell you that the idea behind the scheme is—not moral."

"Mr. Mycroft, you're a dear. But I don't have any morals."

He tilted his head, shrugged, puffed on his pipe. "Are you sure?"

"Well—yes." Jean considered a moment. "I suppose so. Do you want me to go into details?"

"No. I think what I meant to say was, are you sure you know what you want out of life?"

"Certainly. Lots of money."

Mycroft grinned. "That's really not a good answer. What will you buy with your money?"

Jean felt irrational anger rising in her throat. "Oh—lots of things." She rose to her feet. "Just what do I owe you, Mr. Mycroft?"

"Oh—ten dollars. Give it to Ruth."

"Thank you, Mr. Mycroft." She stalked out of his office.

As she marched down the corridor she was surprised to find that she was angry with herself as well as irritated with Mr. Mycroft. He had no right making people wonder about themselves. It wouldn't be so bad if she weren't wondering a little already.

But this was all nonsense. Two million dollars was two million dollars. When she was rich, she'd call on Mr. Mycroft and ask him if honestly he didn't think it was worth a few little lapses.

And today—up to Abercrombie Station. She suddenly became excited.

_____

3

The pilot of the Abercrombie supply barge was emphatic. "No, sir, I think you're making a mistake, nice little girl like you."

He was a chunky man in his thirties, hard-bitten and positive. Sparse blond hair crusted his scalp, deep lines gave his mouth a cynical slant. Webbard, the Abercrombie chief steward, was billeted astern, in the special handling locker. The usual webbings were inadequate to protect his corpulence; he floated chin-deep in a tankful of emulsion the same specific gravity as his body.

There was no passenger cabin and Jean had slipped into the seat beside the pilot. She wore a modest white frock, a white toque, a gray-and-black-striped jacket.

The pilot had few good words for Abercrombie Station. "Now it's what I call a shame, taking a kid like you to serve the likes of them.... Why don't they get one of their own kind? Surely both sides would be the happier."

Jean said innocently, "I'm going up for only just a little bit."

"So you think. It's catching. In a year you'll be like the rest of them. The air alone is enough to sicken a person, rich and sweet like olive oil. Me, I never set foot outside the barge unless I can't help it."

"Do you think I'll be—safe?" She raised her lashes, turned him her reckless sidelong look.

He licked his lips, moved in his seat. "Oh, you'll be safe enough," he muttered. "At least from them that's been there a while. You might have to duck a few just fresh from Earth.... After they've lived on the Station a bit their ideas change, and they wouldn't spit on the best part of an Earth girl."

"Hmmph." Jean compressed her lips. Earl Abercrombie had been born on the Station.

"But I wasn't thinking so much of that," said the pilot. It was hard, he thought, talking straight sense to a kid so young and inexperienced. "I meant in that atmosphere you'll be apt to let yourself go. Pretty soon you'll look like the rest of 'em—never want to leave. Some aren't *able* to leave—couldn't stand it back on Earth if they wanted to."

"Oh—I don't think so. Not in my case."

"It's catching," said the pilot vehemently. "Look, kid—I know. I've ferried out to all the stations, I've seen 'em come and go. Each station has its own kind of weirdness, and you can't keep away from it." He chuckled self-consciously. "Maybe that's why I'm so batty myself.... Now take Madeira Station. Gay. Frou-frou." He made a mincing motion with his fingers. "That's Madeira. You wouldn't know much about that.... But take Balchester Aerie, take Merlin Dell, take the Starhome—"

"Surely, some are just pleasure resorts?"

The pilot grudgingly admitted that of the twenty-two resort satellites, fully half were as ordinary as Miami Beach. "But the others—oh, Moses!" He rolled his eyes back. "And Abercrombie is the worst."

There was silence in the cabin. Earth was a monstrous green, blue, white, and black ball over Jean's shoulder. The sun made a furious hole in the sky below. Ahead were the stars—and a set of blinking blue and red lights.

"Is that Abercrombie?"

"No, that's the Masonic Temple. Abercrombie is on out a ways...." He looked diffidently at her from the corner of his eyes. "Now—look! I don't want you to think I'm fresh. Or maybe I do. But if you're hard up for a job—why don't you come back to Earth with me? I got a pretty nice shack in Long Beach—nothing fancy—but it's on the beach, and it'll be better than working for a bunch of sideshow freaks."

Jean said absently, "No thanks." The pilot pulled in his chin, pulled his elbows close against his body, glowered.

An hour passed. From behind came a rattle, and a small panel slid back. Webbard's pursy face showed through. The barge was coasting on free momentum, gravity was negated. "How much longer to the Station?"

"It's just ahead. Half an hour, more or less, and we'll be fished up tight and right."

Webbard grunted, withdrew.

Yellow and green lights winked ahead. "That's Abercrombie," said the pilot. He reached out to a handle. "Brace yourself." He pulled. Pale blue check-jets streamed out ahead.

From behind came a thump and an angry cursing. The pilot grinned. "Got him good." The jets roared a minute, died. "Every trip it's the same way. Now in a minute he'll stick his head through the panel and bawl me out."

The portal slid back. Webbard showed his furious face. "Why in thunder don't you warn me before you check? I just now took a blow that might have hurt me! You're not much of a pilot, risking injuries of that sort!"

The pilot said in a droll voice, "Sorry, sir, sorry indeed. Won't happen again."

"It had better not! If it does, I'll make it my business to see that you're discharged."

The portal snapped shut. "Sometimes I get him better than others," said the pilot. "This was a good one, I could tell by the thump."

He shifted in his seat, put his arm around Jean's shoulders, pulled her against him. "Let's have a little kiss, before we fish home."

Jean leaned forward, reached out her arm. He saw her face coming toward him—bright wonderful face, onyx, pale rose, ivory, smiling, hot with life....She reached past him, thrust the check-valve. Four jets thrashed forward. The barge jerked. The pilot fell into the instrument panel, comical surprise written on his face.

From behind came a heavy resonant thump.

The pilot pulled himself back into the seat, knocked back the check-valve. Blood oozed from his chin, forming a little red wen. Behind them the portal snapped open. Webbard's face, black with rage, looked through.

When he had finally finished, and the portal had closed, the pilot looked at Jean, who was sitting quietly in her seat, the corners of her mouth drawn up dreamily.

He said from deep in his throat, "If I had you alone, I'd beat you half to death."

Jean drew her knees up under her chin, clasped her arms around and looked silently ahead.

Abercrombie Station had been built to the Fitch cylinder design: a power and service core, a series of circular decks, a transparent sheath. To the original construction a number of modifications and annexes had been added. An outside deck circled the cylinder, sheet steel to hold the magnetic grapples of small boats, cargo binds, magnetic shoes, anything which was to be fixed in place for a greater or lesser time. At each end of the cylinder, tubes connected to dependent constructions. The first, a sphere, was the private residence of the Abercrombies. The second, a cylinder, rotated at sufficient speed to press the water it contained evenly over its inner surface to a depth of ten feet; this was the Station swimming pool, a feature found on only three of the resort satellites.

The supply barge inched close to the dock, bumped. Four men attached constrictor tackle to rings in the hull, heaved the barge along to the supply port. The barge settled into its socket, grapples shot home, the ports sucked open.

Chief Steward Webbard was still smoldering, but now a display of anger was beneath his dignity. Disdaining magnetic shoes, he pulled himself to the entrance, motioned to Jean. "Bring your baggage."

Jean went to her neat little trunk, jerked it into the air, found herself floundering helpless in the middle of the cargo space. Webbard impatiently returned with magnetic clips for her shoes, and helped her float the trunk into the Station.

She was breathing different, rich air. The barge had smelled of ozone, grease, hemp sacking, but the Station.... Without consciously trying to identify the odor, Jean thought of waffles with butter and syrup mixed with talcum powder.

Webbard floated in front of her, an imposing spectacle. His fat no longer hung on him in folds; it ballooned out in an even perimeter. His face was smooth as a watermelon, and it seemed as if his features were incised, carved, rather than molded. He focused his eyes at a point above her dark head. "We had better come to an understanding, young lady."

"Certainly, Mr. Webbard."

"As a favor to my friend, Mr. Fotheringay, I have brought you here to work. Beyond this original and singular act, I am no longer responsible. I am not your sponsor. Mr. Fotheringay recommended you highly, so see that you give satisfaction. Your immediate superior will be Mrs. Blaiskell, and you must obey her implicitly. We have very strict rules here at Abercrombie—fair treatment and good pay—but you must earn it. Your work must speak for itself, and you can expect no special favors." He coughed. "Indeed, if I may say so, you are fortunate in finding employment here; usually we hire people more of our own sort, it makes for harmonious conditions."

Jean waited with demurely bowed head. Webbard spoke on further, detailing specific warnings, admonitions, injunctions.

Jean nodded dutifully. There was no point antagonizing pompous old Webbard. And Webbard thought that here was a respectful young lady, thin and very young and with a peculiar frenetic gleam in her eye, but sufficiently impressed by his importance.... Good coloring too. Pleasant features. If she only could manage two hundred more pounds of flesh on her bones, she might have appealed to his grosser nature.

"This way, then," said Webbard.

He floated ahead, and by some magnificent innate power continued to radiate the impression of inexorable dignity even while plunging headfirst along the corridor.

Jean came more sedately, walking on her magnetic clips, pushing the trunk ahead as easily if it had been a paper bag.

They reached the central core, and Webbard, after looking back over his bulging shoulders, launched himself up the shaft.

Panes in the wall of the core permitted a view of the various halls, lounges, refectories, salons. Jean stopped by a room decorated with red plush drapes and marble statuary. She stared, first in wonder, then in amusement.

Webbard called impatiently, "Come along now, miss, come along."

Jean pulled herself away from the pane. "I was watching the guests. They looked like—" She broke into a sudden giggle.

Webbard frowned, pursed his lips. Jean thought he was about to demand the grounds of her merriment, but evidently he felt it beneath his dignity. He called, "Come along now, I can spare you only a moment."

She turned one last glance into the hall, and now she laughed aloud.

Fat women, like bladder-fish in an aquarium tank. Fat women, round and tender as yellow peaches. Fat women, miraculously easy and agile in the absence of gravity. The occasion seemed to be an afternoon musicale. The hall was crowded and heavy with balls of pink flesh draped in blouses and pantaloons of white, pale blue and yellow.

The current Abercrombie fashion seemed designed to accent the round bodies. Flat bands like Sam Browne belts molded the breasts down and out, under the arms. The hair was parted down the middle, skinned smoothly back to a small roll at the nape of the neck. Flesh, bulbs of tender flesh, smooth shiny balloons. Tiny twitching features, dancing fingers and toes, eyes and lips roguishly painted. On Earth any one of these women would have sat immobile, a pile of sagging sweating tissue. At Abercrombie Station—the so-called "Adipose Alley"—they moved with the ease of dandelion puffs, and their faces and bodies were smooth as butterballs.

"Come, come, come!" barked Webbard. "There's no loitering at Abercrombie!"

Jean restrained the impulse to slide her trunk up the core against Webbard's rotund buttocks, a tempting target.

He waited for her at the far end of the corridor.

"Mr. Webbard," she asked thoughtfully, "how much does Earl Abercrombie weigh?"

Webbard tilted his head back, glared reprovingly down his nose. "Such intimacies, miss, are not considered polite conversation here."

Jean said, "I merely wondered if he were as—well, imposing as you are."

Webbard sniffed. "I couldn't answer you. Mr. Abercrombie is a person of great competence. His—presence is a matter you must learn not to discuss. It's not proper, not done."

"Thank you, Mr. Webbard," said Jean meekly.

Webbard said, "You'll catch on. You'll make a good girl yet. Now, through the tube, and I'll take you to Mrs. Blaiskell."

Mrs. Blaiskell was short and squat as a kumquat. Her head was steel gray, and skinned back modishly to the roll behind her head. She wore tight black rompers, the uniform of the Abercrombie servants, so Jean was to learn.

Jean suspected that she made a poor impression on Mrs. Blaiskell. She felt the snapping gray eyes search her from head to foot, and kept her own modestly downcast.

Webbard explained that Jean was to be trained as a maid, and suggested that Mrs. Blaiskell use her in the Pleasaunce and the bedrooms.

Mrs. Blaiskell nodded. "Good idea. The young master is peculiar, as everyone knows, but he's been pestering the girls lately and interrupting their duties; wise to have one in there such as her—no offense, miss, I just mean it's the gravity that does it—who won't be so apt to catch his eye."

Webbard signed to her, and they floated off a little distance, conversing in low whispers.

Jean's mouth quivered at the corners. Old fools!

Five minutes passed. Jean began to fidget. Why didn't they do something? Take her somewhere. She suppressed her restlessness. Life! How good, how zestful! She wondered, *Will I feel this same joy when I'm twenty? When I'm thirty, forty?* She drew back the corners of her mouth. *Of course I will! I'll never let myself change. . . . But life must be used to its best. Every flicker of ardor and excitement must be wrung free and tasted.* She grinned. Here she floated, breathing the overripe air of Abercrombie Station. In a way it was adventure. It paid well—two million dollars, and only for seducing an eighteen-year-old boy. Seducing him, marrying him—what difference? Of course he was Earl Abercrombie, and if he were as imposing as Mr. Webbard. . . . She considered Webbard's great body in wry speculation. Oh well, two million was two million. If things got too bad, the price might go up. Ten million, perhaps. Not too large a cut out of a billion.

Webbard departed without a word, twitching himself easily back down the core.

"Come," said Mrs. Blaiskell. "I'll show you your room. You can rest and tomorrow I'll take you around."

4

Mrs. Blaiskell stood by, frankly critical, while Jean fitted herself into black rompers. "Lord have mercy, but you mustn't pinch in the waist so! You're rachity and thin to starvation now, poor child; you mustn't point it up so! Perhaps we can find a few airfloats to fill you out; not that it's essential, Lord knows, since you're but a dust-maid. Still, it always improves a household to have a staff of pretty women, and young Earl, I will say this for him and all his oddness, he does appreciate a handsome woman. . . . Now then, your bosom, we must do something there; why, you're nearly flat! You see, there's no scope to allow a fine drape down under the arms, see?" She pointed to her own voluminous rolls of adipose. "Suppose we just roll up a bit of cushion and—"

"No," said Jean tremulously. Was it possible that they thought her so ugly? "I won't wear padding."

Mrs. Blaiskell sniffed. "It's your own self that's to benefit, my dear. I'm sure it's not me that's the wizened one."

Jean bent over her black slippers. "No, you're very sleek."

Mrs. Blaiskell nodded proudly. "I keep myself well shaped out, and all the better for it. It wasn't so when I was your age, miss, I'll tell you; I was on Earth then—"

"Oh, you weren't born here?"

"No, miss, I was one of the poor souls pressed and ridden by gravity, and I burned up my body with the effort of mere conveyance. No, I was born in Sydney, Australia, of decent kind folk, but they were too poor to buy me a place on Abercrombie. I was lucky enough to secure just such a position as you have, and that was while Mr. Justus and old Mrs. Eva, his mother—that's Earl's grandmother—was still with us. I've never been down to Earth since. I'll never set foot on the surface again."

"Don't you miss the festivals and great buildings and all the lovely countryside?"

"Pah!" Mrs. Blaiskell spat the word. "And be pressed into hideous folds and wrinkles? And ride in a cart, and be stared at and snickered at by the home people? Thin as sticks they are with their constant worry and fight against the pull of the soil! No, miss, we have our own sceneries and fetes; there's a pavanne for tomorrow night, a Grand Masque Pantomime, a Pageant of Beautiful Women, all in the month ahead. And best, I'm among my own people, the round ones, and I've never had a wrinkle on my face. I'm fine and full-blown, and I wouldn't trade with any of them below."

Jean shrugged. "If you're happy, that's all that matters." She looked at herself in the mirror with satisfaction. Even if fat Mrs. Blaiskell thought otherwise, the black rompers looked well on her, now that she'd fitted them snug to her hips and waist. Her legs—slender, round and shining ivory—were good, this she knew. Even if weird Mr. Webbard and odd Mrs. Blaiskell thought otherwise. Wait till she tried them on young Earl. He preferred gravity girls; Fotheringay had told her so. And yet—Webbard and Mrs. Blaiskell had hinted otherwise. Maybe he liked both kinds . . . ? Jean smiled, a little tremulously. If Earl liked both kinds, then he would like almost anything that was warm, moved, and breathed. And that certainly included herself.

If she asked Mrs. Blaiskell outright, she'd be startled and shocked.

Good proper Mrs. Blaiskell. A motherly soul, not like the matrons in the various asylums and waifs' homes of her experience. Strapping big women those had been—practical and quick with their hands.... But Mrs. Blaiskell was nice; she would never have deserted her child on a pool table. Mrs. Blaiskell would have struggled and starved herself to keep her child and raise her nicely.... Jean idly speculated how it would seem with Mrs. Blaiskell for a mother. And Mr. Mycroft for a father. It gave her a queer prickly feeling, and also somehow called up from deep inside a dark dull resentment tinged with anger.

Jean moved uneasily, fretfully. *Never mind the nonsense! You're playing a lone hand. What would you want with relatives? What an ungodly nuisance!* She would never have been allowed this adventure up to Abercrombie Station.... On the other hand, with relatives there would be many fewer problems on how to spend two million dollars.

Jean sighed. Her own mother wasn't kind and comfortable like Mrs. Blaiskell. She couldn't have been, and the whole matter became an academic question. *Forget it, put it clean out of your mind.*

Mrs. Blaiskell brought forward service shoes, worn to some extent by everyone at the Station: slippers with magnetic coils in the soles. Wires led to a power bank at the belt. By adjusting a rheostat, any degree of magnetism could be achieved.

"When a person works, she needs a footing," Mrs. Blaiskell explained. "Of course there's not much to do, once you get on to it. Cleaning is easy, with our good filters; still, there's sometimes a stir of dust and always a little film of oil that settles from the air."

Jean straightened up. "Okay, Mrs. B., I'm ready. Where do we start?"

Mrs. Blaiskell raised her eyebrows at the familiarity, but was not seriously displeased. In the main, the girl seemed to be respectful, willing, and intelligent. And—significantly—not the sort to create a disturbance with Mr. Earl.

Twitching a toe against a wall, she propelled herself down the corridor, halted by a white door, slid back the panel.

They entered the room as if from the ceiling. Jean felt an instant of vertigo, pushing herself headfirst at what appeared to be a floor.

Mrs. Blaiskell deftly seized a chair, swung her body around, put her feet to the nominal floor. Jean joined her. They stood in a large round room, apparently a section across the building. Windows opened on space, stars shone in from all sides; the entire zodiac was visible with a sweep of the eyes.

Sunlight came up from below, shining on the ceiling, and off to one quarter hung the half-moon, hard and sharp as a new coin. The room was rather too opulent for Jean's taste. She was conscious of an overwhelming surfeit of mustard-saffron carpet, white paneling with gold arabesques, a round table clamped to the floor, surrounded by chairs footed with magnetic casters. A crystal chandelier thrust rigidly down; rotund cherubs peered at intervals from the angle between wall and ceiling.

"The Pleasaunce," said Mrs. Blaiskell. "You'll clean in here every morning first thing." She described Jean's duties in detail.

"Next we go to—" she nudged Jean. "Here's old Mrs. Clara, Earl's mother. Bow your head, just as I do."

A woman dressed in rose purple floated into the room. She wore an expression of absentminded arrogance, as if in all the universe there were no doubt, uncertainty or equivocation. She was almost perfectly globular, as wide as she was tall. Her hair was silver white, her face a bubble of smooth flesh, daubed apparently at random with rouge. She wore stones spread six inches down over her bulging bosom and shoulders.

Mrs. Blaiskell bowed her head unctuously. "Mrs. Clara, dear, allow me to introduce the new parlor maid; she's new up from Earth and very handy."

Mrs. Clara Abercrombie darted Jean a quick look. "Emaciated creature."

"Oh, she'll healthen up," cooed Mrs. Blaiskell. "Plenty of good food and hard work will do wonders for her; after all, she's only a child."

"Mmmph. Hardly. It's blood, Blaiskell, and well you know it."

"Well, yes, of course, Mrs. Clara."

Mrs. Clara continued in a brassy voice, darting glances around the room. "Either it's good blood you have or vinegar. This girl here, she'll never be really comfortable, I can see it. It's not in her blood."

"No, ma'am, you're correct in what you say."

"It's not in Earl's blood either. He's the one I'm worried for. Hugo was the rich one, but his brother Lionel after him, poor dear Lionel, and—"

"What about Lionel?" said a husky voice. Jean twisted. This was Earl. "Who's heard from Lionel?"

"No one, my dear. He's gone, he'll never be back. I was but commenting that neither one of you ever reached your growth, showing all bone as you do."

Earl scowled past his mother, past Mrs. Blaiskell, and his gaze fell on Jean. "What's this? Another servant? We don't need her. Send her away. Always ideas for more expense."

"She's for your rooms, Earl, my dear," said his mother.

"Where's Jessy? What was wrong with Jessy?"

Mrs. Clara and Mrs. Blaiskell exchanged indulgent glances. Jean turned Earl a slow arch look. He blinked, then frowned. Jean dropped her eyes, traced a pattern on the rug with her toe, an operation which she knew sent interesting movements along her leg. Earning the two million dollars wouldn't be as irksome as she had feared. Because Earl was not at all fat. He was stocky, solid, with bull shoulders and a bull neck. He had a close crop of tight blond curls, a florid complexion, a big waxy nose, a ponderous jaw. His mouth was good, drooping sullenly at the moment.

He was something less than attractive, thought Jean. On Earth she would have ignored him, or if he persisted, stung him to fury with a series of insults. But she had been expecting far worse; a bulbous creature like Webbard, a human balloon.... Of course there was no real reason for Earl to be fat; the children of fat people were as likely as not to be of normal size.

Mrs. Clara was instructing Mrs. Blaiskell for the day, Mrs. Blaiskell nodding precisely on each sixth word and ticking off points on her stubby little fingers.

Mrs. Clara finished, Mrs. Blaiskell nodded to Jean. "Come, miss, there's work to be done."

Earl called after them, "Mind now, no one in my study!"

Jean asked curiously, "Why doesn't he want anyone in his study?"

"That's where he keeps all his collections. He won't have a thing disturbed. Very strange sometimes, Mr. Earl. You'll just have to make allowances, and be on your good behavior. In some ways he's harder to serve than Mrs. Clara."

"Earl was born here?"

Mrs. Blaiskell nodded. "He's never been down to Earth. Says it's a place of crazy people, and the Lord knows, he's more than half right."

"Who are Hugo and Lionel?"

"They're the two oldest. Hugo is dead, Lord rest him, and Lionel is off on his travels. Then under Earl there's Harper and Dauphin and Millicent and Clarice. That's all Mrs. Clara's children, all very proud and portly. Earl is the skinny lad of the lot, and very lucky too, because when Hugo died, Lionel was off gadding and so Earl inherited. . . . Now here's his suite, and what a mess."

As they worked Mrs. Blaiskell commented on various aspects of the room. "That bed now! Earl wasn't satisfied with sleeping under a saddleband like the rest of us, no! He wears pajamas of magnetized cloth, and that weights him against the cushions almost as if he lived on Earth. . . . And this reading and studying, my word, there's nothing the lad won't think of! And his telescope! He'll sit in the cupola and focus on Earth by the hour."

"Maybe he'd like to visit Earth?"

Mrs. Blaiskell nodded. "I wouldn't be surprised if you were close on it there. The place has a horrid fascination for him. But he can't leave Abercrombie, you know."

"That's strange. Why not?"

Mrs. Blaiskell darted her wise look. "Because then he forfeits his inheritance; that's in the original charter, that the owner must remain on the premises." She pointed to a gray door. "That there's his study. And now I'm going to give you a peep in, so you won't be tormented by curiosity and perhaps make trouble for yourself when I'm not around to keep an eye open. . . . Now don't be excited by what you see; there's nothing to hurt you."

With the air of a priestess unveiling mystery, Mrs. Blaiskell fumbled a moment with the door-slide, manipulating it in a manner which Jean was not able to observe.

The door swung aside. Mrs. Blaiskell smirked as Jean jumped back in alarm.

"Now, now, now, don't be alarmed; I told you there was nothing to harm you. That's one of Master Earl's zoological specimens, and rare trouble and expense he's gone to—"

Jean sighed deeply, and gave closer inspection to the horned black creature which stood on two legs just inside the door, poised and leaning as if ready to embrace the intruder in leathery black arms.

"That's the most scary part," said Mrs. Blaiskell in quiet satisfaction. "He's got his insects and bugs there"—she pointed—"his gems there, his old music discs there, his stamps there, his books along that cabinet. Nasty things, I'm ashamed of him. Don't let me know of your peeking in them nasty books that Mr. Earl gloats over."

"No, Mrs. Blaiskell," said Jean meekly. "I'm not interested in that kind of thing. If it's what I think it is."

Mrs. Blaiskell nodded emphatically. "It's what you think it is and worse." She did not expand on the background of her familiarity with the library, and Jean thought it inappropriate to inquire.

Earl stood behind them. "Well?" he asked in a heavy sarcastic voice. "Getting an eyeful?" He kicked himself across the room, slammed shut the door.

Mrs. Blaiskell said in a conciliatory voice, "Now, Mr. Earl, I was just showing the new girl what to avoid, what not to look at, and I didn't want her swounding of heart stoppage if innocent-like she happened to peek inside."

Earl grunted. "If she peeps inside while I'm there, she'll be 'swounding' from something more than heart stoppage."

"I'm a good cook too," said Jean. She turned away. "Come, Mrs. Blaiskell, let's leave until Mr. Earl has recovered his temper. I won't have him hurting your feelings."

Mrs. Blaiskell stammered, "Now, then! Surely there's no harm. . . ." She stopped. Earl had gone into his study and slammed the door.

Mrs. Blaiskell's eyes glistened with thick tears. "Ah, my dear, I do so dislike harsh words. . . ."

They worked in silence and finished the bedroom. At the door Mrs. Blaiskell said confidentially into Jean's ears, "Why do you think Earl is so gruff and grumpy?"

"I've no idea," breathed Jean. "None whatever."

"Well," said Mrs. Blaiskell warily, "it all boils down to this: his appearance. He's so self-conscious of his thinness that he's all eaten up inside. He can't bear to have anyone see him; he thinks they're sneering. I've heard him tell Mrs. Clara so. Of course they're not; they're just sorry. He eats like a horse, he takes gland-pellets, but still he's that spindly and all hard tense muscle." She inspected Jean thoroughly. "I think we'll put you on the same kind of regimen, and see if we can't make a prettier woman out of you." Then she shook her head doubtfully, clicked her tongue. "It might not be in your blood, as Mrs. Clara says. I hardly can see that it's in your blood. . . ."

5

There were tiny red ribbons on Jean's slippers, a red ribbon in her hair, a coquettish black beauty spot on her cheek. She had altered her rompers so that they clung unobtrusively to her waist and hips.

Before she left the room she examined herself in the mirror. *Maybe it's me that's out of step! How would I look with a couple hundred more pounds of grade? No. I suppose not. I'm the gamine type. I'll look like a wolverine when I'm sixty, but for the next forty years—watch out.*

She took herself along the corridor, past the Pleasaunce, the music rooms, the formal parlor, the refectory, up into the bedrooms. She stopped by Earl's door, flung it open, entered, pushing the electrostatic duster ahead of her.

The room was dark; the transpar walls were opaque under the action of the scrambling field.

Jean found the dial, turned up the light.

Earl was awake. He lay on his side, his yellow magnetic pajamas pressing him into the mattress. A pale blue quilt was pulled up to his shoulders, his arm lay across his face. Under the shadow of his arm his eye smoldered out at Jean.

He lay motionless, too outraged to move.

Jean put her hands on her hips, said in her clear young voice, "Get up, you sluggard! You'll get as fat as the rest of them lounging around till all hours. . . ."

The silence was choked and ominous. Jean bent to peer under Earl's arm. "Are you alive?"

Without moving Earl said in a harsh low voice, "Exactly what do you think you're doing?"

"I'm about my regular duties. I've finished the Pleasaunce. Next comes your room."

His eyes went to a clock. "At seven o'clock in the morning?"

"Why not? The sooner I get done, the sooner I can get to my own business."

"Your own business be damned. Get out of here, before you get hurt."

"No, sir. I'm a self-determined individual. Once my work is done, there's nothing more important than self-expression."

"Get out!"

"I'm an artist, a painter. Or maybe I'll be a poet this year. Or a dancer. I'd make a wonderful ballerina. Watch." She essayed a pirouette, but the impulse took her up to the ceiling—not ungracefully, this she made sure.

She pushed herself back. "If I had magnetic slippers I could twirl an hour and a half. Grand jetés are easy. . . ."

He raised himself on his elbow, blinking and glaring, as if on the verge of launching himself at her.

"You're either crazy—or so utterly impertinent as to amount to the same thing."

"Not at all," said Jean. "I'm very courteous. There might be a difference of opinion, but still it doesn't make you automatically right."

He slumped back on the bed. "Argue with old Webbard," he said thickly. "Now—for the last time—get out!"

"I'll go," said Jean, "but you'll be sorry."

"Sorry?" His voice had risen nearly an octave. "Why should I be sorry?"

"Suppose I took offense at your rudeness and told Mr. Webbard I wanted to quit?"

Earl said through tight lips, "I'm going to talk to Mr. Webbard today and maybe you'll be asked to quit....Miraculous!" he told himself bitterly. "Scarecrow maids breaking in at sunup...."

Jean stared in surprise. "Scarecrow! Me? On Earth I'm considered a very pretty girl. I can get away with things like this, disturbing people, because I'm pretty."

"This is Abercrombie Station," said Earl in a dry voice. "Thank God!"

"You're rather handsome yourself," said Jean tentatively.

Earl sat up, his face tinged with angry blood. "Get out of here!" he shouted. "You're discharged!"

"Pish," said Jean. "You wouldn't dare fire me."

"I wouldn't dare?" asked Earl in a dangerous voice. "Why wouldn't I dare?"

"Because I'm smarter than you are."

Earl made a husky sound in his throat. "And just what makes you think so?"

Jean laughed. "You'd be very nice, Earl, if you weren't so touchy."

"All right, we'll take that up first. Why am I so touchy?"

Jean shrugged. "I said you were nice-looking and you blew a skull-fuse." She waved away an imaginary fluff from the back of her hand. "I call that touchiness."

Earl wore a grim smile that made Jean think of Fotheringay. Earl might be tough if pushed far enough. But not as tough as—well, say Ansel Clellan. Or Fiorenzo. Or Party MacClure. Or Fotheringay. Or herself, for that matter.

He was staring at her, as if he were seeing her for the first time. This is what she wanted. "Why do you think you're smarter, then?"

"Oh, I don't know. . . . Are you smart?"

His glance darted off to the doors leading to his study; a momentary quiver of satisfaction crossed his face. "Yes, I'm smart."

"Can you play chess?"

"Of course I play chess," he said belligerently. "I'm one of the best chess players alive."

"I could beat you with one hand." Jean had played chess four times in her life.

"I wish you had something I wanted," he said slowly. "I'd take it away from you."

Jean gave him an arch look. "Let's play for forfeits."

"No!"

"Ha!" She laughed, eyes sparkling.

He flushed. "Very well."

Jean picked up her duster. "Not now, though." She had accomplished more than she had hoped for. She looked ostentatiously over her shoulder. "I've got to work. If Mrs. Blaiskell finds me here she'll accuse you of seducing me."

He snorted with twisted lips. He looked like an angry blond boar, thought Jean. But two million dollars was two million dollars. And it wasn't as bad as if he'd been fat. The idea had been planted in his mind. "You be thinking of the forfeit," said Jean. "I've got to work."

She left the room, turning him a final glance over her shoulder which she hoped was cryptic.

The servants' quarters were in the main cylinder, the Abercrombie Station proper. Jean sat quietly in a corner of the mess hall, watching and listening while the other servants had their elevenses: cocoa gobbed heavy with whipped cream, pastries, ice cream. The talk was high pitched, edgy. Jean wondered at the myth that fat people were languid and easygoing.

From the corner of her eye she saw Mr. Webbard float into the room, his face tight and gray with anger.

She lowered her head over her cocoa, watching him from under her lashes.

Webbard looked directly at her, his lips sucked in and his bulbous cheeks quivered. For a moment it seemed that he would drift at her, attracted by the force of his anger alone; somehow he restrained himself. He looked around the room until he spied Mrs. Blaiskell. A flick of his fingers sent him to where she sat at the end table, held by magnets appropriately fastened to her rompers.

He bent over her, muttered in her ear. Jean could not hear his words, but she saw Mrs. Blaiskell's face change and her eyes go seeking around the room.

Mr. Webbard completed his dramatization and felt better. He wiped the palms of his hands along the ample area of his dark blue corduroy trousers, twisted with a quick wriggle of his shoulders and sent himself to the door with a flick of his toe.

Marvelous, thought Jean, the majesty, the orbital massiveness of Webbard's passage through the air. The full moonface, heavy lidded, placid; the rosy cheeks, the chins and jowls puffed round and tumescent, glazed and oily, without blemish, mar or wrinkle; the hemisphere of the chest, then the bifurcate lower half, in the rich dark blue corduroy: the whole marvel coasting along with the inexorable momentum of an ore barge. . . .

Jean became aware that Mrs. Blaiskell was motioning to her from the doorway, making cryptic little signals with her fat fingers.

Mrs. Blaiskell was waiting in the little vestibule she called her office, her face scene to shifting emotions. "Mr. Webbard has given me some serious information," she said in a voice intended to be stern.

Jean displayed alarm. "About me?"

Mrs. Blaiskell nodded decisively. "Mr. Earl complained of some very strange behavior this morning. At seven o'clock or earlier . . ."

Jean gasped. "Is it possible, that Earl has had the audacity to—"

"*Mr.* Earl," Mrs. Blaiskell corrected primly.

"Why, Mrs. Blaiskell, it was as much as my life was worth to get away from him!"

Mrs. Blaiskell blinked uneasily. "That's not precisely the way Mr. Webbard put it. He said you—"

"Does that sound reasonable? Is that likely, Mrs. B.?"

"Well—no," Mrs. Blaiskell admitted, putting her hand to her chin, and tapping her teeth with a fingernail. "Certainly it seems odd, come to consider a little more closely." She looked at Jean. "But how is it that—"

"He called me into his room, and then—" Jean had never been able to cry, but she hid her face in her hands.

"There, now," said Mrs. Blaiskell. "I never believed Mr. Webbard anyway. Did he—did he—" She found herself unable to phrase the question.

Jean shook her head. "It wasn't for want of trying."

"Just goes to show," muttered Mrs. Blaiskell. "And I thought he'd grown out of that nonsense."

" 'Nonsense'?" The word had been invested with a certain overtone that set it out of context.

Mrs. Blaiskell was embarrassed. She shifted her eyes. "Earl has passed through several stages, and I'm not sure which has been the most troublesome. . . . A year or two ago—two years, because this was while Hugo was still alive and the family was together—he saw so many Earth films that he began to admire Earth women, and it had us all worried. Thank heaven, he's completely thrown off that unwholesome-ness, but it's going to make him all the more shy and self-conscious." She sighed. "If only one of the pretty girls of the Station would love him for himself, for his brilliant mind . . . but no, they're all romantic and they're more taken by a rich round body and fine flesh, and poor gnarled Earl is sure that when one of them does smile his way she's after his money, and very likely true, so I say!" She looked at Jean speculatively. "It just occurred to me that Earl might be veering back to his old—well, strangeness. Not that you're not a nice well-meaning creature, because you are."

Well, well, thought Jean dispiritedly. Evidently she had achieved not so much this morning as she had hoped. But then, every campaign had its setbacks.

"In any event, Mr. Webbard has asked that I give you different duties, to keep you from Mr. Earl's sight, because he's evidently taken an antip-athy to you. . . . And after this morning I'm sure you'll not object."

"Of course not," said Jean absently. Earl, that bigoted, warped, wretch of a boy!

"For today, you'll just watch the Pleasaunce and service the period-icals and water the atrium plants. Tomorrow—well, we'll see."

Jean nodded and turned to leave. "One more thing," said Mrs. Blais-kell in a hesitant voice. Jean paused. Mrs. Blaiskell could not seem to find the right words.

They came in a sudden surge, all strung together. "Be a little careful of yourself, especially when you're alone near Mr. Earl. This is Aber-crombie Station, you know, and he's Earl Abercrombie, and the High Justice, and some very strange things happen. . . ."

Jean said in a shocked whisper, "Physical violence, Mrs. Blaiskell?"

Mrs. Blaiskell stammered and blushed. "Yes, I suppose you'd call it that.... Some very disgraceful things have come to light. Not nice, though I shouldn't be saying it to you, who's only been with us a day. But, be careful. I wouldn't want your soul on my conscience."

"I'll be careful," said Jean in a properly hushed voice.

Mrs. Blaiskell nodded her head, an indication that the interview was at an end.

Jean returned to the refectory. It was really very nice for Mrs. Blaiskell to worry about her. It was almost as if Mrs. Blaiskell were fond of her. Jean sneered automatically. That was too much to expect. Women always disliked her because their men were never safe when Jean was near. Not that Jean consciously flirted—at least, not always—but there was something about her that interested men, even the old ones. They paid lip-service to the idea that Jean was a child, but their eyes wandered up and down, the way a young man's eyes wandered.

But out here on Abercrombie Station it was different. Ruefully Jean admitted that no one was jealous of her, no one on the entire Station. It was the other way around; she was regarded as an object of pity. But it was still nice of Mrs. Blaiskell to take her under her wing; it gave Jean a pleasant warm feeling. Maybe if and when she got hold of that two million dollars—and her thoughts went to Earl. The warm feeling drained from her mind.

Earl, hoity-toity Earl, was ruffled because she had disturbed his rest. So bristle-necked Earl thought she was gnarled and stunted! Jean pulled herself to the chair. Seating herself with a thump, she seized up her bulb of cocoa and sucked at the spout.

Earl! She pictured him: the sullen face, the kinky blond hair, the overripe mouth, the stocky body he so desperately yearned to fatten. This was the man she must inveigle into matrimony. On Earth, on almost any other planet in the human universe, it would be child's play—

This was Abercrombie Station!

She sipped her cocoa, considering the problem. The odds that Earl would fall in love with her and come through with a legitimate proposal seemed slim. Could he be tricked into a position where in order to save face or reputation he would be forced to marry her? Probably not. At Abercrombie Station, she told herself, marriage with her represented almost the ultimate loss of face. Still, there were avenues to be explored. Suppose she beat Earl at chess, could she make marriage the forfeit? Hardly. Earl would be too sly and dishonorable to pay up. It was necessary to make him *want* to marry her, and that would entail making herself desirable in his eyes, which in turn made necessary a revision of Earl's whole outlook. To begin with, he'd have to feel that his own person was not entirely loathsome (although it was). Earl's morale must be built up to a point where he felt himself superior to the rest of Abercrombie Station, and where he would be proud to marry one of his own kind.

A possibility at the other pole: if Earl's self-respect were so utterly blasted and reduced, if he could be made to feel so despicable and impotent that he would be ashamed to show his face outside his room, he might marry her as the best bet in sight. . . . And still another possibility: revenge. If Earl realized that the fat girls who flattered him were actually ridiculing him behind his back, he might marry her from sheer spite.

One last possibility. Duress. Marriage or death. She considered poisons and antidotes, diseases and cures, a straightforward gun in the ribs. . . .

Jean angrily tossed the empty cocoa bulb into the waste hopper. Trickery, sex lure, flattery, browbeating, revenge, fear—which was the most farfetched? All were ridiculous.

She decided she needed more time, more information. Perhaps Earl had a weak spot she could work on. If they had a community of interests, she'd be much further advanced. Examination of his study might give her a few hints.

A bell chimed, a number dropped on a call-board and a voice said, "Pleasaunce."

Mrs. Blaiskell appeared. "That's you, miss. Now go in, nice as you please, and ask Mrs. Clara what it is that's wanted, and then you can go off duty till three."

6

Mrs. Clara Abercrombie, however, was not present. The Pleasaunce was occupied by twenty or thirty young folk, talking and arguing with rather giddy enthusiasm. The girls wore pastel satins, velvets, gauzes, tight around their rotund pink bodies, with frothy little ruffles and anklets, while the young men affected elegant dark grays and blues and tawny beiges, with military trim of white and scarlet.

Ranged along a wall were a dozen stage settings in miniature. Above, a ribbon of paper bore the words: *Pandora in Elis. Libretto by A. Percy Stevanic, music by Colleen O'Casey.*

Jean looked around the room to see who had summoned her. Earl raised his finger peremptorily. Jean walked on her magnetic shoes to where he floated near one of the miniature stage sets. He turned to a mess of cocoa and whipped cream, clinging like a tumor to the side of the set—evidently a broken bulb.

"Clean up that spill," Earl said in a flinty voice.

Jean thought, *He half wants to rub it in, half wants to act as if he doesn't recognize me.* She nodded dutifully. "I'll get a container and a sponge."

When she returned, Earl was across the room talking earnestly to a girl whose globular body was encased in a gown of brilliant rose velvet. She wore rosebuds over each ear and played with a ridiculous little white dog, while she listened to Earl with a halfhearted affection of interest.

Jean worked as slowly as possible, watching from the corners of her eyes. Snatches of conversation reached her: "Lapwill's done simply a marvelous job on the editing, but I don't see that he's given Myras the same scope—" "If the pageant grosses ten thousand dollars, Mrs. Clara says she'll put another ten thousand toward the construction fund. Think of it! a Little Theater all our own!" Excited and conspiratorial whispers ran through the Pleasaunce, "—and for the water scene why not have the chorus float across the sky as moons?"

Jean watched Earl. He hung on the fat girl's words, and spoke with a pathetic attempt at intimate comradeship and jocularity. The girl nodded politely, twisted up her features into a smile. Jean noticed her eyes followed a hearty youth whose physique bulged out his plum-colored breeches like wind bellying a spinnaker. Earl perceived the girl's inattention. Jean saw him falter momentarily, then work even harder at his badinage. The fat girl licked her lips, swung her ridiculous little dog on its leash, and glanced over to where the purple-trousered youth bellowed with laughter.

A sudden idea caused Jean to hasten her work. Earl no doubt would be occupied here until lunchtime—two hours away. And Mrs. Blaiskell had relieved her from duty till three.

She took herself from the hall, disposed of the cleaning equipment, dived up the corridor to Earl's private chambers. At Mrs. Clara's suite she paused, listening at the door. Snores!

Another fifty feet to Earl's chambers. She looked quickly up and down the corridor, slid back the door and slipped cautiously inside.

The room was silent as Jean made a quick survey. Closet, dressing room to one side, sun-flooded bathroom to the other. Across the room was the tall gray door into the study. A sign hung upon the door, apparently freshly made:

PRIVATE.   DANGER.   DO NOT ENTER.

Jean paused to consider. What kind of danger? Earl might have set devious safeguards over his private chamber.

She examined the door-slide button. It was overhung by an apparently innocent guard—which might or might not control an alarm circuit. She pressed her belt-buckle against the shutter in such a way as to maintain an electrical circuit, then moved the guard aside, pressed the button with her fingernail—gingerly. She knew of buttons which darted out hypodermics when pressed.

There was no whisper of machinery. The door remained in place.

Jean blew fretfully between her teeth. No keyhole, no buttons to play a combination on. . . . Mrs. Blaiskell had found no trouble. Jean tried to reconstruct her motions. She moved to the slide, set her head to where she could see the reflection of the light from the wall. . . . There was a smudge on the gloss. She looked closely and a telltale glint indicated a photoelectric eye.

She put her finger on the eye, pressed the slide-button. The door slipped open. In spite of having been forewarned, Jean recoiled from the horrid black shape which hung forward as if to grapple her.

She waited. After a moment the door fell gently back into place.

Jean returned to the outer corridor, stationed herself where she could duck into Mrs. Clara's apartments if a suspicious shape came looming up the corridor. Earl might not have contented himself with the protection of a secret electric lock.

Five minutes passed. Mrs. Clara's personal maid passed by, a globular little Chinese, eyes like two shiny black beetles, but no one else.

Jean pushed herself back to Earl's room, crossed to the study door. Once more she read the sign:

PRIVATE.   DANGER.   DO NOT ENTER.

She hesitated. "I'm sixteen years old. Going on seventeen. Too young to die. It's just like that odd creature to furnish his study with evil tricks." She shrugged off the notion. "What a person won't do for money."

She opened the door, slipped through.

The door closed behind her. Quickly she moved out from under the poised demon-shape and turned to examine Earl's sanctum. She looked right, left, up, down.

"There's a lot to see here," she muttered. "I hope Earl doesn't run out of sheep's-eyes for his fat girl, or decide he wants a particular newspaper clipping...."

She turned power into her slipper magnets, and wondered where to begin. The room was more like a warehouse or museum than a study, and gave the impression of wild confusion arranged, sorted, and filed by an extraordinary finicky mind.

After a fashion, it was a beautiful room, imbued with an atmosphere of erudition in its dark wood-tones. The far wall glowed molten with rich color—a rose window from the old Chartres cathedral, in full effulgence under the glare of free-space sunlight.

"Too bad Earl ran out of outside wall," said Jean. "A collection of stained-glass windows runs into a lot of wallspace, and one is hardly a collection.... Perhaps there's another room...." For the study, large as it was, apparently occupied only half the space permitted by the dimensions of Earl's suite. "But—for the moment—I've got enough here to look at."

Racks, cases, files, walnut-and-leaded-glass cabinets surfaced the walls; glass-topped displays occupied the floor. To her left was a battery of tanks. In the first series swam eels, hundreds of eels: Earth eels, eels from the outer worlds. She opened a cabinet. Chinese coins hung on pegs, each documented with crabbed boyish handwriting.

She circled the room, marveling at the profusion.

There were rock crystals from forty-two separate planets, all of which appeared identical to Jean's unpracticed eye.

There were papyrus scrolls, Mayan codices, medieval parchments illuminated with gold and Tyrian purple, Ogham runes on moldering sheepskin, clay cylinders incised with cuneiform.

Intricate wood carvings—fancy chains, cages within cages, amazing interlocking spheres, seven vested Brahmin temples.

Centimeter cubes containing samples of every known element. Thousands of postage stamps, mounted on leaves, swung out of a circular cabinet.

There were volumes of autographs of famous criminals, together with their photographs and Bertillon and Pevetsky measurements. From one corner came the rich aromas of perfumes—a thousand little flagons minutely described and coded, together with the index and code explanation, and these again had their origin on a multitude of worlds. There were specimens of fungus growths from all over the universe, and there were racks of miniature phonograph records, an inch across, micro-formed from the original pressings.

She found photographs of Earl's everyday life, together with his weight, height and girth measurement in crabbed handwriting, and each picture bore a colored star, a colored square and either a red or blue disc. By this time Jean knew the flavor of Earl's personality. Near at hand there would be an index and explanation. She found it, near the camera which took the pictures. The discs referred to bodily functions; the stars, by a complicated system she could not quite comprehend, described Earl's morale, his frame of mind. The colored squares recorded his love life. Jean's mouth twisted in a wry grin. She wandered aimlessly on, fingering the physiographic globes of a hundred planets and examining maps and charts.

The cruder aspects of Earl's personality were represented in a collection of pornographic photographs, and near at hand an easel and canvas where Earl was composing a lewd study of his own. Jean pursed her mouth primly. The prospect of marrying Earl was becoming infinitely less enchanting.

She found an alcove filled with little chessboards, each set up in a game. A numbered card and record of moves was attached to each board. Jean picked up the inevitable index book and glanced through. Earl played postcard chess with opponents all over the universe. She found his record of wins and losses. He was slightly but not markedly a winner. One man, William Angelo of Toronto, beat him consistently. Jean memorized the address, reflecting that if Earl ever took up her challenge to play chess, now she knew how to beat him. She would embroil Angelo in a game, and send Earl's moves to Angelo as her own and play Angelo's return moves against Earl. It would be somewhat circuitous and tedious, but foolproof—almost.

She continued her tour of the study. Seashells, moths, dragonflies, fossil trilobites, opals, torture implements, shrunken human heads. If the collection represented bona fide learning, thought Jean, it would have taxed the time and ability of any four Earth geniuses. But the hoard was essentially mindless and mechanical, nothing more than a boy's collection of college pennants or signs or match-box covers on a vaster scale.

One of the walls opened out into an ell, and here was communication via a freight hatch to outside space. Unopened boxes, crates, cases, bundles—apparently material as yet to be filed in Earl's rookery—filled the room. At the corner another grotesque and monumental creature hung poised, as if to clutch at her, and Jean felt strangely hesitant to wander within its reach. This one stood about eight feet tall. It wore the shaggy coat of a bear and vaguely resembled a gorilla, although the face was long and pointed, peering out from under the fur, like that of a French poodle.

Jean thought of Fotheringay's reference to Earl as an "eminent zoologist." She looked around the room. The stuffed animals, the tanks of eels, Earth tropical fish and Maniacan polywriggles were the only zoological specimens in sight. Hardly enough to qualify Earl as a zoologist. Of course, there was an annex to the room. . . . She heard a sound. A click at the outer door.

Jean dived behind the stuffed animal, heart thudding in her throat. With exasperation she told herself, *He's an eighteen-year-old boy. . . . If I can't face him down, out-argue, out-think, out-fight him, and come out on top generally, then it's time for me to start crocheting table mats for a living.* Nevertheless, she remained hidden.

Earl stood quietly in the doorway. The door swung shut behind him. His face was flushed and damp, as if he had just recovered from anger or embarrassment. His delft blue eyes gazed unseeingly down the roof, gradually came into focus.

He frowned, glanced suspiciously right and left, sniffed. Jean made herself small behind the shaggy fur. Could he smell her?

He coiled up his legs, kicked against the wall, dived directly toward her. Under the creature's arm she saw him approaching, bigger, bigger, bigger, arms at his sides, head turned up like a diver. He thumped against the hairy chest, put his feet to the ground, stood not six feet distant.

He was muttering under his breath. She heard him plainly. "Damnable insult. . . . If she only *knew! Hah!*" He laughed a loud scornful bark. *Hah!*"

Jean relaxed with a near-audible sigh. Earl had not seen her, and did not suspect her presence.

He whistled aimlessly between his teeth, indecisively. At last he walked to the wall, reached behind a bit of ornate fretwork. A panel swung aside, a flood of bright sunlight poured through the opening into the study.

Earl was whistling a tuneless cadence. He entered the room but did not shut the door. Jean darted from behind her hiding place, looked in, swept the room with her eyes. Possibly she gasped.

Earl was standing six feet away, reading from a list. He looked up suddenly, and Jean felt the brush of his eyes.

He did not move. . . . Had he seen her?

For a moment he made no sound, no stir. Then he came to the door, stood staring up the study and held this position for ten or fifteen seconds. From behind the stuffed gorilla-thing Jean saw his lips move, as if he were silently calculating.

She licked her lips, thinking of the inner room.

He went out into the alcove, among the unopened boxes and bales. He pulled up several, floated them toward the open door, and they drifted into the flood of sunshine. He pushed other bundles aside, found what he was seeking, and sent another bundle after the rest.

He pushed himself back to the door, where he stood suddenly tense, nose dilated, eyes keen, sharp. He sniffed the air. His eyes swung to the stuffed monster. He approached it slowly, arms hanging loose from his shoulders.

He looked behind, expelled his breath in a long drawn hiss, grunted. From within the annex Jean thought, *He can either smell me, or it's telepathy!* She darted into the room while Earl was fumbling among the crates, and ducked under a wide divan. Flat on her stomach she watched Earl's inspection of the stuffed animal, and her skin tingled. *He smells me, he feels me, he senses me.*

Earl stood in the doorway, looking up and down the study. Then he carefully, slowly, closed the door, threw a bolt home, turned to face into the inner room.

For five minutes he busied himself with his crates, unbundling, arranging the contents, which seemed to be bottles of white powder, on shelves.

Jean pushed herself clear of the floor, up against the underside of the divan and moved to a position where she could see without being seen. Now she understood why Fotheringay had spoken of Earl as an "eminent zoologist."

There was another word which would fit him better, an unfamiliar word which Jean could not immediately dredge out of her memory. Her vocabulary was no more extensive than any girl of her own age, but the word had made an impression.

Teratology. That was the word. Earl was a teratologist.

Like the objects in his other collections, the monsters were only such creatures as lent themselves to ready, almost haphazard collecting. They were displayed in glass cabinets. Panels at the back screened off the sunlight, and at absolute zero, the things would remain preserved indefinitely without taxidermy or embalming.

They were a motley, though monstrous group. There were true human monsters, macro- and micro-cephalics, hermaphrodites, creatures with multiple limbs and with none, creatures sprouting tissues like buds on a yeast cell, twisted hoop-men, faceless things, things green, blue, and gray.

And then there were other specimens equally hideous, but possibly normal in their own environment: the miscellany of a hundred life-bearing planets.

To Jean's eyes, the ultimate travesty was a fat man, displayed in a place of prominence! Possibly he had gained the conspicuous position on his own merits. He was corpulent to a degree Jean had not considered possible. Beside him Webbard might show active and athletic. Take this creature to Earth, he would slump like a jellyfish. Out here on Abercrombie he floated free, bloated and puffed like the throat of a singing frog! Jean looked at his face—looked again! Tight blond curls on his head. . . .

Earl yawned, stretched. He proceeded to remove his clothes. Stark naked he stood in the middle of the room. He lookedly slowly, sleepily along the ranks of his collection.

He made a decision, moved languidly to one of the cubicles. He pulled a switch.

Jean heard a faint musical hum, a hissing, smelled heady ozone. A moment passed. She heard a sigh of air. The inner door of a glass cubicle opened. The creature within, moving feebly, drifted out into the room. . . .

Jean pressed her lips tight together; after a moment looked away.

Marry Earl? She winced. *No, Mr. Fotheringay. You marry him yourself, you're as able as I am. . . . Two million dollars?* She shuddered. Five million sounded better. For five million she might marry him. But that's as far as it would go. She'd put on her own ring, there'd be no kissing of the bride. She was Jean Parlier, no plaster saint. But enough was enough, and this was too much.

7

Presently Earl left the room. Jean lay still, listened. No sound came from outside. She must be careful. Earl would surely kill her if he found her here. She waited five minutes. No sound, no motion reached her. Cautiously she edged herself out from under the divan.

The sunlight burned her skin with a pleasant warmth, but she hardly felt it. Her skin seemed stained; the air seemed tainted and soiled her throat, her lungs. She wanted a bath. . . . Five million dollars would buy lots of baths. Where was the index? Somewhere would be an index. There had to be an index. . . . Yes. She found it, and quickly consulted the proper entry. It gave her much meat for thought.

There was also an entry describing the revitalizing mechanism. She glanced at it hurriedly, understanding little. Such things existed, she knew. Tremendous magnetic fields streamed through the protoplasm, gripping and binding tight each individual atom, and when the object was kept at absolute zero, energy expenditure dwindled to near-nothing. Switch off the clamping field, kick the particles back into motion with a penetrating vibration, and the creature returned to life.

She returned the index to its place, pushed herself to the door.

No sound came from outside. Earl might be writing or coding the events of the day on his phonogram. . . . Well, so then? She was not helpless. She opened the door, pushed boldly through.

The study was empty!

She dived to the outer door, listened. A faint sound of running water reached her ears. Earl was in the shower. This would be a good time to leave.

She pressed the door-slide. The door snapped open. She stepped out into Earl's bedroom, pushed herself across to the outer door.

Earl came out of the bathroom, his stocky fresh-skinned torso damp with water.

He stood stock-still, then hastily draped a towel around his middle. His face suddenly went mottled red and pink. "What are you doing in here?"

Jean said sweetly, "I came to check on your linen, to see if you needed towels."

He made no answer, but stood watching her. He said harshly, "Where have you been this last hour?"

Jean made a flippant gesture. "Here, there. Were you looking for me?"

He took a stealthy step forward. "I've a good mind to—"

"To what?" Behind her she fumbled for the door-slide.

"To—"

The door opened.

"Wait," said Earl. He pushed himself forward.

Jean slipped out into the corridor, a foot ahead of Earl's hands.

"Come back in," said Earl, making a clutch for her.

From behind them Mrs. Blaiskell said in a horrified voice, "Well, I never! Mr. Earl!" She had appeared from Mrs. Clara's room.

Earl backed into his room hissing unvoiced curses. Jean looked in after him. "The next time you see me, you'll wish you'd played chess with me."

"Jean!" barked Mrs. Blaiskell.

Earl asked in a hard voice, "What do you mean?"

Jean had no idea what she meant. Her mind raced. Better keep her ideas to herself. "I'll tell you tomorrow morning." She laughed mischievously. "About six or six-thirty."

"Miss Jean!" cried Mrs. Blaiskell angrily. "Come away from that door this instant!"

Jean calmed herself in the servants' refectory with a pot of tea.

Webbard came in, fat, pompous, and fussy as a hedgehog. He spied Jean and his voice rose to a reedy oboe tone. "Miss, miss!"

Jean had a trick she knew to be effective, thrusting out her firm young chin, squinting, charging her voice with metal. "Are you looking for me?"

Webbard said, "Yes, I certainly am. Where on earth—"

"Well, I've been looking for you. Do you want to hear what I'm going to tell you in private or not?"

Webbard blinked. "Your tone of voice is impudent, miss. If you please—"

"Okay," said Jean. "Right here, then. First of all, I'm quitting. I'm going back to Earth. I'm going to see—"

Webbard held up his hand in alarm, looked around the refectory. Conversation along the tables had come to a halt. A dozen curious eyes were watching.

"I'll interview you in my office," said Webbard.

The door slid shut behind her. Webbard pressed his rotundity into a chair; magnetic strands in his trousers held him in place. "Now, what is all this? I'll have you know there've been serious complaints."

Jean said disgustedly, "Tie a can to it, Webbard. Talk sense."

Webbard was thunderstruck. "You're an impudent minx!"

"Look. Do you want me to tell Earl how I landed the job?"

Webbard's face quivered. His mouth fell open; he blinked four or five times rapidly. "You wouldn't dare to—"

Jean said patiently, "Forget the master-slave routine for five minutes, Webbard. This is man-to-man talk."

"What do you want?"

"I've a few questions I want to ask you."

"Well?"

"Tell me about old Mr. Abercrombie, Mrs. Clara's husband."

"There's nothing to tell. Mr. Justus was a very distinguished gentleman."

"He and Mrs. Clara had how many children?"

"Seven."

"And the oldest inherits the Station?"

"The oldest, always the oldest. Mr. Justus believed in firm organization. Of course the other children were guaranteed a home here at the Station, those who wished to stay."

"And Hugo was the oldest. How long after Mr. Justus did he die?"

Webbard found the conversation distasteful. "This is all footling nonsense," he growled in a deep voice.

"How long?"

"Two years."

"And what happened to him?"

Webbard said briskly, "He had a stroke. Cardiac complaint. Now, what's all this I hear about your quitting?"

"How long ago?"

"Ah—two years."

"And then Earl inherited?"

Webbard pursed his lips. "Mr. Lionel unfortunately was off the Station, and Mr. Earl became legal master."

"Rather nice timing, from Earl's viewpoint."

Webbard puffed out his cheeks. "Now then, young lady, we've had enough of that! If—"

"Mr. Webbard, let's have an understanding once and for all. Either you answer my questions and stop this blustering or I'll ask someone else. And when I'm done, that someone else will be asking you questions too."

"You insolent little trash!" snarled Webbard.

Jean turned toward the door. Webbard grunted, thrashed himself forward. Jean gave her arm a shake; out of nowhere a blade of quivering glass appeared in her hand.

Webbard floundered in alarm, trying to halt his motion through the air. Jean put up her foot, pushed him in the belly, back toward his chair.

She said, "I want to see a picture of the entire family."

"I don't have any such pictures."

Jean shrugged. "I can go to any public library and dial the Who's-Who." She looked him over coolly, as she coiled her knife. Webbard shrank back in his chair. Perhaps he thought her a homicidal maniac. Well, she wasn't a maniac and she wasn't homicidal either, unless she was driven to it. She asked easily, "Is it a fact that Earl is worth a billion dollars?"

Webbard snorted. "A billion dollars? Ridiculous! The family owns nothing but the Station and lives off the income. A hundred million dollars would build another twice as big and luxurious."

"Where did Fotheringay get that figure?" she asked wonderingly.

"I couldn't say," Webbard replied shortly.

"Where is Lionel now?"

Webbard pulled his lips in and out desperately. "He's—resting somewhere along the Riviera."

"Hm. . . . You say you don't have any photographs?"

Webbard scratched his chin. "I believe that there's a shot of Lionel. . . . Let me see. . . . Yes, just a moment." He fumbled in his desk, pawed and peered, and at last came up with a snapshot. "Mr. Lionel."

Jean examined the photograph with interest. "Well, well." The face in the photograph and the face of the fat man in Earl's zoological collection were the same. "Well, well." She looked up sharply. "And what's his address?"

"I'm sure I don't know," Webbard responded with some return of his mincing dignity.

"Quit dragging your feet, Webbard."

"Oh, well—the Villa Passe-temps, Juan-les-pins."

"I'll believe it when I see your address file. Where is it?"

Webbard began breathing hard. "Now see here, young lady, there's serious matters at stake!"

"Such as what?"

"Well—" Webbard lowered his voice, glanced conspiratorially at the walls of the room. "It's common knowledge at the Station that Mr. Earl and Mr. Lionel are—well, not friendly. And there's a rumor—a rumor, mind you—that Mr. Earl has hired a well-known criminal to kill Mr. Lionel."

That would be Fotheringay, Jean surmised.

Webbard continued. "So you see, it's necessary that I exercise the utmost caution. . . ."

Jean laughed. "Let's see that file."

Webbard finally indicated a card file. Jean said, "You know where it is; pull it out."

Webbard glumly sorted through the cards. "Here."

The address was: Hotel Atlantide, Apartment 3001, French Colony, Metropolis, Earth.

Jean memorized the address, then stood irresolutely, trying to think of further questions. Webbard smiled slowly. Jean ignored him, stood nibbling her fingertips. Times like this she felt the inadequacy of her youth. When it came to action—fighting, laughing, spying, playing games, making love—she felt complete assurance. But the sorting out of possibilities and deciding which were probable and which irrational was when she felt less than sure. Such as now. . . . Old Webbard, the fat blob, had calmed himself and was gloating. Well, let him enjoy himself. . . . She had to get to Earth. She had to see Lionel Abercrombie. Possibly Fotheringay had been hired to kill him, possibly not. Possibly Fotheringay knew where to find him, possibly not. Webbard knew Fotheringay; probably he had served as Earl's intermediary. Or possibly Webbard was performing some intricate evolutions of his own. It was plain that, now, her interests were joined with Lionel's, rather than Fotheringay's, because marrying Earl was clearly out of the question. Lionel must stay alive. If this meant double-crossing Fotheringay, too bad for Fotheringay. He could have told her more about Earl's "zoological collection" before he sent her up to marry Earl. . . . Of course, she told herself, Fotheringay would have no means of knowing the peculiar use Earl made of his specimens.

"Well?" asked Webbard with an unpleasant grin.

"When does the next ship leave for Earth?"

"The supply barge is heading back tonight."

"That's fine. If I can fight off the pilot. You can pay me now."

"Pay you? You've only done a day's work. You owe the Station for transportation, your uniform, your meals—"

"Oh, never mind." Jean turned, pulled herself into the corridor, went to her room, packed her belongings.

Mrs. Blaiskell pushed her head through the door. "Oh, there you are. . . ." She sniffed. "Mr. Earl has been inquiring for you. He wants to see you at once." It was plain that she disapproved.

"Sure," said Jean. "Right away."

Mrs. Blaiskell departed.

Jean pushed herself along the corridor to the loading deck. The barge pilot was assisting in the loading of some empty metal drums. He saw Jean and his face changed. "You again?"

"I'm going back to Earth with you. You were right. I don't like it here."

The pilot nodded sourly. "This time you ride in the storage. That way neither of us gets hurt. . . . I couldn't promise a thing if you're up forward."

"Suits me," said Jean. "I'm going aboard."

When Jean reached the Hotel Atlantide in Metropolis she wore a black dress and black pumps which she felt made her look older and more sophisticated. Crossing the lobby she kept a wary lookout for the house detective. Sometimes they nursed unkind suspicions toward un-accompanied young girls. It was best to avoid the police, keep them at a distance. When they found that she had no father, no mother, no guardian, their minds were apt to turn to some dreary government institution. On several occasions rather extreme measures to ensure her independence had been necessary.

But the Hotel Atlantide detective took no heed of the black-haired girl quietly crossing the lobby, if he saw her at all. The lift attendant observed that she seemed restless, as with either a great deal of pent enthusiasm or nervous. A porter on the thirtieth floor noticed her searching for an apartment number and mentally labeled her a person unfamiliar with the hotel. A chambermaid watched her press the bell at Apartment 3001, saw the door open, saw the girl jerk back in surprise, then slowly enter the apartment. Strange, thought the chambermaid, and speculated mildly for a few moments. Then she went to recharge the foam dispensers in the public bathrooms, and the incident passed from her mind.

The apartment was spacious, elegant, expensive. Windows overlooked Central Gardens and the Morison Hall of Equity behind. The furnishings were the work of a professional decorator, harmonious and sterile; a few incidental objects around the room, however, hinted of a woman's presence. But Jean saw no woman. There was only herself and Fotheringay.

Fotheringay wore subdued gray flannels and dark necktie. In a crowd of twenty people he would vanish.

After an instant of surprise he stood back. "Come in."

Jean darted glances around the room, half expecting a fat crumpled body. But possibly Lionel had not been at home, and Fotheringay was waiting.

"Well," he asked, "what brings you here?" He was watching her covertly. "Take a seat."

Jean sank into a chair, chewed at her lip. Fotheringay watched her catlike. Walk carefully. She prodded her mind. What legitimate excuse did she have for visiting Lionel? Perhaps Fotheringay had expected her to double-cross him. . . . Where was Hammond? Her neck tingled. Eyes were on her neck. She looked around quickly.

Someone in the hall tried to dodge out of sight. Not quickly enough. Inside Jean's brain a film of ignorance broke to release a warm soothing flood of knowledge.

She smiled, her sharp white little teeth showing between her lips. It had been a fat woman whom she had seen in the hall, a very fat woman, rosy, flushed, quivering.

"What are you smiling at?" inquired Fotheringay.

She used his own technique. "Are you wondering who gave me your address?"

"Obviously Webbard."

Jean nodded. "Is the lady your wife?"

Fotheringay's chin raised a hairbreadth. "Get to the point."

"Very well." She hitched herself forward. There was still a possibility that she was making a terrible mistake, but the risk must be taken. Questions would reveal her uncertainity, diminish her bargaining position. "How much money can you raise—right now? Cash."

"Ten or twenty thousand."

Her face must have showed disappointment.

"Not enough?"

"No. You sent me on a bum steer."

Fotheringay sat silently.

"Earl would no more make a pass at me than bite off his tongue. His taste in women is—like yours."

Fotheringay displayed no irritation. "But two years ago—"

"There's a reason for that." She raised her eyebrows ruefully. "Not a nice reason."

"Well, get on with it."

"He liked Earth girls because they were freaks. In his opinion, naturally. Earl likes freaks."

Fotheringay rubbed his chin, watching her with blank wide eyes. "I never thought of that."

"Your scheme might have worked out if Earl were halfway right-side up. But I just don't have what it takes."

Fotheringay smiled frostily. "You didn't come here to tell me that."

"No. I know how Lionel Abercrombie can get the Station for himself. ... Of course your name is Fotheringay."

"If my name is Fotheringay, why did you come here looking for me?"

Jean laughed, a gay ringing laugh. "Why do you think I'm looking for you? I'm looking for Lionel Abercrombie. Fotheringay is no use to me unless I can marry Earl. I can't. I haven't got enough of that stuff. Now I'm looking for Lionel Abercrombie."

8

Fotheringay tapped a well-manicured finger on a well-flanneled knee, and said quietly, "I'm Lionel Abercrombie."

"How do I know you are?"

He tossed her a passport. She glanced at it, tossed it back.

"Okay. Now—you have twenty thousand. That's not enough. I want two million. ... If you haven't got it, you haven't got it. I'm not unreasonable. But I want to make sure I get it when you do have it. ... So—you'll write me a deed, a bill of sale, something legal that gives me your interest in Abercrombie Station. I'll agree to sell it back to you for two million dollars."

Fotheringay shook his head. "That kind of agreement is binding on me but not on you. You're a minor."

Jean said, "The sooner I get clear of Abercrombie the better. I'm not greedy. You can have your billion dollars. I merely want two million. . . . Incidentally, how do you figure a billion? Webbard says the whole setup is only worth a hundred million."

Lionel's mouth twisted in a wintry smile. "Webbard didn't include the holdings of the Abercrombie guests. Some very rich people are fat. The fatter they get, the less they like life on Earth."

"They could always move to another resort station."

Lionel shook his head. "It's not the same atmosphere. Abercrombie is Fatman's World. The one small spot in all the universe where a fat man is proud of his weight." There was a wistful overtone in his voice.

Jean said softly, "And you're lonesome for Abercrombie yourself."

Lionel smiled grimly. "'Is that so strange?"

Jean shifted in her chair. "Now we'll go to a lawyer. I know a good one. Richard Mycroft. I want this deed drawn up without loopholes. Maybe I'll have to find myself a guardian, a trustee."

"You don't need a guardian."

Jean smiled complacently. "For a fact, I don't."

"You still haven't told me what this project consists of."

"I'll tell you when I have the deed. You don't lose a thing giving away property you don't own. And after you give it away, it's to my interest to help you get it."

Lionel rose to his feet. "It had better be good."

"It will be."

The fat woman came into the room. She was obviously an Earth girl, bewildered and delighted by Lionel's attentions. Looking at Jean her face became clouded with jealousy.

Out in the corridor Jean said wisely, "You get her up to Abercrombie, she'll be throwing you over for one of those fat rascals."

"Shut up!" said Lionel, in a voice like the whetting of a scythe.

The pilot of the supply barge said sullenly, "I don't know about this."

Lionel asked quietly, "You like your job?"

The pilot muttered churlishly, but made no further protest. Lionel buckled himself into the seat beside him. Jean, the horse-faced man named Hammond, two elderly men of professional aspect and uneasy manner settled themselves in the cargo hold.

The ship lifted free of the dock, pushed up above the atmosphere, lined out into Abercrombie's orbit.

The Station floated ahead, glinting in the sunlight.

The barge landed on the cargo deck, the handlers tugged it into its socket, the port sighed open.

"Come on," said Lionel. "Make it fast. Let's get it over with." He tapped Jean's shoulder. "You're first."

She led the way up the main core. Fat guests floated down past them, light and round as soapbubbles, their faces masks of surprise at the sight of so many bone-people.

Up the core, along the vinculum into the Abercrombie private sphere. They passed the Pleasaunce, where Jean caught a glimpse of Mrs. Clara, fat as a blutworst, with the obsequious Webbard.

They passed Mrs. Blaiskell. "Why, Mr. Lionel!" she gasped. "Well, I never, I never!"

Lionel brushed past. Jean, looking over her shoulder into his face, felt a qualm. Something dark smoldered in his eyes. Triumph, malice, vindication, cruelty. Something not quite human. If nothing else, Jean was extremely human, and was wont to feel uneasy in the presence of out-world life. . . . She felt uneasy now.

"Hurry," came Lionel's voice. "Hurry."

Past Mrs. Clara's chambers, to the door of Earl's bedroom. Jean pressed the button; the door slid open.

Earl stood before a mirror, tying a red and blue silk cravat around his bull-neck. He wore a suit of pearl gray gabardine, cut very full and padded to make his body look round and soft. He saw Jean in the mirror, behind her the hard face of his brother Lionel. He whirled, lost his footing, drifted ineffectually into the air.

Lionel laughed. "Get him, Hammond. Bring him along."

Earl stormed and raved. He was the master here, everybody get out. He'd have them all jailed, killed. He'd kill them himself. . . .

Hammond searched him for weapons, and the two professional-looking men stood uncomfortably in the background muttering to each other.

"Look here, Mr. Abercrombie," one of them said at last. "We can't be a party to violence. . . ."

"Shut up," said Lionel. "You're here as witnesses, as medical men. You're being paid to look, that's all. If you don't like what you see, that's too bad." He motioned to Jean. "Get going."

Jean pushed herself to the study door. Earl called out sharply: "Get away from there, get away! That's private, that's my private study!"

Jean pressed her lips together. It was impossible to avoid feeling pity for poor gnarled Earl. But—she thought of his "zoological collection." Firmly she covered the electric eye, pressed the button. The door swung open, revealing the glory of the stained glass glowing with the fire of heaven.

Jean pushed herself to the furry two-legged creature. Here she waited.

Earl made some difficulty about coming through the door. Hammond manipulated his elbows; Earl belched up a hoarse screech, flung himself forward, panting like a winded chicken.

Lionel said, "Don't fool with Hammond, Earl. He likes hurting people."

The two witnesses muttered wrathfully. Lionel quelled them with a look.

Hammond seized Earl by the seat of the pants, raised him over his head, walked with magnetic shoes gripping the deck across the cluttered floor of the study, with Earl flailing and groping helplessly.

Jean fumbled in the fretwork over the panel into the annex. Earl screamed, "Keep your hands out of there! Oh, how you'll pay, how you'll pay for this, how you'll pay!" His voice hoarsened, he broke into sobs.

Hammond shook him, like a terrier shaking a rat.

Earl sobbed louder.

The sound grated on Jean's ears. She frowned, found the button, pushed. The panel flew open.

They all moved into the bright annex, Earl completely broken, sobbing and pleading.

"There it is," said Jean.

Lionel swung his gaze along the collection of monstrosities. The out-world things, the dragons, basilisks, griffins, the armored insects, the great-eyed serpents, the tangles of muscle, the coiled creatures of fang, brain, cartilage. And then there were the human creatures, no less grotesque. Lionel's eyes stopped at the fat man.

He looked at Earl, who had fallen numbly silent.

"Poor old Hugo," said Lionel. "You ought to be ashamed of yourself, Earl."

Earl made a sighing sound.

Lionel said, "But Hugo is dead. . . . He's as dead as any of the other things. Right, Earl?" He looked at Jean. "Right?"

"I guess that's right," said Jean uneasily. She found no pleasure baiting Earl.

"Of course he's dead," panted Earl.

Jean went to the little key controlling the magnetic field.

Earl screamed, "You witch! You witch!"

Jean depressed the key. There was a musical hum, a hissing, a smell of ozone. A moment passed. There came a sigh of air. The cubicle opened with a sucking sound. Hugo drifted into the room.

He twitched his arms, gagged and retched, made a thin crying sound in his throat.

Lionel turned to his two witnesses. "Is this man alive?"

They muttered excitedly, "Yes, yes!"

Lionel turned to Hugo. "Tell them your name."

Hugo whispered feebly, pressed his elbows to his body, pulled up his atrophied little legs, tried to assume a fetal position.

Lionel asked the two men, "Is this man sane?"

They fidgeted. "That of course is hardly a matter we can determine offhand." There was further mumbling about tests, cephalographs, reflexes.

Lionel waited a moment. Hugo was gurgling, crying like a baby. "Well—is he sane?"

The doctors said, "He's suffering from severe shock. The deep-freeze classically has the effect of disturbing the synapses—"

Lionel asked sardonically, "Is he in his right mind?"

"Well—no."

Lionel nodded. "In that case—you're looking at the new master of Abercrombie Station."

Earl protested, "You can't get away with that, Lionel! He's been insane for a long time, and you've been off the Station!"

Lionel grinned wolfishly. "Do you want to take the matter into Admiralty Court at Metropolis?"

Earl fell silent. Lionel looked at the doctors, who were whispering heatedly together.

"Talk to him," said Lionel. "Satisfy yourself whether he's in his right mind or not."

The doctors dutifully addressed Hugo, who made mewing sounds. They came to an uncomfortable but definite decision. "Clearly this man is not able to conduct his own affairs."

Earl pettishly wrenched himself from Hammond's grasp. "Let go of me."

"Better be careful," said Lionel. "I don't think Hammond likes you."

"I don't like Hammond," said Earl viciously. "I don't like anyone." His voice dropped in pitch. "I don't even like myself." He stood staring into the cubicle which Hugo had vacated.

Jean sensed a tide of recklessness rising in him. She opened her mouth to speak.

But Earl had already started.

Time stood still. Earl seemed to move with bewildering slowness, but the others stood as if frozen in jelly.

Time turned on for Jean. "I'm getting out of here!" she gasped, knowing what the half-crazed Earl was about to do.

Earl ran down the line of his monsters, magnetic shoes slapping on the deck. As he ran, he flipped switches. When he finished he stood at the far end of the room. Behind him things came to life.

Hammond gathered himself, plunged after Jean. A black arm apparently groping at random caught hold of his leg. There was a dull cracking sound. Hammond bawled out in terror.

Jean started through the door. She jerked back, shrieking. Facing her was the eight-foot gorilla-thing with the French poodle face. Somewhere along the line Earl had thrown a switch relieving it from magnetic catalepsy. The black eyes shone, the mouth dripped, the hands clenched and unclenched. Jean shrank back.

There were horrible noises from behind. She heard Earl gasping in sudden fear. But she could not turn her eyes from the gorilla-thing. It drifted into the room. The black dog-eyes looked deep into Jean's. She could not move! A great black arm, groping mindlessly, fell past Jean's shoulder, touched the gorilla-thing.

There was screaming bedlam. Jean pressed herself against the wall. A green flapping creature, coiling and uncoiling, twisted out into the study, smashing racks, screens, displays, sending books, minerals, papers, mechanisms, cases and cabinets floating and crashing. The gorilla-thing came after, one of its arms twisted and loose. A rolling flurry of webbed feet, scales, muscular tail and a human body followed—Hammond and a griffin from a world aptly named Pest-Hole.

Jean darted through the door, thought to hide in the alcove. Outside, on the deck, was Earl's spaceboat. She shoved herself across to the port.

Behind, frantically scrambling, came one of the doctors whom Lionel had brought along for a witness.

Jean called, "Over here, over here!"

The doctor threw himself into the spaceboat.

Jean crouched by the port, ready to slam it at any approach of danger.... She sighed. All her hopes, plans, future had exploded. Death, debacle, catastrophe were hers instead.

She turned to the doctor. "Where's your partner?"

"Dead! Oh Lord, oh Lord, what can we do?"

Jean turned her head to look at him, lips curling in disgust. Then she saw him in a new, flattering light. A disinterested witness. He looked like money. He could testify that for at least thirty seconds Lionel had been master of Abercrombie Station. Thirty seconds was enough to transfer title to her. Whether Hugo were sane or not didn't matter because Hugo had died thirty seconds before the metal frog with the knife-edged scissor-bill had fixed on Lionel's throat.

Best to make sure. "Listen," said Jean. "This may be important. Suppose you were to testify in court. Who died first, Hugo or Lionel?"

The doctor sat quiet a moment. "Why, Hugo! I saw his neck broken while Lionel was still alive."

"Are you sure?"

"Oh, yes." He tried to pull himself together. "We must do something."

"Okay," said Jean. "What shall we do?"

"I don't know."

From the study came a gurgling sound, and an instant later, a woman's scream. "God!" said Jean. "The things have got out into the inner bedroom.... What they won't do to Abercrombie Station...." She lost control and retched against the hull of the boat.

A brown face like a poodle dog's, spotted red with blood, peered around the corner at them. Stealthily it pulled itself closer.

Mesmerized, Jean saw that now its arm had been twisted entirely off. It darted forward. Jean fell back, slammed the port. A heavy body thudded against the metal.

They were closed in Earl's spaceboat. The man had fainted. Jean said, "Don't die on me, fellow. You're worth money...."

Faintly through the metal came crashing and thumping. Then came the muffled *spatttt* of proton guns.

The guns sounded with monotonous regularity. *Spatttt . . . spatttt . . . spatttt . . . spatttt . . . spatttt. . . .*

Then there was utter silence.

Jean inched open the port. The alcove was empty. Across her vision drifted the broken body of the gorilla-thing.

Jean ventured into the alcove, looked out into the study. Thirty feet distant stood Webbard, planted like a pirate captain on the bridge of his ship. His face was white and wadded; pinched lines ran from his nose around his nearly invisible mouth. He carried two big proton guns; the orifices of both were white-hot.

He saw Jean; his eyes took on a glitter. "You! It's you that's caused all this, your sneaking and spying!"

He jerked up his proton guns.

"No!" cried Jean. "It's not my fault!"

Lionel's voice came weakly. "Put down those guns, Webbard." Clutching his throat he pushed himself into the study. "That's the new owner," he croaked sardonically. "You wouldn't want to murder your boss, would you?"

Webbard blinked in astonishment. "Mr. Lionel!"

"Yes," said Lionel. "Home again. . . . And there's quite a mess to clean up, Webbard. . . ."

Jean looked at the bankbook. The figures burned into the plastic, spread almost all the way across the tape.

"Two million dollars."

Mycroft puffed on his pipe, looked out the window. "There's a matter you should be considering," he said. "That's the investment of your money. You won't be able to do it by yourself; other parties will insist on dealing with a responsible entity—that is to say, a trustee or guardian."

"I don't know much about these things," said Jean. "I—rather assumed that you'd take care of them."

Mycroft reached over, tapped the dottle out of his pipe.

"Don't you want to?" asked Jean.

Mycroft said with a compressed distant smile, "Yes, I want to. . . . I'll be glad to administer a two-million-dollar estate. In effect, I'll become your legal guardian, until you're of age. We'll have to get a court order of appointment. The effect of the order will be to take control of the money out of your hands; we can include in the articles, however, a clause guaranteeing you the full income—which I assume is what you want. It should come to—oh, say fifty thousand a year after taxes."

"That suits me," said Jean listlessly. "I'm not too interested in anything right now. . . . There seems to be something of a letdown."

Mycroft nodded. "I can see how that's possible."

Jean said, "I have the money. I've always wanted it, now I have it. And now—" She held out her hands, raised her eyebrows. "It's just a number in a bankbook. . . . Tomorrow morning I'll get up and say to myself, 'What shall I do today? Shall I buy a house? Shall I order a thousand dollars worth of clothes? Shall I start out on a two-year tour of Argo Navis?' And the answer will come out, 'No, the hell with it all.' "

"What you need," said Mycroft, "are some friends, nice girls your own age."

Jean's mouth moved in rather a sickly smile. "I'm afraid we wouldn't have much in common. . . . It's probably a good idea, but—it wouldn't work out." She sat passively in the chair, her wide mouth drooping.

Mycroft noticed that in repose it was a sweet generous mouth.

She said in a low voice, "I can't get out of my head the idea that somewhere in the universe I must have a mother and a father. . . ."

Mycroft rubbed his chin. "People who'd abandon a baby in a saloon aren't worth thinking about, Jean."

"I know," she said in a dismal voice. "Oh, Mr. Mycroft, I'm so damn lonely. . . ." Jean was crying, her head buried in her arms.

Mycroft irresolutely put his hand on her shoulder, patted awkwardly.

After a moment she said, "You'll think I'm an awful fool."

"No," said Mycroft gruffly. "I think nothing of the kind. I wish that I . . ." He could not put it into words.

She pulled herself together, rose to her feet. "Enough of this. . . ." She turned his head up, kissed his chin. "You're really very nice, Mr. Mycroft. . . . But I don't want sympathy. I hate it. I'm used to looking out for myself."

Mycroft returned to his seat, loaded his pipe to keep his fingers busy. Jean picked up her little handbag. "Right now I've got a date with a couturier named André. He's going to dress me to an inch of my life. And then I'm going to—" She broke off. "I'd better not tell you. You'd be alarmed and shocked."

He cleared his throat. "I expect I would."

She nodded brightly. "So long." Then she left his office.

Mycroft cleared his throat again, hitched up his trousers, settled his jacket, returned to his work. . . . Somehow it appeared dull, drab, gray. His head ached.

He said, "I feel like going out and getting drunk. . . ."

Ten minutes passed. His door opened. Jean looked in.

"Hello, Mr. Mycroft."

"Hello, Jean."

"I changed my mind. I thought it would be nicer if I took you out to dinner, and then maybe we could go to a show. . . . Would you like that?"

"Very much," said Mycroft.

SHIPPING CLERK

---

by William Morrison

Weight problems are caused by the fact that too much food is coming into the body and not enough is leaving. In "Shipping Clerk" the late William Morrison (Joseph Samachson) concentrates on the source of the intake and what can be done about it.

If there had ever been a time when Ollie Keith hadn't been hungry, it was so far in the past that he couldn't remember it. He was hungry now as he walked through the alley, his eyes shifting lusterlessly from one heap of rubbish to the next. He was hungry through and through, all one hundred and forty pounds of him, the flesh distributed so gauntly over his tall frame that in spots it seemed about to wear through, as his clothes had. That it hadn't done so in forty-two years sometimes struck Ollie as in the nature of a miracle.

He worked for a junk collector and he was unsuccessful in his present job, as he had been at everything else. Ollie had followed the first part of the rags-to-riches formula with classic exactness. He had been born to rags, and then, as if that hadn't been enough, his parents had died, and he had been left an orphan. He should have gone to the big city, found a job in the rich merchant's counting house, and saved the pretty daughter, acquiring her and her fortune in the process.

It hadn't worked out that way. In the orphanage where he had spent so many unhappy years, both his food and his education had been skimped. He had later been hired out to a farmer, but he hadn't been strong enough for farm labor, and he had been sent back.

His life since then had followed an unhappy pattern. Lacking strength and skill, he had been unable to find and hold a good job. Without a good job, he had been unable to pay for the food and medical care, and for the training he would have needed to acquire strength and skill. Once, in the search for food and training, he had offered himself

170

to the Army, but the doctors who examined him had quickly turned thumbs down, and the Army had rejected him with contempt. They wanted better human material than that.

How he had managed to survive at all to the present was another miracle. By this time, of course, he knew, as the radio comic put it, that he wasn't long for this world. And to make the passage to another world even easier, he had taken to drink. Rot gut stilled the pangs of hunger even more effectively than inadequate food did. And it gave him the first moments of happiness, spurious though they were, that he could remember.

Now, as he sought through the heaps of rubbish for usuable rags or redeemable milk bottles, his eyes lighted on something unexpected. Right at the edge of the curb lay a small nut, species indeterminate. If he had his usual luck, it would turn out to be withered inside, but at least he could hope for the best.

He picked up the nut, banged it futilely against the ground, and then looked around for a rock with which to crack it. None was in sight. Rather fearfully, he put it in his mouth and tried to crack it between his teeth. His teeth were in as poor condition as the rest of him, and the chances were that they would crack before the nut did.

The nut slipped and Ollie gurgled, threw his hands into the air, and almost choked. Then he got it out of his windpipe and, a second later, breathed easily. The nut was in his stomach, still uncracked. And Ollie, it seemed to him, was hungrier than ever.

The alley was a failure. His life had been a progression from rags to rags, and these last rags were inferior to the first. There were no milk bottles, there was no junk worth salvaging.

At the end of the alley was a barber shop, and here Ollie had a great and unexpected stroke of luck. He found a bottle. The bottle was no container for milk and it wasn't empty. It was standing on a small table near an open window in the rear of the barber shop. Ollie found that he could get it by simply stretching out his long, gaunt arm for it, without climbing in through the window at all.

He took a long swig, and then another. The liquor tasted far better than anything he had ever bought.

When he returned the bottle to its place, it was empty.

Strangely enough, despite its excellent quality, or perhaps, he thought, *because* of it, the whiskey failed to have its usual effect on him. It left him completely sober and clear-eyed, but hungrier than ever.

In his desperation, Ollie did something that he seldom dared to do. He went into a restaurant, not too good a restaurant or he would never have been allowed to take a seat, and ordered a meal he couldn't pay for.

He knew what would happen, of course, after he had eaten. He would put on an act about having lost his money, but that wouldn't fool the manager for more than one second. If the man was feeling good and needed help, he'd let Ollie work the price out washing dishes. If he was a little grumpy and had all the dishwashers he needed, he'd have them boot the tar out of Ollie and then turn him over to the police.

The soup was thick and tasty, although tasty in a way that no gourmet would have appreciated. The mess was food, however, and Ollie gulped it down gratefully. But it did nothing to satisfy his hunger. Likewise, the stew had every possible leftover thrown into it, and none of it gave Ollie any feeling of satisfaction. Even the dessert and the muddy coffee left him as empty as before.

The waiter had been in the back room with the cook. Now Ollie saw him signal to the manger, and watched the manager hasten back. He closed his eyes. They were onto him; there was no doubt about it. For a moment he considered trying to get out of the front door before they closed in, but there was another waiter present, keeping an eye on the patrons, and he knew that he would never make it. He took a deep breath and waited for the roof to fall in on him.

He heard the manager's footsteps and opened his eyes. The manager said, "Uh—look, bud, about that meal you ate—"

"Not bad," observed Ollie brightly.

"Glad you liked it."

He noticed little beads of sweat on the manager's forehead, and wondered what had put them there. He said, "Only trouble is, it ain't fillin'. I'm just as hungry as I was before."

"It didn't fill you up, huh? That's too bad. I'll tell you what I'll do. Rather than see you go away dissatisfied, I won't charge you for the meal. Not a cent."

Ollie blinked. This made no sense whatever. All the same, if not for the gnawing in his stomach, he would have picked himself up and run. As it was, he said, "Thanks. Guess in that case I'll have another order of stew. Maybe this time it'll stick to my ribs."

"Not the stew," replied the manager nervously. "You had the last that was left. Try the roast beef."

"Hmm, that's more than I was gonna spend."

"No charge," said the manager. "For you, no charge at all."

"Then gimme a double order. I feel starved."

The double order went down the hatch, yet Ollie felt just as empty as ever. But he was afraid to press his luck too far, and after he had downed one more dessert—also without charge—he reluctantly picked himself up and walked out. He was too hungry to spend any more time wondering why he had got a free meal.

In the back room of the restaurant, the manager sank weakly into a chair. "I was afraid he was going to insist on paying for it. Then we'd really have been on a spot."

"Guess he was too glad to get it for free," the cook said.

"Well, if anything happens to him now, it'll happen away from here."

"Suppose they take a look at what's in his stomach."

"He still won't be able to sue us. What did you do with the rest of that stew?"

"It's in the garbage."

"Cover it up. We don't want dead cats and dogs all over the place. And next time you reach for the salt, make sure there isn't an insect powder label on it."

"It was an accident; it could happen to anybody," said the cook philosophically. "You know, maybe we shouldn't have let him go away. Maybe we should've sent him to a doctor."

"And pay his bills? Don't be a sap. From now on, he's on his own. Whatever happens to him, we don't know anything about it. We never saw him before."

The only thing that was happening to Ollie was that he was getting hungrier and hungrier. He had, in fact, never before been so ravenous. He felt as if he hadn't eaten in years.

He had met with two strokes of luck—the accessible bottle and the incredibly generous manager. They had left him just as hungry and thirsty as before. Now he encountered a third gift of fortune. On the plate glass window of a restaurant was the flamboyant announcement: EATING CONTEST TONIGHT AT MONTE'S RESTAURANT! FOR THE CHAMPIONSHIP OF THE WORLD! ENTRIES BEING TAKEN NOW! NO CHARGE IF YOU EAT ENOUGH FOR AT LEAST THREE PEOPLE.

Ollie's face brightened. The way he felt, he could have eaten enough for a hundred. The fact that the contestants, as he saw upon reading further, would be limited to hard-boiled eggs made no difference to him. For once he would have a chance to eat everything he could get down his yawning gullet.

That night it was clear that neither the judges nor the audience thought much of Ollie as an eater. Hungry he undoubtedly was, but it was obvious that his stomach had shrunk from years of disuse, and besides, he didn't have the build of a born eater. He was long and skinny, whereas the other contestants seemed almost as broad and wide as they were tall. In gaining weight, as in so many other things, the motto seemed to be that those who already had would get more. Ollie had too little to start with.

In order to keep the contest from developing an anticlimax, they started with Ollie, believing that he would be lucky if he ate ten eggs.

Ollie was so ravenous that he found it difficult to control himself, and he made a bad impression by gulping the first egg as fast as he could. A real eater would have let the egg slide down rapidly yet gently, without making an obvious effort. This uncontrolled, amateur speed, thought the judges, could only lead to a stomachache.

Ollie devoured the second egg, the third, the fourth, and the rest of his allotted ten. At that point, one of the judges asked, "How do you feel?"

"Hungry."

"Stomach hurt?"

"Only from hunger. It feels like it got nothin' in it. Somehow, them eggs don't fill me up."

Somebody in the audience laughed. The judges exchanged glances and ordered more eggs brought on. From the crowd of watchers, cries of encouragement came to Ollie. At this stage, there was still nobody who thought that he had a chance.

Ollie proceeded to go through twenty eggs, forty, sixty, a hundred. By that time, the judges and the crowd were in a state of unprecedented excitement.

Again a judge demanded, "How do you feel?"

"Still hungry. They don't fill me up at all."

"But those are large eggs. Do you know how much a hundred of them weigh? Over fifteen pounds!"

"I don't care how much they weigh. I'm still hungry."

"Do you mind if we weigh you?"

"So long as you don't stop givin' me eggs, okay."

They brought out a scale and Ollie stepped on it. He weighed one hundred and thirty-nine pounds, on the nose.

Then he started eating eggs again. At the end of his second hundred, they weighed him once more. Ollie weighed one hundred thirty-eight and three-quarters.

The judges stared at each other and then at Ollie. For a moment the entire audience sat in awed silence, as if watching a miracle. Then the mood of awe passed.

One of the judges said wisely, "He palms them and slips them to a confederate."

"Out here on the stage?" demanded another judge. "Where's his confederate? Besides, you can see for yourself that he eats them. You can watch them going down his throat."

"But that's impossible. If they really went down his throat, he'd gain weight."

"I don't know how he does it," admitted the other. "But he does."

"The man is a freak. Let's get some doctors over here."

Ollie ate another hundred and forty-three eggs, and then had to stop because the restaurant ran out of them. The other contestants never even had a chance to get started.

When the doctor came and they told him the story, his first impulse seemed to be to grin. He knew a practical joke when he heard one. But they put Ollie on the scales—by this time he weighed only a hundred thirty-eight and a quarter pounds—and fed him a two-pound loaf of bread. Then they weighed him again.

He was an even one hundred and thirty-eight.

"At this rate, he'll starve to death," said the doctor, who opened his little black bag and proceeded to give Ollie a thorough examination.

Ollie was very unhappy about it because it interfered with his eating, and he felt more hungry than ever. But they promised to feed him afterward and, more or less unwillingly, he submitted.

"Bad teeth, enlarged heart, lesion on each lung, flat feet, hernia, displaced vertebrae—you name it and he has it," said the doctor. "Where the devil did he come from?"

Ollie was working on an order of roast beef and was too busy to reply.

Somebody said, "He's a rag-picker. I've seen him around."

"When did he start this eating spree?"

With stuffed mouth, Ollie mumbled, "Today."

"Today, eh? What happened today that makes you able to eat so much?"

"I just feel hungry."

"I can see that. Look, how about going over to the hospital so we can really examine you?"

"No, sir," said Ollie. "You ain't pokin' no needles into me."

"No needles," agreed the doctor hastily. If there was no other way to get blood samples, they could always drug him with morphine and he'd never know what had happened. "We'll just look at you. And we'll feed you all you can eat."

"All I can eat? It's a deal!"

The humor was crude, but it put the point across—the photographer assigned to the contest had snapped a picture of Ollie in the middle of gulping two eggs. One was traveling down his gullet, causing a lump in this throat, and the other was being stuffed into his mouth at the same time. The caption writer had entitled the shot: THE MAN WHO BROKE THE ICEBOX AT MONTE'S, and the column alongside was headed, Eats Three Hundred and Forty-three Eggs. "I'm Hungry!" he says.

Zolto put the paper down. "This is the one," he said to his wife. "There can be no doubt that this person has found it."

"I knew it was no longer in the alley," said Pojim. Ordinarily a comely female, she was now deep in thought, and succeeded in looking beautiful and pensive at the same time. "How are we to get it back without exciting unwelcome attention?"

"Frankly," said Zolto, "I don't know. But we'd better think of a way. He must have mistaken it for a nut and swallowed it. Undoubtedly the hospital attendants will take X-rays of him and discover it."

"They won't know what it is."

"They will operate to remove it, and then they will find out."

Pojim nodded. "What I don't understand," she said, "is why it had this effect. When we lost it, it was locked."

"He must have opened it by accident. Some of these creatures, I have noticed, have a habit of trying to crack nuts with their teeth. He must have bitten on the proper switch."

"The one for inanimate matter? I think, Zolto, that you're right. The stomach contents are collapsed and passed into our universe through the transfer. But the stomach itself, being part of a living creature, cannot pass through the same switch. And the poor creature continually loses weight because of metabolism. Especially, of course, when he eats."

"Poor creature, you call him? You're too soft-hearted, Pojim. What do you think we'll be if we don't get the transfer back?"

He hunched up his shoulders and laughed.

Pojim said, "Control yourself, Zolto. When you laugh, you don't look human, and you certainly don't sound it."

"What difference does it make? We're alone."

"You can never tell when we'll be overheard."

"Don't change the subject. What are we supposed to do about the transfer?"

"We'll think of a way," said Pojim, but he could see she was worried.

In the hospital, they had put Ollie into a bed. They had wanted a nurse to bathe him, but he had objected violently to this indignity, and finally they had sent in a male orderly to do the job. Now, bathed, shaven, and wearing a silly little nightgown that made him ashamed to look at himself, he was lying in bed, slowly starving to death.

A dozen empty plates, the remains of assorted specialties of the hospital, filled with vitamins and other good things, lay around him. Everything had tasted fine while going down, but nothing seemed to have stuck to him.

All he could do was brood about the puzzled and anxious looks on the doctors' faces when they examined him.

The attack came without warning. One moment Ollie was lying there unhappily, suffering hunger pangs, and the next moment somebody had punched him in the stomach. The shock made him start and then look down. But there was nobody near him. The doctors had left him alone while they looked up articles in textbooks and argued with each other.

He felt another punch, and then another and another. He yelled in fright and pain.

After five minutes, a nurse looked in and asked casually, "Did you call?"

"My stomach!" groaned Ollie. "Somebody's hittin' me in my stomach!"

"It's a tummyache," she said with a cheerful smile. "It should teach you not to wolf your food."

Then she caught a glimpse of his stomach, from which Ollie, in his agony, had cast off the sheet, and she gulped. It was swollen like a watermelon—or, rather, like a watermelon with great warts. Lumps stuck out all over it.

She rushed out, calling, "Doctor Manson! Doctor Manson!"

When she returned with two doctors, Ollie was in such acute misery that he didn't even notice them. One doctor said, "Well, I'll be damned!" and began tapping the swollen stomach.

The other doctor demanded, "When did this happen?"

"Right now, I guess," replied the nurse. "Just a few minutes ago his stomach was as flat as the way it was when you saw it."

"We'd better give him a shot of morphine to put him out of his pain," said the first doctor, "and then we'll X-ray him."

Ollie was in a semicoma as they lifted him off his bed and wheeled him into the X-ray room. He didn't hear a word of the ensuing discussion about the photographs, although the doctors talked freely in front of him—freely and profanely.

It was Dr. Manson who demanded, "What in God's name are those things, anyway?"

"They look like pineapples and grapefruit," replied the bewildered X-ray specialist.

"Square-edged pineapples? Grapefruit with one end pointed?"

"I didn't say that's what they are," returned the other defensively. "I said that's what they look like. The grapefruit could be eggplant," he added in confusion.

"Eggplant, my foot. How the devil did they get into his stomach, anyway? He's been eating like a pig, but even a pig couldn't have gotten those things down its throat."

"Wake him up and ask him."

"He doesn't know any more than we do," said the nurse. "He told me that it felt as if somebody was hitting him in the stomach. That's all he'd be able to tell us."

"He's got the damnedest stomach I ever heard of," marveled Dr. Manson. "Let's open it up and take a look at it from the inside."

"We'll have to get his consent," said the specialist nervously. "I know it would be interesting, but we can't cut into him unless he's willing."

"It would be for his own good. We'd get that unsliced fruit salad out of him." Dr. Manson stared at the X-ray plates again. "Pineapples, grapefruit, something that looks like a banana with a small bush on top. Assorted large round objects. And what looks like a nut. A small nut."

If Ollie had been aware, he might have told Dr. Manson that the nut was the kernel of the trouble. As it was, all he could do was groan.

"He's coming to," said the nurse.

"Good," asserted Dr. Manson. "Get a release, Nurse, and the minute he's capable of following directions, have him sign it."

In the corridor outside, two white-clad interns stopped at the door of Ollie's room and listened. They could not properly have been described as man and woman, but at any rate one was male and the other female. If you didn't look at them too closely, they seemed to be human, which, of course, was what they wanted you to think.

"Just as I said," observed Zolto. "They intend to operate. And their attention has already been drawn to the nut."

"We can stop them by violence, if necessary. But I abhor violence."

"I know, dear," Zolto said thoughtfully. "What has happened is clear enough. He kept sending all that food through, and our people analyzed it and discovered what it was. They must have been surprised to discover no message from us, but after a while they arrived at the conclusion that we needed some of our own food and they sent it to us. It's a good thing that they didn't send more of it at one time."

"The poor man must be in agony as it is."

"Never mind the poor man. Think of our own situation."

"But don't you see, Zolto? His digestive juices can't dissolve such unfamiliar chemical constituents, and his stomach must be greatly irritated."

She broke off for a moment as the nurse came past them, giving them only a casual glance. The X-ray specialist followed shortly, his face reflecting the bewilderment he felt as a result of studying the plate he was holding.

"That leaves only Dr. Manson with him," said Zolto. "Pojim, I have a plan. Do you have any of those pandigestive tablets with you?"

"I always carry them. I never know when in this world I'll run into something my stomach can't handle."

"Fine." Zolto stepped back from the doorway, cleared his throat, and began to yell, "Calling Dr. Manson! Dr. Manson, report to surgery!"

"You've been seeing too many of their movies," said Pojim.

But Zolto's trick worked. They heard Dr. Manson mutter, "Damn!" and saw him rush into the corridor. He passed them without even noticing that they were there.

"We have him to ourselves," said Zolto. "Quick, the tablets."

They stepped into the room, where Zolto passed a small inhalator back and forth under Ollie's nose. Ollie jerked away from it, and his eyes opened.

"Take this," said Pojim, with a persuasive smile. "It will ease your pain." And she put two tablets into Ollie's surprised mouth.

Automatically, Ollie swallowed and the tablets sped down to meet the collection in his stomach. Pojim gave him another smile, and then she and Zolto hurriedly left the room.

To Ollie, things seemed to be happening in more and more bewildering fashion. No sooner had these strange doctors left than Dr. Manson came rushing back, cursing, in a way that would have shocked Hippocrates, the unknown idiot who had summoned him to surgery. Then the nurse came in, with a paper. Ollie gathered that he was being asked to sign something.

He shook his head vigorously. "Not me. I don't sign *nothin'*, sister."

"It's a matter of life and death. Your own life and death. We have to get those things out of your stomach."

"No, sir, you're not cuttin' me open."

Dr. Manson gritted his teeth in frustration. "You don't feel so much pain now because of the morphine I gave you. But it's going to wear off in a few minutes and then you'll be in agony again. You'll have to let us operate."

"No, sir," repeated Ollie stubbornly. "You're not cuttin' me open."

And then he almost leaped from his bed. His already distended stomach seemed to swell outward, and before the astonished eyes of doctor and nurse, a strange new bump appeared.

"Help!" yelled Ollie.

"That's exactly what we're trying to do," said Dr. Manson angrily. "Only you won't let us. Now sign that paper, man, and stop your nonsense."

Ollie groaned and signed. The next moment he was being rushed into the operating room.

The morphine was wearing off rapidly, and he lay, still groaning, on the table. From the ceiling, bright lights beat down upon him. Near his head the anesthetist stood with his cone of sleep poised in readiness. At one side a happy Dr. Manson was slipping rubber gloves on his antiseptic hands, while the attentive nurses and assistants waited.

Two interns were standing near the doorway. One of them, Zolto, said softly, "We may have to use violence after all. They must not find it."

"I should have given him a third tablet," said Pojim, the other intern, regretfully. "Who would have suspected that the action would be so slow?"

They fell silent. Zolto slipped a hand into his pocket and grasped the weapon, the one he had hoped he wouldn't have to use.

Dr. Manson nodded curtly and said, "Anesthetic."

And then, as the anesthetist bent forward, it happened. Ollie's uncovered stomach, lying there in wait for the knife, seemed to heave and boil. Ollie shrieked and, as the assembled medicos watched in dazed fascination, the knobs and bumps smoothed out. The whole stomach began to shrink, like a cake falling in when someone has slammed the oven door. The pandigestive tablets had finally acted.

Ollie sat up. He forgot that he was wearing the skimpy and shameless nightgown, forgot, too, that he had a roomful of spectators. He pushed away the anesthetist who tried to stop him.

"I feel fine," he said.

"Lie down," ordered Dr. Manson sternly. "We're going to operate and find out what's wrong with you."

"You're not cuttin' into me," said Ollie. He swung his feet to the floor and stood up. "There ain't nothin' wrong with me. I feel wonderful. For the first time in my life I ain't hungry, and I'm spoilin' for trouble. Don't nobody try to stop me."

He started to march across the floor, pushing his way through the protesting doctors.

"This way," said one of the interns near the door. "We'll get your clothes." Ollie looked at her in suspicion, but she went on, "Remember? I'm the one who gave you the tablets to make the pain go away."

"They sure worked," said Ollie happily, and allowed himself to be led along.

He heard the uproar behind him, but he paid no attention. Whatever they wanted, he was getting out of here, fast. There might have been trouble, but at a critical point the public address system swung into operation, thanks to the foresight of his intern friends, who had rigged up a special portable attachment to the microphone. It started calling Dr. Manson, calling Dr. Kolanyi, calling Dr. Pumber, and all the others.

In the confusion, Ollie escaped and found himself, for the first time in his life, a passenger in a taxicab. With him were the two friendly interns, no longer in white.

"Just in case any more of those lumps appear in your stomach," said the female, "take another couple of tablets."

She was so persuasive that Ollie put up only token resistance. The tablets went down his stomach, and then he settled back to enjoy the cab ride. It was only later that he wondered where they were taking him. By that time, he was too sleepy to wonder very much.

With the aid of the first two tablets, he had digested the equivalent of a tremendous meal. The blood coursed merrily in his veins and arteries, and he had a warm sensation of well-being.

As the taxi sped along, his eyes closed.

"You transmitted the message in one of the latter tablets?" asked Zolto in their native tongue.

"I have explained all that has happened," replied his wife. "They will stop sending food and wait for other directives."

"Good. Now we'll have to get the transfer out of him as soon as possible. We ourselves can operate and he will never be the wiser."

"I wonder," said Pojim. "Once we have the transfer, it will only be a nuisance to us. We'll have to guard it carefully and be in continual fear of losing it. Perhaps it would be more sensible to leave it inside him."

"Inside him? Pojim, my sweet, have you taken leave of your senses?"

"Not at all. It is easier to guard a man than a tiny object. I took a look at one of the X-ray plates, and it is clear that the transfer switch has adhered to his stomach. It will remain there indefinitely. Suppose we focus a transpositor on that stomach of his. Then, as the objects we want arrive from our own universe in their collapsed condition, we can transpose them into our laboratory, enlarge them, and send them off to Aldebaran, where they are needed."

"But suppose that he and that stomach of his move around!"

"He will stay in one place if we treat him well. Don't you see, Zolto? He is a creature who has always lacked food. We shall supply him such food as his own kind have never dreamed of, complete with pandigestion fluid. At the same time, we shall set him to doing light work in order to keep him busy. Much of his task will involve studying and improving himself. And at night we shall receive the things we need from our own universe."

"And when we have enough to supply the colony on Aldebaran II?"

"Then it will be time enough to remove the transfer switch."

Zolto laughed. It was a laugh that would have been curiously out of place in a human being, and if the taxi driver hadn't been so busy steering his way through traffic, he would have turned around to look. Pojim sensed the danger, and held up a warning finger.

Zolto subsided. "You have remarkable ideas, my wife. Still, I see no reason why this should not work. Let us try it."

Ollie awoke to a new life. He was feeling better than he had ever felt in his entire miserable existence. The two interns who had come along with him had been transformed magically into a kindly lady and gentleman, who wished to hire him to do easy work at an excellent salary. Ollie let himself be hired.

He had his choice of things to eat now, but, strangely enough, he no longer had his old hunger. It was is if he were being fed from some hidden source, and he ate, one might almost have said, for the looks of it. The little he did consume, however, seemed to go a long way.

He gained weight, his muscles hardened, his old teeth fell out and new ones appeared. He himself was astonished at this latter phenomenon, but after his previous experience at the hospital, he kept his astonishment to himself. The spots on his lungs disappeared, his spine straightened. After a time he reached a weight of a hundred and ninety pounds, and his eyes were bright and clear. At night he slept the sleep of the just—or the drugged.

At first he was happy. But after several months, there came a feeling of boredom. He sought out Mr. and Mrs. Zolto, and said, "I'm sorry, I can't stay here any longer."

"Why?" asked the lady.

"There's no room here, ma'am, for advancement," he said, almost apologetically. "I've been studyin' and I got ideas about things I can do. All sorts of ideas."

Pojim and Zolto, who had planted the ideas, nodded solemnly.

Pojim said, "We're glad to hear that, Ollie. The fact is that we ourselves had decided to move to—to a warmer climate, some distance away from here. We were wondering how you'd get along without us."

"Don't you worry about me. I'll do fine."

"Well, that's splendid. But it would be convenient to us if you could wait till tomorrow. We'd like to give you something to remember us by."

"I'll be glad to wait, ma'am."

That night Ollie had a strange nightmare. He dreamed that he was on the operating table again, and that the doctors and nurses were once more closing in on him. He opened his mouth to scream, but no sound came out. And then the two interns were there, once more wearing their uniforms.

The female said, "It's all right. It's perfectly all right. We're just removing the transfer switch. In the morning you won't even remember what happened."

And, in fact, in the morning he didn't. He had only a vague feeling that something *had* happened.

They shook hands with him and gave him a very fine letter of reference, in case he tried to get another job, and Mrs. Zolto presented him with an envelope in which there were several bills whose size later made his eyes almost pop out of his head.

He walked down the street as if it belonged to him, or were going to. Gone was the slouch, gone the bleariness of the eyes, gone the hangdog look.

Gone was all memory of the dismal past.

And then Ollie had a strange feeling. At first it seemed so peculiar that he couldn't figure out what it was. It started in his stomach, which seemed to turn over and almost tie itself into a knot. He felt a twinge of pain and winced almost perceptibly.

It took him several minutes to realize what it was.

For the first time in months, he was hungry.

THE MALTED MILK MONSTER

by William Tenn

Many people who love to eat constantly think about food —they daydream about places where mountains are made of fudge, rivers of flowing chocolate, and so on. Here, the always brilliant William Tenn invites us to visit such a world.

From the moment he opened his eyes and saw the color of the sky, the shape of the clouds, the incredible topography, Carter Broun knew exactly where he was. He didn't really have to identify the blandly sweet smell which filled his nostrils, nor did he particularly have to investigate further the river of dark mahogany coursing, with the gentlest of roars, between two small, cone-shaped hills, two hills of exactly the same dimensions and sporting exactly the same vegetation.

There was just no doubt about it. Not after Carter had contemplated, for ten or fifteen awe-struck seconds, the sky of absolutely uniform and brilliant blue—bluey blue, *that* was the color, he decided morosely— and those oval, pink white clouds spaced so evenly across it. Not to mention those birds flapping into the narrowing distance; from here, each looked like a letter V, the arms of which had been carefully curved outward and down.

Only one place in the universe boasted such a landscape, such an atmosphere, such birds. This was The World of The Malted Milk Monster.

God help me, Carter thought, *now it's my world, too.*

That peculiar, ripping flash inside him, like some sort of lightning of the soul! He'd said good-bye to Lee at the door of her lawn-enclosed home and started down the neat suburban street to where his MG was parked. He'd been rolling the car keys around in his hand and planning the itinerary of his Friday night date with Lee—you either got a girl to your apartment by the second date, he had found, or you flunked out forever—when he'd noticed the Malted Milk Monster watching him unwinkingly from behind a hedge. Probably had followed them all the way from Goldie's Goodie Palace.

Then the flash, the mad sensation of being ripped out of his context and being shoved into another, entirely different place. And opening his eyes here.

It all came, and the knowledge was bitter, of taking your date to an ice cream parlor instead of an honest bar. But a bar didn't seem like the right follow-up to a Sunday afternoon movie in Grenville Acres. Besides, you don't take a schoolteacher to a bar on her home grounds. You pour an inoffensive soda into her, walk her home through the autumn streets, being as gentlemanly charming as possible, you decline the invitation to come in and meet the folks by mentioning the big report you have to prepare for tomorrow's Account Executive conference—a man has his work to do, and that must come first—and back you drive to Manhattan with the pleasant knowledge of a seduction intelligently initiated.

Unfortunately, you don't plan on other factors—unseen powers, for example.

There was not much point in checking, but he might as well check. Once he was really certain, he could begin worrying. And working out an escape.

Carter wandered down to the mahogany river across well-cropped grass and past large tinsel-type flowers. He knelt, dipped a finger in the thick liquid and tasted it. Chocolate. Of course.

Just on the off-chance, he pinched himself long and hard, squeezingly and painfully. It hurt enough. No, he'd known he hadn't been dreaming to begin with. For one thing, in a dream you rarely realize you're dreaming.

This was real.

Chocolate syrup to drink. And for food—

The two little hills were covered with dwarf trees bearing lollipops, the cellophane-wrapped fruit varying slightly in color from tree to tree. Here and there on the level ground were bonbon bushes and sharply triangular Christmas-tree affairs from whose twigs dangled small pies, cakes, and assorted cookies—most of them chocolate.

The sun beat down rosily, rosily, and none of the chocolate melted. The chocolate river, on the other hand, ran interminably and gurglingly. Whatever its sources, wherever it rose, the river evidently had plenty of reserves.

Carter was struck by an especially ugly thought. Suppose, viewing the river's affluence, suppose it *rained* chocolate! Really, one could not put anything past the Malted Milk Monster.

Lee had objected to the name.

"She's just a fat little girl. Rather brilliant, rather neurotic, too. And very curious about the strange, distinguished young man who's buying her teacher a soda."

"All right, but I've been counting," Carter had insisted. "Five chocolate malteds since we came in. *Five!* And the way she sits there at the end of the counter never taking her eyes off us, not even when she unwraps a fresh straw!"

"Most of the children in Grenville have more spending money than is good for them. Dorothy's parents are divorced—mother's a big-time buyer, father's a vice-president of a bank—and they use their money to fight for her affections. She spends practically all of her time in Goldie's. You know, Carter, that psychological equation: when I was small and my parents loved me, they gave me food; therefore, food equals love?"

Carter nodded. He knew all about such psychological equations. As a determined and well-sexed young bachelor, he had studied Freud as intently as a second lieutenant in the First World War might have studied von Clausewitz.

"You're so damned feminine," he announced warmly, underlining the points that, with any luck at all, would shortly be at issue. "Only a gal who was woman all the way through would be able to see in that ball of lard, that pimply Malted Milk Monster—"

"She's no such thing, Carter! What a terrible nickname for such a mixed-up little girl! Although," Lee mused, swirling the long spoon about in the residual muddy bubbles of her soda glass, "although it *is* funny you should think of it. That's what—or something like it—the other kids in the class call her. They tell stories about her—that she can make stones and flowerpots disappear just by staring hard at them. Kids are just like adults, a little more obvious, that's all. They make a witch out of the unpopular one."

He kept trying. "They never made one out of you, that's for sure. Anybody who's the slightest bit sensitive just has to look at you to know that love and loving—"

"It's so pathetic, really," she interrupted without knowing it. "I asked them to write a composition about the happiest day they could remember. Do you know what Dorothy wrote about? A day in her dream world, a day that never ever happened. And yet it was beautifully done, for a child her age. Full of affection-symbols like cake and candy. The world was supposed to smell like an ice cream parlor. Imagine! There was a finely written passage—you appreciate good writing, Carter, I know—about two cute little hills all covered with lollipop trees, each tree bearing a different flavor. And between the hills there wound a stream of purest chocolate!"

Carter gave up. He lit a cigarette and stared over Lee's earnest but nonetheless lovely head. At the grossly heavy little girl whose fat over-flowed the last stool in the ice cream parlor, her mouth sucking steadily at the chocolate malted milk, her eyes as steadily sucking at his. He found himself forced to drop his glance first.

"—even when we have a drawing lesson," Lee was still on it. "She never does anything else. It's absolutely real to the poor child—so lonely, so starved for companionship! I've learned to expect that flat blue sky full of oval pink clouds, those curved-line birds, that chocolate river, and all those bushes filled with goodies. Every single time! For a child of her intelligence, she's somewhat retarded graphically. She draws like a child a year or two younger. But that's to be expected: it's almost purely a verbal, a conceptual intelligence, you might say—"

You might also say the topic had created a highly annoying and useless diversion. Carter bit on the cigarette through his lips, looked up again cautiously. The Malted Milk Monster's eyes were as unwavering as ever. Such *pulling* power—what was so fascinating about him? Well, her father was a Madison Avenue type: the clothes, probably. Carter was justly proud of his wardrobe. His clothes, he knew, were in almost ostentatious good taste—they screamed restraint and expensive low-ness of key.

Yes, that was it. He reminded her of her father. Her rich father.

Carter caught himself preening and stubbed out the cigarette in abrupt harsh disgust. Damn it! That was the trouble with this Madison Avenue music—you laughed at it, you kidded others about it, you even read books satirizing it—and then you found yourself singing to it. He reminded her of her father who was the vice-president of a bank and probably quite well off. Well, so what? Did that say anything good about Carter Broun? Not necessarily at all, at all. Carter Broun was a well-educated, clever and rather lucky young man who had found his way into a well-paying, clever and extremely luck-flavored business.

A young man who had gotten so deeply involved in the superficiali-ties of the business that when a child as obviously and horrifyingly tormented as this little girl came to his attention, all he could see was a neat gag nickname—this kind of shallow, brilliant thing you'd toss off to a client at a sales conference.

Lee, now. Lee's roots were still wrapped around the compact, squirming mass of the human race. She loved her work but she *cared* too; she certainly cared. The way she goes on! The way her eyes shine as she talks!

"—the other children were positively stupefied. Or that time I asked them to make up riddles. Do you know what Dorothy asked when her turn came? Just listen to this, Carter. She asked the class: 'Which would you rather—be eaten by a giant caterpillar, or a million tiny little lions?' Now I maintain that a girl with that much imagination—"

"That much maladjustment," he corrected. "She sounds like a very sick kid. But I'd give a lot," he mused, "to see how she'd do on a Rorschach. A giant caterpillar, or a million tiny little lions . . . and without even ink-blots to go on! Do you know if she's ever had any psychotherapy?"

His companion had smiled grimly. "Her parents are very well off, I told you. I suspect she's had *all* the advantages. Up to and including protracted legal battles as to whether she's to go to poppa's doctor or momma's doctor. What that girl really needs, no one can give her: a different set of parents, or, at the least, one parent who really cares for her."

Carter had disagreed. "Not so much now, not at her age. I'd say it would be much more helpful at this point to have a couple of kids who like and accept her. If there's one thing that Motivational Research brings home to you, it's what thoroughgoing social animals we humans are. Without a matrix of companionship, without the interest and approval of at least a handful of our contemporaries, we're worse than mixed-up—we aren't even people. Hermits aren't people; I don't know what they are, exactly, but they're not people. And so long as that kid is a psychological hermit, she's not really a human person. She's something else."

Somewhere in the next fifteen minutes, he knew that he had clicked with Lee. But by then he was deep in the problem of how one could help a kid like Dorothy to make friends. It had become an MR problem, dealing with the individual, however, rather than the group; and, like all MR problems, of such obsessing interest to him that nothing else mattered.

In the end, it had been Lee who had changed the subject very forcefully; it had been Lee who had to drop hints about their next date. He'd managed to get a grip on himself and began talking about what they'd do when she came into town to meet him next Friday night. All in all, it had worked out quite well.

But as they left the soda shop, Carter had thrown just one last glance behind him through the plate-glass window. The Malted Milk Monster had turned on her stool, straw still in her mouth, eyes following him like a pair of starving sharks.

And then, of course, shadowing them all the way to Lee's home. What had she done to him? How had she done it? *Why?*

He kicked angrily at a loose stone, watched it bounce into the river with a thick brown splash. Was this one of the stones Dorothy had abstracted from the real world? Again, how? Not why, though; it could well have been part of a series of controlled experiments to test the range of her powers.

Powers? Was that the word? Talent, perhaps, or catalytic capacity —that might be more descriptive.

Given a very remarkable mind, given a very strong personality imbedded in a child's brain, given unhappiness, unpopularity, and general neurosis to sharpen that mind, to add even more punch to the personality—and what! *What* would develop?

He suddenly recalled his last thoughts before arriving in this lollipop world. Just after he'd left Lee, his head full of happy thoughts about Friday night, just at the very moment he'd seen the kid staring at him, he'd begun thinking about her problems again. The realization that she had followed them all the way from the soda shop out of sheer murderous loneliness had stimulated him into wondering about her mind.

There had been a sequence. First: *Gee, she's hungry for people.* Then: *Not for people in general, for kids her own age. How would you go about making kids like her? Now* there's *a motivation problem for you!* Then: *Well, the first question is what are her motives; what's it like in her mind?* Good professional MR unraveling technique.

And then that terrible flash, that mental rip, and he'd opened his eyes here.

In other words, he'd had something to do with it. It hadn't been all her. He'd been wide open psychologically, trying to visualize the inside of her mind, just as she had—as she had done something.

No, it still required something from her, for all this to have happened. And no matter what you called it—talent, powers, catalysis— she had it. And she'd used it on him.

Carter shivered suddenly, remembering the riddle she'd made up.

He was adrift in the fantasy life of that kind of kid. He wished he had paid attention to Lee's earlier discussion in the ice cream parlor instead of forcing the conversation back into more lucrative channels. To get out safely, to survive, he could use every scrap of information on Dorothy that had ever existed.

After all, her most meager wishes were now the fixed and immutable natural laws under which he had to operate.

He was no longer alone, he observed. He was surrounded by children. They had seemingly materialized all around him, yelling, playing, scrambling, jumping. And where the yelling was loudest, where the games were thickest, there was Dorothy. The Malted Milk Monster. The children gamboled about her like so many fountains against a central statue.

She stood there, still staring at him. And her stare was as uncomfortable as ever. A little more so, for that matter, than he remembered it. She wore the same blue jeans and yellow cashmere sweater with smudges on it. She was taller than life-size, a bit taller than the other children. She was slenderer, too. Now, in all fairness, you could not call her more than plump.

And she had no pimples.

Carter was irritated at how fast he'd had to drop his eyes. But to keep them open and aimed at her was like looking directly into the beam of an antiaircraft searchlight.

"Looka me, Dorothy!" the kids yelled. "I'm jumping! Looka how high I can jump!"

"How about playing tag, Dorothy?" they yelled. "Let's play tag! You choose who should be It!"

"Make up a new game, Dorothy! Make up one of the good games you always make up!"

"Let's have a picnic, huh, Dorothy?"

"Dorothy, let's have a relay race!"

"Dorothy, let's play house!"

"Dorothy, let's jump rope!"

"Dorothy—"

"Dorothy—"

"Dorothy—"

When she started to speak, every one of the kids shut up. They stopped running, they stopped yelling, they stopped whatever they were doing and turned to look at her.

"This nice man," she said. "He'll play with us. Won't you, mister?"

"No," Carter said. "I'd like to, but I'm afraid I—"

"He'll play a game of ball with us," she went on imperturbably. "Here, mister. Here's the ball. You're a nice man to play with us."

When she moved toward him, holding out a large striped ball which had suddenly appeared in her hands, the bulk of the children moved with her.

Carter was still searching for words wherewith to explain that, while he had no interest at the moment in playing a game of ball, he was much interested in a private conversation with Dorothy herself, an audience, so to speak—when the ball was thrust into his fingers and he found himself playing.

"You see, I don't usually—" he began as he threw the ball and caught it, threw the ball and caught it.

"Very busy right now, but some other ti—" he continued as he caught the ball and threw it, caught the ball and threw it.

No matter in which direction he threw the ball, no matter how many eager pairs of child hands made a grab for it, it was always Dorothy who received it and threw it back to him.

"Yay, Dorothy!" the children yelled. "This is *fun!*"

"Be glad to play with you kids as soon as I finish my—" Carter puffed, finding it fantastically tough exercise.

"Yay, Dorothy! This is a real good game!"

"Such a nice man!"

"So much fun!"

Dorothy threw the ball straight up in the air and it disappeared. "Let's play leapfrog," she said. "Would you like to play leapfrog with us, mister?"

"Sorry," Carter gasped as he bent, his hands on his knees, so that she could leap over his back from behind. "I haven't played leapfrog in years and I don't intend to st—" He ran forward, placed his hands in the small of Dorothy's back, sailed across, bent forward again in expectation of her jump. "Leapfrog is one game that I never—"

They played leapfrog until he was wobbling with dizziness, until every breath felt as if it had been clawed out of his chest.

Dorothy seated herself gracefully on the ground and gathered the children in an adoring cluster. "Now we'd like to hear a story. Please, mister, tell us a story?"

Carter started an agonized protest. It was somehow transformed into the story of Goldilocks and the Three Bears, told wheezingly and punctuated with heaving gulps for air. Then he told the story of Little Red Riding Hood. Then he told the story of Bluebeard.

Somewhere near the end of that particular work, Dorothy disappeared. But the children remained, and Carter continued the story, willy-nilly. The kids began to look frightened. Some shivered, others moaned and cried.

It had been getting darker for the past few minutes, and just as Carter finished the last lines of Bluebeard and, without stopping, launched into "Once upon a time there was a poor but honest woodcutter who had two children named Hansel and Gretel," a huge black cloud slid across the sky and swooped down at them.

A terrifying scarlet face with an enormous nose and flashing white teeth came out of the cloud and roared till the ground shook. Then it stopped and began to gnash its teeth. This sounded like an explosion in a crockery warehouse.

The children screamed in pure eye-popping terror and ran. "Dorothy!" they shrieked. "Dorothy, save us! The Bad Old Man! Save us, Dorothy, save us! Dorothy, where are you?"

Carter sank to the grass, released and utterly exhausted. He was far too tired to run or even look up, far too upset to care what happened to him anymore. It seemed like the first time in hours that his body was his again to command; but his body wasn't worth very much at the moment.

"Hey, Mac," a voice queried sympathetically over his head. "They givin' you a hard time?"

It was the scarlet face from the cloud. It no longer looked terrifying, merely concerned in a friendly fashion. And it was shrinking rapidly in size until it was in correct proportion to the normal human body under it. When it was a rather ordinary red and grizzled face, dirty with a few days' growth of beard around the red and busily veined nose, its owner knelt on the edge of the cloud and leaped to the ground, a distance, by this time, of half a dozen feet.

He was an oldish man of middle height, wearing a pair of solid gray pants, a torn brown shirt which hung outside it down to his hips and, on his bare feet, two frayed and filthy canvas shoes, one of which was split at the sole. He looked familiar, as every bum somehow looks like every other bum. He was archetypically the shambling, sodden derelict, a pure example of absolute human junk, but—

He was an adult.

Carter sprang up and offered his hand joyfully. It was shaken in a flabby, uncertain, half-cringing way, like a newly paroled prisoner taking his farewell of the warden.

"Could you use a drink, Mac?"

"I sure as hell could," Carter told him heartily. "Am I glad to see you!"

The derelict nodded vaguely, reached up, and pulled the black cloud even closer. He fumbled inside and pulled a bottle out. It was about half full, but though the fluid it contained was the proper shade of amber, it was clear glass all the way around. No label.

He held out this beggar's choice. "Name's Eddie. What they call me Shirttail. You need a glass to drink from? Ain't no glasses."

Carter shrugged. He sterilized the open top of the bottle with the palm of his hand, put it to his mouth and took a broad gulp.

"Whouch!" he said.

He found himself coughing so hard that he almost dropped the bottle. Shirttail took it away from him solicitously. "Awful, ain't it?" he asked, then proceeded to belt down a third of the stuff.

Awful, Carter decided, was not quite the word for it. It tasted like whiskey, all right, somewhere way down at the bottom, but with an overlay consisting of iodine, ammonia, camphor, and dilute hydrochloric acid. His tongue squirmed in his mouth like a trapped snake.

Shirttail removed the bottle from his mouth, shuddered, grimaced, and licked his lips. "That's what *she* thinks whiskey tastes like."

"Who? Dorothy?"

"Atsit. The kid—whatever she thinks something tastes like, that's what it tastes like. But it's better'n nothing, better'n no booze at all. Wanna come up to the place? We can sit a while."

He was pointing to the cloud which hung low over them, a dark and misshapen dirigible. Doubtfully, Carter grabbed some of its tenuous material and pulled himself up. It was like swimming through fog that felt solid only at the places your hands touched it.

A soaring black cavern of a room. Off in a corner—a niche, rather, since there were no corners—stood an army cot covered with ragged plaid blankets, a tableful of cracked cups and saucers and three sagging, garbagey-looking easy chairs. An unshaded light bulb hung from a thin wire over the cot and burned tinily, resentfully, in the piles of gloom. Whether or not the area behind the cot could properly be called a wall, it was covered from top to bottom with glossy pictures of naked women.

"Not my idea—hers," Shirttail explained as he clambered up through the floor. "Everything's hers, every idea, everything. What she once saw the inside of a night-watchman's shack, I figure. What to her I'm the same kinda guy as the night-watchman, so that's the layout I get. But thank God for the bottle. The pictures, far as I'm concerned, you can have, but the bottle—thank God for the bottle."

He offered it to Carter, who shook his head and hand in a no. They sat in two facing easy chairs, each of which immediately settled off to one side in opposite directions. Damn it, Carter thought, I *have* seen him before. But where?

"Take a slug, Mac, go ahead, take a slug. One good thing she's got here, that kid—the bottle gets full as fast as you kill it. You ain't takin' nothin' from me when you help yourself. And if you don't drink regular, you'll be talkin' to yourself. What you won't talk sense."

Carter considered the point and saw it might well be valid. He took another drink. It was fully as bad as the first but the effects of the alcohol came through more strongly now and tended to insulate against the flavor. He sighed and swallowed some more. No doubt about it, the world—even Dorothy's world—looked better.

He handed the bottle back and studied his companion. Hardly the right type for this place, when you came right down to it. A bum. A very average old bum. Why him as The Bad Old Man?

"How long have you been here?" Carter asked him.

Shirttail shrugged and stared loose-lipped over the top of the bottle. "A year, maybe. Two years, maybe. What there's no way to figure. Sometimes winter one day, sometimes summer tomorrow. What even my beard don't grow no more after I came. I feel like years and years *and* years and years. Worsen stir, worsen anything. The things I been through here, Mac, the things I been through!"

"Bad?" Carter asked sympathetically.

"Bad?" Shirttail indicated just how bad by rolling his red eyes in an emphatic upward arc. "Bad don't come near. I got to go out and scare those kids whenever she wants me to. What I'm in the sack, what I got other things on my mind, don't make no difference. Dorothy gives out with a think: 'Come a-runnin' and start a-scarin'.' I got to drop whatever

I'm doin'. I'm in the sack, what the hell, I got other things on my mind, I got to drop it and start a-scarin'. I blow up big like you just saw me, I got to scream and bang my choppers, I got to zoom on down. Then the kids yell: 'Dorothy, save us!' and she starts takin' me apart. What I mean apart. The things she's done to me, *biff! bam! pow! pam!,* slapped me silly, up, down, around, every which way, for a-scarin' those kids! What it wasn't my idea in the first place. I just do it 'cause she gives out with a think and makes me do it."

"Ever try resisting, refusing?" Carter inquired. "I mean what happens if you say no?"

"Mac, you don't say ,no. You just don't. Everything here goes her way. When she itches, you scratch. When she sneezes, you wipe your nose. What I used to call her all kindsa names to myself, just to pass the time—Mac, I don't remember a single one now. I try to remember one dirty name and I can't, to save my skin. She's just Dorothy. That's all I can call her. You know what I mean? Everything goes her way, even inside your head. The only leeway you get is to stay the kinda guy she sees you as in the first place. But otherwise it's her way, and the longer you stick around, the more her way it is."

Carter remembered with dismay how little he had wanted to play ball or leapfrog and how thoroughly he had played. Worse, how he had told stories when he had intended to protest. And worse yet, he hadn't —even in his own mind—used the phrase The Malted Milk Monster for some time now! He had thought of her, had referred to her, only as Dorothy.

"And the longer you stick around—"

He had to get out of here, had to find some way to smash out of this world—fast!

Shirttail was offering the bottle again. Carter refused it impatiently. Escape, breaking out, that came first. And for that he'd need his mind at its clearest. The alternative was being slowly absorbed, psychologically as well as physically, into Dorothy's dream world, until even his thoughts would be only slightly eccentric versions of her image of him, and he would be caught, like a fly immortalized by amber, in whatever habitation and whatever role she visualized for The Nice Man.

The Nice Man! He shivered. What a way to spend the rest of his life! No, now, while he was still more or less himself, Carter Broun, while his brain still glittered with the edge of a bright young motivational research executive in the real world, *now* was the time to break through.

The real world. As good a name for it as any other. Carter was a mystic never and a Freudian only when the occasion suited him. His credo was simple: anything that *is* is real. So . . .

Postulate a cosmos sufficiently long in extension and sufficiently broad in possibility, and there has to be room somewhere in all its infinities for every kind of world that Man could imagine.

Or a child dream up.

And suppose a child, out of overpowering longing and loneliness, out of some incredible innate talent, perhaps, is able to break through the folds of cosmic enormities into the one cranny where its dream world exists as a tangible, everyday truth. Not much of a step from there to switching other individuals, adults even, stones and flowerpots certainly, from one universe to the other. The original supposition, Carter decided, was the difficult one. Once that was accepted, the others were easy.

In an unlimited number of parallel worlds, to find the true home of one's mind . . .

Was that what Dorothy had done? And, in that case, which would be the dream world, which the real? You could probably die in either with equal ease—so *that* was no criterion.

Well, what difference did it make? The real world, for Carter, was the world from which he had been pulled, the world in which he had standing, individuality and personal purpose. The world he liked and intended to return to. And this, this other world, no matter how substantial unto itself in its peculiar space-time matrix, was the dream world—the world he must flee. The world that he had to prove, against the logic of his very senses, did not exist—by leaving it, or by destroying it somehow.

Destroying . . .

He stared hard at Shirttail. No wonder the derelict had looked so familiar!

It had been the briefest glimpse, weeks ago, possibly months, but the word brought back the sententious caption under that unforgettable photograph.

A tabloid newspaper on a print-wet, newly arrived pile he'd noticed over his shoulder as he'd been passing the newsstand at Fifty-third Street, just off Madison. And he'd had to stop and take another look at the photograph spreading its shock value over a sector of the front page. A MAN WHO DESTROYED HIMSELF was the caption's headline.

The caption went on to explain, in the most appalled journalese, that this was what you might expect to look like if you spent the rest of your life not working, sleeping in doorways, and drinking, instead of eating, your meals. "Even hardened interns and nurses at the hospital averted their faces from this terrible thing that had once been a man."

But the photograph *did* show a terrible thing that had once been a man. He was shown in the alley as he'd been found, shown just as the stretcher was being lifted, and you weren't likely to forget him for a long, long time.

The worst part of it was that he was alive. The eyes stared into the lens of the camera without any pretense of seeing. There was no mark on the face or body, no blood, nothing but dirt, and yet you had the feeling that this was a man who had fallen out of a window ten stories up or been hit by a car speeding at ninety miles an hour—and not been killed. Not completely killed, anyway, just partially killed.

The body lay and the eyes stared and the man was alive, but nothing more than that could be said. Looking at the picture, you suddenly thought of complex organic compounds that were almost living creatures but had not yet made the grade. The flabby, sheer nonconsciousness of this yet-sentient creature made catatonia seen in comparison a rather jolly, extremely active state.

According to the caption, he had been found looking like this in an alley; he had been removed to a large city hospital, and, after ten hours, the doctors had not been able to do a single thing with him. No response at all.

Carter remembered the picture well. It had been a picture of Shirttail.

Somewhere, at this very moment, possibly in a hospital in Grenville Acres, before the eyes of a terrified, a nauseated Lee, there was another body that bore a physical resemblance to one Carter Broun, but that in every important respect looked exactly like that horrible photograph. A body that was barely alive, that would not respond to any stimuli, that could do no more than exist—since its consciousness was elsewhere.

Here, in Dorothy's private chocolate-candy world.

He had to get out of this place. No matter what, he was *going* to get out of this place.

Only he'd need something close to dynamite. Psychological dynamite.

"—even cut my throat," Shirttail was going on heavily. "Oh, I maybe coulda cut my throat at the beginning, if I'da thoughta it. Too late now: I'm stopped cold any time I try. What I tried starving myself, but no go. Only candy to eat ina first place. Anybody can kick candy—it don't do no good, though. You don't hafta eat here, don't even hafta breathe. You stop breathin', you don't croak. Fact, Mac, fact. I done it. Hours and hours you can hold your breath: nothin' happens. Nothin' happens but what she wants to happen. And that's all. That's it."

Carter suggested, desperately trying to drag an elementary idea out of the concept of parallel universes, "How about the two of us getting together here and talking things over, just as we're doing? If we mapped out some workable sort of plan right now, it would be something she wouldn't like to have happen—but if we did, it would be real—it would have happened."

"Mac, you still don't get it. If you and me are together talkin', then someway or other that's the way *she* wants it. What she figures we go together, like, and we oughta be talkin' or bein' together. Meanwhile, she's workin' it out. What she's gonna do next. What we ain't gonna like it one damn bit, but so what?—far's she's concerned."

Carter frowned, not at Shirttail's last remarks, but at an unexpected and highly uncomfortable corroboration. He had suddenly felt an enormous tugging sensation in both his mind and body. Something was pulling at him to leave the cloud and descend to the candied surface.

Dorothy was coming back. She wanted him on the spot once more. She had a new sequence. Carter fought the tug grimly. He began to perspire.

The tug grew stronger. And stronger.

He squeezed his hands into tight, painful fists. "The Malted Milk Monster," he forced himself to say between clenched teeth. "Remember—*The Malted Milk Monster.*"

Shirttail looked up, intrigued. "Hey," he said. "Do me a favor, Mac—cuss her out. It'll do me good, honest, to hear a coupla good, first-class cuss words. Even if I won't remember them worth a damn, I'd still like to hear them again, just for old time's sake. Hey, Mac?"

Carter, thrashing about in the chair, elbows digging into his sides, immersed in his own private struggle, shook his head. "No," he gasped. "Can't. Not now."

"I know. It's tough. What I mean, tough. Like when I first come, I used to battle it out the same way, every time I feel her give out with a think. I battle and I battle, and it's no go. I been moochin' all day, see, up and down the East Fifties, Sutton Place, all like that. I been moochin' for the price of a flop, for the price of a shot, but not a chance. What it's so cold, my back's draggin' the sidewalk, but the whole goddamn world's got its pocket buttoned. Comes night, no flop. The whole night, I carry the banner. I stay awake, I keep walkin', what I don't wanna freeze. Five, six o'clock in the mornin', there's this can, there's half a fifth right on top in a bagfulla garbage. I hit it, oh, I hit it good."

Against his most determined mental opposition, Carter found himself getting to his feet. He knew his face was turning purple with the effort. He had to stop her now. He had to. It was the only way to invalidate her world.

But the Malt—*Dorothy* was calling him.

Shirttail rubbed a trembling filthy forefinger up and down the neck of the bottle. "And then I see this little alleyway between the buildings, what there's supposed to be a gate locking it off but it's been left open. I go in, it's dark, but there's a grating, hot air coming up from a basement and I'm outa the wind. Sack time. What I think I'm one lucky old bum, but it's the last time I think about luck. I wake up, it's light, there's this kid, this Dorothy lookin' at me. Lookin', lookin'. She's got a big ball in her hands and she's standin' there lookin' at me. She points to the bottle.

" 'That's my daddy's bottle,' she says. 'He threw it out last night, after the party. But it's his bottle.' I don't want no trouble with kids in this neighborhood, and I don't like the way it feels the way she looks. 'Scat, kid,' I say, and I sack out again. What I wake up next, here I am. I got the bottle and that's all I got. Mac, from that time on, it's rough. What I mean, *rough*. She had things here then, big things, things with legs and all kindsa—"

As if he were willing and even desirous of doing it, Carter turned his back on The Bad Old Man and began walking down through black fog. Behind him, the words continued to splash out like liquid from a steadily shaken glass. Carter's legs walked in direct contradiction to the nerve impulses they were receiving.

He couldn't refuse, couldn't resist. That much was obvious. As well try to refuse, to resist, the flood of forty days and forty nights, or the sun that Joshua made to stand still. Another way. He must find another way to fight. Meanwhile, he had to come as she demanded.

Dorothy was waiting for him on a patch of well-mown grass near a pink and green bonbon bush. As he came down beside her, she glanced away from him for a moment and at the dark cloud.

It disappeared.

What happened to Shirttail, Carter wondered—had he been wiped out for good? Or temporarily relegated to some sort of Limbo of reverie?

And then he really saw Dorothy—and the changes she had made.

She was still wearing the blue jeans, but the cashmere sweater was clean, perfectly clean. A bright, brand-new yellow. And she was taller. And she was even more slender than she had been before.

But that yellow cashmere sweater!

It was filled with two impossibly protruding breasts that belonged on a poster in front of a cheap movie house announcing the triumphant attributes of a Hollywood love goddess.

The rest of her body was still childlike, seemingly even more so than when he had first seen her, but this was due to the caricature effect of that incredible bosom.

Except—

Yes, except for the smear of red across her lip, the lumps of mascara at the tips of the eyelashes, and the clashing, smashing colors on her fingernails. Did this mean—

He shook his head uncertainly, irritably. He hadn't counted on anything like this. Whatever it was.

"So," Dorothy simpered at last. "We meet again."

"It was meant to be," Carter found himself breathing. "We two have a common destiny. We live under the same strange star."

Talk about your precocious kids! But where did she get the dialogue, he wondered frantically—movies? Television drama? Books? Or out of her own neurosis-crammed head? And what did he represent in it? *Her* role was obvious: she was blatantly competing with Lee.

There was a struggling wisp of uncombed thought: Lee and who else? But over and around it was the horrified knowledge that he was saying things he would never say of his own volition. How soon before he'd be *thinking* such clichés?

And there was a memory at the back of his mind—he had a name for her that was very much his own creation, very hard to remember, but he had to remember it, something like, rather like, let's see now— *Dorothy*. The only name for her there was.

But that hadn't been it. No.

He thought in pitiful, despairing wing-flaps, like an ostrich trying to fly. *Awful, awful.* He had to touch his own real personality somehow. He had to break through.

Shatter—

"Is your love then so strong, so truly true?" she demanded. "You have not forgotten me after all this time? Look into my eyes and tell me so. Tell me that your heart still belongs to me alone."

No, I won't, he groaned. He looked into her eyes. *I can't! Not such absolute baloney. And she's a kid—a little girl!*

"Do you doubt me, my darling?" he said softly, the sentences coming out of him in so many punched-out breaths. "Don't ever, *ever* doubt me. You are the only one for me, forever and always, as long as there is a sky overhead and an earth beneath. You and I, forever and always."

He had to *stop.* She was getting complete control over him. He said whatever she wanted him to say. And he was going to think it, too. But he couldn't prevent the words from flowing out of his mouth, once it was his turn, once she had finished and was waiting—

Dorothy looked off into the distance toward the two hills of equal height. Her eyes were misty, and, in spite of himself, Carter felt a catch in his throat. *Ridiculous! And yet how sad . . .*

"I almost feared your love," she mused. "I grew lonely and came to believe—"

Now. While she was doing the talking. While the full force of her mind was not turned compellingly upon him. Make it real. That's the way to bust this dream world. Make it real.

He reached for her.

"—that you had forgotten and found another. How was I to know—"

He grabbed at her.

He made it real.

There was an instant when the ground shook under his feet, when there was ripping sound from one end to another of the solid blue sky. There was just one instant when he exulted.

Then Dorothy turned wide, terror-stricken eyes at him. And screamed!

Her scream was the loudest thing in the universe. It went on and on and on, deafeningly. Yet he wasn't deafened, because he heard it all, every bit of it from the beginning, in each and every note of its immense range, all of its skull-powdering volume, all of its volcanic fear.

Not only Dorothy screamed. The candy trees screamed. The cookie bushes screamed. The two hills screamed. The chocolate river stood up between its screaming banks and screamed. The stones, the very air screamed.

And the ground fell apart and Carter Broun dropped into it. He dropped for centuries, he dropped for eons, he dropped for galactic eternities. Then he stopped dropping, stopped screaming himself, took his hands from his ears and looked around.

He was inside a dull gray, perfectly spherical, perfectly featureless vault. There were no doors and no windows, no seams and no cracks anywhere in the curving surface all about him. It was absolutely impenetrable and absolutely soundproof.

It had to be, he began to realize, as he scuttled dizzily around and around inside it. It had to be impenetrable and soundproof. It had to be at the bottommost bottom of the dream world, so that no sight and no sound from it should ever reach Dorothy's consciousness.

It was a total repression, this chamber of her mind, built to hide the deadly dangerous memory that was himself—built to last as long as Dorothy lasted.

THE FOOD FARM

by Kit Reed

They call them food farms or fat farms or health spas, but what they really are are diet prisons. Herd the obese together, starve them en masse, force them to exercise, that's how the theory goes. Ah, but what if the inmates revolted?

So here I am, warden-in-charge, fattening them up for our leader, Tommy Fango; here I am laying on the banana pudding and the milkshakes and the cream-and-brandy cocktails, going about like a technician, gauging their effect on haunch and thigh when all the time it is I who love him, I who could have pleased him eternally if only life had broken differently. But I am scrawny now, I am swept like a leaf around corners, battered by the slightest wind. My elbows rattle against my ribs, and I have to spend half the day in bed so a gram or two of what I eat will stay with me, for if I do not, the fats and creams will vanish, burned up in my own insatiable furnace, and what little flesh I have will melt away.

Cruel as it may sound, I know where to place the blame.

It was vanity, all vanity, and I hate them most for that. It was not my vanity, for I have always been a simple soul: I reconciled myself early to reinforced chairs and loose garments, to the spattering of remarks. Instead of heeding them I plugged in, and I would have been happy to let it go at that, going through life with my radio in my bodice, for while I never drew cries of admiration, no one ever blanched and turned away.

But they were vain and in their vanity my frail father, my pale, scrawny mother saw me not as an entity but a reflection on themselves. I flush with shame to remember the excuses they made for me. "She takes after May's side of the family," my father would say, denying any responsibility. "It's only baby fat," my mother would say, jabbing her elbow into my soft flank. "Nelly is big for her age." Then she would jerk furiously, pulling my voluminous smock down to cover my knees. That

204

was when they still consented to be seen with me. In that period they would stuff me with pies and roasts before we went anywhere, filling me up so I would not gorge myself in public. Even so I had to take thirds, fourths, fifths, and so I was a humiliation to them.

In time I was too much for them and they stopped taking me out; they made no more attempts to explain. Instead they tried to think of ways to make me look better; the doctors tried the fool's poor battery of pills; they tried to make me join a club. For a while my mother and I did exercises; we would sit on the floor, she in a black leotard, I in my smock. Then she would do the brisk one-two, one-two and I would make a few passes at my toes. But I had to listen, I had to plug in, and after I was plugged in naturally I had to find something to eat; Tommy might sing and I always ate when Tommy sang, and so I would leave her there on the floor, still going one-two, one-two. For a while after that they tried locking up the food. Then they began to cut into my meals.

That was the cruelest time. They would refuse me bread, they would plead and cry, plying me with lettuce and telling me it was all for my own good. Couldn't they hear my vitals crying out? I fought, I screamed, and when that failed I suffered in silent obedience until finally hunger drove me into the streets. I would lie in bed, made brave by the Monets and Barry Arkin and the Philadons coming in over the radio, and Tommy (there was never enough; I heard him a hundred times a day and it was never enough; how bitter that seems now!). I would hear them and then when my parents were asleep I would unplug and go out into the neighborhood. The first few nights I begged, throwing myself on the mercy of passersby and then plunging into the bakery, bringing home everything I didn't eat right there in the shop. I got money quickly enough; I didn't even have to ask. Perhaps it was my bulk, perhaps it was my desperate subverbal cry of hunger; I found I had only to approach and the money was mine. As soon as they saw me, people would whirl and bolt, hurling a purse or wallet into my path as if to slow me in my pursuit; they would be gone before I could even express my thanks. Once I was shot at. Once a stone lodged itself in my flesh.

At home my parents continued with their tears and pleas. They persisted with their skim milk and their chops, ignorant of the life I lived by night. In the daytime I was complaisant, dozing between snacks, feeding on the sounds which played in my ear, coming from the radio concealed in my dress. Then, when night fell, I unplugged; it gave a certain edge to things, knowing I would not plug in again until I was ready to eat. Some nights this only meant going to one of the caches in my room, bringing forth bottles and cartons and cans. On other nights I had to go into the streets, finding money where I could. Then I would lay in a new supply of cakes and rolls and baloney from the delicatessen and several cans of ready-made frosting and perhaps a flitch of bacon or some ham; I would toss in a basket of oranges to ward off scurvy and a carton of candy bars for quick energy. Once I had enough I would go back to my room, concealing food here and there, rearranging my nest of pillows and comforters. I would open the first pie or the first half-gallon of ice cream and then, as I began, I would plug in.

You had to plug in; everybody that mattered was plugged in. It was our bond, our solace and our power, and it wasn't a matter of being distracted, or occupying time. The sound was what mattered, that and the fact that fat or thin, asleep or awake, you were important when you plugged in, and you knew that through fire and flood and adversity, through contumely and hard times there was this single bond, this common heritage; strong or weak, eternally gifted or wretched and ill-loved, we were all plugged in.

Tommy, beautiful Tommy Fango, the others paled to nothing next to him. Everybody heard him in those days; they played him two or three times an hour but you never knew when it would be so you were plugged in and listening hard every living moment; you ate, you slept, you drew breath for the moment when they would put on one of Tommy's records, you waited for his voice to fill the room. Cold cuts and cupcakes and game hens came and went during that period in my life, but one thing was constant; I always had a cream pie thawing and when they played the first bars of "When a Widow" and Tommy's voice first flexed and uncurled, I was ready, I would eat the cream pie during Tommy's midnight show. The whole world waited in those days; we waited through endless sunlight, through nights of drumbeats and monotony, we all waited for Tommy Fango's records, and we waited for that whole unbroken hour of Tommy, his midnight show. He came on live at midnight in those days; he sang, broadcasting from the Hotel Riverside, and that was beautiful, but more important, he talked, and while he was talking he made everything all right. Nobody was lonely when Tommy talked; he brought us all together on that midnight show, he talked and made us powerful, he talked and finally he sang. You have to imagine what it was like, me in the night, Tommy, the pie. In a while I would go to a place where I had to live on Tommy and only Tommy, to a time when hearing Tommy would bring back the pie, all the poor lost pies . . .

Tommy's records, his show, the pie . . . that was perhaps the happiest period of my life. I would sit and listen and I would eat and eat and eat. So great was my bliss that it became torture to put away the food at daybreak; it grew harder and harder for me to hide the cartons and the cans and the bottles, all the residue of my happiness. Perhaps a bit of bacon fell into the register; perhaps an egg rolled under the bed and began to smell. All right, perhaps I did become careless, continuing my revels into the morning, or I may have been thoughtless enough to leave a jelly roll unfinished on the rug. I became aware that they were watching, lurking just outside my door, plotting as I ate. In time they broke in on me, weeping and pleading, lamenting over every ice cream carton and crumb of pie; then they threatened. Finally they restored the food they had taken from me in the daytime, thinking to curtail my eating at night. Folly. By that time I needed it all, I shut myself in with it and would not listen. I ignored their cries of hurt pride, their outpourings of wounded vanity, their puny little threats. Even if I had listened, I could not have forestalled what happened next.

I was so happy that last day. There was a Smithfield ham, mine, and I remember a jar of cherry preserves, mine, and I remember bacon, pale and white on Italian bread. I remember sounds downstairs and before I could take warning, an assault, a company of uniformed attendants, the sting of a hypodermic gun. Then the ten of them closed in and grappled me into a sling, or net, and heaving and straining, they bore me down the stairs. I'll never forgive you, I cried, as they bundled me into the ambulance. I'll never forgive you, I bellowed as my mother in a last betrayal took away my radio, and I cried out one last time, as my father removed a hambone from my breast: I'll never forgive you. And I never have.

It is painful to describe what happened next. I remember three days of horror and agony, of being too weak, finally, to cry out or claw the walls. Then at last I was quiet and they moved me into a sunny, pastel, chintz-bedizened room. I remember that there were flowers on the dresser and someone watching me.

"What are you in for?" she said.

I could barely speak for weakness. "Despair."

"Hell with that," she said, chewing. "You're in for food."

"What are you eating?" I tried to raise my head.

"Chewing. Inside of the mouth. It helps."

"I'm going to die."

"Everybody thinks that at first. I did." She tilted her head in an attitude of grace. "You know, this is a very exclusive school."

Her name was Ramona and as I wept silently, she filled me in. This was a last resort for the few who could afford to send their children here. They prettied it up with a schedule of therapy, exercise, massage; we would wear dainty pink smocks and talk of art and theater; from time to time we would attend classes in elocution and hygiene. Our parents would say with pride that we were away at Faircrest, an elegant finishing school; we knew better—it was a prison and we were being starved.

"It's a world I never made," said Ramona, and I knew that her parents were to blame, even as mine were. Her mother liked to take the children into hotels and casinos, wearing her thin daughters like a garland of jewels. Her father followed the sun on his private yacht, with the pennants flying and his children on the fantail, lithe and tanned. He would pat his flat, tanned belly and look at Ramona in disgust. When it was no longer possible to hide her, he gave in to blind pride. One night they came in a launch and took her away. She had been here six months now, and had lost almost a hundred pounds. She must have been monumental in her prime; she was still huge.

"We live from day to day," she said. "But you don't know the worst."

"My radio," I said in a spasm of fear. "They took away my radio."

"There is a reason," she said. "They call it therapy."

I was mumbling in my throat, in a minute I would scream.

"Wait." With ceremony, she pushed aside a picture and touched a tiny switch and then, like sweet balm for my panic, Tommy's voice flowed into the room.

When I was quiet she said, "You only hear him once a day."

"No."

"But you can hear him any time you want to. You hear him when you need him most."

But we were missing the first few bars and so we shut up and listened, and after "When a Widow" was over we sat quietly for a moment, her resigned, me weeping, and then Ramona threw another switch and the Sound filtered into the room, and it was almost like being plugged in.

"Try not to think about it."

"I'll die."

"If you think about it you *will* die. You have to learn to use it instead. In a minute they will come with lunch," Ramona said and as The Screamers sang sweet background, she went on in a monotone: "A chop. One lousy chop with a piece of lettuce and maybe some gluten bread. I pretend it's a leg of lamb—that works if you eat very, very slowly and think about Tommy the whole time; then if you look at your picture of Tommy you can turn the lettuce into anything you want, Caesar salad or a whole smorgasbord, and if you say his name over and over you can pretend a whole bombe or torte if you want to and ..."

"I'm going to pretend a ham and kidney pie and a watermelon filled with chopped fruits and Tommy and I are in the Rainbow Room and we're going to finish up with Fudge Royale ..." I almost drowned in my own saliva; in the background I could almost hear Tommy and I could hear Ramona saying, "Capon, Tommy would like capon, canard à l'orange, Napoleons, tomorrow we will save Tommy for lunch and listen while we eat ..." and I thought about that, I thought about listening and imagining whole cream pies and I went on, "...lemon pie, rice pudding, a whole Edam cheese ... I think I'm going to live."

The matron came in the next morning at breakfast, and stood as she would every day, tapping red fingernails on one svelte hip, looking on in revulsion as we fell on the glass of orange juice and the hard-boiled egg. I was too weak to control myself; I heard a shrill sniveling sound and realized only from her expression that it was my own voice: "Please, just some bread, a stick of butter, anything, I could lick the dishes if you'd let me, only please don't leave me like this, please ..." I can still see her sneer as she turned her back.

I felt Ramona's loyal hand on my shoulder. "There's always toothpaste, but don't use too much at once or they'll come and take it away from you."

I was too weak to rise and so she brought it and we shared the tube and talked about all the banquets we had ever known, and when we got tired of that we talked about Tommy, and when that failed, Ramona went to the switch and we heard "When a Widow," and that helped for a while, and then we decided that tomorrow we would put off "When a Widow" until bedtime because then we would have something to look forward to all day. Then lunch came and we both wept.

It was not just hunger: after a while the stomach begins to devour itself and the few grams you toss it at mealtimes assuage it so that in time the appetite itself begins to fail. After hunger comes depression. I lay there, still too weak to get about, and in my misery I realized that they could bring me roast pork and watermelon and Boston cream pie without ceasing; they could gratify all my dreams and I would only weep helplessly, because I no longer had the strength to eat. Even then, when I thought I had reached rock bottom, I had not comprehended the worst. I noticed it first in Ramona. Watching her at the mirror, I said, in fear:

"You're thinner."

She turned with tears in her eyes. "Nelly, I'm not the only one."

I looked around at my own arms and saw that she was right: there was one less fold of flesh above the elbow; there was one less wrinkle at the wrist. I turned my face to the wall and all Ramona's talk of food and Tommy did not comfort me. In desperation she turned on Tommy's voice, but as she sang I lay back and contemplated the melting of my own flesh.

"If we stole a radio we could hear him again," Ramona said, trying to soothe me. "We could hear him when he sings tonight."

Tommy came to Faircrest on a visit two days later, for reasons that I could not then understand. All the other girls lumbered into the assembly hall to see him, thousands of pounds of agitated flesh. It was that morning that I discovered I could walk again, and I was on my feet, struggling into the pink tent in a fury to get to Tommy, when the matron intercepted me.

"Not you, Nelly."

"I have to get to Tommy. I have to hear him sing."

"Next time, maybe." With a look of naked cruelty she added, "You're a disgrace. You're still too gross."

I lunged, but it was too late; she had already shot the bolt. And so I sat in the midst of my diminishing body, suffering while every other girl in the place listened to him sing. I knew then I had to act; I would regain myself somehow, I would find food and regain my flesh and then I would go to Tommy. I would use force if I had to, but I would hear him sing. I raged through the room all that morning, hearing the shrieks of five hundred girls, the thunder of their feet, but even when I pressed myself against the wall I could not hear Tommy's voice.

Yet Ramona, when she came back to the room, said the most interesting thing. It was some time before she could speak at all, but in her generosity she played "When a Widow" while she regained herself, and then she spoke:

"He came for something, Nelly. He came for something he didn't find."

"Tell about what he was wearing. Tell what his throat did when he sang."

"He looked at all the *before* pictures, Nelly. The matron was trying to make him look at the *afters* but he kept looking at the *befores* and shaking his head and then he found one and put it in his pocket and if he hadn't found it, he wasn't going to sing."

I could feel my spine stiffen. "Ramona, you've got to help me. I must go to him."

That night we staged a daring break. We clubbed the attendant when he brought dinner, and once we had him under the bed we ate all the chops and gluten bread on his cart and then we went down the corridor, lifting bolts, and when we were a hundred strong we locked the matron in her office and raided the dining hall, howling and eating everything we could find. I ate that night, how I ate, but even as I ate I was aware of a fatal lightness in my bones, a failure in capacity, and so they found me in the frozen food locker, weeping over a chain of link sausage, inconsolable because I understood that they had spoiled it for me, they with their chops and their gluten bread; I could never eat as I once had, I would never be myself again.

In my fury I went after the matron with a ham hock, and when I had them all at bay I took a loin of pork for sustenance and I broke out of that place. I had to get to Tommy before I got any thinner; I had to try. Outside the gate I stopped a car and hit the driver with the loin of pork and then I drove to the Hotel Riverside, where Tommy always stayed. I made my way up the fire stairs on little cat feet and when the valet went to his suite with one of his velveteen suits I followed, quick as a tigress, and the next moment I was inside. When all was quiet I tiptoed to his door and stepped inside.

He was magnificent. He stood at the window, gaunt and beautiful; his blond hair fell to his waist and his shoulders shriveled under a heartbreaking double-breasted pea green velvet suit. He did not see me at first; I drank in his image and then, delicately, cleared my throat. In the second that he turned and saw me, everything seemed possible.

"It's you." His voice throbbed.

"I had to come."

Our eyes fused and in that moment I believed that we two could meet, burning as a single, lambent flame, but in the next second his face had crumpled in disappointment; he brought a picture from his pocket, a fingered, cracked photograph, and he looked from it to me and back at the photograph, saying, "My darling, you've fallen off."

"Maybe it's not too late," I cried, but we both knew I would fail.

And fail I did, even though I ate for days, for five desperate, heroic weeks; I threw pies into the breach, fresh hams and whole sides of beef, but those sad days at the food farm, the starvation and the drugs have so upset my chemistry that it cannot be restored; no matter what I eat I fall off and I continue to fall off; my body is a halfway house for foods I can no longer assimilate. Tommy watches, and because he knows he almost had me, huge and round and beautiful, Tommy mourns. He eats less and less now. He eats like a bird and lately he has refused to sing; strangely, his records have begun to disappear.

And so a whole nation waits.

"I almost had her," he says, when they beg him to resume his midnight shows; he will not sing, he won't talk, but his hands describe the mountain of woman he has longed for all his life.

And so I have lost Tommy, and he has lost me, but I am doing my best to make it up to him. I own Faircrest now, and in the place where Ramona and I once suffered I use my skills on the girls Tommy wants me to cultivate. I can put twenty pounds on a girl in a couple of weeks and I don't mean bloat, I mean solid fat. Ramona and I feed them up and once a week we weigh and I poke the upper arm with a special stick and I will not be satisfied until the stick goes in and does not rebound because all resiliency is gone. Each week I bring out my best and Tommy shakes his head in misery because the best is not yet good enough, none of them are what I once was. But one day the time and the girl will be right—would that it were me—the time and the girl will be right and Tommy will sing again. In the meantime, the whole world waits; in the meantime, in a private wing well away from the others, I keep my special cases; the matron, who grows fatter as I watch her. And Mom. And Dad.

THE ARTIST OF HUNGER

by Scott Sanders

*Scott Sanders is one of the very best young writers work-
ing in the science fiction field. In "The Artist of Hunger" he
displays his talent in a moving story about a man with a very
special talent for food.*

It was not a very convincing dawn. Near the eastern horizon the sky
was the color of chicken liver simmering in butter. Flocks of birds
melted against the sunrise in chocolate tones. Banks of clouds surged
down from the north like a tide of mashed potatoes, and dainty popcorn
clouds lingered in the south.

Edible, yes, but one could hardly call it convincing. Gripping a lightbrush in one hand and a mug of malto in the other, Sir Toby Moore
reclined upon a couch and brooded on his wretched painting. The
image shimmered above him on the vaulted ceiling of his studio, a
miniature of the image that would later be projected onto the domes of
malls in five continents. With the lightbrush he added another touch of
butter yellow to the sunrise. Rather a vulgar mixture of foods, he had to
confess, what with chicken giblets and chocolates. Why could he paint
nothing but banquet skies? They had become a fixation with him, these
firmaments stuffed with meats and candies, poultries, and pastries. He
took a chilly swig of malto, then lay back on the couch and set the mug
upon his prominent belly.

Sir Toby's belly was prominent in two respects: it was huge and it
was famous. Its conspicuous bulk was due to his zeal for eating, his
distaste for exercise, and his steadfast refusal to undergo a slenderizing
operation. His rotund silhouette had become famous, belonging as it
did to one of the most celebrated mall-artists in North America, an
artist, moreover, whose sponsor, MEGA Corporation, owned The Sleek
of Araby, the leading chain of slenderizing shops. He was not what
anyone would regard as a walking exhibit of the virtues of slimness.

213

Nonetheless, he liked to think of himself as being only physically fat, and not metaphysically so. In his heart and brain he was no fatter than the next person. Indeed, for the first twenty-odd years of his life he had not even been especially fat in body. Plump, maybe. Only since moving into the Rogue River Mall six years earlier had he begun to put on weight, and to keep putting on weight, season after season, like an iceberg accumulating each winter's snow.

Journalists christened him Sir Tubby, Sir Roly-Poly. Camera crews delighted in filming him while he escorted his petite lady friend, Lyla Bellard, from restaurant or cinema. On video he would loom beside her, huge and pale, like a leashed polar bear.

One such video exposure aired while Sir Toby was engaged in perusing his chicken-liver sunrise. He was quickly informed of this new publicity by a MEGA vice-president, whose bony face materialized on the phonescreen. "You just can't stay away from the cameras, can you?" said the woman in an exasperated voice.

"Can I help it if the photographers hide in the plastic shrubbery and ambush me every time I stir from my apartment?" replied Sir Toby.

"Not only do we see you from all angles, with your tiny mistress standing next to you as if to represent the human scale, but afterward they show a panel of three doctors who're trying to guess your weight and your life expectancy." The vice-president forced a smile, like a doctor trying to cheer up a terminal patient. The taut skin of her cheeks reminded Sir Toby of trampolines. "We've already had several hundred complaints from stockholders."

"They want my head on a platter," he suggested.

"They'd rather have your belly, and maybe half of each haunch. Enough to slim you down to respectable proportions."

Knowing, or at least hoping, that he was too valuable a property for MEGA to lose, he said boldly: "So fire me. I'll take my stool into the mall and go back to doing laser portraits."

"Don't play the grand man. It doesn't suit you."

"So I was on video. All right. Shoot the cameraman. What else do you want?"

"I want to appeal to your dignity."

Sir Toby half lifted the mug from his belly, and then, bethinking himself, lowered it again. He was famished. The woman on the phonescreen kept smiling grimly. All these corporate-image people had too many teeth. "My dignity?"

"When people think of The Sleek of Araby, Sir Toby, we want them to *think thin.* We want them to imagine twigs, not stumps."

"I assure you," he bluffed, "being a stump is far more weighty and consequential than being a twig. Do you, for instance, truly enjoy being scrawny as a stick? What do your male friends hold on to?"

The vice-president's grin froze, an expanse of teeth floating on the screen like a half-moon. "Listen, our competitors have mounted posters of you in their shops, identifying you as The Sleek of Araby mascot. As our *symbol.*"

Sir Toby groaned. He was only too familiar with those competitors and their revolting names: Fat-Away Farms, Rub-a-Dub-Tubby's, The Beauty and the Feast, The Incredible Shrinking Man, Ipso Fatso, Gorge Us George's, each of them with outlets in malls across the country, vying with one another in the electronic war against obesity. The mere thought of these shops, their glistening needles and microwave vaporizers, made Sir Toby queasy. On several occasions he had gone so far as to deposit himself on the slenderizing couch in a Sleek of Araby parlor, only to flee in terror once he caught sight of the fat-extraction devices. The whole enterprise struck him as an unholy alliance between modern electronics and medieval torture.

"I can't help the way your competitors decorate their shops," he said.

"But you can. A series of operations . . ."

"Out of the question."

"MEGA would raise your fee . . ."

He lurched upright on the couch and glared into the phonescreen. "Madam, I'm an artist, not a rack for displaying clothes. Nor a video star. It so happens I am content with my present shape. I have no desire to resemble a weasel or a lightning rod. If MEGA doesn't approve of my physique, then I'll get someone else to broadcast my skies."

The professional smile faltered. "I only meant to suggest a possibility."

"An impossibility."

"You won't even consider it?"

"I have considered, and the answer is no. I won't have my body milked and shriveled by any imbecile machinery."

"Could you at least arrange for a larger mistress. Miss Bellard makes you appear so—"

Sir Toby flung the empty mug at the screen. Plastic bounced harmlessly against plastic, freezing the vice-president in midsentence. With the angry punch of a button he erased her image. Those extravagant teeth were the last of her to wink into oblivion.

He longed to gather all these corporate-image makers, tie them in a sack, and dump them in the Rogue River—assuming one could still *find* the river, down in its concrete channel far beneath the mall. They would never quit meddling with a person. When they insisted on changing his name from Thurgood Moranski to Toby Moore, he had been annoyed, but he could see their point. Placing the "Sir" in front of it (when neither he nor any of his ancestors had ever so much as visited England, let alone been knighted by the king) had seemed to him more comical than sinister. But next they ordered him to shave his beard, give up wearing plaid dinner jackets, take up wearing square-toed shoes, and then he began to grow irritable. (He now wore plaid coats and even plaid trousers at every opportunity, to spite them, and his blond beard reached halfway down his chest.) Once they offered to hire a svelte actor, some moronic whippet, to make all his public appearances, but Sir Toby had threatened to strangle the man on sight.

And now this really was too much, when they began dictating the size of his mistress. He adored Lyla, every cubic centimeter of her. The less of her there was, the more affection he could invest per gram. She was the only woman who had ever succeeded in making him feel graceful. "It's not a matter of bulk," she told him early in their friendship. "It's how the soul moves." The way she said it made him feel that his soul was as tangible as his fleecy beard. When their friendship had matured sufficiently to afford him an opportunity of examining her naked body, he had searched her belly for the telltale puncture scars from slenderizing operations. He had seen the scars on so many others, on men in saunas and shower rooms, on women in swimming pools and in less public places, those tiny puckerings of skin like pursed lips marking where the needles had done their work. But the skin on Lyla's belly was as smooth and unblemished as a freshly laundered sheet. "However do you manage to stay thin without subjecting yourself to those barbarous operations?" he asked her. "I only eat when I'm hungry," she told him. "So do I," he said. To which she replied, "Ah, yes, but you're hungry all the time."

That was unfortunately true. Hunger gnawed at him relentlessly, like a rat trying to escape from his stomach. Even while recollecting that first delightful survey of Lyla's belly, he was munching pretzels and sipping yet another mug of malto. He could only stop thinking about food when he was sleeping or, strangely enough, when he was at Lyla's apartment. She utterly refused to live in the mall, or even to visit him there, complaining that its hives of bedrooms and clanging shops made her ill. She lived instead in one of the military research installations, out in the Cascade Mountains. "Why don't you come live with me?" she had urged him on many occasions. But he had always refused. Since childhood, he had dreamed of growing rich enough to live forevermore inside a mall. Each mall was like ancient Rome, the empire's center, into which all the tributary streams of civilization constantly poured. That childhood vision still held so firm a grip on his imagination that nothing less than the powerful lure of Lyla could ever persuade him to venture outside.

Between thoughts of Lyla and the infuriating telephone call, Sir Toby was too stirred up to resume painting. So he left the image of his half-finished sky shimmering on the roof of his studio and trudged out into the mall. Some piece of trash was playing overhead on the domescreen: it looked rather like the effects of a hurricane on a mattress factory, interspersed with fireworks. Gaudy junk. He withdrew his gaze just as the ad bloomed across the screen: a close-up of a woman sucking on a straw. Slurp, slurp. Luscious lips. That would be Cravin' Haven. "Food for the Famished." He knew all the icons by heart.

Dodging a pack of kids, who were bearing down on him in a zipcart, Sir Toby clutched a plastic tree for support and nearly uprooted it. That was one of the humiliations of being fat in a world of skinny people: you had to lean on things, on chairbacks and railings, and could never feel confident they would bear your weight. An alarm rang and a guard immediately appeared. "Who's messing with the vegetation?" Sir Toby retreated, explaining the accident, but not before the guard had recognized him. Lifted eyebrows. "Hey, you that painter?"

"No, no, somebody else entirely," Sir Toby insisted, stepping onto a pedbelt, which soon delivered him from the inquiring guard.

Music blaring overhead announced a change of program, and he made the mistake of looking up. An ad for Sleek of Araby burst on the screen: twin portraits of a young man, in the first of which he appeared grotesquely swollen, his eyes mere slits, his jowls bulging over his collar, while in the second portrait, taken after the slenderizing operation, he looked lithe as an undersea creature. An electric eel, say, or a muskrat, thought Sir Toby sourly. "LET THE SLEEK OF ARABY MAKE YOU LOOK LIKE YOUR REAL SELF AGAIN," the announcer boomed. The artists had taken great pains to make the withered young man appear handsome and fetching, but in Sir Toby's eyes he looked sadly shrunken, like a helium balloon abandoned at night in plump grandeur near the ceiling, discovered next morning in a shriveled heap of rubber on the floor.

As he rode the crowded belts through the avenues of the mall, he noticed the other riders drawing away from him, their scrawny bodies encircling him like a stockade fence about a blockhouse. He was painfully accustomed to this isolation. The halo of space they left around him bore less resemblance to the aura of respect surrounding a king than to a *cordon sanitaire*. Their distance kept him in quarantine, as if they feared an epidemic of obesity would spread outward from him to infect the planet.

Most of his fellow belt-riders were nibbling snacks and guzzling drinks from cans. The noise of munching and swallowing was louder than the soundtrack that accompanied the domeshow. As the belt slithered past food shops, the empty-handed riders stepped off to replenish their supplies, and new riders hopped aboard with jaws grinding. Sir Toby was feeling momentarily virtuous amid all this eating until he realized that he was actually holding a nearly empty bag of salties in his hand. He stopped in mid-chew. Where had they come from? Probably his pocket. Food seemed always to hide in his coats and trousers, even though he could rarely remember putting it there. Maybe he was being followed by a malicious pickpocket who, instead of removing his wallet, stuffed Sir Toby's pockets with grub. After hesitating briefly, he shook the remaining salties into his mouth, then jammed the crumpled sack into the handkerchief pocket of his plaid sportcoat. Inside, his fingertips discovered several lumps of hard candy, stored there like a squirrel's acorns. With an effort of will he forced himself to leave the candies in place.

When his hand came out of the pocket empty, he was overwhelmed by such an intense craving for sugar that he lost his balance and staggered a few steps along the pedbelt. The other riders cleared away from him, keeping out of range in case he should fall. He felt panicky with hunger. The sound of chomping reverberated in his ears. He had to get off, get away from all these stares, go somewhere to eat in secret. As he lurched to the rim of the belt, the people making way for him muttered, "It's about time!" "They'll have their work cut out for them!" "It's a desperate case!" Glancing up, he saw the lurid neon lights of a Rub-a-Dub-Tubby's looming into view. Beyond that shone the lights of Fat-Away Farms and Gorge Us George's. Sir Toby teetered on the edge of the pedbelt, unwilling to let the skinny riders think he was going into one of those shops for an operation. But someone shoved him in the back with a blunt object (perhaps a sausage or a loaf of rye bread, he imagined in his hunger), and he stumbled onto the pavement, nearly bumping into an emaciated woman who was just emerging from the door of Fat-Away Farms.

"Sir Roly-Poly!" the woman exclaimed.

"Moore," he answered stiffly.

She grinned up at him with her newly shrunken face. A series of fresh scars along her throat and jaw stood out like scarlet stitches. "Just like in your picture," she breathed.

" 'Picture'?"

"That poster they've got hanging inside there," she said, as she brushed past him to hop on the belt.

And it was true, there on the rear wall of the slenderizing parlor hung a life-size portrait of him, in corpulent profile and living color. He stood in the doorway, mesmerized by his unflattering likeness. It dominated the shop, like some evil icon for frightening passersby into the clutches of the fat-removal machines. The caption below read: PRODUCED BY THE SLEEK OF ARABY. One of the operators glanced at him, then at the poster, then back again at Sir Toby, eyes widening, needle poised above the beefy thigh of a carefully draped customer.

"You're all a pack of leeches and ghouls!" bellowed Sir Toby through the open door. "Fat-suckers and walking cadavers!" A dozen operators glared at him now and a dozen customers stirred beneath their draperies. Then as an afterthought, backing away, he shouted, "May every needle hit a nerve!"

Fuming, he avoided the pedbelt, with its cargo of chomping scarecrows, and ambled down the walkway past Gorge Us George's and Ipso Fatso's. He stole a glance through the window of each shop, and in each he saw his grotesque portrait.

He walked hurriedly on, feeling morose and hungry. Within moments he was puffing. At least, in his unhappiness, he was burning calories. Lyla would be proud of him, out exercising vigorously like this. She despised pedbelts and elevators, insisted on using her own legs to go everywhere. Such legs! Not thin, really. In fact, nicely rounded. They were merely small and delightfully proportioned, like all the rest of her, as if she had been designed to fit a daintier world than the one other mortals inhabited.

Outside the window of a Cravin' Haven his exercise came to a halt, and he stared in like a tramp at the diners seated along the counter. His mouth opened and shut in voracious sympathy with theirs. At about the third bite he tasted chocolate, having unconsciously stuffed his mouth with joybars, which he had fished from some forgotten hiding place in his voluminous suit. The taste of chocolate always dissolved his last vestiges of self-restraint. Transfixed before the window of the snack shop, he pulled from his pockets and devoured in rapid succession the hard candies (butterscotch), a box of raisins, a rather stale pastry, and a packet of crushed soy-chips. After the last hiding place had been ransacked he went on thrusting hands into pockets, opening and closing his coat, slapping his thigh and rump, in search of more food. He gave up searching only when he noticed that the diners inside Cravin' Haven were watching his pantomime with great amusement, pointing at him with drinking straws and half-eaten burgers. Several of them appeared to be mouthing his name, or some slanderous variation on his name.

Again he walked on through the mall, sunk in gloom, wondering how far he would have to trudge in order to burn up all the calories he had just consumed. It was hopeless. His exercise would never catch up with his eating. He could sympathize with people who every day sank more deeply into debt. Still he was ravenous. It was absurd, it was humiliating, to be so thoroughly a creature of one's belly. "Where on earth does this appetite come from?" he had asked Lyla, and then, mockingly, he had suggested, "From my artistic temperament?" "It comes from staying in the mall—that constant bombardment—," she said, "and from not living with me."

Bombardment. Perhaps she had something there, he conceded, as he shuffled past eateries, Eros parlors, feelie shops, costume boutiques, arcades. And there were the perpetual domeshows and ads blaring down.

What was playing right now, for example? Peering up, he was startled to see a rerun of one of his own vintage sky-paintings. Cumulus clouds that actually looked like clouds instead of mashed potatoes; Chinese dragon kites playing against a lavender haze; a flight of Canada geese beating their way across the face of a woozy late-afternoon sun; around the horizon a rim of hills topped by the spire-points of conifers.

He had painted that sky at least a dozen years earlier, when still a teenager, long before moving into the mall. It already showed his characteristic strokes with the lightbrush. Yet, by comparison with his recent work, overstuffed with allusions to food, this early painting seemed to him fresh and powerful. Every detail in it was authentic, something he had *seen* rather than vaguely hungered for. It was a creation of the eye, not the belly.

Had he lost so much power? he wondered, standing there outside a Never Say Diet store ("Open for Eating 25 Hours a Day"), weeping, a bloated silhouette so familiar that shoppers paused to gape at him. The tears slithered through his beard and rolled down the hidden folds of his chin.

For such profound misery there was only one antidote—Lyla. He barged straight for her, like a draft horse headed for the barn, riding the shuttle through its translucent tube out to the research installation in the Cascade Mountains. She would scold him for bothering her at work, something he had never done before. But he didn't care. This was an emergency. Most likely she would be dousing rats with exotic rays, turning them into lizards or spoons, and how important was that by comparison with the salvation of her lover?

He did not even begin to understand Lyla's research, and was not certain he wanted to. It involved poking about in the brain with vibrations, or perhaps devising ways of preventing *others* from poking about in the brain, or some such business. All very mathematical—which meant, so far as he was concerned, that it might just as well have been carried on in the language of dolphins. Never having progressed much beyond the multiplication tables, Sir Toby resolutely avoided any commerce with numbers or equations. He was grateful that he did not need to understand electronics in order to use a lightbrush, or to understand holographics in order to have his skies broadcast in malls.

The shuttle quivered to a halt. He glanced at the signboard: two more stops to go. Ads glowed on walls and ceilings. Announcers kept up a sales patter: buy me, buy me. During the lull in the station, the sounds of chewing wafted like subdued applause from seats all around him. Then he remembered with a feeling akin to despair that he had emptied his pockets in the mall. There were vending machines two cars down, but he could not bring himself to squeeze his way along the aisle past all those staring faces. Lyla would very likely have nothing to eat in her lab. She seemed to subsist entirely on air and moisture, like the mint green plant he kept hanging in his bathroom.

He would just have to endure the hunger. Only two more stops. Surely there would be a snack bar at the research center. Or perhaps he could persuade a guard to sell the contents of his lunch bucket.

At thought of the guard, a worry suddenly arose in his mind. What if they refused to let him in? Didn't one have to be investigated back seven generations in order to work in these military places? And nobody trusted an artist. Who could tell, he might snoop around, memorize a few things, and paint some wiring diagrams into his next sky. Broadcast military secrets in malls around the world. Spies would stop in the middle of their shopping, gaze up at his revelations, snap quick photos to smuggle back to enemy governments.

No, they would never let him in.

Another quiver of the shuttle. His stop. He might as well try. Charge the gate with head lowered. All they could do was shoot him. Perhaps Lyla could vouch for him, fit him with a blindfold and lead him by the hand to her ratmaze lab. He stood up, smacked his jacket and trousers into some semblance of neatness, and shuffled on to the platform. No one else left the shuttle (all of them doubtless intending, like sensible people, to cross the mountains into eastern Oregon or Idaho), and no one stood on the platform waiting. There were no vending machines, no benches or ticket booths. In fact, so far as he could see, the station consisted of a single windowless room, white enamel over metal, with a formidable-looking door at one end and warning signs plastered on all the walls.

Before he could read the warnings, a video camera swiveled down to focus on him from a perch above the door, and a voice boomed from some hidden speaker: "STATE YOUR BUSINESS! CLEARANCE CODE! KEYWORD!"

Sir Toby blinked at the camera. "I merely wanted to visit a friend."

Evidently this answer stunned the guard, for several seconds of electronic hum ensued. Presently the same male voice, but considerably humbled now, inquired: "Excuse me, sir, but you wouldn't be the guy who paints the skies, would you? Sir Toby Something?"

"Moore," Sir Toby answered, bowing slightly. "I've come to see Dr. Bellard on urgent business. May I speak with her please? I promise not to kidnap her or to steal away any portion of your laboratory."

A moment later the combined breathing of several onlookers, who had evidently gathered at the microphone, was audible through the speakers. "Look," whispered a female voice. "It's him all right." There was a muffled discussion, of which he could decipher only two words, Toby and Lyla. This conference was terminated by a harsh laugh, and then the first guard's chastened voice: "One moment, sir, while I page Dr. Bellard."

Sir Toby, who was beginning to feel rather like a zoo exhibit here in his steel cage, turned away from the camera to wait. Out of habit, he searched all his pockets once again, plaid coat and trousers, vest and shirt. Much to his surprise, he actually discovered a chocolate joybar in one of his watchpockets. To his even greater surprise, he felt no desire to eat it. Indeed, he felt crammed to the gullet, as if he could easily go a month before his next meal. With a shiver of revulsion, he slipped the joybar back into its hiding place. What was happening to him? He studied the bare white walls of his cubicle suspiciously. Maybe they were beaming rays at him to quench his hunger. They did such things at these psy-labs, he was sure of that. Poking about in the brain.

He felt suddenly faint. There being no seat, he backed into a corner of the cell and propped himself against the two walls. Lyla would make them stop experimenting on him. Would she appear on the screen, or through a door? Then again, she might not even be here today, might be off testing a new weapon at the desert firing range.

So intent he was on calculating these various possibilities that he did not hear the door open or the footsteps lightly approach.

"Toby, darling," came a gentle voice, "whatever's the matter?"

It was as if someone had set off a recording of birdsong in his heart. He staggered out of the corner like a punchdrunk boxer and engulfed her in an enormous hug, murmuring, "Lyla, Lyla, they're tormenting me."

"Who?" she cried indignantly, drawing back far enough to gaze at him with fierce brown eyes.

"Everybody. The journalists with their infernal cameras. The Sleek of Araby bosses with their teeth and their needles. People who gawk at me in the mall. And even here," he protested, gesturing at the camera's glass eye, "the guards are beaming some kind of"—he groped for a word—"*fullness* rays at me."

" 'Fullness rays'?" she repeated skeptically.

He explained to her about the uneaten chocolate bar, the full stomach, the faintness.

"Don't be silly." Her small hand played like a mouse in his beard.

"Do you think I'd step in here if they were irradiating this cubicle? It's okay. Really." As if to reassure him about the wholesomeness of the cell, she lifted her arms and turned once around, lithe and caressable in a rust-colored jumpsuit, the laboratory insignia attached on one shoulder and her rank stitched on a breast pocket. It was always disconcerting for him to be reminded that this tiny woman, with her ponytail and mice-size hands, actually worked for the psy-war division of the Pentagon.

"I just feel awfully strange," he said.

"Why don't you take a vacation from the mall?" she suggested, as she had so often suggested before. "Stay out here at my place?"

"The evening news would love that."

"So what more can they say about us than they've said already?"

He wavered. "Yes, but I've got a sky-mural due in two days."

"I'll fetch a lightbrush and projector from the lab."

"But I've already got part of a sky shining on my ceiling."

"We'll have the tapes buzzed out here. Easy." She looked at him intently, a slight smile on her face. "Have you run out of excuses?"

He shrugged and returned her smile. He had always offered the same excuses. Publicity. Work. Deadlines. Yet, in his heart of hearts—or perhaps his stomach of stomachs—he had been reluctant to leave the mall itself, with its eateries and domeshows and pleasure arcades. Now the mere thought of food filled him with loathing. And as for pleasure, there was always Lyla.

"The change might do me some good," he agreed at last.

"Delightful!" She took one of his great paws in her tiny one, and with her other hand she waved at the camera. The featureless door clicked open. Someone had been watching, of course.

The partially finished sky glimmered on the ceiling of Lyla's apartment: chicken-liver sunrise, chocolate birds, mashed-potato clouds. But after three hours of frowning at this confection, Sir Toby still could not bring himself to add one stroke of the lightbrush. Lyla had scoffingly called it "the great flying smorgasbord," and he was inclined to agree with her. Only a starving man had any business painting such toothsome skies, and Sir Toby, lounging like a walrus upon Lyla's couch, could no longer pretend to be starving. He still had cravings aplenty, but not for food. With the flick of a switch he erased it all, the popcorn and giblets, the gravies and syrups, the sugary constellations. He closed his eyes and waited for some new image to creep into his inward vision.

He was still contemplating the dark interstellar spaces when Lyla called to him from the guest bedroom. Ordinarily he avoided this room, for it housed a colony of white rats, quick little beasts that, having served their purpose in the laboratory, had been saved by Lyla from extermination. "I have something to show you," she said.

With a sigh, he shuffled down the hallway, but only after tucking his pantslegs into his socks as a precaution against the inquisitive rats.

Lyla stood just outside a low Plexiglas gate that sealed the doorway. "Closer," she insisted, drawing him up to the threshold by his elbow. The room was bare except for dishes of food, some rodent-scale exercise equipment, a pair of plastic mazes, and the population of rats, which were skittering nervously about like dancers practicing their steps before curtain-rise. "Now watch," said Lyla, pushing a button in the wall.

The ceiling was quickly suffused with a rose-colored glow, gradually darkening to the color of tomato soup. Within that goop, creamy pasta-shapes began to congeal. Sir Toby immediately recognized this as the overture to one of his recent skies, broadcast within the past six months. "How did you get hold of it?" he asked.

"Military channels," she answered darkly. "Just watch what happens."

He knew only too well what would happen. After the tomato soup would come lasagne, eggplant Parmesan, and so on through a five-course Italian meal, all smeared across the ceiling in shades of catsup. He could not bear to watch. In any case, he was distracted by a scrabbling noise. When he looked down, afraid the beasts might be assaulting his stockinged feet, he saw the rats galloping pell-mell toward the food dishes, fighting for position at the trough, gorging themselves. Bits of grain flew in all directions as the white jaws snapped. Watching them made his skin crawl. The rats nipped at one another in their frenzy to get at the food. They hauled themselves from dish to dish, sometimes with engorged bellies actually dragging on the floor.

"They'll kill themselves," he said with horror.

"Some of them would, if I left it running long enough."

"My sky is doing that?" Standing in the doorway, he realized that a feeling of hunger was mixing with his nausea.

"Not your sky, but what your sponsor blended in with it." Lyla tucked her hand under one of his arms. "Stick your head inside the room and see how it feels."

Fascinated, frightened, he leaned over the threshold and was immediately seized by an overwhelming craving. He clutched at his stomach, screaming, "Turn it off!"

Lyla quickly extinguished the painting, drew him back into the hallway, put her arms around as much of him as she could encompass. "I'm sorry, sweetheart, but you wouldn't have believed me if I'd just told you about it."

"What—?" he began, but he was too dazed even to formulate a question. He sympathized with the rats, which now lay on their sides, paws outstretched, swollen bellies laboriously heaving.

"They spliced into your sky-tape an overlay that directly stimulates the hunger center in the brain," Lyla explained. "You get a more concentrated charge in here than you get in a mall, but this gives you an idea of the effect."

"They can *do* that?"

"Yes, they most certainly can, and they *have* been doing it for six or seven years."

"Keeping everybody hungry?"

She nodded. "Twenty-four hours a day. In every mall and shuttle, in the stadiums and domes."

"But not here?" he said, thinking of the military quarters, the labs and warehouses that spread around them in a labyrinth of windowless buildings.

"No, our heads have to be kept clear." With heavy irony, she added, "National security."

He gazed in at the bloated rats. A few weeks of such eating, and they would all need slenderizing operations. From trough to needle. Then back to trough? With a sudden bitter rush of insight, he understood: food shops and slenderizing parlors, Cravin' Havens and Sleek of Araby's, they were the opposite poles of the same mad orbit, hounded into eating and then shamed into shrinking, driven by the impulses that showered down from the domes.

In a voice filled with dismay, he asked, "Do you know how it works?"

"I helped develop the process," said Lyla.

"You! For the malls?"

"No, of course not. For the military. It was only supposed to be used in war. But the generals weren't interested in stimulating hunger, so the Pentagon licensed these civilian applications."

"What were the generals looking for?"

"The sorts of things that would immobilize an enemy."

"Like what?"

"Like sleep or panic. Like blind anger or lust. With slight variations in impulse you can trigger any of the basic responses."

He glowered at her. "It's *evil.*"

"It's necessary. Or so they keep telling me. The world's dangerous."

"Even the hunger? Is that necessary? The feed-troughs and needles?"

"I didn't want that," Lyla replied hotly. "I had no part in this stupid business of the malls."

"But it's going on out there right now," he bellowed, pointing in the vague direction of the nearest mall, "your hunger-storm, your poisonous rain!"

"It's not mine!"

"You let it happen!" He charged angrily down the hall, away from her, away from the swollen rats.

"Thurgood," she called after him in a restrained voice, using his real name, the name she sometimes whispered when they were making love. He paused in the hallway, his back to her. And she said: "I didn't have to show you my little demonstration with the rats, did I? I'd never told you the truth before because I was afraid you'd condemn me. I kept trying to get you to move out of the mall, because I wanted to save you from that constant bombardment. That hunger-storm, as you call it. But you wouldn't come."

He resumed his angry march into the living room, where he began putting on his shoes.

"Maybe I should have kept lying to you," she cried. "Left you in your sweet ignorance."

In the middle of the living room, he swung round, a shoe dangling from one finger. "How can you go to that lab every day, knowing how people live in the malls?"

She closed on him rapidly, with the blind fury of a miniature dog attacking a rhinoceros. Both fists raised, she pounded him on the chest, tipping him backward onto the couch. "Hasn't your work been used for things you don't believe in?" Lyla shouted. "Haven't they bought your creations and used them to manipulate people? Haven't they?"

"I had no way of knowing," he protested.

She leaned over him, tiny and fierce, arms akimbo and fists on hips. "You knew enough. Maybe not about the hunger-probes, but you knew MEGA owns both ends of the food-and-fat circuit, all those slenderizing parlors and glutton shops with their stupid names. You saw the ads. You hummed the tunes in your sleep. You knew your paintings were luring people onto the tables, shoving them under the needles."

"I never..." he began. Then he faltered into silence, for she was right, he had let his work be used to sell whatever MEGA wanted to sell. Food. Needles. They had provided him with an empty canvas, huge blank domes in a thousand shopping malls, and because they had let him spread his visions there, he had closed his eyes to the ads. Now he felt profoundly ashamed. For the second time that day, he had been forced to look at his own unflattering portrait, and for the second time he cried.

"Thurgood?" said Lyla. "Sweetheart?"

He felt the weight of her on his lap, her legs straddling him and her knees resting on the couch. With both hands she stroked his forehead, as if smoothing a handkerchief.

"I know what you feel," she murmured. "I've lived with it a long time."

For supper there was yogurt and salad. Lyla knew how to find such arcane foods, perhaps through "military channels." Though it was delicious, Sir Toby could not bring himself to finish his meal. Every bite made him think of those rats, of the munching passengers aboard the shuttle, of the chewing faces at the counter in Cravin' Haven. As he picked at his plate, Lyla said, "Keep this up, and you'll melt away to nothing."

He laughed, relieved that they still loved each other. "Sure, like an iceberg, in about ten years of hot weather."

The image of the iceberg reminded him of that vice-president from MEGA, her professional teeth floating on the screen, and he was immediately sunk into gloom once again. He couldn't go on doing Sleek of Araby skies. But what could he paint? Where could he get his murals shown?

Sensing this change in mood, Lyla said, "Never mind, we'll find other work. There must be some things we can do with our hands and brains that don't involve turning people into puppets."

"Let's hope so." He rose to clear the table and load the dishes into the washer. He was handling the last plate, blank of mind, when he noticed a hairline crack in the glaze. Immediately he set the plate down, rushed into the living room, grabbed the lightbrush, and began sketching feathery shapes on the ceiling. The crack had jarred some image loose in him, and the pattern was rapidly materializing in the white space overhead, branched and feathery, a delicate tracery of lines.

Lyla soon nestled against him, gazing up at the emerging design. "It's lovely," she said.

He worked along furiously for a spell, until he felt the shape was there, the essential body of the thing, all crosshatches and webs, delicate interlacing wisps. "I can't remember what it is," he said, "but that's what it looks like."

Lyla stared for a few moments. Then she said, "It's frost. Frost on a window."

Yes, of course. He was elated. Where had the memory lingered in him? Perhaps he had seen it at his grandparents' home, out in the Oregon woods, frost on the window of a winter morning.

So there were paintings in him still, even ones as delicate and unforeseen as this tracery on the ceiling. Paintings! Suddenly he had an idea, an idea so outrageous that he began hopping around the apartment in delight. "Oh, Lyla! Oh, Lyla!"

"What is it?" She spun about in consternation as he circled her in his lumbering dance.

"I want to broadcast one last sky!" he whooped. "That one right there," pointing at the ceiling. "Frost! And I want you to have it doctored up for me, have those impulse-things stuck in. Not hunger this time. No, no. This time it's going to be sex. The Sleek of Araby brings you an orgy! Think of it. The dome lights up, my frost creeps over the screen, and soon everyone in malls on seven continents is grabbing the nearest warm body, ripping away clothes, tumbling onto the carpeted floors! Shopkeepers flop down in the aisles. Customers wrestle one another onto counters. The guards unbutton their uniforms. Every mall in the network turns into a pleasure pit, a heap of writhing lovers. What do you say? That would put MEGA and the rest of them out of the impulse-business, wouldn't it?"

As he danced in circles around her, his arms waving and beard wagging, Lyla gasped at him from the center of the living room, like a bear-handler whose pet had suddenly gone berserk. "That's utterly crazy," she breathed.

"Sure it is, sure it is. But you'll do it for me, won't you, sweetums?"

"I couldn't do anything like *that*," she murmured, but she said it without conviction.

"Hah!" He beamed at her. Wrapping his great arms around her, he lifted her from the floor and shook her playfully, a bear with a rag doll. For a moment her smile was uncertain, and then it brightened into glee.

QUITTERS, INC.

by Stephen King

Many dieters know there is a close relationship between weight loss and smoking—a reduction in one often results in an increase in the other. Here, one of America's best-selling authors provides the perfect solution to this perplexing problem.

Morrison was waiting for someone who was hung up in the air traffic jam over Kennedy International when he saw a familiar face at the end of the bar and walked down.

"Jimmy? Jimmy McCann?"

It was. A little heavier than when Morrison had seen him at the Atlanta Exhibition the year before, but otherwise he looked awesomely fit. In college he had been a thin, pallid chain smoker buried behind huge horn-rimmed glasses. He had apparently switched to contact lenses.

"Dick Morrison?"

"Yeah. You look great." He extended his hand and they shook.

"So do you," McCann said, but Morrison knew it was a lie. He had been overworking, overeating, and smoking too much. "What are you drinking?"

"Bourbon and bitters," Morrison said. He hooked his feet around a bar stool and lighted a cigarette. "Meeting someone, Jimmy?"

"No. Going to Miami for a conference. A heavy client. Bills six million. I'm supposed to hold his hand because we lost out on a big special next spring."

"Are you still with Crager and Barton?"

"Executive veep now."

"Fantastic! Congratulations! When did all this happen?" He tried to tell himself that the little worm of jealousy in his stomach was just acid indigestion. He pulled out a roll of antacid pills and crunched one in his mouth.

"Last August. Something happened that changed my life." He looked speculatively at Morrison and sipped his drink. "You might be interested."

My God, Morrison thought with an inner wince. Jimmy McCann's got religion.

"Sure," he said, and gulped at his drink when it came.

"I wasn't in very good shape," McCann said. "Personal problems with Sharon, my dad died—heart attack—and I'd developed this hacking cough. Bobby Crager dropped by my office one day and gave me a fatherly little peptalk. Do you remember what those are like?"

"Yeah." He had worked at Crager and Barton for eighteen months before joining the Morton Agency. "Get your butt in gear or get your butt out."

McCann laughed. "You know it. Well, to put the capper on it, the doc told me I had an incipient ulcer. He told me to quit smoking." McCann grimaced. "Might as well tell me to quit breathing."

Morrison nodded in perfect understanding. Nonsmokers could afford to be smug. He looked at his own cigarette with distaste and stubbed it out, knowing he would be lighting another in five minutes.

"Did you quit?" he asked.

"Yes, I did. At first I didn't think I'd be able to—I was cheating like hell. Then I met a guy who told me about an outfit over on Forty-sixth Street. Specialists. I said what do I have to lose and went over. I haven't smoked since."

Morrison's eyes widened. "What did they do? Fill you full of some drug?"

"No." He had taken out his wallet and was rummaging through it. "Here it is. I knew I had one kicking around." He laid a plain white business card on the bar between them.

QUITTERS, INC.
Stop Going Up in Smoke!
237 East 46th Street
Treatments by Appointment

"Keep it, if you want," McCann said. "They'll cure you. Guaranteed."

"How?"

"I can't tell you," McCann said.

"Huh? Why not?"

"It's part of the contract they make you sign. Anyway, they tell you how it works when they interview you."

"You signed a *contract*?"

McCann nodded.

"And on the basis of that—"

"Yep." He smiled at Morrison, who thought: Well, it's happened. Jim McCann has joined the smug bastards.

"Why the great secrecy if this outfit is so fantastic? How come I've never seen any spots on TV, bilbboards, magazine ads—"

"They get all the clients they can handle by word of mouth."

"You're an advertising man, Jimmy. You can't believe that."

"I do," McCann said. "They have a ninety-eight percent cure rate."

"Wait a second," Morrison said. He motioned for another drink and lit a cigarette. "Do these guys strap you down and make you smoke until you throw up?"

"No."

"Give you something so that you get sick every time you light—"

"No, it's nothing like that. Go and see for yourself." He gestured at Morrison's cigarette. "You don't really like that, do you?"

"Nooo, but—"

"Stopping really changed things for me," McCann said. "I don't suppose it's the same for everyone, but with me it was just like dominoes falling over. I felt better and my relationship with Sharon improved. I had more energy, and my job performance picked up."

"Look, you've got my curiosity aroused. Can't you just—"

"I'm sorry, Dick. I really can't talk about it." His voice was firm.

"Did you put on any weight?"

For a moment he thought Jimmy McCann looked almost grim. "Yes. A little too much, in fact. But I took it off again. I'm about right now. I was skinny before."

"Flight 206 now boarding at Gate 9," the loudspeaker announced.

"That's me," McCann said, getting up. He tossed a five on the bar. "Have another, if you like. And think about what I said, Dick. Really." And then he was gone, making his way through the crowd to the escalators. Morrison picked up the card, looked at it thoughtfully, then tucked it away in his wallet and forgot it.

The card fell out of his wallet and onto another bar a month later. He had left the office early and had come here to drink the afternoon away. Things had not been going so well at the Morton Agency. In fact, things were bloody horrible.

He gave Henry a ten to pay for his drink, then picked up the small card and reread it—237 East Forty-sixth Street was only two blocks over; it was a cool, sunny October day outside, and maybe, just for chuckles—

When Henry brought his change, he finished his drink and then went for a walk.

Quitters, Inc., was in a new building where the monthly rent on the office space was probably close to Morrison's yearly salary. From the directory in the lobby, it looked to him like their offices took up one whole floor, and that spelled money. Lots of it.

He took the elevator up and stepped off into a lushly carpeted foyer and from there into a gracefully appointed reception room with a wide window that looked out on the scurrying bugs below. Three men and one woman sat in the chairs along the walls, reading magazines. Business types, all of them. Morrison went to the desk.

"A friend gave me this," he said, passing the card to the receptionist. "I guess you'd say he's an alumnus."

She smiled and rolled a form into her typewriter. "What is your name, sir?"

"Richard Morrison."

Clack-clackety-clack. But very muted clacks; the typewriter was an IBM.

"Your address?"

"Twenty-nine Maple Lane, Clinton, New York."

"Married?"

"Yes."

"Children?"

"One." He thought of Alvin and frowned slightly. "One" was the wrong word. "A half" might be better. His son was mentally retarded and lived at a special school in New Jersey.

"Who recommended us to you, Mr. Morrison?"

"An old school friend. James McCann."

"Very good. Will you have a seat? It's been a very busy day."

"All right."

He sat between the woman, who was wearing a severe blue suit, and a young executive type wearing a herringbone jacket and modish sideburns. He took out his pack of cigarettes, looked around, and saw there were no ashtrays.

He put the pack away again. That was all right. He would see this little game through and then light up while he was leaving. He might even tap some ashes on their maroon shag rug if they made him wait long enough. He picked up a copy of *Time* and began to leaf through it.

He was called a quarter of an hour later, after the woman in the blue suit. His nicotine center was speaking quite loudly now. A man who had come in after him took out a cigarette case, snapped it open, saw there were no ashtrays, and put it away—looking a little guilty, Morrison thought. It made him feel better.

At last the receptionist gave him a sunny smile and said, "Go right in, Mr. Morrison."

Morrison walked through the door beyond her desk and found himself in an indirectly lit hallway. A heavyset man with white hair that looked phony shook his hand, smiled affably, and said, "Follow me, Mr. Morrison."

He led Morrison past a number of closed, unmarked doors and then opened one of them about halfway down the hall with a key. Beyond the door was an austere little room walled with drilled white cork panels. The only furnishings were a desk with a chair on either side. There was what appeared to be a small oblong window in the wall behind the desk, but it was covered with a short green curtain. There was a picture on the wall to Morrison's left—a tall man with iron gray hair. He was holding a sheet of paper in one hand. He looked vaguely familiar.

"I'm Vic Donatti," the heavyset man said, "if you decide to go ahead with our program I'll be in charge of your case."

"Pleased to know you," Morrison said. He wanted a cigarette very badly.

"Have a seat."

Donatti put the receptionist's form on the desk and then drew another form from the desk drawer. He looked directly into Morrison's eyes. "Do you want to quit smoking?"

Morrison cleared his throat, crossed his legs, and tried to think of a way to equivocate. He couldn't. "Yes," he said.

"Will you sign this?" He gave Morrison the form. He scanned it quickly. The undersigned agrees not to divulge the methods or techniques or et cetera, et cetera.

"Sure," he said, and Donatti put a pen in his hand. He scratched his name, and Donatti signed below it. A moment later the paper disappeared back into the desk drawer. Well, he thought ironically, I've taken the pledge. He had taken it before. Once it had lasted for two whole days.

"Good," Donatti said. "We don't bother with propaganda here, Mr. Morrison. Questions of health or expense or social grace. We have no interest in why you want to stop smoking. We are pragmatists."

"Good," Morrison said blankly.

"We employ no drugs. We employ no Dale Carnegie people to sermonize you. We recommend no special diet. And we accept no payment until you have stopped smoking for one year."

"My God," Morrison said.

"Mr. McCann didn't tell you that?"

"No."

"How is Mr. McCann, by the way? Is he well?"

"He's fine."

"Wonderful. Excellent. Now . . . just a few questions, Mr. Morrison. These are somewhat personal, but I assure you that your answers will be held in strictest confidence."

"Yes?" Morrison asked noncommittally.

"What is your wife's name?"

"Lucinda Morrison. Her maiden name was Ramsey."

"Do you love her?"

Morrison looked up sharply, but Donatti was looking at him blandly. "Yes, of course," he said.

"Have you ever had marital problems? A separation, perhaps?"

"What has that got to do with kicking the habit?" Morrison asked. He sounded a little angrier than he had intended, but he wanted—hell, he *needed*—a cigarette.

"A great deal," Donatti said. "Just bear with me."

"No. Nothing like that." Although things *had* been a little tense just lately.

"You just have the one child?"

"Yes. Alvin. He's in a private school."

"And which school is it?"

"That," Morrison said grimly, "I'm not going to tell you."

"All right," Donatti said agreeably. He smiled disarmingly at Morrison. "All your questions will be answered tomorrow at your first treatment."

"How nice," Morrison said, and stood.

"One final question," Donatti said. "You haven't had a cigarette for over an hour. How do you feel?"

"Fine," Morrison lied. "Just fine."

"Good for you!" Donatti exclaimed. He stepped around the desk and opened the door. "Enjoy them tonight. After tomorrow, you'll never smoke again."

"Is that right?"

"Mr. Morrison," Donatti said solemnly, "we guarantee it."

He was sitting in the outer office of Quitters, Inc., the next day promptly at three. He had spent most of the day swinging between skipping the appointment the receptionist had made for him on the way out and going in a spirit of mulish cooperation—*Throw your best pitch at me, buster.*

In the end, something Jimmy McCann had said convinced him to keep the appointment—*It changed my whole life.* God knew his own life could do with some changing. And then there was his own curiosity. Before going up in the elevator, he smoked a cigarette down to the filter. Too damn bad if it's the last one, he thought. It tasted horrible.

The wait in the outer office was shorter this time. When the receptionist told him to go in, Donatti was waiting. He offered his hand and smiled, and to Morrison the smile looked almost predatory. He began to feel a little tense, and that made him want a cigarette.

"Come with me," Donatti said, and led the way down to the small room. He sat behind the desk again, and Morrison took the other chair.

"I'm very glad you came," Donatti said. "A great many prospective clients never show up again after the initial interview. They discover they don't want to quit as badly as they thought. It's going to be a pleasure to work with you on this."

"When does the treatment start?" Hypnosis, he was thinking. It must be hypnosis.

"Oh, it already has. It started when we shook hands in the hall. Do you have cigarettes with you, Mr. Morrison?"

"Yes."

"May I have them, please?"

Shrugging, Morrison handed Donatti his pack. There were only two or three left in it, anyway.

Donatti put the pack on the desk. Then, smiling into Morrison's eyes, he curled his right hand into a fist and began to hammer it down on the pack of cigarettes, which twisted and flattened. A broken cigarette end flew out. Tobacco crumbs spilled. The sound of Donatti's fist was very loud in the closed room. The smile remained on his face in spite of the force of the blows, and Morrison was chilled by it. Probably just the effect they want to inspire, he thought.

At last Donatti ceased pounding. He picked up the pack, a twisted and battered ruin. "You wouldn't believe the pleasure that gives me," he said, and dropped the pack into the wastebasket. "Even after three years in the business, it still pleases me."

"As a treatment, it leaves something to be desired," Morrison said mildly. "There's a newsstand in the lobby of this very building. And they sell all brands.

"As you say," Donatti said. He folded his hands. "Your son, Alvin Dawes Morrison, is in the Paterson School for Handicapped Children. Born with cranial brain damage. Tested IQ of forty-six. Not quite in the educable retarded category. Your wife—"

"How did you find that out?" Morrison barked. He was startled and angry. "You've got no goddamn right to go poking around my—"

"We know a lot about you," Donatti said smoothly. "But, as I said, it will all be held in strictest confidence."

"I'm getting out of here," Morrison said thinly. He stood up.

"Stay a bit longer."

Morrison looked at him closely. Donatti wasn't upset. In fact, he looked a little amused. The face of a man who has seen this reaction scores of times—maybe hundreds.

"All right. But it better be good."

"Oh, it is." Donatti leaned back. "I told you we were pragmatists here. As pragmatists, we have to start by realizing how difficult it is to cure an addiction to tobacco. The relapse rate is almost eighty-five percent. The relapse rate for heroin addicts is lower than that. It is an extraordinary problem. *Extraordinary.*"

Morrison glanced into the wastebasket. One of the cigarettes, although twisted, still looked smokeable. Donatti laughed goodnaturedly, reached into the wastebasket, and broke it between his fingers.

"State legislatures sometimes hear a request that the prison systems do away with the weekly cigarette ration. Such proposals are invariably defeated. In a few cases where they have passed, there have been fierce prison riots. *Riots,* Mr. Morrison. Imagine it."

"I," Morrison said, "am not surprised."

"But consider the implications. When you put a man in prison you take away any normal sex life, you take away his liquor, his politics, his freedom of movement. No riots—or few in comparison to the number of prisons. But when you take away his *cigarettes*—wham! bam!" He slammed his fist on the desk for emphasis.

"During World War I, when no one on the German home front could get cigarettes, the sight of German aristocrats picking butts out of the gutter was a common one. During World War II, many American women turned to pipes when they were unable to obtain cigarettes. A fascinating problem for the true pragmatist, Mr. Morrison."

"Could we get to the treatment?"

"Momentarily. Step over here, please." Donatti had risen and was standing by the green curtains Morrison had noticed yesterday. Donatti drew the curtains, discovering a rectangular window that looked into a bare room. No, not quite bare. There was a rabbit on the floor, eating pellets out of a dish.

"Pretty bunny," Morrison commented.

"Indeed. Watch him." Donatti pressed a button by the windowsill. The rabbit stopped eating and began to hop about crazily. It seemed to leap higher each time its feet struck the floor. Its fur stood out spikily in all directions. Its eyes were wild.

"Stop that! You're electrocuting him!"

Donatti released the button. "Far from it. There's a very low-yield charge in the floor. Watch the rabbit, Mr. Morrison!"

The rabbit was crouched about ten feet away from the dish of pellets. His nose wriggled. All at once he hopped away into a corner.

"If the rabbit gets a jolt often enough while he's eating," Donatti said, "he makes the association very quickly. Eating causes pain. Therefore, he won't eat. A few more shocks, and the rabbit will starve to death in front of his food. It's called aversion training."

Light dawned in Morrison's head.

"No, thanks." He started for the door.

"Wait, please, Mr. Morrison."

Morrison didn't pause. He grasped the doorknob . . . and felt it slip solidly through his hand. "Unlock this."

"Mr. Morrison, if you'll just sit down—"

"Unlock this door or I'll have the cops on you before you can say Marlboro Man."

"Sit down." The voice was cold as shaved ice.

Morrison looked at Donatti. His brown eyes were muddy and frightening. My God, he thought, I'm locked in here with a psycho. He licked his lips. He wanted a cigarette more than he ever had in his life.

"Let me explain the treatment in more detail," Donatti said.

"You don't understand," Morrison said with counterfeit patience. "I don't want the treatment. I've decided against it."

"No, Mr. Morrison. *You're* the one who doesn't understand. You don't have any choice. When I told you the treatment had already begun, I was speaking the literal truth. I would have thought you'd tipped to that by now."

"You're crazy," Morrison said wonderingly.

"No. Only a pragmatist. Let me tell you all about the treatment."

"Sure," Morrison said. "As long as you understand that as soon as I get out of here I'm going to buy five packs of cigarettes and smoke them all on the way to the police station." He suddenly realized he was biting his thumbnail, sucking on it, and made himself stop.

"As you wish. But I think you'll change your mind when you see the whole picture."

Morrison said nothing. He sat down again and folded his hands.

"For the first month of the treatment, our operatives will have you under constant supervision," Donatti said. "You'll be able to spot some of them. Not all. But they'll always be with you. *Always.* If they see you smoke a cigarette, I get a call."

"And I suppose you bring me here and do the old rabbit trick," Morrison said. He tried to sound cold and sarcastic, but he suddenly felt horribly frightened. This was a nightmare.

"Oh, no," Donatti said. "Your wife gets the rabbit trick, not you."

Morrison looked at him dumbly.

Donatti smiled. "You," he said, "get to watch."

After Donatti let him out, Morrison walked for over two hours in a complete daze. It was another fine day, but he didn't notice. The monstrousness of Donatti's smiling face blotted out all else.

"You see," he had said, "a pragmatic problem demands pragmatic solutions. You must realize we have your best interests at heart."

Quitters, Inc., according to Donatti, was a sort of foundation—a nonprofit organization begun by the man in the wall portrait. The gentleman had been extremely successful in several family businesses —including slot machines, massage parlors, numbers, and a brisk (although clandestine) trade between New York and Turkey. Mort "Three-

Fingers" Minelli had been a heavy smoker—up in the three-pack-a-day range. The paper he was holding in the picture was a doctor's diagnosis: lung cancer. Mort had died in 1970, after endowing Quitters, Inc., with family funds.

"We try to keep as close to breaking even as possible," Donatti had said: "But we're more interested in helping our fellowman. And of course, it's a great tax angle."

The treatment was chillingly simple. A first offense and Cindy would be brought to what Donatti called "the rabbit room." A second offense, and Morrison would get the dose. On a third offense, both of them would be brought in together. A fourth offense would show grave cooperation problems and would require sterner measures. An operative would be sent to Alvin's school to work the boy over.

"Imagine," Donatti said, smiling, "how horrible it will be for the boy. He wouldn't understand it even if someone explained. He'll only know someone is hurting him because Daddy was bad. He'll be very frightened."

"You bastard," Morrison said helplessly. He felt close to tears. "You dirty, filthy bastard."

"Don't misunderstand," Donatti said. He was smiling sympathetically. "I'm sure it won't happen. Forty percent of our clients never have to be disciplined at all—and only ten percent have more than three falls from grace. Those are reassuring figures, aren't they?"

Morrison didn't find them reassuring. He found them terrifying.

"Of course, if you transgress a *fifth* time—"

"What do you mean?"

Donatti beamed. "The room for you and your wife, a second beating for your son, and a beating for your wife."

Morrison, driven beyond the point of rational consideration, lunged over the desk at Donatti. Donatti moved with amazing speed for a man who had apparently been completely relaxed. He shoved the chair backward and drove both of his feet over the desk and into Morrison's belly. Gagging and coughing, Morrison staggered backward.

"Sit down, Mr. Morrison," Donatti said benignly. "Let's talk this over like rational men."

When he could get his breath, Morrison did as he was told. Nightmares had to end sometime, didn't they?

Quitters, Inc., Donatti had explained further, operated on a ten-step punishment scale. Steps six, seven, and eight consisted of further trips to the rabbit room (and increased voltage) and more serious beatings. The ninth step would be the breaking of his son's arms.

"And the tenth?" Morrison asked, his mouth dry.

Donatti shook his head sadly. "Then we give up, Mr. Morrison. You become part of the unregenerate two percent."

"You really give up?"

"In a manner of speaking." He opened one of the desk drawers and laid a silenced .45 on the desk. He smiled into Morrison's eyes. "But even the unregenerate two percent never smoke again. We guarantee it."

The Friday Night movie was *Bullitt,* one of Cindy's favorites, but after an hour of Morrison's mutterings and fidgetings, her concentration was broken.

"What's the matter with you?" she asked during station identification.

"Nothing . . . everything," he growled. "I'm giving up smoking."

She laughed. "Since when? Five minutes ago?"

"Since three o'clock this afternoon."

"You really haven't had a cigarette since then?"

"No," he said, and began to gnaw his thumbnail. It was ragged, down to the quick.

"That's wonderful! What ever made you decide to quit?"

"You," he said. "And . . . and Alvin."

Her eyes widened, and when the movie came back on, she didn't notice. Dick rarely mentioned their retarded son. She came over, looked at the empty ashtray by his right hand, and then into his eyes. "Are you really trying to quit, Dick?"

"Really." And if I go to the cops, he added mentally, the local goon squad will be around to rearrange your face, Cindy.

"I'm glad. Even if you don't make it, we both thank you for the thought, Dick."

"Oh, I think I'll make it," he said, thinking of the muddy, homicidal look that had come into Donatti's eyes when he kicked him in the stomach.

He slept badly that night, dozing in and out of sleep. Around three o'clock he woke up completely. His craving for a cigarette was like a low-grade fever. He went downstairs and to his study. The room was in the middle of the house. No windows. He slid open the top drawer of his desk and looked in, fascinated by the cigarette box. He looked around and licked his lips.

Constant supervision during the first month, Donatti had said. Eighteen hours a day during the next two—but he would never know *which* eighteen. During the fourth month, the month when most clients backslid, the "service" would return to twenty-four hours a day. Then twelve hours of broken surveillance each day for the rest of the year. After that? Random surveillance for the rest of the client's life.

For the rest of his life.

"We may audit you every other month," Donatti said. "Or every other day. Or constantly for one week two years from now. The point is, *you won't know*. If you smoke, you'll be gambling with loaded dice. Are they watching? Are they picking up my wife or sending a man after my son right now? Beautiful, isn't it? And if you do sneak a smoke, it'll taste awful. It will taste like your son's blood."

But they couldn't be watching now, in the dead of night, in his own study. The house was grave-quiet.

He looked at the cigarettes in the box for almost two minutes, unable to tear his gaze away. Then he went to the study door, peered out into the empty hall, and went back to look at the cigarettes some more. A horrible picture came: his life stretching before him and not a cigarette to be found. How in the name of God was he ever going to be able to make another tough presentation to a weary client, without that cigarette burning nonchalantly between his fingers as he approached the charts and layouts? How would he be able to endure Cindy's endless garden shows without a cigarette? How could he even get up in the morning and face the day without a cigarette to smoke as he drank his coffee and read the paper?

He cursed himself for getting into this. He cursed Donatti. And most of all, he cursed Jimmy McCann. How could he have done it? The son of a bitch had *known*. His hands trembled in their desire to get hold of Jimmy Judas McCann.

Stealthily, he glanced around the study again. He reached into the drawer and brought out a cigarette. He caressed it, fondled it. What was that old slogan? *So round, so firm, so fully packed.* Truer words had never been spoken. He put the cigarette in his mouth and then paused, cocking his head.

Had there been the slightest noise from the closet? A faint shifting? Surely not. But—

Another mental image—that rabbit hopping crazily in the grip of electricity. The thought of Cindy in that room—

He listened desperately and heard nothing. He told himself that all he had to do was to go to the closet door and yank it open. But he was too afraid of what he might find. He went back to bed but he didn't sleep for a long time.

In spite of how lousy he felt in the morning, breakfast tasted good. After a moment's hesitation, he followed his customary bowl of corn-flakes with scrambled eggs. He was grumpily washing out the pan when Cindy came downstairs in her robe.

"Richard Morrison! You haven't eaten an egg for breakfast since Hector was a pup."

Morrison grunted. He considered *since Hector was a pup* to be one of Cindy's stupider sayings, on a par with *I should smile and kiss a pig.*

"Have you smoked yet?" she asked, pouring orange juice.

"No."

"You'll be back on them by noon," she proclaimed airily.

"Lot of goddamn help you are!" he rasped, rounding on her. "You and anyone else who doesn't smoke, you all think ... ah, never mind."

He expected her to be angry, but she was looking at him with something like wonder. "You're really serious," she said. "You really are."

"You bet I am." *You'll never know* how *serious. I hope.*

"Poor baby," she said, going to him. "You look like death warmed over. But I'm very proud."

Morrison held her tight.

Scenes from the life of Richard Morrison, October-November:

Morrison and a crony from Larkin Studios at Jack Dempsey's bar. Crony offers a cigarette. Morrison grips his glass a little more tightly and says: *I'm quitting.* Crony laughs and says: *I give you a week.*

Morrison waiting for the morning train, looking over the top of the *Times* at a young man in a blue suit. He sees the young man almost every morning now, and sometimes at other places. At Onde's, where he is meeting a client. Looking at 45s in Sam Goody's, where Morrison is looking for a Sam Cooke album. Once in a foursome behind Morrison's group at the local golf course.

Morrison getting drunk at a party, wanting a cigarette—but not quite drunk enough to take one.

Morrison visiting his son, bringing him a large ball that squeaked when you squeezed it. His son's slobbering, delighted kiss. Somehow not as repulsive as before. Hugging his son tightly, realizing what Donatti and his colleagues had so cynically realized before him: love is the most pernicious drug of all. Let the romantics debate its existence. Pragmatists accept it and use it.

Morrison losing the physical compulsion to smoke little by little, but never quite losing the psychological craving, or the need to have something in his mouth—cough drops, Life Savers, a toothpick. Poor substitutes, all of them.

And finally, Morrison hung up in a colossal traffic jam in the Midtown Tunnel. Darkness. Horns blaring. Air stinking. Traffic hopelessly snarled. And suddenly, thumbing open the glove compartment and seeing the half-open pack of cigarettes in there. He looked at them for a moment, then snatched one and lit it with the dashboard lighter. If anything happens, it's Cindy's fault, he told himself defiantly. I told her to get rid of all the damn cigarettes.

The first drag made him cough smoke out furiously. The second made his eyes water. The third made him feel light-headed and swoony. It tastes awful, he thought.

And on the heels of that: My God, what am I doing?

Horns blatted impatiently behind him. Ahead, the traffic had begun to move again. He stubbed the cigarette out in the ashtray, opened both front windows, opened the vents, and then fanned the air helplessly like a kid who has just flushed his first butt down the john.

He joined the traffic flow jerkily and drove home.

"Cindy?" he called. "I'm home."

No answer.

"Cindy? Where are you, hon?"

The phone rang, and he pounced on it. "Hello? Cindy?"

"Hello, Mr. Morrison," Donatti said. He sounded pleasantly brisk and businesslike. "It seems we have a small business matter to attend to. Would five o'clock be convenient?"

"Have you got my wife?"

"Yes, indeed." Donatti chuckled indulgently.

"Look, let her go," Morrison babbled. "It won't happen again. It was a slip, just a slip, that's all. I only had three drags and for God's sake *it didn't even taste good!*"

"That's a shame. I'll count on you for five then, shall I?"

"Please," Morrison said, close to tears. "Please—"

He was speaking to a dead line.

At 5 P.M. the reception room was empty except for the secretary, who gave him a twinkly smile that ignored Morrison's pallor and disheveled appearance. "Mr. Donatti?" she said into the intercom. "Mr. Morrison to see you." She nodded to Morrison. "Go right in."

Donatti was waiting outside the unmarked room with a man who was wearing a SMILE sweatshirt and carrying a .38. He was built like an ape.

"Listen," Morrison said to Donatti. "We can work something out, can't we? I'll pay you. I'll—"

"Shaddap," the man in the SMILE sweatshirt said.

"It's good to see you," Donatti said. "Sorry it has to be under such adverse circumstances. Will you come with me? We'll make this as brief as possible. I can assure you your wife won't be hurt . . . this time."

Morrison tensed himself to leap at Donatti.

"Come, come," Donatti said, looking annoyed. "If you do that, Junk here is going to pistol-whip you and your wife is still going to get it. Now where's the percentage in that?"

"I hope you rot in hell," he told Donatti.

Donatti sighed. "If I had a nickel for every time someone expressed a similar sentiment, I could retire. Let it be a lesson to you, Mr. Morrison. When a romantic tries to do a good thing and fails, they give him a medal. When a pragmatist succeeds, they wish him in hell. Shall we go?"

Junk motioned with the pistol.

Morrison preceded them into the room. He felt numb. The small green curtain had been pulled. Junk prodded him with the gun. This is what being a witness at the gas chamber must have been like, he thought.

He looked in, Cindy was there, looking around bewilderedly.

"Cindy!" Morrison called miserably. "Cindy, they—"

"She can't hear or see you," Donatti said. "One-way glass. Well, let's get it over with. It really was a very small slip. I believe thirty seconds should be enough. Junk?"

Junk pressed the button with one hand and kept the pistol jammed firmly into Morrison's back with the other.

It was the longest thirty seconds of his life.

When it was over, Donatti put a hand on Morrison's shoulder and said, "Are you going to throw up?"

"No," Morrison said weakly. His forehead was against the glass. His legs were jelly. "I don't think so." He turned around and saw that Junk was gone.

"Come with me," Donatti said.

"Where?" Morrison asked apathetically.

"I think you have a few things to explain, don't you?"

"How can I face her? How can I tell her that I . . . I . . ."

"I think you're going to be surprised," Donatti said.

The room was empty except for a sofa. Cindy was on it, sobbing helplessly.

"Cindy?" he said gently.

She looked up, her eyes magnified by tears. "Dick?" she whispered. "Dick? Oh . . . Oh God . . ." He held her tightly. "Two men," she said against his chest. "In the house and at first I thought they were burglars and then I thought they were going to rape me and then they took me someplace with a blindfold over my eyes and . . . and . . . oh it was h-horrible—"

"Shhh," he said. "Shhh."

"But why?" she asked, looking up at him. "Why would they—"

"Because of me," he said. "I have to tell you a story, Cindy—"

When he finished he was silent a moment and then said, "I suppose you hate me. I wouldn't blame you."

He was looking at the floor, and she took his face in both hands and turned it to hers. "No," she said. "I don't hate you."

He looked at her in mute surprise.

"It was worth it," she said. "God bless these people. They've let you out of prison."

"Do you mean that?"

"Yes," she said, and kissed him. "Can we go home now? I feel much better. Ever so much."

The phone rang one evening a week later, and when Morrison recognized Donatti's voice, he said, "Your boys have got it wrong. I haven't even been near a cigarette."

"We know that. We have a final matter to talk over. Can you stop by tomorrow afternoon?"

"Is it—"

"No, nothing serious. Bookkeeping really. By the way, congratulations on your promotion."

"How did you know about that?"

"We're keeping tabs," Donatti said noncommittally, and hung up.

When they entered the small room, Donatti said, "Don't look so nervous. No one's going to bite you. Step over here, please."

Morrison saw an ordinary bathroom scale. "Listen, I've gained a little weight, but—"

"Yes, seventy-three percent of our clients do. Step up, please."

Morrison did, and tipped the scales at one-seventy-four.

"Okay, fine. You can step off. How tall are you, Mr. Morrison?"

"Five eleven."

"Okay, let's see." He pulled a small card laminated in plastic from his breast pocket. "Well, that's not too bad. I'm going to write you a prescrip for some highly illegal diet pills. Use them sparingly and according to directions. And I'm going to set your maximum weight at . . . let's see . . ." He consulted the card again. "One eighty-two, how does that sound? And since this is December first, I'll expect you the first of every month for a weigh-in. No problem if you can't make it, as long as you call in advance."

"And what happens if I go over one-eighty-two?"

Donatti smiled. "We'll send someone out to your house to cut off your wife's little finger," he said. "You can leave through this door, Mr. Morrison. Have a nice day."

Eight months later:

Morrison runs into the crony from the Larkin Studios at Dempsey's bar. Morrison is down to what Cindy proudly calls his fighting weight: one-sixty-seven. He works out three times a week and looks as fit as whipcord. The crony from Larkin, by comparison, looks like something the cat dragged in.

Crony: Lord, how'd you ever stop? I'm locked into this damn habit tighter than Tillie. The crony stubs his cigarette out with real revulsion and drains his scotch.

Morrison looks at him speculatively and then takes a small white business card out of his wallet. He puts it on the bar between them. You know, he says, these guys changed my life.

Twelve months later:
Morrison receives a bill in the mail. The bill says:

QUITTERS, INC.
237 East 46th Street
New York, N.Y. 10017

1 Treatment	$2500.00
Counselor (Victor Donatti)	$2500.00
Electricity	$ .50
TOTAL (Please pay this amount)	$5000.50

Those sons of bitches! he explodes. They charged me for the electricity they used to ... to ...

Just pay it, she says, and kisses him.

Twenty months later:
Quite by accident, Morrison and his wife meet the Jimmy McCanns at the Helen Hayes Theatre. Introductions are made all around. Jimmy looks as good, if not better, than he did on that day in the airport terminal so long ago. Morrison has never met his wife. She is pretty in the radiant way plain girls sometimes have when they are very, very happy.

She offers her hand and Morrison shakes it. There is something odd about her grip, and halfway through the second act, he realizes what it was. The little finger on her right hand is missing.